INTRIGUE

Seek thrills. Solve crimes. Justice served.

The Killer Next Door
Amanda Stevens

What Lies Below
Carol Ericson

MILLS & BOON

THE KILLER NEXT DOOR
© 2024 by Marilyn Medlock Amann
Philippine Copyright 2024
Australian Copyright 2024
New Zealand Copyright 2024

First Published 2024
First Australian Paperback Edition 2024
ISBN 978 1 867 92167 3

WHAT LIES BELLOW
© 2024 by Carol Ericson
Philippine Copyright 2024
Australian Copyright 2024
New Zealand Copyright 2024

First Published 2024
First Australian Paperback Edition 2024
ISBN 978 1 867 92167 3

MIX
Paper | Supporting
responsible forestry
FSC® C001695
www.fsc.org

Published by
Harlequin Mills & Boon
An imprint of Harlequin Enterprises (Australia) Pty Limited
(ABN 47 001 180 918), a subsidiary of HarperCollins
Publishers Australia Pty Limited
(ABN 36 009 913 517)
Level 19, 201 Elizabeth Street
SYDNEY NSW 2000 AUSTRALIA

Cover art used by arrangement with Harlequin Books S.A.. All rights reserved.

Printed and bound in Australia by McPherson's Printing Group

The Killer Next Door

Amanda Stevens

MILLS & BOON

Amanda Stevens is an award-winning author of over fifty novels, including the modern gothic series The Graveyard Queen. Her books have been described as eerie and atmospheric and "a new take on the classic ghost story." Born and raised in the rural South, she now resides in Houston, Texas, where she enjoys binge-watching, bike riding and the occasional margarita.

Visit the Author Profile page
at millsandboon.com.au.

CAST OF CHARACTERS

Detective Sydney Shepherd—While on suspension from the police department, Sydney becomes convinced her next-door neighbor is a serial killer. Desperate to prevent the next murder, she agrees to work with a washed-up detective she helped get fired.

Trent Gannon—The disgraced police detective turned private investigator agrees to help Sydney with an off-the-books investigation. But can he put aside past grievances long enough to catch the Seaside Strangler?

Brandan Shaw—Is he a lone wolf or following in the footsteps of a mentor?

Lieutenant Dan Bertram—Sydney's superior is all too familiar with the unsolved serial murders that plagued the area two decades ago. He was in a position not only to cover his tracks, but also to groom his protégé.

Martin Swann—Twenty years ago, Sydney's landlord took a troubled adolescent under his wing, but to what end?

Richard Mathison—His youngest son stands accused of murdering his girlfriend. Is his other son—his forgotten son—a serial killer desperate for his father's attention?

Gabriel Mathison—Is he innocent of murder or the product of a dark legacy?

Chapter One

Suspended.

The dreaded word reverberated like a drumbeat inside Detective Sydney Shepherd's head, keeping time with the dull throb from her concussion. Her stomach churned as she mentally replayed the high-speed chase that had culminated in a single-vehicle car crash and a trip to the nearest ER in Seaside, Texas.

Even now she shuddered at the weightless sensation of being airborne and then the sickening crunch of metal against pavement as her vehicle rolled not once but twice before coming to a spinning stop that had left her battered, disoriented and upside down. A cacophony of honking horns and screeching brakes had finally propelled her into action. Untangling herself from the seat belt, she'd climbed through the shattered window to make sure no one else had been injured.

Later at the hospital, the ER doctor had been blunt. *You're lucky to be alive, young lady.*

Yeah, no kidding. Not that she needed his censure. She'd done nothing but berate herself since crawling through that broken window.

What were you thinking, pursuing a vehicle at that speed?
I was thinking I wanted to catch a killer before he fled

*the country. I was thinking I wanted to wipe that smug smile
from Gabriel Mathison's face once and for all. I was thinking of that moment when I could finally slap the cuffs on
his wrists and read him his rights.*

*Liar. You weren't thinking at all. You let adrenaline and
obsession take the wheel. You're damn lucky to be alive and
even more fortunate that you didn't kill or maim someone
else in the process.*

Maybe death wouldn't have been such a bad option, she
decided. Which was worse—living with the nagging tor-
ment of what could have happened or the sinking dread of
what was about to happen?

Not to mention the fiery agony of a fractured ankle and
the suffocating pressure from a bruised rib. It hurt to talk,
it hurt to cough, it hurt to breathe. She lay flat on her back
and stared at the ceiling in gloomy silence. *You deserve
every bit of this misery. Thanks to you, Gabriel Mathison
is now untouchable. He's probably out there at this very
moment celebrating his victory.*

"Syd? Did you hear what I said?"

She dropped her gaze from the ceiling to the middle-
aged man at the foot of the bed. Drawing a painful breath,
she released it slowly. "Yes, I heard you. You said I'm suspended without pay, pending a full investigation."

"I said more than that." For a moment, Lieutenant Dan
Bertram let his professional demeanor slip, and a fatherly
concern flickered across his careworn features. "Are you
in a lot of pain?"

She used every ounce of her strength not to groan.
"Nothing I can't handle."

His tone turned gruff. "You don't have to do that, you
know. Pretend you're unbreakable. This is me you're talking to. I used to patch up your skinned knees when you

were little. You don't always have to be the toughest cop in the room."

Yes, I do. Not everyone is like you.

Even in this day and age, there were those in the department who would relish the chance to cut her down to size if they caught even a shred of vulnerability. The suit of armor she'd donned in the academy had eventually become a second skin, one never to be shed on duty or off. But she decided to throw the lieutenant a bone. "Okay, even my eyeballs hurt. Is that what you wanted to hear?"

"If it's the truth. When I got the call—" he paused as a myriad of emotions flashed across his features "—they sent me a photo of your car. I didn't know what to expect when I walked through that door."

"I'm sorry to worry you. The doctor says I'll be fine."

"Thank God for that." He seemed to wear the weight of the world on his slumping shoulders as he stood gazing down at her. His uniform was starting to tug across the middle and beneath his receding hairline, his brow had deepened into a perpetual scowl. He'd been divorced for nearly a decade, but he still sometimes fiddled with an imaginary wedding ring when he was worried or deep in thought. Before Sydney's dad had died, the two men had been partners and later close friends. Dan Bertram had been the nearest thing she'd had to a doting uncle long before he'd become her mentor and finally her commander. He expected a lot from her, and his obvious disappointment was a hard pill for Sydney to swallow.

"It could have been worse," she said.

"Much worse," he agreed. "You're young. You'll heal. And the suspension isn't permanent."

"We both know that's a mere formality. Even if by some miracle I'm allowed to stay on the force, I'll be busted down to patrol or desk duty. I'll never be allowed anywhere near the Criminal Investigations Unit again. Richard Mathison will see to that. He promised to rain hell down upon me if I went after his son. It wasn't an idle threat."

"Yet, you went after him anyway."

"I followed the evidence. You would have done the same."

The lieutenant sighed. "We're talking about you right now and the consequences of your actions. I'll ask the chief to have a word with Mathison. They're old friends. Maybe she can get him to call off the dogs. Avoiding a lawsuit will go a long way toward rehabilitating your reputation within the department."

Sydney wasn't buying it. "Why would the chief go out on a limb for me? Why would you, for that matter? You've got your own career to consider."

"Don't worry about me. I know how to protect myself. As to why… I made a promise years ago that I'd look out for you, and I don't go back on my word. Besides—" a rare smile tugged at his cheeks "—I see something of my younger self in you. I know what it's like to have a fire in your belly. That burning need to make a name for yourself. I know how dangerous it can be, too. Your dad cut me a break once when I was still green and ambitious, and I'm willing to do the same for you on one condition."

Her gaze narrowed. "What?"

"Use your recovery time to reflect on your choices. I'm dead serious about that. You need to reevaluate your priorities. Your dad set a high bar, and no one knows better than I the difficulty of living up to Tom Shepherd's standards." The lieutenant leaned in. "But here's the thing you need to remember. He wasn't born a hero. His legacy wasn't created overnight. He made mistakes along the way just like everyone else. You've been a detective for less than two years. You've still got a lot to learn. If Tom were here now, he'd be the first to tell you that patience and discretion are virtues. You have to know when to back off."

The advice didn't sit well with Sydney. She didn't like being manipulated, and she didn't believe for a moment that her dad would have let a guy like Gabriel Mathison walk because his family had clout and money. "You mean back off when the suspect has a wealthy father who also happens to be a member of the town council?"

The lieutenant's demeanor hardened in the face of her defiance. "It's called politics. Living to fight another day. You let your emotions get the better of you this time. You became so single-minded in your pursuit of Gabriel Mathison that you allowed him to goad you into making it personal."

Anger bubbled despite her best efforts. She took a calming breath and counted to ten. "Mathison thinks he's above the law. He thinks he can get away with murder because of who his father is. You and I both know he killed Jessica King. He attacked her with a blunt force instrument, strangled her while she lay unconscious and dumped her body on the side of the road. Then he partied with his friends for the rest of the night. If that isn't cold-blooded, I don't know what is."

"Knowing and proving are two different things. And, unfortunately, those same friends have given him an alibi for the time in question."

"Then we need to break them. We need to persuade one of them to come forward and tell the truth."

"You've tried that already."

"Obviously, I didn't try hard enough. That's on me." She paused to tamp down her emotions yet again. "I know you don't want to hear this, but what if I'm right? What if Jessica King wasn't his first victim? He has a violent history that his father has worked very hard to conceal. What if Gabriel Mathison was the perpetrator of at least two other unsolved homicides in the past year?"

Her steely resolve deepened his scowl. "You're right. I don't want to hear it. That's the kind of overreach that got you into trouble in the first place."

"I know that."

"Do you? Because your actions suggest otherwise." She tried to protest, but he put up a hand to halt her. "Just listen for once. I stuck my neck out for you. You were allowed to take lead on the Jessica King case at my request. Your first homicide investigation should have been a big opportunity for you, but you went too far. You couldn't nail Mathison on the case you were assigned, so you started digging for connections that were at best weak and at worst far-fetched. You acted impulsively, some might say irrationally, and now here we are."

His frank assessment of her performance was like a dagger through her heart. Turning her head to the narrow window, she fixed her gaze on the parking lot while blinking back hot tears. "Do you really think it's a coincidence that the victim's best friend was transferred to another state after claiming Jessica was afraid of Gabriel? Or that the witness who saw a physical altercation between Gabriel and Jessica the night she was murdered suddenly decided to recant her story? Richard Mathison is cleaning up his son's mess just like he's always done. Why would he go to all that trouble if Gabriel is innocent? Three victims in the past year, all strangled, their bodies found along the interstate just miles from the Mathison beach house. I suppose that's also a coincidence."

"Think about what you just said. Why would he dispose of bodies so close to his family's property?"

She turned back to him. "Why not, if he thinks he's untouchable?"

"Okay." The lieutenant's voice became deceptively calm, but any hint of patience or support had long since vanished. "Let's go through this one more time. The first victim was found in the trunk of an abandoned car, the second a few months later in a shallow grave. Both had been bound and strangled, both had close ties to the drug trade. That's a dangerous lifestyle. Executions are as common as handshakes. Jessica King was an associate at a respected law firm. She came from a good family with no known ties to the cartels or any other criminal enterprise. Despite your efforts to the contrary, you haven't been able to link her murder to the other two homicides."

"Except for how she was murdered. Two strangulations might be a coincidence, but three is a pattern," Sydney insisted.

"You're doing it again. You just can't help yourself, can you?"

Her chin came up. "All I know is that sweeping inconvenient facts under the rug won't make them go away. Something very real and very dark is happening in our little community. A killer is out there preying on young women. I don't know how or why, but every instinct is telling me that Gabriel Mathison is somehow involved."

"That kind of talk doesn't leave this room, Detective." The formality of his admonishment underscored his warning. He was no longer a caring friend or even a concerned mentor, but a commanding officer putting her on notice. "The last thing we want is to scare people into thinking we have an active serial killer in the area.

"As for Mathison—" he straightened and returned to the foot of her bed "—he's no longer your concern. Under no circumstances will you make contact with him. If you pass him on the street, look the other way. From this moment forward, that man is dead to you. Am I clear?"

She swallowed a retort and nodded.

"Keep your mouth shut and your head down until this situation is resolved one way or another. In the meantime, I would advise that you give some thought to what you'll say if and when you go before the review board. Don't get defensive and don't be afraid to show remorse. A little humility can go a long way."

Defiance crept into her reply despite her best efforts. "Even when I know I'm right?"

His icy glare spoke volumes. "Learn to play the game, or get used to writing parking tickets."

SYDNEY CONTEMPLATED THE lieutenant's warning while she waited for the doctor to return. Depending on the results of the CT scan, she could be released as soon as her broken bone was set. That was her hope, at least. A night in the hospital was the last thing she wanted. The teeming misery of the emergency room made her long for the quiet sanctuary of her tiny garage apartment.

She also needed access to her laptop. As luck would have it, she'd downloaded her case notes to the hard drive, enabling her to continue a virtual investigation while she recuperated at home. The powers that be could remove her physically from the case and muzzle her contacts within the department, but they had no control over what she did on her own time in the privacy of her own home.

You're doing it again, Syd. The lieutenant's admonishment lingered like a bitter aftertaste. *You just can't help yourself, can you?*

Okay, so maybe he was right. A little reflection might be warranted after such a monumental screwup. Maybe she had allowed herself to become obsessed and single-minded. Maybe she did need to take a step back and regroup. But soul-searching had never been her strong suit. An honest evaluation required owning up to several unpleasant peccadillos, including a tendency toward hubris.

It didn't matter that her pride and arrogance came from a place of self-doubt. Deep down, she was daunted by the expectation of living up to her father's legacy and bedeviled by the fear that she would never escape his shadow. Her particular combination of fervency and aloofness was off-putting. She had no real friends, no close relationships. Even her own mother kept her distance. But that particular rabbit hole was an exploration for another day.

A nurse came in a little while later to recheck her vitals and to inform her that she was being moved to a private room. When Sydney expressed dismay, he gave her a sympathetic smile. "Don't worry. You'll be out of here before you know it. For now, though, we'd like to keep an eye on you overnight. As soon as the order comes through, someone will be in to take you upstairs. But that may be a while, so just sit tight, okay? We don't want to lose you in all the confusion."

Sydney couldn't tell if he was joking or not.

While she waited alone in the tiny room, she practiced visualizing the pain leaving her body in a wisp of gray-green smoke. Guided imagery sometimes helped with the tension headaches she brought home from work. Normally, she tried to avoid strong painkillers, but right now she'd give her last paycheck for a shot of something to knock her out.

Forcing herself to concentrate on the imagery of that coil of smoke, she lay back against the pillow and closed her eyes. Surprisingly, she managed to drift off. She had the strangest dream about being wheeled into a section of the hospital under construction and left to fend for herself. When she tried to get up from the gurney, she discovered her wrists and ankles were shackled to the metal bed rails. She couldn't move or call for help. All she could do was watch in horror as a masked surgeon, whose eyes looked an awful lot like Gabriel Mathison's, materialized at her side with arms outstretched toward her neck.

She awoke on a gasp, her hand to her throat.

"You okay?" a voice asked from the doorway.

She turned her head toward the sound. A man stood just inside the room reading a file he'd plucked from the plastic holder on the door. He also wore a mask, but his head was bowed to the chart, so she couldn't see his eyes.

Her pulse accelerated as she watched him. He wasn't the doctor who had examined her earlier, and he didn't appear to be a nurse or attendant. He didn't look as if he belonged in the hospital at all, dressed as he was in faded jeans, sneakers and a plaid shirt that he wore open over a gray T-shirt. It came to her in a flash that he might be someone the Mathisons had sent to finish her off. She wanted to laugh at her imagination, but knowing what she knew about that family, the notion didn't seem that absurd.

She tried to project authority into her voice. "Who are you?"

He didn't glance up. "I just came by to see how you're doing."

"Are you a doctor?" Something about his voice, about

the way he kept his head lowered just enough so that she couldn't get a good look at him… "Where's Dr. Parnell?"

"I'm sure he'll be along soon." He dropped the file back in the holder and turned. "How's the pain?"

"Manageable." She gripped the edge of the bed, realizing how completely at this stranger's mercy she was. She couldn't run, much less fight, though she wouldn't go down without trying. "Who are you again?"

He strode into the room as if he had every right in the world to be there. When he got to the foot of the bed, he removed the paper mask and stuffed it in his shirt pocket.

She gaped at him in astonishment. *"Trent Gannon?"*

His gaze raked her from head to toe. "You remember my name. I'd say that's a good sign considering the head injury."

She swallowed back her shock. "Not necessarily. Some people are hard to forget under any circumstances."

"Thank you."

"It wasn't a compliment." She forced her gaze to remain steady when she really wanted to glance away from the boldness of his gray eyes. Of all the disgraced former police detectives to come strolling into her room. "How did you get back here anyway? They have restrictions on who can come and go from this area."

He shrugged. "I've always found that if you act like you belong, most people are reluctant to question you."

"Someone should speak to security about that," she muttered. *Trent Gannon.* She shook her head in disbelief. How long had it been anyway? She'd lost track of him years ago. "You still haven't told me why you're here."

"I was visiting a friend in the hospital. He had the TV on, and I heard your name mentioned in conjunction with a high-speed chase that ended in a crash. The local news showed a picture of the car." He gave a low whistle. "That's one less vehicle in the city fleet."

"So you came by to gloat?"

He lifted a brow at her curt tone. "Do you really think I'd take pleasure in someone else's misfortune?"

"Yes, I do. Don't you remember what you said to me the last time we met face-to-face?"

"That wasn't one of my better days." He moved back so that he could lean a shoulder against the wall. Disgraced or not, his presence filled that tiny room, so much so that Sydney found it a little difficult to catch her breath. She resisted the urge to pull the sheet up to her chin even though she was still fully clothed. "I'd just surrendered my shield and firearm and packed up my desk. I said a lot of things to a lot of people on my way out. But that was a long time ago. Water under the bridge as they say. I don't hold a grudge."

Sydney bristled. "I should hope not, considering everything that happened was your fault. You had to know you were risking your career when you decided to show up drunk to a crime scene."

Something that might have been regret flickered in his eyes. "When someone starts drinking on the job, they usually aren't thinking too clearly, period."

"I guess not." She hesitated, then said in a softer tone, "For the record, no one enjoyed watching your downfall."

His smile turned wry. "I don't know if that's entirely true."

"It is. A lot of people covered for you for as long as they could. Longer than they should have."

His smile disappeared. "But not you."

She met his gaze without flinching. "I had no choice. I was asked point-blank by my commanding officer what I witnessed at that crime scene. I had to tell the truth. You were becoming a danger to yourself and others."

"You did the right thing."

His response took her aback. He wasn't at all the way she remembered him. He'd once been considered the best detective in the Criminal Investigations Unit, someone who commanded respect and admiration from his peers and superiors alike. But at the height of his career, he'd already displayed a tendency to self-destruct. Considering the gossip and her memory of his ignominious departure, she would have expected an attack on her character or, at the very least, pushback on her recall of events. Instead, his easy acceptance of her criticism left her momentarily speechless.

In the ensuing silence, she tried to study his demeanor without being obvious. She'd once found Trent Gannon attractive, but that was back when he was still a hotshot detective with an unparalleled record for closing cases. His downward spiral had changed her perception of him, and in time he'd become a cautionary tale. Now she found herself unsettled by the similarities to her current trajectory.

"As you said, it was a long time ago," she murmured, for lack of anything better to offer.

"Three years can seem like a lifetime. I was headed down a bad path. It took me a long time to admit that you actually did me a favor. Losing my job made me take a cold, hard look at myself. I knew I needed to make changes. First, I had to stop drinking. I woke up one morning and decided to quit cold turkey."

"That couldn't have been easy."

"It wasn't, but probably not as hard as you imagine. I don't say that to diminish the hell others go through to get and stay sober. For me, booze was always more of a crutch than a craving. A liquid bandage. I didn't miss it after I quit. I sure as hell didn't miss the hangovers."

Why had she never wondered before what had driven him to drink? Why had she never been curious enough to ask? Too caught up in her own ambition, she supposed. She felt ashamed now to admit that her initial thought upon his departure from the department was that a spot in the Criminal Investigations Unit had finally opened up.

"I'm glad you're doing well," she said and meant it, though she wasn't sure if she believed him. Had he really changed his ways? His careless appearance would suggest otherwise. "It's admirable that you turned your life around, but I still don't understand what any of this has to do with me. We haven't spoken since you left. We were barely acquaintances even back then. Now here you are acting as if we're long-lost friends. I'd like to know why."

The inscrutable look he gave her sent a shiver of alarm down her spine. "It's simple. You helped me once. I'd like to return the favor."

"How?"

He came around to the side of the bed and pulled up a stool. "May I?" He sat without waiting for her consent. His nearness made her even more uneasy, but she didn't want to call attention to her distress by asking him to leave. If he was here to make amends, she didn't want to be the one to set him back.

She scanned his features, noting the fine lines around his eyes and mouth, the hairstyle that had grown a little too shaggy and the clothing that had seen better days. She wondered suddenly what his life had been like since he left the department. No one ever talked about him. It was as if Trent Gannon had vanished into thin air when he walked out the door that day.

"I've been following your case," he said. "For what it's worth coming from me, I think you're right about Gabriel

Mathison. Something is off about that guy. There've been rumors about him for years and how he likes to play rough with women. I don't know if he killed his girlfriend, but he's hiding something."

He had her full attention now. "What do you mean? Give me specifics."

He quelled her excitement. "I can't. It's instinct more than anything else. A gut feeling after watching his body language at his father's press conference. I'm still pretty good at reading people."

"Richard Mathison gave a press conference? That was fast. And…not good," she fretted. "For me, at least."

Trent nodded. "They played it off as improvised, but everyone knows he has the local media in his pocket. Not just the media. Plenty of important people in this town owe him favors. Some of them work for the police department. I've seen firsthand how evidence can disappear and witnesses will clam up after a single phone call from his office. But the kind of money that can be used to bribe and coerce can also make people arrogant and careless. Gabriel Mathison doesn't have his father's discipline. He's not capable of committing the perfect murder. If he's guilty, sooner or later, he'll let something slip. He'll talk to the wrong person. His ego won't allow him to remain silent."

She said on a resigned sigh, "I hope you're right, but I won't be the one to bring him in. I've been removed from the investigation and suspended without pay. If I go near Gabriel Mathison, I face termination and possibly a lawsuit." She cast a worried glance toward the hallway door. "I shouldn't even be talking to you about the case."

He lowered his voice. "I understand. They've put you on a short leash. Forget the nuts and bolts of the investigation. Tell me about the accident."

"Why?"

"I'd just like to hear from you what happened."

Sydney still didn't trust his motives. What if this amiable side of Trent Gannon was an act to disguise his vendetta? What if he was here to take advantage of her current vulnerability to somehow hasten her downfall? Anything was possible, but for the time being, she decided to give him the benefit of the doubt if for no other reason than the conversation distracted her from the searing pain in her ankle.

"I received an anonymous call that a plane was fueled and waiting on a private airstrip to fly Mathison across the border," she said. "Long story short, I staked out his place and then followed him onto the interstate when he left his house. He accelerated. I accelerated. Next thing I knew, a third vehicle came out of nowhere and cut me off. I swerved, hit the shoulder and rolled."

"Do you think you were set up?"

"I've wondered about that. But how could he have been so certain I'd take the bait, let alone that I'd lose control of my vehicle?"

"He knew you wouldn't take a chance on letting him leave the country. The third car was either meant to take you out or make the pursuit appear more dangerous and reckless than it was. Even without the crash, a high-speed chase would have been enough to trigger an investigation into your conduct. You likely would have been removed from the case regardless."

Sydney grimaced. "He outmaneuvered me. The lieutenant was right. I let my emotions get the better of me, and now I'm stuck in here while he's out there free to do as he pleases."

"That's why I'm here," Trent said. "If you're willing to take a chance on me, I can help you nail him. I can be your eyes and ears and even your driver until you're up and around and able to navigate on your own."

His offer stunned her. She searched for a telltale crack or twitch in his features as she wondered yet again why he'd turned up out of the blue the way he had. It couldn't be as simple as making amends. "As intriguing as I find the offer, you'll understand why I'm a little concerned about your motive."

"I just want to help."

Did he? "Even if I wanted or needed your help, I'm not allowed to go anywhere near Gabriel Mathison. If I so much as glance at him sideways, my suspension becomes permanent."

"True, but I'm a private citizen. I can do whatever I want within the law. Besides—" he leaned forward, his eyes still shadowed with something she couldn't read "—we both know you are never going to let this go, regardless of the consequences."

"You don't know anything about me."

A faint smile flickered. "I know a driven person when I see one. I'm offering you a way around your suspension. I do all the legwork and conduct the interviews. Your hands stay clean."

She frowned. "What do you want in return?"

He got up and moved back to the foot of the bed, as if what he had to say required a little distance. "For the past couple of weeks, I've been doing a deep dive into a series of murders that occurred in Southeast Texas from the late 1990s through the early 2000s. Roughly a quarter of a century ago. The bodies of seven young women were found in as many years along the I-45 corridor from Houston to Galveston. Are you familiar with those cases?"

"No, but I would have been a little kid back then. I was in kindergarten during the whole Y2K thing."

He nodded. "I was a few years older, but I didn't remember them, either, until I recently interviewed a retired Houston police detective on my podcast. He said—"

She cut him off. "Hold on. Your *podcast*?"

He looked amused. "Not what you expected from a former drunk?"

Hardly. Never in a million years would she have associated Trent Gannon with anything remotely connected to a podcast or social media in general. If someone had told her that he'd been found dead in a ditch somewhere or that he was serving time in a state penitentiary, yeah. Either of those scenarios would have been more believable.

His smile turned deprecating. "I'll admit, it's not the career I would have chosen for myself, but desperate times called for desperate measures. I started the podcast as a side hustle after I was fired. A way to make a few bucks while drumming up business for my private detective agency—"

She cut him off a second time. "You're a private detective now? Since when?"

"Since I needed to eat and pay bills and no one would hire me," he said with brutal honesty. "I was more surprised than anyone when the podcast took off, but that's a story for another day."

She took a moment to digest his revelations and to adjust her perception of him. Not dead in a ditch or serving time, but a man who'd pulled himself up from a very dark place and carved out a new career for himself. Would she have the courage to do the same?

He gave her a knowing look as if he could tell what she was thinking. "Should I go on?"

She nodded.

"The MO on those cases was all over the place. Shootings, stabbings, strangulations—"

"Strangulations?" Sydney bolted upright despite the bruised rib. Then she clutched her side and eased back down. "Sorry. Please continue."

"Different causes of death and bodies found in different locations. No apparent similarities or connections among the victims. No physical resemblances other than an age range. Nothing in common except for the fact that their murders went unsolved. By every indication, the homicides were random. Each case was investigated individually by the appropriate jurisdiction. Despite the disparities, a detective assigned to one of the cases began to suspect a single killer was responsible and requested assistance from the FBI. The information gathered from the various law enforcement agencies was consolidated and a common thread eventually identified. Articles of clothing and jewelry had been taken from each of the victims. Initially, it was assumed the items had been lost during captivity or a struggle. An earring, a scarf, a handbag. In every single case, at least one shoe was missing. Always the left shoe."

Sydney rubbed a hand up and down her arm where chill bumps had suddenly surfaced. "Why the left shoe?"

"Possibly some kind of fetish or disorder. Or a misdirection to fool the police." He shrugged. "One victim a year for seven years, and then the murders stopped. For whatever reason, the killer went dormant and the trail went cold. Very few people in the area ever realized that a serial predator had lived among them. May still live among us."

Sydney stared at him for the longest moment, almost afraid to say aloud the conclusion she'd immediately jumped to. "Are you suggesting he's active again?"

He seemed hesitant to answer. "It's a longshot. Odds are the killer is dead or in prison for another crime. But my gut tells me that maybe, just maybe, he's still out there. I'm trying to find another piece of the puzzle, no matter how small or seemingly insignificant. You may be able to help me."

"How?"

"Your dad was the local cop who brought in the FBI."

"What?" She pushed herself up against the pillows. "Are you sure?"

"Yes. You didn't know?"

She tried to conceal her shock. The conversation had taken a turn she hadn't expected. "He wouldn't have mentioned anything about it at home. My mother didn't like hearing about his cases."

"That's usually for the best." Something in his tone made her wonder again about his private life. "The fifth body was found in a wooded area off the freeway, but within the Seaside city limits. Your dad took lead. He'd been working the case for over a year when another body turned up in a remote area of Galveston County. This time, there were enough similarities to his case that he started to look into past unsolved homicides in the region. He began to suspect they were looking for a single perpetrator clever enough to disguise his movements and proclivities by varying his MO, victim selection and location. Rather than trying to coerce cooperation from the various jurisdictions, he decided to request assistance from the feds."

Sydney sat riveted. "What was the cause of death in his case?"

"Victim number five was the first of three strangulations."

"*Three* strangulations?" She tried to fight off a growing unease as something clicked into place. Maybe she did have a vague recollection of those cases. An overheard conversation between her parents niggled at the back of her mind.

Don't let her play outside alone until we catch the bastard.

She's a handful, Tom. I can't watch her twenty-four hours a day.

Trent pounced on her silence. "What's wrong? Did you remember something?"

"Not really. Nothing helpful." But the memory kept tugging. *She's a handful, Tom. I can't watch her twenty-four hours a day.* Even with the threat of a serial killer on the loose?

"Are you sure?" he pressed.

She sighed. "Like I said, I was just a little kid back then. As for my dad, he died a few years ago. And there's no way I can get my hands on his casefiles, if that's where you're going with this."

"You still have friends in the department, don't you?"

"No one who'll stick their neck out for me."

Except for Dan Bertram, although she'd done a pretty good job of burning that bridge earlier. Still, he'd been her dad's partner for years. The two had been like brothers for a time. Even if he hadn't been actively involved in the investigation, he would have known about the cases. Why hadn't he mentioned them in conjunction to the recent strangulations?

Trent said something, drawing her attention back to their conversation. "I'm sorry. What?"

"I asked about your dad's notebooks. Did he keep any records at home?"

"His personal belongings were put in storage when I sold the house. It would take hours to go through all the boxes."

"I'm willing if you are."

She gave him a long, penetrating stare. "Why didn't you tell me the truth from the start instead of trying to play me?"

"What do you mean?"

Her gaze narrowed. "Admit it. You don't give a damn about helping me. You just want access to my dad's files."

"Why can't it be both?"

At least he didn't insult her with a flat-out denial. "Why are you so interested in these cases anyway? What's in it for you? Are you trying to prove something? Or is it just about content for your podcast?"

"You didn't mention justice." ·

She folded her arms.

"Okay, you're right. It was about content in the beginning," he admitted. "The interview with the former HPD detective was one of my most popular shows. Thousands of new subscribers in a matter of days after I uploaded the video. Some of the clips from the episode went viral and racked up so many views that I decided to turn it into a series. People love police procedurals and unsolved mysteries. Podcasts are the new medium for true crime fanatics. But the deeper I dug…" He hesitated as if unsure how much he wanted to reveal. "Let's just say, I now have a more compelling reason for exploring these murders."

"What reason?"

"That's something I'm not yet ready to discuss."

"Being cryptic won't help your cause," she warned. "And anyway, I don't know that I'm comfortable letting you dig through my dad's things. He was a very private person."

"Will you at least think about it?"

She gave a vague nod. "I need to rest now."

"Yeah, I can see that. This isn't the time or place anyway. I'll be in touch. In the meantime, take care of yourself. I don't just mean physically." He came back around to the side of her bed and stared down at her. "Don't make the mistake of thinking the department will have your back. The moment

Richard Mathison files a lawsuit, they'll circle the wagons. You have no idea how bad it can get."

"I'm starting to have an inkling," she murmured.

He removed a card from his shirt pocket and placed it on top of the sheet. "If you find yourself out in the cold, give me a call."

Chapter Two

Late that afternoon, Sydney was moved upstairs to a private room with a nice view of downtown. The doctor had gone over the X-rays and CT scans, and then her temporary ankle splint was replaced with a fiberglass cast. If all went well for the next four to six weeks, she would then be fitted with a walking boot.

The cast was lightweight, but already her skin felt hot and itchy inside and elevating her foot soon became unbearable. She was tired of lying on her back, tired of being poked and prodded, just plain tired, period. But she reminded herself that a fractured ankle was nothing in the scheme of things. She'd made it through her father's death and had finally come to terms with her mother's indifference. A broken bone wasn't going to keep her down for long.

However, by the time the dinner hour rolled around, her spirits had flatlined, and she found herself nearly comatose with pain. Her tray came and went untouched. She tried to practice visualization as she waited for the pain meds to take effect. Checking emails and returning text messages only distracted her for a little while. Finally, she switched on the TV and dozed to the background drone of a garden show.

Drifting in and out, she noted the deepening shadows

outside her window as the nursing shift changed and a new face came in to check on her. When she finally fell into a deep sleep, she awakened abruptly, alarmed and disoriented as one often was in a strange place. She lay very still as her eyes adjusted to the darkness. A dull throb at her temples and the rigidity of the cast around her ankle brought everything back. The car crash, the suspension, the unexpected visit from Trent Gannon. She knew where she was and how she'd gotten there, but something seemed…not right.

She remained motionless as she tried to attune her senses to her surroundings. She heard the faint peal of a ringtone as someone moved down the hallway outside her door and the more distant ping of the elevator. She could smell roses. Someone must have brought in a bouquet while she slept. That was surprising. For a moment she wondered—hoped—the arrangement might be from her mother, but when had Lori Shepherd ever thought of anyone but herself? That was unfair. She probably didn't even know about the accident unless Dan Bertram had thought to call her.

Shaking off the remnants of sleep, Sydney started to reach for the light switch, then froze as she realized what had awakened her. Why goose bumps prickled at her nape. Someone was in her room.

She stifled a gasp as a silhouette took shape in the weak illumination from the bathroom nightlight. A man stood at the foot of her bed gazing down at her.

Her first instinct was to reach for her weapon until she remembered she'd surrendered her firearm to the lieutenant. She remained motionless in the dark, wanting desperately to believe that a nurse had come to check on her, but she knew better.

How long had he been standing there?

She ran through the possibilities as she lay perfectly still on the outside, but bracing herself on the inside.

It couldn't be Trent Gannon. He'd left hours ago, and he had no reason to return unless she called him. And the lieutenant or any of her colleagues wouldn't visit her room at such a late hour. Most of them would probably want to steer clear of her anyway for fear of being tainted by her suspension. The wagons had undoubtedly started to circle, leaving her out in the cold as Trent had predicted.

Gabriel Mathison. The name came with an icy certainty that set her heart to pounding. Adrenaline pulsed through her veins, tingling at her fingertips and the base of her spine. Still, she remained frozen, though a muscle in her wounded foot had started to twitch uncontrollably.

"I know you're awake." His voice sounded silky smooth in the shadowy room, edged with the kind of ingrained superiority that excess too often bred. Beneath the scent of the roses, she caught a hint of his cologne, something woodsy and expensive and suppressive. Something that reminded her of death.

"I can see you in the moonlight," he said. "Your eyes are wide open and gleaming. Are you frightened?"

In response, she slid her hand across the sheet, groping for the call button.

"It's not there," he informed her. "I put the controls and your phone out of reach. I thought it best we not be interrupted."

She swallowed back her fear. "I could scream. The nurse's station is just down the hall."

"You could, but you won't." He sounded supremely confident. "Your curiosity won't let you. Or maybe *obsession* is a better word."

Prove him wrong. Scream for help at the top your lungs.

Instead, she hoisted herself up against the pillows so that she didn't feel quite so vulnerable. "I'm not obsessed," she said. "I'm determined."

"And look where that got you." He leaned against the rail, tracing his finger down the side of her cast.

"Don't touch me." She jerked her foot away, sending a spasm of pain up her leg.

He gave a low laugh. "Don't worry. You're not my type. I've never cared for dirty blondes. But it seems you do have an admirer."

Her vision had adjusted to the darkness so that she could see him more clearly now, the dark hair falling just so across his forehead, the perfectly symmetrical features, the taunting smile. He might have been considered extraordinarily handsome if not for a weak jawline and the glint of cruelty in his eyes.

She needed to moisten her dry lips but she didn't want to give him the satisfaction of knowing how badly he unnerved her. Was she frightened? Yes. If her suspicions were true, he'd killed at least once and gotten away with it. Why wouldn't he think he could do so again?

"What admirer?" she found herself asking.

He gave a nod to the table beside her bed. "The white roses on your nightstand. At least two dozen, I would guess. Too extravagant to be from a friend or colleague. Someone obviously wants to make an impression." She could sense his smirk. "Shall I read the card to you?"

"Just tell me why you're here."

"See you soon, Sydney."

"What?"

"No signature on the card. Just…*See you soon, Sydney.*"

She swallowed back a wave of panic. "How do you know what the card says?"

"I took a peek while you were sleeping."

He'd been in her room long enough to read the message that came with the roses. To remove the call button and take her phone. He'd been that close while she lay sleeping. What else had he done?

Moving around to the side of the bed, he placed his body between her and the hallway door. He wasn't a big man. Two or three inches shy of six feet with a slim build. But she knew from her research that he was a kickboxer. He also held black belts in karate and aikido, and like his father, he had a fascination for antique weapons.

All of this ran through her mind while she sized up her chances of making a run for the door with a broken ankle.

He peered down at her. "You don't look so good."

She forced steel into her tone. "At least I'm alive. That's more than I can say for Jessica King."

He seemed unfazed by the mention of his dead girlfriend. "Yes, poor Jessie. So tragic. She was very nearly the perfect woman except for one tiny flaw." He leaned in so close that he could have easily slid his fingers around Sydney's throat or stuffed a pillow over her face. "Like you, she had the bad habit of sticking her nose where it didn't belong."

"Is that why you killed her?"

"See what I mean? Always asking questions."

"What happened?" Sydney struggled to keep her emotions static. Mathison was all about being in control. *Let him believe he has the upper hand. He might let something slip.* "Did she find out something about your father's business? About you? Did you kill her to keep her quiet?"

"You seem to think you have all the answers. You tell me." His voice was deceptively passive.

She gave a curt nod. "I think you attacked her in a fit of jealous rage. She was a beautiful, successful woman with any number of admirers. You didn't like her getting all that attention, so you decided to teach her a lesson. Rough her up a little. Show her who was really in control. But she fought you, didn't she? That's why you had to hit her. So hard you fractured her skull. Then you strangled her as she lay unconscious. You couldn't take a chance that she might survive. That she might wake up and tell someone what you'd done to her. Am I close? Come on," she coaxed. "Tell me what really happened. There's no one here but us. It'll be your word against mine."

"And who would ever believe you over me?" His eyes glittered dangerously as he stared down at her.

"Exactly," she agreed, even though the truth irked her. "You've already bested me. I've been removed from the case. Suspended without pay indefinitely. My credibility is shot and my career is over. No matter what you say, I can't touch you. So tell me what I missed. Tell me where I went wrong." She tried to keep her tone even as her fingers curled into fists beneath the covers. "That's why you're here, isn't it? To rub your win in my face."

"I'm here to make sure you got the message. But you're right about one thing. Your career is over. You tried to tarnish the Mathison name, and my old man won't stand for that. You have no idea how far he'll go to protect his precious reputation. This…" He waved a hand toward her cast. "Trust me, what happened to you in that crash is nothing compared to what's coming."

"I'm not afraid of your father. I'm not afraid of you, either," she lied. "You think you've gotten away with murder, but someone like you doesn't commit the perfect crime. Your ego makes you careless. You'll have overlooked some small detail, or maybe one of your friends will decide to rat you out. Badge or no badge, I'll be watching. I'll be waiting."

He gave an exaggerated shudder. "You're making me shiver."

"Sneer all you want," she said. "But this isn't over."

"You're right about that, too." He leaned down suddenly, placing his lips against her ear. "See you soon, Sydney."

TRENT GLANCED AT his phone on the table beside his worn-out beach chair. The metal frame creaked as he leaned sideways, and for the umpteenth time, he wondered when the thing would collapse altogether. He'd found it discarded behind the garage when he moved in last year, so he figured he and the chair had been living on borrowed time ever since.

He checked the clock on the screen as he'd done repeatedly for the past half hour. Nearly midnight. Finally. He'd been up since five that morning, going strong all day, and now he longed for the comfort of his bed. Instead, he stretched out his legs and waited.

The June night was unseasonably hot and sticky. Lightning flickered in the distance. He could smell ozone on the warm breeze that blew in from the water. Rain would be nice. The bedraggled tomato plant at the corner of his backyard could use a long drink. Maybe a storm would cool things off. Wishful thinking. Summer on the Gulf Coast could be brutal weatherwise. Droughts, flash flooding, the occasional hurricane to worry about. Not to mention mosquitos.

He thought about walking down to the dock and dangling his feet in the water while he waited. His neighbors, mostly retirees and ex-military, had long since turned in, so he didn't have to worry about making idle chitchat. Didn't have to pretend to care about fishing or cards or any of the mundane activities that filled their long days. He liked living alone for a reason. He briefly flirted with the idea of a quick dip, but instead he settled deeper into the chair. He was comfortable right where he was, so why bother? Besides, the view from his yard was hard to beat. Most people desired oceanfront property, but he preferred the bay. The water was calmer, his surroundings quieter. Sometimes a little too quiet, but he was used to the solitude.

Before the heat had set in, he sometimes slept on the screened porch, lulled by the breeze and the sound of lapping water as he drifted in and out of his dreams. For the last few nights, however, he'd taken to sleeping inside even when the weather was mild. He'd gotten into the habit of making an extra round through the house just to check the locks before he allowed his head to hit the pillow. On restless nights, he'd stand at the sliding glass door in the den and stare out over the moonlit water until he spotted the barest hint of a silhouette on the horizon.

He judged the vessel to be around forty feet with the clear outline of a cabin. Probably a dual-engine cruiser with a hard top. The boat had appeared just hours after the second episode in his current podcast series had gone live. Exactly one week to the day after his initial interview with the retired Houston police detective.

His follow-up guest had been the sister of the seventh and final victim. Eileen Ballard had been eager for the interview and seemed to find solace in being able to speak at length about her sister's murder. She recalled in vivid detail the last time she'd seen her sister, what they'd talked about and what the victim had been wearing.

She always took such care with her clothing and makeup. I used to tease her that she'd been born in the wrong era. Our grandmother had left her a collection of vintage jewelry and accessories that she cherished. When she left for work that morning, she had on her favorite silk scarf. She'd tied it around her neck and pinned it to her dress with a silver brooch. They recovered the brooch with the body, but the scarf never turned up. I always found it odd that the killer took the time to unfasten the brooch only to leave it behind.

The memory floated away as Trent focused his gaze on the water. He hadn't placed much importance on the sightings at first. The presence of a boat on moonlit water seemed innocuous. Someone out night fishing or enjoying a midnight cruise. He couldn't even be sure it was the same vessel that returned night after night. But then he started paying attention to the routine. The boat always glided into his line of sight at precisely midnight. Stopped in the same location, establishing a pattern that he could no longer deny. Someone was out there watching the shoreline. Watching his house.

On the one night when the cruiser failed to appear, Trent had taken his neighbor's boat out for a close encounter. Rocking on the waves, he'd kept watch for well over an hour, but the phantom vessel never showed. After that, he remained onshore, observing from his window or the patio as a dark premonition had started to creep in with the mist.

Picking up his phone, he counted down the seconds to midnight. *Three, two, one...* He set the phone aside and scanned the horizon. There it was. Sailing across the glassy water like a ghost ship. Like a figment of his imagination. Each night, edging a bit closer to the shoreline, or so it seemed from his vantage.

He lifted his night-vision binoculars and trained the lenses on the horizon. Even with the aid of thermal imaging, he'd never been able to detect anyone onboard, much less make out a name on the hull. The vessel really did seem to be a mirage, but the icy suspicion that tingled his scalp was all too real.

That same chill feathered along his bare arms as he skimmed the boat from stem to stern. *Who are you? What the hell are you doing out there?*

A movement near the cabin caught his attention and adrenaline pulsed. Never before had he detected even a slight movement. The boat came and went as if guided by an invisible hand. Not tonight, though. As he peered through the eyepiece, a human form took shape.

Was he seeing things? He glanced away, blinked and refocused.

Still there.

As if somehow intuiting Trent's doubt, the figure moved out of the shadows and stepped boldly into the moonlight so there could be no mistaking his presence. But he kept his head turned away as if he knew someone would be watching. This new development puzzled and intrigued Trent even as his trepidation deepened. For the longest time, he remained fixated on the silhouette. He couldn't make out even grainy features from this distance.

Minutes ticked by before he set aside the binoculars and got up to stride down to the water's edge. The surf swirled around his ankles as he stood gazing out toward the cruiser. *Come on, you bastard. Tell me to my face what you want.* He thought about waving the vessel ashore, but that might be an invitation he'd soon regret.

The night was so quiet he imagined he could detect the low idle of the inboard motors. He could definitely hear the quieter tinkle of the wind chimes that hung from a neighbor's boathouse. He waded out, letting the water rise to his thighs and then to his waist before he dove under and resurfaced neck-deep. The cruiser remained stationary in the face of his dare, pitching on the waves before the prow finally turned toward the open water. Within minutes the boat had disappeared in the darkness.

Trent's gaze remained glued to the spot, then he abruptly returned to shore. He started walking with no destination in mind. Past the tinkling chimes. Past rickety docks with bobbing boats. Past a long line of darkened houses. A few minutes earlier, he'd wanted nothing so much as to crawl between cool sheets and close his eyes. Now he was too keyed up to sleep. Something had been nagging at him ever since the boat had first appeared on the horizon a week ago. *He knows who you are and where you live. He knows you're looking for him.*

An elusive monster that preyed on young women.

The Seaside Strangler.

The name sounded like something from a low-budget horror movie, which had been the point. He'd wanted to grab attention for his podcast series. Mission accomplished, if the mysterious boat was any indication. In hindsight, the moniker seemed a little too contrived and not really apt since the murders had taken place in seven different communities, including Houston. Still, if Trent was right, the killer had ties to this town. In a sense, the *strangler* in him had been born here. For whatever reason, he'd been resurrected. To find him, Trent needed the help of a certain police detective who found herself in a place he'd been three years ago. A blue-eyed blonde who had the reputation of being impulsive, reckless and tough as nails.

What makes you think you can trust her? She turned on you once. How do you know she won't do it again?

"I don't trust her," he muttered.

He didn't trust anyone. But Sydney Shepherd was the only cop he knew willing to put herself on the line no matter the consequences. She was still inexperienced as a detective. Not the partner he would have chosen if he had his pick, but she possessed something no one else had—access to her late father's records. One way or another, Trent intended to get inside that storage unit. Her cooperation would make things easier, but a refusal wouldn't stop him.

Scouring the empty horizon one last time, he returned home and put away his gear. Then he made the rounds through the bungalow, pausing in his office to scan the whiteboard he'd picked up from a junk shop. He followed a trail of blue x's all up and down the map of the I-45 corridor. The blue marks signified the seven original murders. A small cluster of three red x's indicated where the bodies of the three recent victims had been found—all in or near Seaside. Radiating from each of the marks was a series of intersecting lines and spirals that would appear chaotic and meaningless to the untrained eye, but to Trent they represented days and nights of painstaking research in order to establish even the smallest connection among the victims, past and present.

He studied the board, moving sticky notes like chess pieces until everything started to blur. Turning out the light in his office, he went down the hallway to his bedroom, collapsing on the mattress with a heavy sigh. He threw an arm over his eyes and slept.

A noise roused him sometime later. He swung his legs over the side of the bed and sat with his ear cocked toward the hallway, listening intently to the familiar night sounds. He heard nothing out of the ordinary, and yet the hair at the back of his neck lifted.

Easing the nightstand drawer open, he removed a weapon and rose to slip across the room to the door. He navigated down the narrow hallway, instinctively avoiding the creaking floorboards in the center. He checked the front door first and then went from room to room, methodically searching every corner and closet and peering through windows and out the back door. Nothing seemed amiss.

Satisfied that no one had invaded his sanctuary, he returned the firearm to the nightstand drawer and went out to the kitchen for a glass of water. He stood staring out the window over the sink as he drank. The moon was up, illuminating his neglected garden and the weed-strewn pathway that led down to the water. He could still hear the faint tinkle from the boathouse. For a moment, he imagined a shoulder brushing against the chimes and then a hand lifting to silence them. Maybe he shouldn't have been so quick to put away his weapon, he thought, and then shrugged off his lingering unease. *No one's there.*

But even as he turned back toward the bedroom, another sound halted him. He eased through the tiny foyer and peered through the glass panes out to the porch. Then he turned the dead bolt and jerked open the door. His neighbor's orange tabby darted up the porch steps and shot past him into the house.

Already on edge, Trent jumped at the unexpected intrusion, then swore. Closing the door, he turned with another muttered oath. Larry had jumped up on the armchair he'd claimed for himself when Trent had first moved in. From the start, the tabby had made himself at home. Sometimes he'd curl up for a snooze while Trent edited videos or watched TV. The cat never remained inside for more than an hour or two at a time. He seemed to know better than to overstay his welcome, which was far more intuitive than most humans Trent knew.

Rather than settling down in his usual spot on the cushion, Larry perched on the arm and began to yowl and paw frantically at whatever the neighbor's granddaughter had tied around his neck. The kid had a penchant for torturing the poor cat, though not maliciously. She merely wanted to dress Larry up like one of her dolls, much to his chagrin. He'd once turned up on Trent's porch with a pearl necklace wound around his throat.

"Take it easy," Trent murmured as he knelt beside the chair. "What's she done to you this time?" The cat batted Trent's hand when he tried to unfasten the knot. "Do you want my help or don't you?"

He finally managed to remove the scarf from the distraught feline's neck, and then he took a moment to examine the fabric. He was no expert, but even he recognized the quality of the silk and the name of the designer stitched unobtrusively into the hem. The scarf looked old but well preserved except for a small brown stain that covered two tiny holes. Recognition niggled.

Leaving Larry to his leisurely bath, Trent headed down the hallway to his office, where he plopped down behind his computer and opened an audio file. The interview with Eileen Ballard was still fresh on his mind, but he had to be sure—

There it was. The description of the dead woman's scarf. *Navy with swirls of green, pink and yellow.* It had been pinned around the victim's neck when she left for work that morning. She hadn't come home that night. Five days later, her body had been discovered in an abandoned warehouse in Houston. She was still fully clothed except for the missing scarf and her shoes.

Trent took a closer look at the stain. Blood? Possibly the victim's or the perpetrator's DNA? He folded the scarf almost reverently before slipping it into a protective bag.

A silk scarf belonging to a woman who'd been murdered

twenty years ago in Houston had turned up tied around a cat's neck in Seaside. Any humor or irony in the absurd situation was lost on Trent. Any doubt he had as to the occupant of the mysterious boat vanished.

The killer was back. And he wanted to play.

Chapter Three

Sydney was released from the hospital the following afternoon. She'd been dressed and ready to go since early that
morning. The lieutenant had called at nine to see if she
needed a ride home, but she declined his offer. She wasn't
yet ready to face him after the way they'd ended things the
day before. His voice on the phone had sounded stilted, and
their conversation was so strained that she found herself
ending the call without mentioning the visit from Gabriel
Mathison.

For as long as she could remember, Dan Bertram had
been a constant in her life—a mentor, a champion and
sometimes a confidant. Someone she could always count
on to have her best interests at heart. But her recent behavior had caused him to lose confidence in her. If she told
him that Mathison had shown up in her hospital room in
the dead of night, he might suspect she was lying to prove
a point. Worse than that, she'd begun to doubt herself. A
part of her wondered if she'd dreamed Gabriel Mathison at
her bedside. If his threats had been nothing more than a fe-
verish hallucination brought on by trauma and painkillers.

One thing was certain. She hadn't imagined the white
roses. She read the card a few times, trying to figure out
who had sent them. Finally coming to the conclusion that

the Mathisons were playing mind games with her, she asked the nurse to give the flowers to another patient.

While she waited for her release papers, she practiced walking up and down the hallway on crutches. Every part of her body screamed for relief, but she ignored the aches and pains. The sooner she became mobile, the sooner she could get back to work. The prospect of sitting in her apartment and doing nothing for the next six weeks made her anxious. Already she had cabin fever after a single night in the hospital. However, by the time the attendant wheeled her downstairs to the waiting car service, her muscles trembled from exhaustion, and home had never sounded better.

Sunday afternoon traffic was light. She checked her messages on the ride to her apartment and then stared out the window until the car turned down her block. At her direction, the driver pulled all the way to the end of the driveway. He got out and opened the door for her, then held her crutches while she awkwardly disembarked.

"You live up there?" He nodded to the garage apartment. "Are you sure you can climb the stairs?"

She wasn't at all sure, but she gave him a confident nod. "Yeah, no worries. I've got this." She waited until he backed out of the driveway before clomping over to the steps, pausing at the bottom to psyche herself up for the climb. She tried to remember the advice she'd been given before she left the hospital. Weight concentrated on her hands, lead with her good foot going up.

"Need some help?"

She'd been so deep in concentration that the male voice, seemingly coming from nowhere, startled her. She jumped, dropped a crutch and had to grab onto the banister to keep from toppling over.

Her first assumption was that her landlord had come out

to check on her. He was a quiet, solitary man who spent most of his days reading on his patio or working in his garden. He spoke when spoken to, but other than the necessary conversations regarding repairs and upkeep, he left Sydney to her own devices, which suited her fine.

Rather than the older Martin Swann, however, the man who emerged from the overgrown hedge looked to be in his early to midthirties, tall and fit with wavy black hair and the most extraordinary blue eyes Sydney had ever looked into. The irises were so vivid, in fact, she thought he must surely wear tinted contacts to enhance them.

He lifted a hand in a friendly wave, and the smile he flashed was utterly disarming. Sydney gawked, then caught herself and closed her mouth. Since when had she become so susceptible to a handsome face? She decided to blame the concussion.

"You startled me," she said with a frown.

"I'm sorry." He crossed the narrow expanse of grass. "I saw you through the bushes. You seemed to have difficulty getting out of the car. I thought you might need a hand."

"Thank you, but I'm fine." Balancing on one foot, she leaned down for the crutch. Who the heck was he, anyway? And what business did he have spying on her? The thought crossed her mind that he might have been hired by Richard Mathison to keep an eye on her. Or worse, harass her in some way. Maybe she was being paranoid, but his own son had warned her the worst was yet to come.

"Here, let me get that for you. It's the least I can do." He closed the distance between them and bent to retrieve the crutch. Clinging to the banister, Sydney gave him a careful inspection while his head was lowered. A line she'd read somewhere came to mind: *Beware the tall, dark stranger.*

He straightened and handed her the crutch, squinting

past her up the stairs. "Not to be a pessimist, but those steps look pretty steep. Are you sure you can manage?"

"I guess we'll find out." Now that she had both crutches tucked underneath her arms, she was starting to regain her equilibrium. There was something about the stranger that rang a faint bell. She was certain they'd never met—who could forget those eyes?—yet he seemed vaguely familiar. She couldn't put her finger on why. "You said you saw me through the hedge?" An accusatory note crept into her tone as she continued to observe him.

He looked sheepish, as if he'd been caught with his hand in the proverbial cookie jar. "Yes, sorry. I know how that must sound, but I swear I wasn't being nosy on purpose. I heard the car and thought it might be my uncle. I'm still getting used to the comings and goings around here." He motioned over his shoulder to the row of oleanders. "I just moved in a few days ago. I'm Brandon, by the way. Brandon Shaw."

"Sydney Shepherd. What happened to Mrs. Dorman?"

"Who?"

She lifted a brow. "The previous owner? Nice elderly lady with white hair?"

"Oh, *that* Mrs. Dorman." He slid his hands in his pockets and rocked back with a quick grin. "The name didn't ring a bell at first. I've never actually met the woman."

"Then how did you end up in her house?" She wondered if she sounded as suspicious to him as she did to her own ears. Normally, she wouldn't have cared, but she didn't want to scare him off until she figured out whether or not he had a connection to the Mathisons.

He didn't seem to mind the question. He answered with an easygoing shrug. "She was called away on a family emergency. Something about a sister in Florida having hip surgery. She'll be gone for several weeks at least. Uncle

Marty knew that I was looking for a quiet place near the water for the summer. He suggested a short-term lease, and Mrs. Dorman agreed. The arrangement works well for both of us. I'm less than ten minutes from the marina, and she has someone looking out for her place while she collects a rent check to help with expenses."

A perfectly logical explanation, but Sydney still wasn't convinced. In her experience, someone who looked like Brandon Shaw didn't just appear out of the blue. "You keep referring to your uncle. You don't mean Martin Swann, do you?"

"Yes. Why does that surprise you?"

"I wasn't aware he had any family. I've lived here for nearly two years, and I've never known him to have a single visitor." She thought of the older man bent over his tasks in the garden, seemingly oblivious to the rest of the world. She'd always felt a bit sorry for him, although she wasn't sure why. She was alone, too, and she frequently reminded herself that was how she liked it.

"I suppose I'm the last of his family." Brandon Shaw fell silent for a moment as he glanced back over his shoulder toward Martin's patio. "We aren't blood relatives, but he was like a surrogate uncle to me when I was a kid. We lost touch for many years after my family moved away. When we finally reconnected, I was surprised to see how much he'd changed. He's grown older, of course. And sadder, I think. I don't know that he ever got over losing his wife. The Uncle Marty from my childhood was gregarious and playful. We used to follow him around like little lost puppy dogs."

"We?"

A frown played across his brow as he nodded toward the house next door. "My siblings and I. We lived here when we were children. It's strange being back on my own. I thought there might be ghosts, but no. It's just a house."

"You grew up in Seaside?"

"I wish," he said with a sigh. "We were only here for a short time, but this place made an impression. I've always wanted to come back and spend more time here."

"Well, I hope it lives up to your memories." Despite her reservations, he intrigued her. Had their paths crossed as children? Was that why he seemed familiar? "It's a nice place to vacation if you don't mind the quiet."

"The quiet is one of the best things about it. But I don't think of my time here as a vacation. Not in the usual sense. It's more of a hiatus," he explained. "A necessary pause from my regular routine to recharge and regroup. I was burned out with my work and a little depressed in the city. The constant whir of activity can start to wear you down. Not to mention the noise. Jackhammers and blaring horns everywhere you go. So loud you can't think. So much smog and exhaust you can't breathe. After a while, you become numb to the chaos…"

He trailed off, as if he'd shared more than he'd intended. He tried to downplay his revelations with another quick shrug. "Anyway, a friend suggested a change of scenery, and I immediately thought of this place. It's a short drive away if I need to get back, and the slower pace is just what I've been craving. Unfortunately, I'd already committed to teaching a summer writing course, but other than that, I don't plan to do anything for the next few weeks except fish and swim."

"Oh, you're a writer," Sydney said. "That's interesting."

"I dabble a bit. You know what they say about those who can't." His self-deprecating smile turned knowing. "Any other questions I can answer for you?"

She tried to look contrite. "Sorry. I didn't mean to give you the third degree."

"Force of habit, I would imagine. You're a police detective, right?" He placed a foot on the bottom step and leaned against the banister. "Marty mentioned you'd be my neighbor. Imagine my surprise when I heard your name on the local news this morning. They showed a photograph of the car you were driving. An unmarked sedan, the best I could tell."

"You're very observant."

"And you're lucky to be alive."

"That seems to be the consensus."

He glanced up the steps once again. "So, those stairs…"

She drew a breath and released it. "Yes. The stairs."

"Tell you what. I'll follow you up. If you lose your balance, I'll catch you."

"Or I'll knock you down and we'll both break our necks."

"There is that," he agreed. "I'm willing to risk it."

Sydney's internal alarm sounded again. Why was he going out of his way to be so helpful? Was she that jaded? Had she lost the ability to accept an act of kindness at face value? The answer was yes. She was exactly that jaded. "Thank you, but I couldn't ask you to do that," she protested. "I've taken up too much of your time as it is."

"I have nothing but time." He motioned toward the stairs. "Shall we?"

She didn't see how she could gracefully refuse, so she turned and gripped her crutches. *Weight on your hands, lead with your good foot. Check your balance before moving on to the next step.*

"Steady as she goes," he echoed. "One step at a time. Nice and slow…"

The climb was torturous. Sydney liked to think of herself as decently in shape. She ran. She trained. She took the occasional Pilates class. But by the time she reached the top step, she was breathing hard and her muscles quivered. She stepped onto the narrow wraparound landing and leaned against the wall to steady her balance. "That was even harder than I thought it would be."

"You'll get the hang of it," he said cheerfully. "Going down might be a bit daunting at first."

"I'll cross that bridge when I come to it." Propping one crutch against the wall, she searched through her bag for a house key rather than retrieving the one she kept hidden beneath a flower pot. Brandon Shaw might be a genuinely nice person, and the fact that Martin Swann knew him personally helped to ease her mind, but he was still a stranger, and sometimes the person with the easiest smile concealed the darkest secrets.

"May I?" He took the key from her hand, turned the lock and pushed open the door for her. Then he dropped the key in her palm and moved back to the top of the stairs as if to let her know he didn't expect—or even want—to be invited inside.

"Thanks again for your help."

"Anytime. I mean that. If you need anything, just let me know."

He went down a few steps before turning to glance back up at her. "Something just occurred to me. It seems you'll have a lot of time on your hands for the next few weeks, and I'm guessing you're not a binge-watcher. If you get bored, you can always check out my writing class. I post new lectures on Tuesday and I live stream every Thursday evening at seven. The chat section can get pretty lively, especially when I read aloud from class assignments. Just hit the notification bell so you'll be alerted when I upload."

"I'll check them out, but I won't be able to contribute," she said. "I don't know anything about writing."

"That's the point of taking a class, isn't it? To learn something new? You might surprise yourself. I'll wager there's more than a story or two inside your head. Just give it some thought. If you get bored."

"I'll think about it." She shifted her weight on the crutches, wanting nothing more than to retreat inside. She needed to rest and elevate her foot. She needed a shower and some food. She needed to be alone. The past twenty-four hours had taken a mental and physical toll. Her ankle hurt, her head hurt, her bruised rib hurt. Not to mention her ego. On top of all that, she'd probably lost a career she loved. Police work was all she'd ever wanted to do. What was she supposed to do now?

For some reason, Trent Gannon popped into her head. If anyone could understand her angst at the moment, it would be him.

She was readying her excuse to disappear inside when the back gate slammed shut, and they both glanced down the driveway in unison. Martin Swann stood on the pavement gazing back at them. He clutched a large box in his arms. Unlike Brandon Shaw, her landlord would never be noticed in a crowd. His appearance was completely nondescript from his pressed khaki pants to his crisp button-down shirt. Yet there was the gleam of curiosity and keen intelligence behind his wire-rimmed glasses.

His gaze darted from Sydney to Brandon, then back to Sydney. "I'm glad I caught you." He shifted the box to his hip. "I heard about the accident. Are you okay? You weren't seriously hurt?"

"A little banged up, but I'll live."

"I'm so relieved to hear it." He seemed to remember the

package and hurried over to the stairs. "This came for you yesterday. The delivery service left it on my front porch."

"Must be my new printer, judging by the size of the box."

"People still use printers?" Brandon teased.

"You might be surprised how often," she said.

"It's bulky." Martin shifted the weight yet again. "Shall I bring it up for you?"

"Let me save you the trouble." Before Sydney could utter a word, Brandon Shaw breezed down the stairs and took the box from Martin. His back was to Sydney. She couldn't hear the exchange between the two men, but Martin looked annoyed before he relinquished the box and lifted his gaze to Sydney.

"I'm glad you're okay," he said.

She nodded. "Thank you. And thank you for bringing over my delivery."

Brandon bounded up the steps with the oversized package as if it weighed no more than an ounce or two. The thought crossed Sydney's mind that he'd done it on purpose just to flaunt his youth and vitality in the older man's face. But she didn't know either man well enough to make such a judgment.

"Where do you want it?" Brandon asked.

"What? Oh, you can just leave it here on the porch," Sydney said. "I'll take it in later."

"Are you sure? I'm already here, willing and able."

Again, he was so friendly and accommodating she could hardly refuse. "All right. Just put it inside the door if you don't mind."

"Not at all." He pushed open the door with his hip and disappeared inside.

She glanced down the steps where Martin Swann still waited as if he expected her to say or do something. Normally, he was the one who broke off their brief exchanges. She gave him a wave. "Thanks again."

He turned without another word and walked back toward his gate.

She left the door open when she went inside. Brandon had placed the box on the floor and was now surveying her place with unabashed curiosity. "It's smaller than I remembered."

"You've been here before?" she asked in surprise.

"Years ago. It wasn't an apartment back then. Uncle Marty used the space as a kind of den. A man cave, if you will. He would come up here when his wife had her bridge parties in the main house. She was a lot more social than Marty. He got on far better with us kids than he did with adults." He looked momentarily lost in memories. "A friend and I used to sneak up here when Marty was at work or out of town and pretend the place was our clubhouse. We even left our initials inside the bedroom closet. But I'm sure that wall has been painted over many times since then."

"No initials that I've noticed." Sydney hovered just inside the door.

He didn't take the hint, but instead he crossed the room and glanced out the window that overlooked the backyard and pool area next door. His eyes glinted when he turned. "That's quite a view. No skinny-dipping for me."

"Your pool, your rules." She moved aside to give him room to exit. "Thanks again for your help."

"It was my pleasure." He grinned as he moved past her through the door. "Don't forget about the writing class. Just do a search on my name. The videos should pop up."

"I'll remember." She followed him out to the porch and watched as he descended the stairs, glad to see the last of him but admiring and envying his agility at the same time.

When he got to the bottom, he glanced over his shoulder with another smile. "See you soon, Sydney."

SEE YOU SOON, SYDNEY.

The expression was common. People said it all the time. Just another way to communicate "goodbye" or "so long" or "take care." But she had a hard time believing that particular wording was a coincidence. First the anonymous message that came with the roses, then Gabriel Mathison whispering in her ear. Now a stranger uttering the exact same catchphrase from the bottom of her steps.

Her suspicions were triggered enough that she decided to run a background check on Brandon Shaw. She opened her laptop to log into the department's database. Password denied. She repeated the process until the system locked her out for too many false tries. She stared at the screen in frustration even as she reminded herself that limiting access during a suspension was protocol. But someone—probably the lieutenant—had certainly acted fast, maybe because he had reason to believe she wasn't coming back.

Or he knew she wouldn't sit around twiddling her thumbs for the next six weeks.

What was she supposed to do? It wasn't like she enjoyed prying into someone's personal business, but her new neighbor was just a little too perfect, a little too helpful and his arrival next door a little too timely. Maybe he was exactly who he seemed—an uncommonly handsome man looking to escape the pressures and intrusions of the modern world—but that little voice in her head reminded her that appearances were often deceiving.

She couldn't run a background check, but she could certainly talk to her landlord. She would be very interested in hearing Martin's take on their past. Would his recollection corroborate Brandon Shaw's story, or would his memories destroy a carefully fabricated life? Something about the younger man's account didn't quite ring true. Maybe she was being cautious to the point of paranoia, but she'd be a fool not to take Mathison's threats seriously. *Sometimes when you think someone is out to get you, they really are out to get you.*

Still reflecting on the encounter, she closed and locked the door, then hobbled over to the window to glance out. She'd always admired Mrs. Dorman's shady backyard and pool area. Like Martin, the older woman spent most of her time outdoors. Gardening seemed more of a passion that a pastime. She was fastidious in her upkeep. Would she really abandon her beloved flowers for the entire summer? Did she even have a sister in Florida?

Okay, now you really do sound paranoid. Take a pain pill and chill.

She did neither. Instead, she lingered at the window, searching the shadowy corners of the yard and peering into the sunroom. The blinds were up, but the bright daylight allowed her a glimpse into the space. She detected no sign of life inside or outside the house. Maybe he'd stopped by to visit with Martin. If they'd been as close as he'd insinuated earlier, they probably had a lot of catching up to do.

But what about that odd moment over the printer box? Had she imagined the sudden tension? She wasn't in a good place. Pain and trauma could too easily alter a person's perception. Already, she could feel the gossamer tentacles of obsession starting to latch on. She told herself to let it go. Focus on something else. But she couldn't. She kept coming back to that brief moment at the bottom of the steps. Maybe Martin wasn't all that happy to have a surrogate nephew turn up in his life after so many years. Maybe their past hadn't been quite as harmonious as Brandon would have her believe.

With a little muscle and a lot of determination, she managed to scoot her dad's old recliner next to the window. She'd be able to keep an eye on the house next door while remaining inconspicuous behind the blinds. Not to mention keeping her foot elevated. When she had the recliner positioned, she dragged over a side table to hold her laptop, remote and all the other paraphernalia she would need to keep herself occupied. She fussed until she had the niche just so, then she went through the apartment rolling up throw rugs and relocating items on the floor that might trip her up in the middle of the night.

By the time she finished, she'd worked up a sweat. Pulling a plastic cast cover over her ankle, she managed to take a shower and wash her hair. Every little task required prodigious effort and seemed to take forever. Climbing over the side of the tub without falling. Balancing on one foot to dry off. Finding a pair of sweatpants loose enough to slip over her cast.

Hobbling back into the living room, she abandoned the idea of a late lunch and headed straight for the recliner. Exhaustion claimed her within minutes, and she fell into a deep sleep with her ankle propped up on the footrest and her head nestled against the worn leather.

She dreamed. Not about the Mathisons or Brandon Shaw or Martin Swann, though the strange quartet had certainly drifted in and out of her thoughts for the past twenty-four hours. She dreamed about Trent Gannon. She literally hadn't thought of him in years, and like a bad penny, he'd turned up at the hospital when she was at her worst. When she desperately needed someone in her corner whether she wanted to admit it or not.

Did she trust him? No. Maybe he really had managed to let go of an old grudge, but he definitely had an agenda. She gave him credit for owning up to the real reason he'd come to see her.

Her cell phone startled her awake. For a moment, she hadn't a clue where she was. The pain medication made her groggy and disoriented. She felt momentary panic until the familiar sounds and scents enveloped her, and she sighed in relief. She was home.

The ringtone pealed again. She tried to blink away the cobwebs as she glanced at the screen. The number was unfamiliar. She started to let the call go to voicemail, then decided it might be important. She pressed the Accept button and put the phone on speaker.

"Hello?" Using the lever on the side of the chair, she adjusted the back to a sitting position.

"Are you watching the press conference?"

She frowned at the phone. "Who is this?"

"Trent Gannon."

Trent Gannon. Bad penny, indeed. "How did you get my number?"

"A mutual friend."

"What friend?"

He ignored the question. "Turn on channel four."

"Why? What's going on?" She used the remote to turn on the flat-screen. When Richard Mathison's face appeared in her living room, she bolted upright. "Is this from yesterday's press conference?"

"No, it's live outside city hall right now. You're just catching the end of it. Hold on a second." She could hear the blare of his television in the background until he muted the sound. "He's not taking questions, apparently. Just reading from a prepared script. The guy on the left is one of his attorneys."

"He looks formidable," Sydney muttered.

"Exactly the reaction he'd want you to have."

She tried to dispel the feeling of doom that had settled over the room with the appearance of Richard Mathison on her TV screen. "What did he say? Mathison, I mean."

"You're not going to like it," Trent warned.

She clutched the arm of the chair. "Just tell me."

"He's threatening a major lawsuit against the Seaside PD for misconduct, harassment, endangerment and a host of other grievances. His attorneys are prepared to file the paperwork by the end of the week unless they can reach an agreement with the department."

"What are they asking for?"

"Your head on a platter, basically. They want you fired."

Her heart sank. "Mathison actually said that? He used my name?"

"He claims you acted irrationally, recklessly and in a manner unbecoming to your profession and to your community. He wants to make an example of you."

She leaned back against the leather and closed her eyes. What would her father say if he could see her now? His record had been exemplary to the very end of his career. He'd been an asset to the department and a true hero to the community. She was almost relieved that he wasn't around to witness her epic downfall.

I blew it, Dad.

Then own it, Syd. Make it right no matter what it takes.

Okay, but how was she supposed to do that, exactly?

"You still there?"

"Yeah." She turned her head to the window, staring down into the garden next door.

Trent's voice softened unexpectedly. "Are you okay?

Maybe I shouldn't have been so blunt. Tact has never been my thing."

She sighed. "It's not like I haven't been expecting it. The suspension was just the first step. In all honesty, my career was probably over the moment I took on the Mathisons."

"But you did it anyway. That took guts."

She winced. "I did my job. Poorly, as it turns out. My actions were anything but courageous."

"I disagree." He was quiet for a moment. "This probably won't mean much to you at the moment, but I have a pretty good idea of how you're feeling."

She appreciated the sentiment, but his commiseration didn't help at all. Different detectives, different circumstances. Then she chided herself for making the distinction. She was hardly in a position to feel superior. She hadn't shown up intoxicated to a crime scene, but some might argue that her actions had been even more irresponsible and dangerous.

"I'm glad you told me," she said. "And for the record, you don't have to walk on eggshells around me. I can handle bluntness. What I can't abide is someone using weasel words to let me down easy. Or mislead me."

"Fair enough. I don't know if what I'm about to say falls under that category or not, but I would remind you that you haven't been fired yet. There's always a possibility the powers that be will call Mathison's bluff."

"A very slim possibility. Aren't you the one who warned me about circling wagons?"

"Yes, but you have something I didn't have when I came up against the machine. You have a decorated lieutenant with clout and seniority in your corner."

"You mean Dan Bertram. Even if he's still on my side— which is a very big if at this point—I don't want him risking his career for me." She tucked a pillow underneath her foot. Her ankle had started to throb again. She reached for the bottle on the side table and gulped a pain pill without water. "What else did Mathison say?"

"Actually, he presented an interesting theory," Trent told her. "He brought up the two unsolved homicides from last year that you were keen to pin on Gabriel Mathison."

"I wasn't *keen* to pin anything on him," she said. "I looked into the possibility of a connection based on the killer's MO."

"Sorry. Poor choice of words. Anyway, Mathison claims the police department allowed you to scapegoat his son in an effort to distract from their incompetence and corruption."

"Wow," she said in surprise. "He's throwing the whole department under the bus. So much for his friendship with the chief. I wonder what she thinks about this press conference."

"You can bet every word he utters has been vetted and serves an agenda. He insists the police knew all three murders are connected but they withheld the information from the public."

"Wait. He *admitted* the murders are connected?"

"Don't get too excited," Trent cautioned. "Remember what I said about every word serving an agenda. According to him, Jessica King's law firm represents one of the most powerful drug kingpins in this part of the state. If she came across information that legally bound her to notify the authorities, then her murder was likely a professional hit. Mathison says the police department has known about the drug link all along but have been threatened or bribed into holding their silence while allowing you to harass his son."

"*I* harassed *him*? That's a good one," she muttered. "I researched Jessica's law firm. They're well respected. I never saw or heard anything that suggested a nefarious clientele."

"That's not something they'd advertise. But I take it you're not buying Mathison's theory."

"It's just a smokescreen," she said in frustration. "He's being deliberately misleading. I agree the cases are related, but I think Gabriel Mathison is the missing link, not some two-bit drug lord."

"What if you're both wrong?"

That stopped her cold. "You still think a killer who disappeared twenty years ago has suddenly become active again?"

"Put it this way. The probability that I'm onto something is a lot higher today than it was yesterday."

"Why?"

"There's been a new development. I would call it significant."

"What's the development?"

"It'll take some explaining," he said. "I'd rather we meet in person."

"That's problematic for me." She lifted her foot as if he could see the effort. "In case you forgot, I'm not exactly mobile at the moment."

"I'll come to you, then. What's the address?"

Was she in the mood for company? Not really. The pain pill was already starting to take effect. She could easily close her eyes and drift back to sleep, but the prospect of spending an hour or two with Trent Gannon didn't sound half bad. If nothing else, he'd be a distraction. Left to her own devices, she'd spend too much time napping and fretting.

She glanced at the phone, realizing Trent was still talking. "I'm sorry, what did you say?"

"I said the sooner we can meet, the better. I'd like to get your take on something that happened last night."

"Is it about the new development?"

"It's all related, but I should warn you up front, this could get hairy. Given your current physical limitations, I thought long and hard before calling you. This guy...this killer..." He paused. "If I'm right, he already knows who I am and where I live. Dragging you into this may not end well for either of us."

The pulse in her throat jumped. If anyone else had delivered such a grim caveat, she might have dismissed their concerns as melodramatic. But not Trent Gannon. She had a feeling he was just being blunt.

He misinterpreted her silence. "You've got a lot on your plate at the moment. Feel free to tell me to take a hike. That's what I'd do."

"No, you wouldn't."

"You don't know the whole story yet." She heard his chair squeak as he got up, probably to pace. "Before I say anything else, I need assurance that any involvement on your end will remain discreet. The last thing I want is to bring any kind of danger to your doorstep. Agreed?"

"You're serious about this."

"Dead serious."

She'd never been one to shy away from danger. Some would argue that she had a tendency to run headlong toward it. Whether that was a good thing or not remained to be seen. "As you said, given my current limitations, keeping a low profile is pretty much a necessity."

"This isn't just about going through your dad's files," he warned. "Although I'd still like to take a look at his notes whenever you're ready. To be brutally honest, I'm alone on this hunt. A fresh pair of eyes and ears could make all the difference."

"And you trust my input?" *Even after all my screwups? You really are desperate.* "Anything I can do to help."

He still sounded unsure. "In that case, let me give you something to mull over before we meet. Supposing those old cases really are connected to the more recent strangulations. Think about what I told you yesterday. Seven murders in seven years, then nothing. The trail went cold. Two decades later, three more bodies have been discovered in less than a year. What does that suggest?"

"He's not only active again, he's escalating from his old pattern. Assuming we're dealing with the same suspect."

"He's escalating and he's taking chances," Trent said. "No one else is looking for him. It's just us. If we don't pick up the trail soon, he'll kill again. He'll keep killing until we stop him. Or he stops us."

She rubbed the back of her neck where goose bumps still prickled. "In that case, you'd better come right over."

Chapter Four

After the call ended, Sydney sat in the recliner digesting Trent's information. The prospect of a new investigation excited her, but even as she jotted down a few notes from their conversation, a part of her had already started to question his true intent.

She wanted to believe he valued her skills and experience as a detective, but her suspension would suggest otherwise. Even on her best day, she still had a lot to learn. So why her?

Maybe the better question was, who else but her? He didn't have a lot of friends left in the department. Most had written him off a long time ago. Could his willingness to work with her be a simple matter of two discredited cops finding themselves out in the cold together?

Whatever his intent, she wasn't about to turn down the opportunity. Bringing an elusive killer to justice would be its own reward, but a part of her had already started to analyze the related benefits. A takedown of that magnitude could go a long way toward the rehabilitation of her reputation, particularly with Dan Bertram. It might even neutralize Richard Mathison's ultimatum and save her career.

Her thoughts chugged on in that hopeful vein as she hoisted herself out of the chair and reached for her crutches. Hobbling back into the bedroom closet, she searched the top shelf for a plastic bin containing a few of her father's possessions. Most everything else had been placed in storage, but she'd brought a few sentimental items to her apartment, including his detective shield and the revolver in her nightstand that had been passed down from her grandfather.

Using one of her crutches to drag the container to the edge of the shelf, she teetered on her good foot until she could grab the handles. Ignoring the pain in her injured ankle, she lowered herself to the floor and dug through the contents until she found the key to the storage unit. Then she spent the next few minutes sorting through the bin before removing a pair of binoculars her dad had kept in the trunk of his car for stakeouts.

Memories came flooding back as she looped the leather strap around her neck. She'd been all of twelve years old, hot and fidgety in a sweltering car as she sat with her dad outside an apartment complex waiting for a suspect to emerge. To keep her entertained, he'd lectured her on the finer points of stakeouts.

Without proper predicate, surveillance is nothing more than snooping. A violation of a basic right that should never be taken lightly. Since I'm off duty you might ask if what we're doing crosses a line. The answer is no, because of an exception called probable cause. I have reason to believe the suspect is engaged in illegal activity, so I need to keep track of his movements. You'll come across cops— maybe even someone you've known and admired in the past—who'll try to persuade you to ignore procedure for the sake of expediency, but that's not what we're about, okay? We follow the law. We observe protocol. Nothing comes back on us.

Then he'd walked her through the basics of wiretapping, trackers and a host of other surveillance devices that required warrants. Despite the heat and her discomfort, Sydney had hung on his every word. She'd thrilled to his use of "we," making it seem as if they were partners. Perched beside him on the front seat of his hot car, he'd seemed bigger than life, a hero to be admired and revered and emulated. And that was the very day she'd decided to follow in his footsteps.

She went back out to the living room and placed the binoculars on the end table beside the recliner. Computer, phone, notebook and now binoculars. *Quite the little spy nest you've built for yourself.* She felt a momentary prickle of guilt. Did she have the proper predicate to surveil her new neighbor? Did she have probable cause to keep track of his movements? Less than twenty-four hours ago, she'd been threatened by Gabriel Mathison. Then a stranger had turned up next door. A man who, by his own admission, had been watching her through the hedge. She had every right to be suspicious. She'd be a fool not to take precautions. For now, the spy nest stayed.

While she waited for Trent, she tidied up the place as best she could. Ten minutes later, she was just coming down the hallway when a knock sounded on the door.

"It's open!"

He came in balancing a paper bag and a drink tray in one hand. "I hope you don't leave your door unlocked all the time."

"I knew you were coming." She leaned on the crutches. "What's all this?"

"I didn't know if you'd eaten, so I stopped by a food truck on the way over. Two-for-one tacos. I hope you're hungry."

"Starving. I haven't been able to eat much since before the accident."

He gave her an admonishing look. "That's not good.

You'll need all the strength you can muster just to get around on those crutches. Speaking of…how are you managing?"

"I've had better days," she admitted.

"Sore?"

"You have no idea."

"I've had my share of bruised ribs, so I sympathize. Those stairs must have been fun."

She grimaced. "I don't look forward to my first trip down them."

"Sit and scoot would be my advice."

The banter was surprisingly companionable considering their acrimonious past and the fact they barely knew one another. Maybe their separate experiences in the hot seat had accelerated a comradery that would never have existed without their respective transgressions. Whatever the case, Sydney was glad she'd agreed to the meeting. If nothing else, Trent's visit beat an afternoon of wallowing in pain and self-pity.

He glanced around with unabashed curiosity. "So, this is your place. Not what I expected, but I like it."

She tried to imagine the apartment through his eyes. Small and sparsely furnished. *Utilitarian* was the word that came to mind. But the residential neighborhood of older homes suited her and the view through some of the windows, particularly at night, made her feel as if she were floating in the trees. "What did you expect?" she asked curiously.

He thought about it for a minute. "I guess I figured you for one of those modern places with all the amenities. Indoor swimming pool, coffee lounge, a big shiny workout room."

She glanced down at her sweatpants. "Really? That seems my speed to you?"

He shot her a quick grin. "I may have had preconceived notions about you based on our past experiences."

"At least you're willing to admit it." She followed his gaze around the space. "It may not look like much, but it suits me fine. The neighborhood is quiet. No one above, below or on either side of me."

"It's off the beaten track," he agreed. "How did you find this place anyway?"

"Someone posted an ad on the station bulletin board. I was actively looking for a new apartment, so it seemed like it was meant to be." She pointed to her tiny dining table when he held up the paper bag. "Over there." Then she instructed him where to find plates and napkins while she grabbed her notebook. Taking a seat, she scribbled the date on a blank page as she surreptitiously watched him move about her tiny kitchen. He was dressed much as he had been the day before. Worn jeans, sneakers and a T-shirt with a hardware store logo on the back. His attire could charitably be described as thrift store chic, but the worn clothing somehow suited him. He could seamlessly blend into a crowd, yet there was something about him that elicited a second look when you met him face-to-face.

If someone had told her twenty-four hours ago that she'd be sneaking second, third and fourth glances at Trent Gannon in her own apartment, she wouldn't have been able to fathom such an unlikely scenario. But here they were.

He came over to the table and sat down across from her. "Dig in. I can personally vouch for the food. A buddy of mine owns the truck. He and his wife do all the cooking. Good people. I usually end up eating there a few times a week."

Funny, she would never have thought of him as having buddies or even casual friendships. He gave off strong loner vibes, but maybe she was projecting her own preconceptions.

She unwrapped a taco. "We should get started. I took a pain pill earlier, so my concentration may start to fade at some point."

He gave her a quick assessment. "None of my business, but be careful with the pills they give you for pain. They're stronger than you might think. Take it from someone who knows."

Again, she wondered what had set him on a bad path before his departure from the department. "I'll take that under advisement," she said with a nod. "Do you mind if I ask a personal question?"

"Go for it."

"What happened three years ago?" She quickly added, "You don't have to answer if you don't want to."

A frown flickered. "No, I get it. If we're doing this together, you need to know I won't go off on a bender and leave you hanging." He reached for the container of green sauce but left it unopened. "I lost someone close to me. It wasn't sudden."

"I'm sorry."

He gave a brief nod. "Watching someone you love suffer day after day, month after month…" He trailed off. "Turned out, she was a lot stronger than I was. The most heroic person I've ever known. My actions were cowardly by comparison. I started having a drink in the hospital parking lot just to get up enough courage to go inside. Then a few drinks when I got home to get through the night. Next thing I knew, I was the cop who kept a flask in his desk."

The haunted look in his eyes made Sydney regret her question. She hadn't meant to open a wound that was obviously still raw. "People handle grief in different ways."

"People handle grief every day and manage not to throw away a career they love," he said. "I don't make excuses for myself."

"But you're okay now."

He shrugged. "I no longer drink and I never will again. But as far as being okay…that's a relative term."

"Don't I know it," she muttered. "Thank you for telling me."

"Like I said, you have a right to know who you're getting into bed with, so to speak. Is there anything you want to tell me?"

She thought about his question for a moment. "No, I think I'm good."

He grinned at that, seemingly falling back into their easy companionship. He drenched his taco in green sauce and scarfed it down in a few big bites. Then he pushed aside his plate and wiped his hands and mouth on a paper napkin. All this occurred while she was still assessing his revelation. Who was the woman he lost and what had she been to him?

"Hungry?" she asked in amusement.

"That'll tide me over so that I can talk while you eat. I'll try not to take up too much of your time. I know you need to rest."

"I've already had my fill of rest. I can only imagine my mood after six weeks of being cooped up in here. I'm glad you called. I'm still not sure how much help I can be, but—" she picked up her pen "—let's give it a go. Do you mind if I take notes?"

"Notes might help. The story is complicated and gets more so all the time. Lots of names, lots of individual investigations. I guess the best place to start is where I left off yesterday—my podcast interview with the retired HPD detective."

"I don't remember you mentioning his name."

"Doug Carter." He waited until she jotted it down, then said, "For the sake of clarity, I'll refer to the seven victims by the number in which they were murdered rather than by name. No disrespect intended. I don't mean to reduce their humanity to a number or statistic, but if I start throwing a bunch of names at you all at once, it'll make it that much harder to keep track. And chronology is important in this case. Chronology is everything. You'll see why as we go along."

"It's your story. You can tell it however you like." She sampled her taco while she waited for him to begin.

He gave a vague nod as if he were already deep in thought. "Doug Carter was the lead investigator on the seventh and final case. He put me in touch with the victim's sister, a woman named Eileen Ballard. Like Carter, she's worked tirelessly for the past two decades trying to keep her sister's murder in the public forefront. Countless interviews. Letters and phone calls by the hundreds if not thousands. She still haunts HPD headquarters every single week for an update on her sister's case."

"Have her efforts been successful?"

He sighed. "You know how that goes. Twenty years is a long time. People move on and forget. A fresh crime or catastrophe captures the public's attention. It was only by happenstance that I learned about her sister's case and the six previous murders from another podcaster. If Doug Carter hadn't agreed to an interview, I would have moved on, too."

"Or found someone else to talk to about the murders."

"I like to think so, but who knows? Anyway, I managed to book Eileen for my podcast a week ago last Friday, one week after the interview with Doug Carter. She was excellent. Smart, quick, articulate. Sympathetic without being maudlin."

"Where can I listen to these interviews?"

"I'll give you the links. According to Eileen, she and her sister were very close. They shared an apartment and made a point of sitting down to breakfast every morning before they left for work. Eileen recounted in great detail everything about their last morning together. What they talked about, what they ate, even her sister's outfit. Apparently, she had a collection of vintage scarves and jewelry that had belonged to their grandmother. She wore her favorite scarf that day and fastened it around her neck with a silver brooch. The brooch was found with the body, but the scarf was never recovered. I stress these details because that scarf will be important later," he said.

Sydney wiped her hands, then scribbled *scarf* in her notebook and underlined the word three times before glancing up. "Was the victim strangled with the scarf?"

"No. The bruising patterns were consistent with someone's hands around her throat. Thumbs like so, the killer facing her." He demonstrated in the air. "That, too, will be important."

A shiver went through Sydney as she made a note in the margin.

"Here's where the story gets really interesting," he said, "at least from my point of view. Several hours after the interview went live, something strange occurred at my place, although I didn't think much of it at the time."

Sydney leaned forward in anticipation. "What happened?"

"I have a house on the bay just south of here. I was sitting outside enjoying the breeze when I noticed a boat a hundred yards or so out from shore. The lights were off, but I could see the silhouette of the vessel in the moonlight.

It stopped directly out from my house, stayed for about twenty minutes and then headed back out toward the gulf. As I said, I didn't think much about it at the time. Could have been someone night fishing or someone up to a more nefarious pastime. Lots of drug activity in this area, as you well know. I went to bed and forgot about the incident. But the boat came back the next night and the next night and the next. Always precisely at midnight. Always stopping straight out from my house except for the one night when I took my neighbor's boat out to intercept. That was the only time he didn't show."

Sydney felt a stir of excitement in the pit of her stomach. This was getting good—or bad, depending on one's perspective. "You think he was watching you?"

"How else would he have known I was on the water?"

"Is there a chance this could all be a coincidence? How can you be sure it's even the same boat?"

"I'm sure."

She tended to believe him. He didn't strike her as someone prone to exaggeration or an overactive imagination—the opposite, in fact. And the pattern he'd laid out was hard to ignore. "Did you try again to intercept?"

"No, but I started to observe the vessel through a pair of night-vision binoculars. Even with an image intensifier, I could never detect any sign of life onboard. No movement whatsoever. He was that careful. Last night everything changed. He came out of the cabin and stood in the moonlight for a good ten minutes as if to make sure I saw him. As if he wanted me to know that he knew I was watching him."

"Could you make out his features?"

"He was too far out and he kept his face turned away. After the boat disappeared, I took a long walk and then went to bed. Something woke me up from a deep sleep. A sound. An instinct. You know that feeling when something isn't right. I got up and checked all around the house. The only thing I found was my neighbor's cat on the porch. That's not unusual. My house has become Larry's second home. He comes and goes at all hours."

"Larry?"

"A big orange tabby. As soon as I opened the door, he shot inside. He had something tied around his neck and was frantic to get it off. That's not unusual, either. My neighbor's granddaughter likes to pretend Larry is one of her dolls. When I was finally able to remove the scarf—"

"Scarf?"

He gave a brief nod. "A vintage silk scarf with bright splashes of color. Exactly like the one Eileen Ballard had described earlier during our interview."

Sydney's first impulse was to accept the revelation and run with it, but she forced herself to play devil's advocate. "That doesn't mean it's the same scarf. After so many years, I'd say the chances are extremely slim. Isn't it more likely that someone heard the podcast and decided to mess with you? You said the sister described the scarf in vivid detail."

"The chances of *that* are extremely slim," Trent countered. "It's the same scarf. I'd stake my life on it. For one thing, the designer on the label is long dead. You can't just go out and buy another scarf like it. I also found tiny holes in the silk where the brooch had been fastened, along with a small stain that could be blood from a pinprick."

"Let's assume it is the same scarf," Sydney said. "Why would he give you a piece of evidence that could incriminate him in at least seven homicides?"

"I've given that a lot of thought," Trent said. "Maybe it's ego. Maybe it's control. He's had a twenty-year hiatus, and now he wants someone to know that he's back."

"That seems a simplistic explanation."

"Not really. Do you know anything about the BTK Killer? He would sometimes go years between kills, leaving notes in the interim for the Wichita police so they would know he was still around. It gave him a feeling of superiority and control. When he was finally captured, he said the anticipation he experienced from stalking and planning helped to sustain him during his dormant periods."

"But why would the killer contact you?"

"I've wondered about that, too. It's possible, maybe even probable that he heard my podcast. My interest in the murders gives us a connection."

Sydney studied him for a moment as her thoughts raced. "Do you realize what you're saying?"

"I know exactly what I'm saying. If DNA can be lifted from the stain, then I could be the only person on the planet with the means of identifying a serial killer who went to ground two decades ago."

"You left out the most important part," she said. "He knows who you are and where you live."

His gaze locked onto hers. "I warned you it could get dangerous."

The tension in the room had become so palpable they both jumped when someone knocked on her door. Sydney's gaze flew to the entrance and then back to Trent. *At least I'm not the only one on edge.*

He scooted back his chair. "Do you want me to get that for you? Are you expecting someone?"

"No." She took a quick breath. "You don't think—"

"No one followed me here. I made certain."

"Sorry. I guess I'm a little spooked." She gave a shaky laugh. "As if a serial killer would come knocking on my door in broad daylight."

A SUNTANNED MAN wearing swim trunks and an unbuttoned shirt stood on the porch with one hand planted on the door-frame. Trent's first thought when he opened the door and saw the pose was *Who the hell is this guy?* His second impression was more disciplined. Somewhere in his thirties. Six feet or a little less. One sixty, one-sixty-five. Dark hair, blue eyes. No visible scars or tattoos, but memorable nonetheless. Memorable and vaguely familiar.

The man looked equally surprised to see Trent at the door. He straightened with an affable smile that was meant to disarm but didn't. "Is Sydney here?"

Trent's response was blunt. "Who wants to know?"

"I'm her neighbor. Sorry for the interruption. I didn't realize she had company." Sydney clomped up to the door on her crutches and the stranger's smile broadened. "There you are. I apologize for dropping by like this."

"No, it's fine," she said. "What's up?"

He made a vague gesture toward the yard below. "I'm having a few people over for an impromptu pool party. We're cooking out. Nothing fancy. Just burgers and grilled vegetables. I wondered if I could bring you a plate when everything is ready. Or better yet, you're welcome to join us if you like."

"That's a very nice offer, but we've got tons of leftovers from a late lunch. As to the pool party..." She stuck out her cast. "I don't think I'm up for that just yet."

"A raincheck, then?"

"Of course."

The man's attention had vectored in on Sydney from the moment she walked up to the door. No big mystery there. She was an attractive woman. But Trent detected something in her response that intrigued him. Her expression and tone remained cordial, yet there was a subtle rigidity to her posture that made him think her guard had gone up. He wondered why.

If the neighbor noticed, he didn't let on. His benign expression never wavered. "If you change your mind later, just come on over. Both of you." His gaze slid back to Trent.

Sydney said quickly, "Oh, sorry. Trent Gannon, this is Brandon Shaw. He just moved in next door. Trent is…an old friend."

Her hesitation amused Trent. She obviously didn't know how to classify their relationship. It was a little complicated, he had to admit.

Brandon's gaze narrowed as he cocked his head. "You look familiar. Have we met?"

"I was wondering the same thing," Trent said. "Any chance you came through the Seaside Police Department prior to three years ago?"

"Is that a subtle way of asking whether or not I've ever been arrested?" He gave Sydney a wink.

Trent shrugged. "Not at all. You could have come in to pay a parking ticket."

"I've never been inside the Seaside Police Station or any police station, for that matter. In fact, I've only been in town a few days. Interesting that your mind would go there, though. Are you also a detective…Trent?"

"Yes, but I don't work for the police department."

"Private security?" That seemed to perk the man's interest. "As it happens, I might be in the market for a new security system."

"Doesn't Mrs. Dorman already have an alarm?" Sydney asked.

"It's an antiquated system. I don't think it's been activated in years. But I'm not worried about my stay here. I'm interested in an upgrade for my home in the city."

"I'm afraid I wouldn't be able to help you," Trent said. "My specialty is surveillance and background checks."

"Cheating spouses and insurance fraud, eh?"

"Among other things."

"I'll certainly keep that in mind." His eyes glinted as he turned back to Sydney. "If you need anything, you know where to find me."

"Thank you again."

He started to exit, then pivoted. "See you both soon, I hope."

Trent waited until the man had bounded down the steps, then he closed the door and turned. "What's the deal with that guy?"

"What do you mean?"

He searched her features. "Maybe I'm wrong, but I thought you seemed tense. Any particular reason why?"

"We only just met today. It's my nature to be cautious around people I don't know. Including you," she added.

"As well you should be," Trent said, unoffended. "But what I sensed was more than a vague misgiving. What's going on?"

She gave him a sidelong glance as she moved away from the door. "Was it really that obvious?"

"I told you, I'm good at reading people. But don't worry. I doubt it would ever occur to your neighbor that anyone he encounters is less than bowled over by his looks and presence. Still, I'd be careful with that guy. If he senses your resistance, he might take it as a challenge."

Her tone was dismissive. "He can take it however he wants. I know how to shut down unwanted attention." She maneuvered over to the window and glanced out. "Besides, I don't think any interest he has in me is romantic or even personal."

"Meaning?"

She hesitated. "I really hadn't planned to get into this right now. We have other things to discuss, and besides, you'll just think I'm paranoid."

"Now you have to tell me."

She sat down on the arm of an old recliner, placing her back to the window as she propped her crutches against the side of the chair. In her baggy sweatpants and tank top, with the cuts and scratches from the accident still fresh on her face and arms, she looked almost fragile, though Trent suspected she would take exception to that description. From the little he'd known of her before he left the department, she'd lived up to her reputation. He knew from experience she could be tough, relentless and prickly to the point of standoffish.

Even now, he couldn't say she was overly approachable. That she had allowed him to invade her personal space was probably a big concession for her. And possibly a mistake. If she hoped to keep her job, she wasn't doing herself any favors by associating with the likes of him. But he suspected her version of doing the right thing might differ considerably from the department's. She came across as an independent thinker, and he liked that about her. He liked a lot of things about her, and that revelation had come as a surprise, considering his previous opinion.

She looked pensive, as if assessing how much she wanted to tell him. "This stays between us?"

"Goes without saying."

She nodded, but still seemed uneasy. "I think he could be working for Richard Mathison. If I'm right, he moved into the house next door to keep tabs on me." She glanced up to gauge his reaction. "See? Paranoid."

Trent moved over beside her and picked up the binoculars. He lifted them to his eyes and adjusted the focus ring as he peered out the window. "Who's keeping tabs on who?"

She grabbed the strap and pulled the binoculars from his hand. "Don't judge. I could be a bird-watcher for all you know."

He couldn't imagine anyone who struck him less like a bird-watcher. Not that there was anything wrong with the pastime. He was a big nature lover himself. But that was all beside the point…

"A notion like that doesn't just pop into your head out of the blue," he said. "What makes you think he's working for Richard Mathison?"

Her voiced hardened. "Because Gabriel Mathison threatened me, that's why. He said I had no idea how far his father would go to protect his precious reputation. His words. He implied that the injuries I sustained in the car accident are nothing compared to what's coming."

Trent scowled. "When did this happen?"

"He came to me see me last night in the hospital. I woke up, and there he was at the foot of my bed watching me sleep." She gave an exaggerated shudder. "Talk about creepy. I thought I was having a nightmare at first."

"What did you do?"

"Nothing I could do. He'd placed both my phone and the call button out of reach while I slept. I could have screamed, I suppose, but a part of me wanted to hear what he had to say. And I didn't want to give him the satisfaction of knowing he'd frightened me."

Tough as nails. "You don't think the threat was a bluff?"

"Do you? I mean, you heard the press conference. Richard Mathison is coming after me with a vengeance. He doesn't just want me fired. You said it yourself. He wants to make an example of me."

"But that doesn't explain why you think your new neighbor is involved."

"Because he *is* my new neighbor."

He gazed down at her in puzzlement. "There has to be more to it than that."

She tucked stray strands of hair behind her ears and sighed. "Like I said, I really didn't want to get into all this right now, but here goes. When I got home from the hospital earlier, he came through the hedge and struck up a conversation. He said he heard the car and thought it might be my landlord, but in hindsight, I think he was waiting for me."

"How would he know you'd been released from the hospital?"

"The same way one of my witnesses got relocated and another recanted her statement. Richard Mathison's reach is long and powerful."

"I've known that for a long time," he agreed. "Did Shaw say anything specific to trigger your suspicion?"

"It was a lot of little things. For instance, he told me that he'd leased the house next door for the summer, but he didn't even know the owner's name."

"Mrs. Dorman?"

"See? Even you remember. He said she'd gone to Florida to take care of her sister, but now I'm wondering if she even has a sister."

"That should be easy enough to find out," Trent said. "I'll make a few calls."

She was instantly defensive. "You don't have to go to all that trouble just to humor me. Besides, I'm perfectly capable of checking things out for myself. At least…I was."

"Let me guess. You've already been reprovisioned."

She looked up in alarm. "How did you know?"

"Standard operating procedure. Your passwords were

probably reset the minute you surrendered your badge and weapon. That's fine. Plenty of ways around a lockout. I'll let you know what I find out."

She looked as if she wanted to argue, then backed off with a nod. "Thanks. If it helps, he has history with the house. He said he lived there for a short time as a kid. He claims Martin Swann was like a surrogate uncle to him."

"Who's Martin Swann?"

"My landlord. He called him Uncle Marty." She wrapped the leather cord around the binoculars and set them aside. "Maybe it was just my imagination—or my paranoia—but when I saw them together earlier, I sensed a weird vibe between them. Like maybe Martin wasn't so happy to see him."

"Maybe we need to check out Uncle Marty, too," Trent suggested.

"He's lived in Seaside for a long time. He once told me that he's owned this property for over thirty years."

Trent glanced over his shoulder, taking in the small living area and compact kitchen. "Has he always rented out this space?"

"Just since his wife died, I think. Brandon mentioned that Martin used the apartment as a retreat whenever his wife had guests. Apparently, she was a lot more social than he was. Or is. He seems to be pretty much a hermit these days, but I'm not one to talk. I don't exactly have a bunch of friends knocking down my door to see how I'm doing."

He smiled. "I'm here."

"Yes, but you're not a friend. Not really. Not yet." She gave him a questioning look. "I'm not exactly sure what we are. Partners? Associates? Coconspirators?"

"How about a pair of shunned detectives working toward a common goal? A pair of misfits who have more in common than either of us would have ever thought twenty-four hours ago."

She gave a little laugh. "I guess that's true. And it doesn't even sound so bad when you put it that way."

He was relieved that she took his assessment in the light-hearted spirit in which he'd intended. Her smile was brief but warm. Almost electric. In the split second before she glanced away, something unexpected flashed between them. Not attraction, though Trent found himself drawn to her despite his past perceptions and her current reservations. Not *only* attraction, he amended, but a unique connection that only two people who had each walked an ill-fated path could experience.

"Trent? Did you hear what I said?" She scowled up at him. "You looked like you were a million miles away just now. Where did you go all of a sudden?"

"Nowhere. Just thinking. Anything else you remember about your conversation with Brandon Shaw?"

"It wasn't a lengthy discussion," she said. "But there is one more odd thing that happened. Someone brought two dozen white roses to my hospital room last night while I was asleep. Gabriel Mathison made a point of telling me about the message on the card. He had it memorized. At first, I thought he just wanted me to know how long he'd been in my room before I woke up. Now I think his intent was more sinister."

"What did the card say?"

"*See you soon, Sydney.* No name, no address, nothing else. Gabriel whispered that same message in my ear before he left my room. Then earlier, Brandon Shaw said the same thing to me at the bottom of the stairs. *See you soon, Sydney.* It's a common catchphrase. I know that. But the timing just seems—I don't know—too coincidental."

"I'm not big on coincidences," Trent said. "But let's play this out for a minute. If the Mathisons did plant him next door, you have to wonder about their endgame. What do they hope to gain by their continued harassment?"

"Just plain old revenge," Sydney said. "These are not good people."

"Agreed, but you've been taken off the case and suspended from the department. The prudent move would be to back off and keep a low profile before another witness decides to come forward. My guess is, you've got them spooked. Is it possible you stumbled across something incriminating that you don't even realize yet? The fact that Gabriel came to your hospital room in the middle of the night smacks of desperation."

"Or cockiness."

"I don't think either of them are as confident as they'd have us believe." A peal of laughter drew Trent's attention back to the window. He stared down into the backyard of the house next door, where two young women in bikinis had suddenly appeared in the water. "Looks like the pool party has turned out to be an intimate affair."

Sydney craned her neck. "I don't see Brandon."

"Maybe he's tending the grill."

She struggled out of the chair, and they stood side by side at the window watching the women giggle and shriek as they tried to mount air floats. "Something just occurred to me," Sydney mused. "He brought up a delivery for me earlier. Brandon, I mean. Maybe we could lift his prints from the cardboard box."

"Packages from a major carrier pass through dozens of hands before they get left at a front door. Lifting a clear set of prints might be difficult. But we can give it a go. Do you have a kit?"

"Not here. Do you?"

"Not on me. I'll bring one by tomorrow."

They returned their attention to the window. After a few minutes, Brandon came out of the house and sat down on the edge of the pool, kicking water toward the young women, who squealed and tried to paddle away. He jumped in after them and grabbed the nearest raft, dunking the occupant. She tried to surface, but he was on her in a flash, holding her under water until her companion came to her rescue by pounding on his back and tugging at his arms.

Trent muttered, "What the hell…?"

The woman came up sputtering and cursing and setting off another shrill yelp from her friend. They both climbed back on the air mattresses and paddled away as Brandon hitched himself out of the pool. Legs dangling, he leaned back on his elbows and lifted his gaze to Sydney's window, as if he knew they were there. As if he was amused rather than embarrassed that they'd witnessed the disturbing horseplay.

Sydney grabbed Trent's arm and tried to pull him away from the window. She lost her balance and would have tumbled to the floor if he hadn't caught her.

"You okay?"

Something that might have been surprise glinted in her eyes. Had she felt it, too? That little spark of awareness upon contact?

She swallowed. "Do you think he saw us?"

"Probably, but there's a glare on the window. He couldn't have seen much more than shadows." Trent glossed over the awkwardness of their interaction as he dropped his hands from her arms and reached for her crutches.

She gave a little hop to regain her balance. "I think that's being optimistic."

"Does it matter? His guests are making a lot of noise over there. It's only natural we'd get curious."

"Yes, but I don't want him to think I'm spying on him."

"Probably best not to let him see the binoculars, then."

She cut him a glance. "I'm serious. We shouldn't have been standing at the window like that. I know better. I was taught how to surveil by the best in the business."

Trent sobered. "I know you know what you're doing, but it bears repeating. Be careful with that guy. What we just witnessed was more than innocent roughhousing. He crossed a line."

To Trent's surprise, she accepted his warning without challenge. She may even have been grateful for his concern. "I'll be on guard," she promised. "Should we get back to our other business?"

Tempting, but he could see the weariness in her eyes. She was about done in, though she wouldn't likely admit it. "I think we've talked enough for one day. I'll call you tomorrow. We can pick back up when we're both fresh."

She walked him out to the porch. "I'm glad you came over. Everything you told me about those murders…it's a lot to take in. Fascinating but a bit overwhelming. I can see how you got caught up after the first interview."

He nodded. "It's hard to believe how under the radar they've remained."

She grew reflective. "What did you mean earlier when you said chronology is everything?"

"Remember yesterday when I told you the FBI eventually concluded the killer was clever enough to evade capture by varying his MO? I have a different theory. He was clever, but he was also evolving. I'll explain more tomorrow. I did warn you it's complicated."

"And getting more so all the time," she murmured.

"That's why I appreciate having another perspective. I can sometimes get lost in the weeds when I'm working alone."

She shrugged off his gratitude. "You know what they say. Two disgraced cops are better than one."

He grinned and started down the steps, turning to glance over his shoulder when she called his name.

She stared down at him, her expression solemn. "Be careful. Dealing with the Mathisons is one thing, but this strange little game you're playing with a serial killer is next level."

Chapter Five

After Trent left, Sydney put away the food and wiped the table. Normally, she would have taken the trash to the outside bin, but her first trip down the steps would have to wait until she felt less wobbly on crutches. She could always ask for help, of course, but that went against her nature. She'd always been independent. A broken ankle might slow her down, but she didn't intend to remain helpless or housebound for the full six weeks of her recovery.

Tonight, however, solitary confinement didn't seem so bad. The mundane task of tidying up had sapped her strength. She was glad that Trent had come over, but she was also relieved to be alone. She had a lot of thinking to do.

Lowering herself onto the recliner, she adjusted the blinds so that she could see out, but anyone looking up at the window wouldn't be able to see her. Then she opened her laptop and clicked on the links to Trent's podcast. The interview with the HPD detective popped up on her screen as a video. She hit Play with the intent of watching for only a few minutes to get a taste, but the material was so compelling she soon lost track of time.

When she finally finished the nearly two-hour interview, the sun had dipped beneath the treetops. At some point, the party next door had broken up or moved inside. The deserted air mattresses looked forlorn and slightly deflated, drifting on the surface of the pool. One of the women had left a pair of white sandals on the deck. Sydney fixated on the high-heel slides for a moment as she thought about all those missing left shoes. All those young lives cut short because of a predator's lust for taking them. What if Trent's hunch proved right? What if that same killer had returned with an even more voracious appetite?

The light faded rapidly with the setting sun. Dusk rolled in on a mild breeze. Sydney would have expected lights to come on in the house next door, but the windows remained dark as the garden grew shadowy. Where had everyone gone? She hadn't heard a car engine, and it was too far to walk to the nearest bars and restaurants. And those shoes remained poolside.

If Brandon and his guests hadn't left the property, what were they doing inside that dark house?

She wanted to believe her suspicions about him were unfounded. Maybe she really was prone to paranoia. Maybe she needed to take a step back and reevaluate, not only her priorities but also her motivation. But putting aside his timely appearance next door, something about him continued to niggle her. The horseplay in the pool earlier only reiterated her qualms about her new neighbor. There was more to Brandon Shaw than met the eye.

She watched the property for another few minutes before diving into Trent's second interview.

Doug Carter's story had been fascinating, but Eileen Ballard's account of the last moments she'd spent with her sister held Sydney enthralled. The woman's twenty-year crusade for justice had honed her storytelling skills. Sydney found herself holding her breath in places and gasping aloud in others. She started out taking notes but soon gave up and just listened intently.

Surprisingly, Trent was an unobtrusive host. Once again Sydney marveled at how vastly different her impression of him had been from the reality. She couldn't help but admire a man who had hit rock bottom but had somehow found the necessary desire and grit to reinvent himself. If she could get past her bruised pride and innate stubbornness, she just might learn a thing or two from him.

What to make of that smile they'd shared? That brief, knowing glance? It had been a while since she'd experienced the thrill of attraction brought on by a mere glance or touch. She'd concentrated on her career to the near exclusion of a social life. She told herself she didn't miss the complications of a relationship. She was in so much trouble at work, the last thing she wanted or needed was a romantic entanglement no matter how fleeting.

Keep right on telling yourself that. Keep reminding yourself that twenty-four hours ago, you wouldn't have given Trent Gannon the time of day.

But things changed. Sometimes in the blink of an eye, it seemed.

She couldn't help but wonder about his past, about the heroic woman he'd mentioned with such deep sorrow and regret. Maybe she'd ask the lieutenant about Trent's past the next time she saw him, although that might be a bit tricky, considering his contentious departure from the department.

Her place turned gloomy with only the computer screen for illumination. When the second episode finally concluded, she felt simultaneously exhausted and agitated. She put aside the laptop and sat in the dark, rehashing key points of the discussion. She heard a door open and close next door. She sat up straighter and lifted a blind with her fingertip so that she had a clearer view of the backyard.

A shadow slipped across the dark yard toward the side door of the garage. She heard the metallic rattle of the garbage cans and thought her neighbor might be taking the trash to the curb. Instead, he made several trips back and forth from the house to the garage. The overhead door rumbled as it lifted. A few minutes later, Brandon Shaw's car slowly backed down the driveway. Sydney couldn't make out any passengers, and she hadn't seen his guests exit the house. Maybe the women had parked their car down the street and had left through the front door.

Or…

Don't go there. Overreach is what got you in trouble in the first place.

Out on the street, the headlights arced as the vehicle turned east and then south at the intersection. She wondered how long he'd be gone. Now would be the perfect time to search his place—except for the fact that she could barely get around in her own apartment, let alone navigate an unfamiliar layout in the dark. And that was beside the dual obstacles of her steep stairs and his locked doors.

Bad idea. Tempting but not at all wise and went against everything her dad had taught her.

She watched until the taillights disappeared, and then she glanced at the clock on her phone. Barely ten o'clock. Still early by her pre-accident standards.

The podcast had left her restless and moody. She needed to talk to someone about what she'd just heard and about all the disturbing images floating around in her head.

She tapped Trent's number in the Recent Calls on her phone, then immediately had second thoughts. Too late. He answered on the first ring.

She tried to sound casual. "Hey, it's Sydney."

"Hey. Everything okay?"

Already his voice had become familiar to her and, in a way, comforting. Maybe because he was her only ally at the moment. "Everything is fine. Am I calling too late?"

"No, I'm up."

His slight hesitation only intensified her trepidation. What if he really had been asleep? Or worse, what if he had company? She knew next to nothing about his personal life except what he'd revealed earlier. Three years was a long time. He could have a serious girlfriend for all she knew. Or a wife. The absence of a wedding ring meant nothing. "Are you sure I'm not interrupting anything? We can talk tomorrow."

"I'm sitting here alone on my patio enjoying the evening breeze. So, no. You aren't interrupting anything."

She realized she'd been gripping the phone. She relaxed her fingers. "Are you waiting for the boat?"

"It's still a little early, but I'm keeping an eye out."

She took another breath. "Are you armed?"

There was a slight hesitation before he said, "Let's just say, I'm prepared."

She didn't know what that meant but sincerely hoped he knew what he was doing. "I'm glad you're taking precautions. This is no time to let down your guard. From what you told me earlier, he could already be nearby, watching your place. He could be observing you at this very moment, and you wouldn't even know it."

"That might be a good thing."

His response astounded her. "How could that be a good thing?"

"Any deviation from his pattern makes him vulnerable.

He's already taking risks. Getting bolder. Eventually, he'll make a mistake, and that's how we'll catch him."

"By using yourself as bait?"

"By luring him out into the open."

"You make it sound so easy," she said.

He gave a low chuckle. "That sounds easy to you?"

She wasn't amused. "You know what I mean. You're downplaying the danger. It's one thing to put yourself on the line, but he's not just watching your place, is he? How could he know about that little girl and her cat unless he's been watching your neighbor's house, too?"

"I know." His tone turned serious. "If it puts your mind at ease, the child and her mother left for Phoenix early this morning."

"Because of what happened?"

"No, the trip was already planned. They won't be back for several weeks. Plenty of time for us to do what needs to be done."

"I don't like this," Sydney said. "You're putting yourself in harm's way without any backup. And what about your neighbor? Shouldn't you warn him about the possibility of a killer lurking in the area?"

"I've briefed him. He's former military. Special Forces would be my guess, because he won't talk about his time in the service. Again, if it makes you feel any better, he's built like a tank and armed to the teeth. I couldn't ask for better backup."

"That's a relief, I guess." She glanced down into the shadowy yard next door. The moon was up, but the night seemed darker than usual and eerily silent. No passing cars. No barking dogs. She had the sudden and disquieting notion that someone could be watching her at that very moment.

She imagined a human shadow down by the oleanders. The silhouette vanished as she peered into the darkness.

"This whole discussion seems surreal," she said with a shiver. "Yesterday, my only concern was stopping Gabriel Mathison from leaving the country. Now I've been suspended from a job I love, and I'm working off the books helping a man I barely know to track a serial killer."

"Interesting turn of events, isn't it?"

"Interesting? That's one word for it." She tried to imagine him sitting in the dark, eyes peeled on the water in anticipation. Alert yet restless and edgy. But maybe that was another projection. He seemed pretty calm at the moment. More deliberate and self-possessed than he had a right to be under the circumstances. She was the one with jitters.

"You haven't told me why you called," he said. "Are you sure everything is okay over there? No more run-ins with Brandon Shaw?"

"He's not home. He left a little while ago. But he's not why I called." She put the phone on speaker as she tried to recapture her train of thought. "I just finished the interview with Eileen Ballard. It got me to thinking about the scarf you found and all the implications of that bloodstain. If there's even a slight chance that you're in possession of the killer's DNA, or the victim's, you have to go to the police."

"I came to you. You are the police."

She winced. "Probably not for long. And at the moment, my options are limited, as you've pointed out. There isn't much I can do to help besides offer an ear and moral support. Still, I have to say this again. You can't sit on evidence that important."

"Think about what you're advising me to do." His voice was a low rumble in her ear. Steady yet enigmatic. "What do you think will happen if I waltz into the station and claim the scarf I found tied around a cat's neck belonged to a woman who was murdered twenty years ago? How do you think they'll respond?"

She cringed. "Ugh. When you put it that way…"

"Exactly. It sounds ridiculous even to me, and I'm the one who found the damn thing. I don't have all that much credibility with the Seaside Police Department to begin with. How long do you think it would take for rumors to start swirling about my mental health? Or that I'm drinking again?"

She couldn't dispute his reasoning. "What if I talk to Dan Bertram?"

Something shifted in his voice. "I'd rather you didn't."

"Why not?"

"Let's just say, I don't hold him in the same regard as you and leave it at that."

She bristled at the implication. "Come on. You can't drop an innuendo like that and expect me to let it go without an explanation. I've known the man my whole life. Since my dad died, he's been more of a parent to me than my own mother. I deserve to know what you mean."

"I shouldn't have said anything."

"But you did."

He hesitated as if he really didn't want to get into it but recognized the very real possibility that she wouldn't let it go until he did. "Before you trust him to have your back, look into his connections to Richard Mathison."

She suppressed a gasp. "What connections? What are you talking about?"

"All I know is that I witnessed firsthand what you and I discussed earlier. You were right when you said Richard Mathison's reach is long and powerful. And I was right when I told you he has people in the police department who owe him favors."

"Dan Bertram isn't one of them," she insisted. "You're mistaken about him."

"Maybe I am. I hope so. But for now, neither of us should count on any help from that quarter. It's just you and me. That is, if you're still willing."

She took offense at the suggestion. "Do you think I'm so fickle or thin-skinned that I'd back out over one disagreement? Give me a little more credit than that."

"To be honest, you strike me as the opposite of fickle and thin-skinned."

She supposed that was meant as a compliment. "I won't say anything to the lieutenant. He probably wouldn't believe me anyway. He might even think I'm trying to divert attention from my own situation. A discredited cop crying wolf." She closed her eyes as the bitterness of her current reality sank in. "It seems we're both in the same boat when it comes to credibility. But I still say the DNA evidence on that scarf is too important to sit on. What about taking it to Doug Carter? He must have friends in the Houston Police Department. Technically, the seventh murder is still their case."

"The problem with that is timing and urgency," Trent said. "Houston is one of the largest human trafficking hubs in the country. The crime lab is backed up anywhere from six months to two years. A twenty-year-old cold case wouldn't be considered a priority. They could take the scarf and back-burner a DNA test indefinitely."

She sighed in frustration. "Then what do you suggest we do?"

"Our best bet at the moment is an independent lab. I know someone who knows someone who owes me a favor.

I'll push for a rush. With any luck, we could have the results by the end of the week."

"And then what? I hate to point out the obvious, but unless you know someone who knows someone in the FBI, we won't have access to any of their databases."

"One thing at a time," Trent said. "It's doubtful we'd turn up a match anyway. Otherwise, he wouldn't have risked leaving that scarf. He knows his DNA isn't in the system."

"Or he knows the blood belongs to the victim. You said he wants someone to know he's back."

"That would leave little doubt," Trent agreed. "But as I said, first things first. We need to find out if the stain is human blood. Then we'll go from there."

She checked the time on her phone. "No sign of the boat yet?"

"Unless he breaks another pattern, he won't show until straight-up midnight."

"Brandon Shaw said he rented the house next door to be close to the marina," she murmured.

"What?"

"He said he wanted to do nothing but fish and swim this summer. Probably doesn't mean anything." Neither did the white sandals abandoned on his pool deck. "I'm not even sure why I brought it up."

Trent was silent for a moment. "He couldn't have been more than nine or ten at the time of the first murder."

"I know. He just…"

"He bears watching for other reasons," Trent said.

She glanced out her window, trailing her gaze along the oleanders where she had spotted a shadow earlier. All was quiet next door, the house still dark. Her gaze went back to those sandals, and a shiver traced up her spine for no good reason.

"You still there?" Trent asked.

"There's a full moon tonight. Is that a good thing or bad?"

"It's to our advantage. The illumination will enhance thermal imaging. I'll be able to see farther and more clearly. Maybe he'll get careless and I'll even catch a glimpse of his face."

"Do you think he'll make contact again tonight?"

"Another scarf tied around a cat's neck? He won't be able to repeat that trick. Larry is safe inside, snoozing on his favorite chair. He'll start yowling to go out as soon as he wakes up, but too bad. Tonight, he's an indoor kitty."

She found his concern for the cat rather touching. A day ago, she would have thought it out of character, but she was learning each time they spoke that Trent Gannon was full of surprises and not at all how she had imagined him.

On impulse, she said, "I found the key to the storage locker. We can go through my dad's things together if you're still interested."

"I'm definitely interested. Tomorrow good for you? I can swing by your place in the afternoon and pick you up."

"I'll be here. I don't know what you hope to find, but I guess it can't hurt to take a look."

He was so quiet she thought he might be distracted by the boat. Then he said, "Your dad never mentioned Doug Carter?"

"Not that I recall. Why?"

"They shared information on their investigations for years. Doug had a lot of respect for your dad."

She tensed. "Why am I sensing a *but*?"

"The last few times they spoke, Doug felt your dad was holding out on him."

Sydney was quick to refute. "He wouldn't do that. He was the most honest, by-the-book cop I've ever known. There's no way he would have withheld important information on a murder investigation."

"No one is suggesting he did," Trent said. "Evidence and fact go into the official casefile. A good detective will keep his hunches close to the vest if he feels the need to."

The exact opposite of what she'd done in the Gabriel Mathison case. If she'd been a little more discreet and circumspect, she might not be in her current situation. "So that's why you want to look through his notes. You're hoping to find something that never made it to the official record."

"You knew him better than anyone. What do you think?"

"I can tell you that he was a stickler for detail."

"That could be all we need."

Now she was the one who fell silent. "Can I ask you something? It may sound far-fetched, but do you think it's possible the suspect made contact with my dad like he has with you? I mean, think about it. Dad was the first one who identified a single perpetrator. He was the one who brought in the FBI. Seems logical if the killer wanted to communicate with the police, he would have reached out to the one cop who had begun to figure him out."

"Not out of the realm of possibility," Trent said. "It certainly has precedent. Go back to the BTK Killer, who left notes and packages all over town for the police. Or the Zodiac killer, who sent all those cryptic messages and cyphers to the media. The list goes on and on. Why? Did you remember something?"

"Nothing concrete. Just something he said to my mother once." She paused. *"Don't let her go outside alone until we catch the bastard."*

"I take it she was referring to you?" Trent didn't sound

convinced. "That's a pretty generic warning. He could have been talking about any criminal."

"I told you it would sound far-fetched."

He tried to soften his skepticism. "I'm the one who found a bloodstained scarf tied around a cat's neck, remember? Just because it sounds far-fetched doesn't mean it's not true."

"Thanks for that." She reclined in the chair and elevated her injured foot. "I don't know why that conversation suddenly came back to me. Who knows if it's even real? But in my mind, I can hear him as clear as day."

"You don't remember anything more specific?"

She thought about her mother's response. "Nothing relevant. His concern really doesn't make sense, because I would have been a little kid at the time of those murders. I didn't fit the victim profile. The killer went after young women. So why was he afraid for my safety unless…"

"He had reason to be."

"Maybe it was the tone of his voice or a look in his eyes," she said. "Or maybe I'm taking too much pain medication and my thinking is all muddled. I just can't help wondering if the killer knew about me. If he somehow used me to send a message to my dad like he did with your neighbor's granddaughter."

Trent's voice took on a note of caution. "Let's see what turns up in your dad's notes before we jump to conclusions. In the meantime, get some rest. I keep forgetting that you just survived a major car crash and you were released from the hospital only a few hours ago. Try and put everything we discussed out of your head for the night. The interviews, too. We can pick back up tomorrow."

But that proved easier said than done. Sydney sat staring out into the night for a long time after the call ended.

Trent was right. She needed to sleep, but her mind wouldn't settle. How much of her anxiety could be attributed to the mess she'd made at work or to a new medication, she didn't know. She wasn't herself. Pain and exhaustion had taken a toll. Made her think things that would never have occurred to her in a less stressful state.

But recognizing her current vulnerabilities did little to ease her mind. She couldn't let go of the notion that the killer had known about her when she was a child. And he'd been waiting all these years for her to grow up.

TRENT SET THE alarm on his phone while he waited for the boat. Not that he was in any danger of falling asleep before midnight. As the hour approached, he'd never felt more alert. Nothing out of the ordinary would escape his attention tonight, no matter how slight a movement or sound. If the killer decided to come ashore, he was armed and ready. But as prepared as he was, the vibration of the silenced alarm still startled him. He turned off the sound and lifted his binoculars.

There he was. Right on time.

Trent's every muscle tensed as he watched the ghostlike vessel glide across the dark water, pausing as it always did directly out from the bungalow. Maybe it was his imagination, but the boat seemed farther away tonight, as if the pilot had calculated the necessary distance from shore to maintain his anonymity when observed through a night-vision lens.

Trent rose and strode barefoot down the path to the water's edge. Not that a few extra feet would enhance his visibility, but he supposed it was a psychological thing. A hollow act of bravado. He stood in ankle-deep water and adjusted the focus ring. For several long minutes, nothing happened. The only motion he could detect was the gentle rise and fall of the hull.

Then, just like the night before, a figure appeared starboard. The person looked to be wearing something over his head, like a cap or a hood to disguise his features. Despite the distance, he kept his face turned away from the shoreline.

He moved about the deck, coming in and out of view before disappearing for several minutes inside the cabin. When he came back out, he carried what looked to be a trash bag in one hand. Moving up to the rail, he flung the bag into the water.

Trent's attention remained riveted. Judging by the size and the ease with which the bag had been tossed, he couldn't be disposing of a body. Not an intact body, at least. *Then what the hell was it?* He doubted someone would make a midnight journey out to the bay just to dump their everyday garbage.

The figure went back inside the cabin and returned a moment later with yet another bag, which he also hurled into the water. Then he stood peering over the rail until presumably the items sank. After a few minutes, he turned his head toward the shoreline. Toward Trent.

For a moment, Trent could have sworn they made eye contact. Strange, because the distance was so great that he couldn't see the man clearly despite the moonlight. He appeared little more than a grainy silhouette against a green field. And yet Trent experienced a flash of familiarity that turned his blood cold.

He watched until the boat disappeared into the darkness, and then he made his way slowly back to the patio. He tried to keep the man's silhouette fresh in his mind as he searched his memory banks for an image or a trigger that would give him a name or a face.

But in the next instant, he scoffed at the notion. The killer had been active when Trent was a kid. Sydney's theory about a connection through her dad was at least somewhat plausible. Trent had no reason to believe his path had ever crossed with the killer's. He wasn't thinking straight. The adrenaline rush that had sustained him throughout the previous night and most of the day faded as grim reality set in. He hadn't been a cop for nearly three years. Even before his dismissal, he'd never dealt with the ruthless cunning of a serial predator. What made him think he could match wits now?

Because you were once a good detective and sooner or later, even the cleverest of killers slip up. Because if you don't find him, who will?

Plopping down in the creaky lawn chair, he lifted the binoculars one last time to make certain the cruiser had vanished. The moonlit water looked deceptively calm. He thought about waking up his neighbor and asking for his boat key. With a little luck, he might be able to find whatever had been tossed overboard. But even knowing the approximate location, he'd still have to search a long stretch of ocean floor and his diving experience was limited at best. A night dive presented a whole new set of challenges.

Maybe Sydney was right. Maybe it was time to bring in the professionals, but he had a bad feeling about the outcome. Even if by some miracle he could get someone to take him seriously, a police presence might do nothing but drive the killer deeper underground. Besides, he'd made contact with Trent for a reason. What that reason was, he had no idea, but he intended to find out.

As the minutes ticked by, the waiting started to get to him. He told himself to go inside, lock the doors and keep watch from the window. Exhaustion bred carelessness. But he ignored his better instincts and remained outside until he was certain the boat had had time to come ashore.

He sat in the dark and listened for the sound of a car engine or stealthy footfalls slipping through the shadows. Earlier, Larry had been caterwauling to get out, but all was silent now except for the occasional tinkle of the wind chimes on the boathouse. An hour went by without incident. He relaxed and even caught himself nodding off. Told himself once again to go inside, get some sleep. He'd been running on fumes for the past twenty-four hours. He was starting to hear things. See things.

Slapping his cheeks to revive himself, he sat up straighter in the chair. He'd definitely sensed something out of the ordinary.

The hair at his nape prickled. Not his imagination. He was no longer alone.

His gun lay on the ground beside his chair. Sliding his hand between the seat and the armrest, he closed his fingers around the handle and brought the weapon to his side as he slowly rose.

The wind chimes had gone silent. He could hear no sound at all except for the gentle ripple along the shoreline. Yet his every instinct told him the killer was somewhere in the dark, watching and waiting.

Trent moved from the moonlit patio into the yard where he took cover in the landscaping. He crouched behind a palmetto, his senses on high alert as he slowly scanned his surroundings. Nothing. All was quiet.

He was beginning to think he had imagined a presence when something brushed against his leg. He looked down into Larry's upturned face. Then he knelt and ran his hand along the cat's backbone. "How the hell did you get out?" he whispered.

Turning back to the bungalow, he scanned the porch and then trailed his gaze over every darkened window. Had the killer been inside his house? Was he there now, hiding under a bed or at the back of a closet until Trent was asleep and at his most vulnerable?

He couldn't have gained entry through the unlocked back door without Trent seeing him from the patio. The front door was dead-bolted. A forced entry through a window would surely have attracted his attention.

Staying low, he circled the premises, looking for an entry point. When he didn't find anything suspicious, he returned to the back of the house and eased up the steps onto the porch, then through the tiny mudroom into the kitchen. He knew every inch of the bungalow. The shadowy shapes of his furniture. The creaking floorboards in the hallway. Even the smell of it. When weather permitted, he kept his windows open to keep the musty scent at bay. Living so close to the water in an old house, mold and mildew were constant callers. Tonight, he could detect another scent, foreign and so elusive as to be nothing more than his imagination.

He moved quickly from room to room, scanning all the hiding places, and then he went back through for a more thorough search. His senses still on alert, he paused in the hallway outside his office as an unexpected draft skimmed along his bare arms. His office was on the opposite side of the house from the patio, making it a likely entry point. But he hadn't noticed an open window in his initial reconnaissance of the perimeter. Which meant someone had possibly gone out the window after Trent had entered the house.

He remained motionless, listening for the slightest sound that would signal an intruder's whereabouts. Then he sidled up to the door, checking the corners in one sweeping glance before stepping inside. Weapon in his right hand steadied with his left, he searched the room and adjoining closet. He was certain every window in the house had been closed and locked earlier, but the wooden frames were weathered and splintered in places and the latches rusted. It wouldn't take much muscle or skill to pry open a catch.

He stood sideways to the window so that he could search the site without turning his back to the hallway. The only movement he could detect was the flutter of leaves in the breeze. If someone had been inside the house, they were gone now. To be on the safe side, Trent shut and locked the window before once again combing the premises.

This time he turned on lights as he checked every room. When he found nothing else amiss, he went back to his office. He didn't know what he expected to find. Another article of bloodstained clothing or a left shoe perhaps.

It took him several minutes to realize that the whiteboard had been subtly altered.

SYDNEY WAS SO tired by the time she finally turned in that she made quick work of brushing her teeth and washing her face. Instead of undressing, she merely kicked off her shoes and collapsed on top of the covers in her sweatpants and tank top, her crutches within easy reach in case she needed to get up during the night.

She felt certain she'd fall asleep instantly, she was that exhausted, but the moment her head hit the pillow, the pain in her ankle intensified. She tried propping her foot up, but the elevation put even more pressure on her bruised rib so that every breath she took was pure agony. To make matters worse, she couldn't even toss and turn in the hopes of finding a more comfortable position. She could do nothing but lie on her back and stare up at the ceiling in abject misery.

When she could stand it no longer, she reached for a pain pill and washed it down with water from the bottle on her nightstand. She wanted to heed Trent's advice to go easy on the medication, but enough was enough. She needed to sleep. Tomorrow she would start tapering off. The pain would be easier to tolerate when she had something to occupy her mind with. Right now, all she could think about was the pulsing ache inside the hot, itchy cast.

When the throbbing finally eased and she was able to doze off, she slept deeply.

Sometime later she was startled awake by a noise. She fought her way up through a thick curtain of cobwebs, certain that someone had been banging on her door. But already the sound had faded, and she realized she must have been dreaming. No one would come beating on her door at this hour. No one with innocent intent.

Pushing herself back against the headboard, she picked up the phone to check the time. Just after two. She'd only been asleep for an hour or so. She'd stayed up late listening to podcasts in case Trent decided to call and let her know about the boat. The phone had remained annoyingly silent. She could have called him, of course, but she thought it best not to distract him. If he really intended to use himself as bait, he needed to be fully alert.

The pain in her ankle had subsided, but the reprieve hadn't come without a cost. She felt groggy and disoriented. Unsettled.

She would definitely ease off the pain medication. Trent wasn't the only one who needed to remain alert. From now on, she'd rely on willpower and an over-the-counter painkiller if she grew desperate enough—

Another sound intruded. She wasn't dreaming this time. She was cognizant enough to distinguish the difference.

The noise came again. Not a sharp knock or rap, but a thump, muted and distant. Normally, she wasn't the type to overreact to an unidentified sound in the middle of the night. She knew how to take care of herself. But her injuries made her vulnerable and more cautious.

Swinging her legs over the side of the bed, she grabbed her crutches. Maneuvering through the dark apartment, she paused at the front window to glance out at the narrow porch and landing area. She couldn't see anyone outside her door or at the bottom of the stairs. Whatever noise she'd heard had ceased once she got up.

She put her eye to the peephole. Still nothing.

"Who's there?" she called from behind her locked door. "I'm armed," she warned.

Silence.

She moved back to the window and searched for a moment longer before she opened the door and stepped out on the porch. The moon was still up but now partially shrouded by clouds that had rolled in from the gulf. She could smell rain in the breeze that ruffled the leaves and intensified the perfume from her landlord's garden. His place was dark, as were all the other houses up and down the street. The whole neighborhood seemed preternaturally silent. Shivering, she swept her gaze over the yard and into the shadows.

If someone had climbed the steps moments earlier to knock on her front door, the person had departed as soon as they realized she was up. She discarded the idea of an intruder. She hadn't heard footfalls on the steps. It was hard to descend a creaky wooden staircase without making a sound.

Another notion niggled. What if they hadn't gone down the steps? The landing extended a few feet around the corner of the apartment. Someone could be crouched against the wall, waiting for her to go back inside. Or waiting to spring out of the darkness and push her down the stairs.

Instinctively, she moved back into the doorway, shielding herself in the deep shadows. She told herself to play it safe. A serial killer resurrected from her dad's past might well be on the prowl. *Go back inside, lock the door and grab a weapon.* Instead, she waited. When no sound came to her, she eased along the wall until she could peer around the corner. No one was there.

She let out a quick breath of relief. The sound must have been a tree limb brushing against the side of the building or across the roof. Or the bump of a loose shutter somewhere nearby. The sound had filtered into her dream and manifested the knock on her door.

As she turned to go inside, a movement in the yard next door checked her. She pressed back into the shadows as Brandon Shaw came around the corner of his garage. He gazed across the backyard for a moment before he strode around the pool and picked up the abandoned sandals. Returning to the garage, he lifted the lid on the trash can and dropped the shoes inside.

He made another pass around the pool and garden area, his attention focused on the ground as if he were searching for something. After a few minutes, he disappeared through the back door of the house. No lights came on. Maybe he'd gone straight to bed. It was very late. Was he just now returning from wherever he'd gone to earlier? Sydney hadn't heard a car engine, but she'd been asleep until the phantom sound at her door had awakened her.

She eased back around the corner of the building only to pause yet again as something below caught her eye. She remained frozen as her eyes adjusted to the darkness and a silhouette took shape.

Martin Swann seemed oblivious to her presence as he hunkered in the oleanders, his gaze fixed on the house next door.

Chapter Six

"I haven't been able to find out much about your next-door neighbor," Trent told Sydney the following day as he sat across from her at her dining table. It was early afternoon, and he'd brought over enough barbeque to feed an army. Neither of them stood on ceremony. They removed the plastic lids from the containers and dug in. Potato salad, baked beans, brisket. Sydney happily filled her plate. Her appetite had returned with a vengeance, and she resolved to getting back to the gym sooner rather than later.

"I should clarify," Trent said, "I haven't been able to find anything yet. But I will. If this guy has skeletons, I'll dig them up."

"*We'll* dig them up," she clarified. "Just because I'm suspended doesn't mean I'm completely without means. I do have resources outside the police department." She picked up her fork. "Thank you for bringing this over, by the way. I haven't had a meal like this in ages."

He played down the gesture. "The restaurant was on the way and we both have to eat."

"Reminds me of when I was a kid and Dad would bring barbecue home from this little hole-in-the-wall joint on Market Street. We'd eat on the deck, just the two of us, and

I'd tell him about my day. Those conversations must have been boring to him, but he never let on."

"What about your mom?"

Sydney waited a beat, then tried to say matter-of-factly, "She left when I was thirteen."

"I'm sorry. I didn't mean to pry."

"No, it's okay." She shrugged. "I came to terms with her indifference a long time ago. Or at least, I pretend that I have. She'd be the first to admit that she was never cut out to be a wife and mother. Especially a mother. She didn't have the patience or the desire to deal with a difficult child."

He lifted a brow. "You were difficult?"

"Difficult by her standards. Meaning I didn't sit in my room and read all day. I liked to wander. Which, come to think of it, probably also suited her fine so long as I stayed out of her hair. My dad was the one who worried. He'd come out looking for me if I wasn't home by dark. Probably had something to do with the kind of people he dealt with all day."

"No doubt. Do you still see your mom?"

"Not very often. She lives in Austin with her artist boy-friend. I've driven up a couple of times for a visit. It was awkward. We don't have much in common. I think we're better off in a long-distance relationship. Anyway…" She poured warm barbecue sauce over her brisket. "What about you? Does your family live around here?"

"My parents were killed in a car wreck when I was in college. I lost my sister three years ago…" He paused. "It's just me now."

"I'm so sorry." Sydney didn't know what else to say. Then something occurred to her. "You were talking about your sister yesterday. You said she was the most heroic person you ever knew."

He nodded. "She was a lot younger than me. Just a kid when our parents died. I moved back home after the accident. Technically, I raised her, but she took care of me, too. She got sick her freshman year of college. A rare kind of bone cancer. She endured one treatment after another until…" He trailed off again. "We spent a lot of time in the hospital."

Sydney reached over and touched his hand briefly. "I can't imagine how hard that must have been."

"It's been a few years. I've had time to make peace."

In the face of his loss and suffering, she felt petty for her estrangement with her mother. *Maybe I'll call her when this is all over.*

"Things got a little deep there." His smile was still strained. "It wasn't my intent to unload on you like that. You've had a pretty rough go of it yourself." He seemed to shake off his dark mood as he pointedly observed her full plate. "But I'm glad to see you're feeling better."

She appreciated his effort and responded in kind. "Should I be embarrassed?"

"For being hungry? Not in my book. Nothing wrong with having a healthy appetite. Like I said, you'll need all your strength for getting around on those crutches. Speaking of…seems like your mobility has improved since yesterday. You've been practicing."

"You might not think so if you'd seen me stumble on the way to the door," she told him. "But maybe we should get back to Brandon Shaw. I didn't expect you to get started on a background check so soon. You have a lot more important things on your mind at the moment. Like using yourself as bait to lure a serial killer out of hiding…and keeping yourself alive in the process."

"No reason I can't do all of the above," he said between bites.

Her fork paused in midair as she stared across the table at him. "You're so nonchalant about this whole thing. I worry you're not taking the necessary precautions."

"Believe me, I am."

"So, what happened last night? Did the boat show up?"

"Yes, but we'll get into all that later. I'd rather focus on your neighbor right now."

Before she could press him about the boat, he said, "It's a little strange for someone his age to be so conspicuously absent from social media. No posts, tweets or images on any of the major platforms."

"He's not completely absent," she told him. "He teaches an online class in creative writing. I found his videos with a simple internet search."

"I saw those, too." Trent paused to swig his ice tea. "The videos look pretty damn polished. I know a little something about the editing process. It's a lot more time consuming than most people realize. Makes you wonder. If he's working for Richard Mathison, why go to all that trouble to create an elaborate cover? Why not just say he's on vacation since he's only supposed to be here for the summer?"

"I've thought about that. For one thing, it gives him an excuse for having video equipment. He could have a camera trained on my place twenty-four hours a day for all we know." She glanced toward the window and shuddered. "And for another, maybe he really is a down-and-out writer looking to make some extra cash. I would guess he's close to Gabriel Mathison's age. Maybe they knew each other at college, and he's done side jobs for the family for years. Or who knows? Maybe they met in a bar, and it's a strangers-on-a-train situation."

Trent looked amused. "That's thinking outside the box."

"I'm just saying. Every good cover has a hint of truth in

it. Brandon Shaw could be his pen name. Maybe that's why you haven't been able to locate his social media accounts."

He nodded his approval. "It's a leap, but I like where you're going with this. If he's using an alias, that would explain why I haven't been able to find him in any of the usual government databases. No tax, property or employment records. No arrests, tickets or warrants. Have you talked to your landlord? Maybe he knows the guy's real name."

"I haven't had a chance. But I'm glad you brought up Martin. I've got something to tell you about him, too."

"I'm all ears."

She blotted her lips on a paper napkin, marveling at the easy nature of their banter. Not only was she comfortable in Trent's company, she was also starting to look forward to his visits. He'd come over today ostensibly to pick her up so that they could search the storage unit for her dad's notebooks. When he showed up at her door with food, she could hardly turn him down. Not that she'd wanted to. As much as she valued her independence, she had to admit it was nice having someone look out for her for a change.

She was still amazed at how quickly her attitude had changed. Three years ago, she could never have imagined working with Trent Gannon in any capacity. Now she could hardly think of anything else. He'd offered her an interesting proposition when she badly needed a distraction, and he'd suggested an intriguing partnership when most of her colleagues had turned their backs on her. Already she was starting to think of him as a friend.

More than a friend, if she were honest, but it was best to keep things low-key while they got to know each other. She appreciated his honesty. It couldn't have been easy revisiting past tragedies and mistakes. Regardless of her new attitude, there was no need to rush into anything. She'd made that mistake before, and it hadn't ended well. She was a lot more careful these days. Besides, he might not even feel the same way, although she'd caught a lingering glance on more than one occasion when he thought her attention was diverted elsewhere. Like now, as he watched her intently from across the table.

He cocked his head. "Well? Don't leave me hanging."

"What?"

"You were going to tell me what you found out about Martin Swann."

She shook off her momentary reverie and forced her focus back to the matter at hand. "It's not so much what I found out. It's where I saw him. He was hiding in the bushes last night. Or early this morning, to be precise. Must have been around two."

His brows shot up. "That's not a euphemism, I take it. You literally saw him hiding in the bushes?"

She recounted the events of the previous evening while he ate.

"Did he see you?" Trent asked when she paused.

"I don't think so. His attention seemed laser-focused on the house next door."

"Why do you think he was spying on Shaw?"

"I have no idea. I told you yesterday I sensed a strange vibe between them. After last night, I'm really curious about their relationship. I have a feeling there's more to their back-story than Brandon wanted me to know."

Trent contemplated her revelation for a moment. "Maybe we should go downstairs and have a chat with Martin Swann."

"I don't know if that's a good idea. He likes to keep to himself. I'm not sure he'd even answer his door if he spotted you. Besides, I thought you were in a hurry to get to the storage unit."

"We've got all afternoon. That is, unless you're in a rush for some reason."

"No, but I think I should talk to Martin alone. He's used to having me around. I'll just casually work Brandon into the conversation without appearing to pry. Or without letting on that I saw him hiding in the bushes last night."

"That's one way to go about it," Trent said. "Or you could just ask him point-blank why he was spying on the neighbor. Catching him off guard might be illuminating."

"It might also put him on the defensive, and then I wouldn't find out anything."

"It's your call." Trent clicked the plastic lids onto the food containers and stood. "Are you done? Should I put the leftovers in the fridge so you'll have something to munch on later?"

"You don't have to wait on me." She scooted back her chair. "I'm doing okay. See?" Balancing on one foot, she stacked her dishes.

He continued to gather up the leftovers. "It doesn't make you weak to accept help, you know."

"Now you sound like Lieutenant Bertram."

He gave her an enigmatic look but didn't respond.

"You're never going to convince me he's a dirty cop," she said.

He looked as if he wanted to argue, then shrugged. "Just watch your back, okay? That's good advice, regardless."

"I'm not the one using myself as bait, but your point is taken."

He nodded and changed the subject. "You say Brandon Shaw left earlier in the evening with the two women we saw in the pool?" He picked up the leftovers and headed for the kitchen.

"I assumed so. I saw his car drive off just before I called

you. I didn't see another vehicle arrive or depart. But that's another odd thing." His question brought back the strange incident with the abandoned shoes, and she quickly filled him in.

Trent came back to the table. "You're right. That does sound a little odd. You'd think he'd have the courtesy of returning the shoes or at least hanging on to them until the owner could come back for them. But I can't say I'm surprised after what we witnessed in the pool yesterday. Holding a woman's head underwater until her friend has to come to her rescue isn't exactly gentlemanly behavior."

"I've had a bad feeling about him from the start," Sydney said.

"I know you have." Trent walked over to the window to stare down into the yard next door. "What's he been up to today?"

"I haven't seen him. Maybe he's sleeping in after a late night. Or maybe he's working on a new video." She hobbled over to the window. "He told me yesterday that he posts new videos on Tuesdays and hosts a live chat every Thursday evening so that his students and viewers can ask questions and participate in critiques. He made a point of inviting me to join in."

"What prompted that?"

"He seemed to think I'd get bored with too much time on my hands. He's not wrong about that," she said. "I didn't think much about the invitation at first. School was never my thing, so I more or less brushed him off. But in hindsight, I have to wonder why he even mentioned the classes to me in the first place."

"Maybe he was reinforcing his cover," Trent suggested.

"Or there's something he wants me to see or hear in those videos."

"Like what?"

She shook her head, deep in thought. "All I know for sure is that I'm now more inclined to take his bloody classes."

"Who knows? You may learn something," Trent teased. "Then you can write a book about our exploits."

Our exploits? "I can guarantee I won't be writing any books. I struggle to get through my incident reports. Paperwork is one thing I won't miss about being a cop, scorned or otherwise."

"I hear that."

She plopped down on the recliner and opened her laptop. "I want to show you something."

"About Shaw?"

"About his videos and what he may or may not want me to see. Maybe I'm reaching, but…" She scrolled through her bookmarked sites. Before she could tilt the laptop so that Trent had a view of the screen, he sat down on the side of the chair and threw an arm across the back. His nearness made her self-conscious. Made her heart beat a little faster so that she had to quickly remind herself the point of his visit.

"What are we looking for?" he asked.

"Like I said, I could be grasping at straws, but I found something curious about these videos. I checked the time stamp. Brandon Shaw uploaded the first one last Tuesday. I know it was shot next door because I recognize Mrs. Dorman's sunroom. See all those shelves behind the desk? That's where she displayed her rare houseplants and her favorite pottery. She was extremely proud of her collection. She said it took years to assemble, and some of the pieces had become quite valuable."

"You're using the past tense."

"What?" She turned to meet his gaze. He was so close

she could see the dark rim around his gray irises and a tiny freckle at the corner of his bottom lip. She swallowed. "Slip of the tongue, I guess."

He didn't look convinced. "You really think Brandon Shaw did something to her, don't you?"

"I know it sounds ridiculous. Maybe it's all the talk about a serial killer. I'm not usually this paranoid, but I actually thought about searching his house when I saw him drive off last night."

Trent looked alarmed. "That's a really bad idea."

"I know. My dad would turn over in his grave. Besides…" She lifted her injured foot. "I can't exactly run these days if I'm caught in the act."

"Running might not do you much good when he knows where you live." Trent's tone was light, but his expression had sobered. "Promise you won't do anything that risky unless I'm around to have your back."

"Says the man trying to single-handedly trap a serial killer."

"I don't have a broken ankle."

She sighed. "You don't have to keep reminding me. I'm painfully aware of my limitations."

"You say that now, but once boredom sets in, you may be tempted to mix things up. Being cooped up for too long makes people like us edgy."

"People like us?"

"We get bored, we get anxious, we get impulsive. Sometimes to the detriment of ourselves and those around us."

"You've got me all figured out, do you?"

Their gazes met again, and she found herself fixating on the freckle at the corner of his mouth. Why had she never noticed before the fullness of his bottom lip or the barest hint of a dimple in his chin? And why was she wondering now what kind of kisser he'd be? Did he employ finesse and technique, or was he more aggressive and impulsive, a real balls-to-the-wall type?

Apparently, she wasn't going to find out anytime soon. He continued their conversation without missing a beat. "At least give me a chance to look into Brandon Shaw's background before you take matters into your own hands."

She nodded and glanced back down at the laptop screen. Pausing the video, she went to a full-screen view. "Assuming he needed a day or two to shoot and edit the video before he uploaded, he's been in that house for at least a week. But I didn't meet him until yesterday. He led me to believe that he'd only moved in a few days ago."

"A week is a few days," Trent said.

"No, a week is several days, but the point is, he's been here longer that he let on, and he's removed all of Mrs. Dorman's things. Now, why would he do that? He only has a short-term lease. If she's coming back soon, why go to the trouble of getting rid of her plants and boxing up her pottery?"

"Isn't it possible Mrs. Dorman packed up her collection before she left? Maybe she didn't want to take a chance with anything breakable or valuable. She could have given the plants to a friend or neighbor to look after."

"Sounds perfectly plausible."

"But?"

"He's installed himself in an elderly woman's home and has removed her personal belongings. If that doesn't send up a red flag, I don't know what would."

"Talk to Martin Swann," Trent said. "Find out what he knows before we jump to any more conclusions."

The loud peal of her ringtone interrupted the discussion. She glanced at the screen before she picked up her phone. "It's Lieutenant Bertram."

"Go ahead and answer it."

She vacillated. "I don't think I want to hear what he has to say."

"Maybe it's good news." Trent rose. "Just answer the damn phone. I'll step outside and give you some privacy."

"You don't need to go. Just…" She held up a finger as she greeted the lieutenant and then listened for a moment before setting the phone aside.

"That was quick," Trent observed.

"Turns out I can't go to the storage unit with you, after all." She picked up the key from the side table and dropped in his hand. "You go without me. The lieutenant wants to see me at the station a-sap."

"Did he say why?"

"No, but he sounded tense." She worried her bottom lip. "That can't be good."

"Again, don't jump to conclusions," he advised. "And don't go in with an attitude. No matter what happens, try to keep your cool. Don't be goaded into losing your temper or saying something in the heat of the moment that might come back to bite you later."

She tried to muster a smile. "Voice of experience?"

"You know it. Do as I say, not as I've done."

"Things haven't turned out so badly for you."

His amusement faded. "I've made the best of a bad situation, but I'm not a cop and I never will be again. That's not the outcome I want for you."

Before she had time to prepare, his hand came up to feather along her cheek. His touch was gentle and so brief as to be an afterthought. The fleeting contact probably meant nothing at all, Sydney told herself. But her heart fluttered just the same.

TRENT WANTED TO drop her at the station and wait outside for moral support, but she declined the offer. She needed a little distance. And if the meeting ended as she feared, she'd prefer to be alone on that long ride home. Besides, the lieutenant had insisted on sending a car for her. She wanted to take the gesture as a good sign, but given everything that had gone down in the past forty-eight hours, she'd be naive not to brace for the worst.

After Trent left, she spent a few minutes freshening up before tackling the outside staircase. She took his advice and scooted down the steps. Not a very dignified descent, but at least she made it to the bottom without incident. While she waited at the curb for her ride, she cast a doubtful glance at the sky. Clouds had moved in, and she could feel an occasional raindrop, but she wasn't about to go back up the stairs for an umbrella.

Next door, Brandon Shaw backed his vehicle out of the garage and reversed down the driveway. He seemed so preoccupied that he didn't even notice her at first. When he finally spotted her, he gave a brief wave before he turned the vehicle and accelerated toward the intersection.

Sydney wondered where he was going in such a hurry. She watched until his car disappeared around the corner, and then she turned to glance up his driveway. The oleanders obscured her view of the pool area, but she knew from memory that the trash can where he'd tossed the white sandals sat against the garage wall. Shifting her position, she wavered for a moment as she recalled Trent's warning about not doing anything reckless without backup. Surely a peek inside a trash can didn't constitute rash behavior. Besides, the lieutenant's car would arrive at any moment. She probably had five minutes at the most to explore.

She checked up and down the street and then over her

shoulder. None of her neighbors were out and about, including Martin Swann. Without the deterrent of prying eyes, she found it a little too easy to throw caution aside. With one final scan of her surroundings, she stepped through the oleanders into the neighboring yard. Now she was officially trespassing. She excused the transgression by reminding herself that sometimes it was necessary to be proactive.

Pausing yet again to reconnoiter, she swept her gaze over the house. The style was a seventies ranch with lots of windows and sliders. The blinds were up in the sunroom. She was tempted to crutch over and peer through the glass. It would be interesting to see if anything else had changed besides Mrs. Dorman's shelf decor. Given the time constraint, she had to content herself with searching the trash can.

Maneuvering up the driveway to the garage, she leaned a crutch against the wall to free one hand. The moment she lifted the lid, a foul odor emanated from the depths of the receptacle, triggering her gag reflex. Slamming the lid down, she waved aside a fly as she hopped back from the stench.

She was no stranger to the various odors of a crime scene. Her jurisdiction was close enough to Houston on one side and to the border on the other that drug- and human-trafficking-related homicides often trickled down into the smaller communities. Not to mention the occasional murder for hire and crime of passion. She knew what death smelled like. The reek rising from the trash can was more akin to rotting meat than human decomposition. That was some comfort, she supposed.

Covering her mouth and nose with her shirt, she tentatively lifted the lid and peered inside. The makeshift mask did little to smother the pungent smell. Swallowing back her revulsion, she used a stick to poke around in the garbage.

Food scraps, empty wine bottles, a few things in plastic bags that she couldn't identify. No white sandals. At least not lying on top of the refuse, as she would have expected. Maybe Brandon had had second thoughts and fished them out. Maybe he was returning them to their owner even now. Somehow, she doubted it.

She poked and prodded for another few minutes before replacing the lid and tossing aside the stick. Grabbing her crutch, she rounded the corner, intent on having a quick search of the pool area, but then she noticed that the side door of the garage stood open. That gave her pause.

It was one thing to go through someone's garbage, quite another to enter a neighbor's premises without invitation or a warrant or even probable cause. She was walking a very thin line. She could almost hear her father's stern admonition.

Don't do it, Syd. Don't you cross that line on nothing but a hunch.

Okay, but what if Brandon Shaw really did work for Richard Mathison? What if he was staying in the house in order to familiarize himself with her habits and weaknesses? Finding out what he was up to could give her an advantage or at least even the playing field.

Of course, she was going to check inside the garage. There had never really been any doubt. She'd come this far, and her suspicions regarding Brandon Shaw had only intensified since last night. She was more certain than ever that he wasn't the amiable neighbor he pretended to be.

Pushing the door wider, she swung inside on the crutches. The garage was dim despite windows on either side, and the space seemed cavernous without any vehicles. Mrs. Dorman parked her tiny Fiat beneath the attached carport on the other side of the house. She preferred to use the garage for storage. Despite all the gardening tools and equipment, the area was tidy and well organized, with plenty of space for a single vehicle. The smaller tools and equipment were tucked away in a cabinet or hanging from a wall or ceiling hook. Bags of potting soil and mulch were stacked against the wall while organic fertilizers and pesticides were stored on open shelving. The only thing that seemed out of place for an avid gardener was the enormous chest-style freezer that hummed at the back of the garage. Why would an elderly woman who lived alone need that much freezer space?

Just another oddity in a litany of inexplicable things, Sydney decided. Like the fact that Mrs. Dorman had been called away to tend to her sister at the same time Brandon Shaw had been looking for a short-term rental in the area. Like how he'd removed her houseplants and prized pottery pieces so quickly, as if he didn't expect her to return. Like how he had uttered the exact same catchphrase that had been written on the card that had accompanied the white roses from an anonymous admirer.

A refrigerator for keeping cold drinks handy would be understandable, especially for someone who spent so much time outdoors. But the size and shape of Mrs. Dorman's freezer reminded Sydney a little too much of a coffin. She started to imagine all sorts of dire possibilities. *You really think Brandon Shaw did something to her, don't you?*

By this time, she'd moved several feet into the garage. She glanced over her shoulder toward the open door. Coast was still clear. She inched farther into the shadowy interior, the rubber tips on her crutches thumping on the concrete floor. The stench from the trash can was still trapped in her nostrils when she paused in front of the freezer. Or was the smell only in her imagination?

She held her breath and reached for the latch, tested the lid and then lifted it gingerly. Condensation drifted from the opening. She hesitated to push the top all the way back, afraid of what she might find beneath the vapor—

"What do you think you're doing?"

Chapter Seven

Sydney's heart leaped into her throat. She thought at first Brandon Shaw had returned, and she braced herself for a confrontation even as she tried to come up with a plausible excuse for invading his private space. In the next instant, she recognized the voice and let out a breath of relief, though an encounter with her landlord would still be awkward under the circumstances. The only thing she had going for her was that "Uncle Marty" didn't belong here, either.

The freezer lid closed with a swoosh as she turned and said casually, "The same thing you are, I imagine. I'm looking for Brandon."

"In *there*?"

She couldn't tell if he was joking or not. Glancing back at the freezer, she said with a shrug, "Oh, that? No. I was just checking on something." She hurried to change the subject. "Have you seen him this morning?"

"He's not here. I heard his car leave a little while ago." Martin's expression never wavered. Was he suspicious? Annoyed? Curious? Sydney couldn't read him at all.

"Then you're not here looking for him?" she asked.

"I came over to retrieve a rake I lent to Mrs. Dorman. I'm still cleaning up in the garden from the storm that blew through last week."

Sydney's gaze flicked to the wall of tools behind him. His excuse was much better than hers. He probably had come over to grab his rake. Her mind raced as he turned and walked over to one of the hooks. What was it Trent had said when he came to visit her in the ER? *Act like you belong, and people are generally reluctant to question you.*

She tried to stand straighter, but the crutches made it difficult. "I came over to talk to him about his online writing class. I guess I'll have to catch him later."

Instead of retreating with the garden tool, Martin positioned himself between her and the door. His posture and demeanor were nonthreatening, but a warning shiver stole up her spine just the same. After all, how well did she really know him? She'd lived in his garage apartment for two years, but they didn't socialize. And she wasn't aware of anyone else in town who seemed to know much about him, despite the fact that he'd owned property in Seaside for more than thirty years. By every indication, he'd kept to himself even before his wife had died. His solitary lifestyle was certainly no indictment, but it made her current uneasiness somewhat understandable.

"An online writing class?" He dropped the rake to his side. "Are you sure you didn't misunderstand him?"

"No, he was very clear about it. I'm surprised he never mentioned it to you. I must say, I find it very exciting living next door to a writer."

"Yes, well…" He cleared his throat. "I'm sure he finds it equally as exciting to have a police detective next door."

She shifted on the crutches and gave him an ironic smile. "Not that I would be of much help these days. Anyway, as I was saying, he invited me to join his class when we met yesterday. I just dropped by to tell him that I've decided to take him up on the offer. It'll give me something to do while I'm out of commission with this ankle. When I came through the hedge, I noticed that the side door to the garage was open, and I thought he might be in here working."

Martin's gaze shifted to the freezer. "You said you were checking on something."

She gave him a contrite smile. "I was, but most people would call it just plain snooping. Please don't tell Mrs. Dorman."

"I'm not in contact with Mrs. Dorman, but I don't imagine she'd appreciate anyone poking through her private things." His tone altered almost infinitesimally, going from semi-cordial to slightly accusing.

Sydney winced. "Of course not. I should know better, and I'll be sure and offer an apology when I see her. This is no excuse, but I couldn't help wondering why someone who lives alone would need so much storage space. Mrs. Dorman is tiny and the freezer is massive. You could easily accommodate a side of beef in that thing… Or a body if you were so inclined." When he didn't respond to Sydney's macabre quip, she muttered, "Sorry. Cop humor."

"Yes, well—"

She cut him off before he could end the conversation. "Speaking of Mrs. Dorman's belongings, do you know what happened to her plants and pottery collection? She used to keep them on the shelves in her sunroom. They seemed to have disappeared."

He looked surprised. "You've been inside the house since she left?"

"No, but I noticed they were missing in one of the videos Brandon posted. Just seemed odd to me that she would pack them all up or give them away when she's only going to be gone a short time."

"I wouldn't know anything about that."

"You don't know anything about her missing posses-sions, or you don't know when she'll be back?"

"Either." He shifted the rake to his other hand, and whether consciously or not, he mimicked her leaning stance with the crutches.

Sydney kept her tone conversational as she probed. "I'm surprised she didn't share her schedule with you. Aren't you the one who arranged the short-term lease agreement with Brandon?"

"I played a very small role. She happened to mention a few days ago that she would be away for a while. She was worried about finding a house sitter and asked if I'd mind keeping an eye on the place. That's the only reason I got involved."

"I wonder why she didn't come to me," Sydney mused.

"You spend long hours at work. Or you did before the accident. I'm home all day. I would notice any strange cars or suspicious activity around the premises."

She nodded. "That makes sense."

"I knew…" He faltered. "Brandon was looking for a place to lease for the summer, so I gave Mrs. Dorman his number. They worked out the terms themselves. I had noth-ing to do with the arrangement."

Sydney's ears perked up at his hesitation. She started to ask about a pen name or alias, but something held her back. Martin Swann had always been unfailingly polite to her, and more importantly, he was a conscientious landlord. She'd never thought twice about being alone with him, but for some reason, her guard had gone up the moment she'd turned to find him behind her.

He was the only one who knew her immediate where-abouts. The overhead door to the garage was still closed, so no one could see in from the street. She was suddenly all too aware of her isolated surroundings and the impediment of a broken ankle. And the fact that Martin had armed himself with a heavy-duty steel rake with sharp tines. What if he tried to stop her from leaving? What if he knocked her in the head or stabbed her and stuffed her body in the freezer? How long before anyone would find her?

She tried to shake off the notion. No reason in the world to even think such a thing, yet her mind still went there. For a moment, she let herself imagine how she would defend herself, given her injuries. She could use one of the crutches to disarm him or even as a bludgeon if it came to it. A well-placed chop to the knees or groin could halt if not incapacitate him.

But why on earth would Martin Swann attack her when he'd never shown the slightest inclination for violence or even confrontation?

All this raced through her mind as she smiled pleasantly. "Regardless, I'm sure Mrs. Dorman appreciated the effort. It's probably reassuring to her that you know Brandon personally. He told me the two of you go way back. He said he and his family lived in this house for a time when he was a kid. You made such an impression that he still calls you Uncle Marty."

She sensed that same strange tension she'd noticed the day before when he delivered her printer. It wasn't fear or even disapproval, but a kind of wary excitement. She told herself now would be a good time to make her exit. For all she knew, Detective Bertram's car might already be waiting for her at the curb. That was some comfort. If she didn't turn up soon, she'd surely get a call or text.

Instead, she continued to try and draw him out. She told herself she wouldn't be much of a detective if she allowed this opportunity to pass her by. Wasn't that the purpose of her foray into Brandon Shaw's private domain? To find out all she could about her enigmatic neighbor?

"He told me he's always wanted to come back and spend more time in Seaside. He's looking forward to the peace and quiet of a small town. Nothing to do but fish and swim. His words."

Martin said in a strained voice, "I'm afraid you're laboring under a misconception, Detective Shepherd. Or perhaps you've made an assumption. Donnie didn't live here with his family."

She lifted a brow. "Who's Donnie?"

"You know him as Brandon. Donnie was his nickname as a boy."

"If he didn't live here, then why did he tell me that he did?"

Martin sighed. "You should ask him. It really isn't my place."

She wasn't going to let him off the hook that easily. "I couldn't help noticing yesterday that you seemed a bit anxious in his presence."

"Not anxious. Cautious."

"Why?"

He glanced over his shoulder toward the open door. "I don't like talking out of turn…"

"Please speak your mind," Sydney encouraged when he trailed off. "There's no one here but us."

"I knew Donnie a long time ago, and circumstances can change after so many years. People change. I've always believed that everyone deserves a second chance."

She'd been a cop long enough to know that not everyone deserved a reprieve, but she merely nodded. "I won't say anything to him. You have my word."

"He lived here but not with his family. Not his real family," he hurried to add when she started to interrupt. "He and the other boys were sent here after their release from juvenile detention."

Sydney tried to hide her shock, though deep down, she wasn't really surprised. Despite his charm and affable demeanor, Brandon Shaw had a disturbing, disruptive air about him. "They lived with Mrs. Dorman?"

"This was before the Dormans bought the property and renovated. For a short time, the building was used as a halfway house for troubled youth. A place where adolescents could assimilate back into society before returning to their parents or to foster care. Or in some cases, back to juvenile detention."

"I had no idea." The revelations about Brandon Shaw were fascinating, but it was Martin's willingness to speak to her so candidly that floored Sydney. She couldn't remember him ever uttering more than a few sentences when she sought him out, let alone carrying on a mostly one-sided conversation. The topic of Brandon Shaw—Donnie— seemed to have triggered a need for disclosure.

"I'm not surprised you don't remember," he said. "It was a long time ago. The neighborhood has changed a lot over the years. People come and go. The elderly forget." His expression turned pensive. "I knew from the start that Brandon was different from the other boys. He was intelligent, charming and uncommonly clever. He'd been on his own for a long time, so he didn't respond well to the program or to being mentored."

"You were his mentor?"

"Unofficially, I suppose. Officially, the program used local volunteers. Teachers, businessmen, police officers. People in positions of authority. They devoted a lot of time and effort to the boys, but there is only so much that can be undone when the damage starts so early. Eventually, you have to accept the fact that some people are beyond help."

"Was Brandon?"

He glanced away. "I didn't think so at first. For whatever reason, he took a liking to me. He would follow me around the garden and soak up everything I taught him. He was like a sponge when a subject interested him. He liked working with his hands. He was a quick learner and a hard worker when he set his mind to it. My wife and I never had children of our own, so I enjoyed spending time with him. I hoped I could eventually make a difference, but…" He sighed. "He still had so much to learn when the halfway house was shut down and the boys were sent away. It was a shame what happened."

"What did happen?"

He gave her an enigmatic look. "Before I continue, I want you to understand something."

She nodded.

"I don't like gossip. I mind my own business and I expect others to do the same. I'm telling you about the past for a reason." His pause was nearly imperceptible. "You're a young woman alone. You have a right to know who's living next door to you."

A thrill tingled down her spine. She didn't bother pointing out her profession or denying her current vulnerabilities. She merely nodded. "I appreciate that."

"I used to travel for my work two or three nights a week. Once, while I was away, Donnie and another boy broke into our house. My wife woke up and caught them going through our things. They were looking for cash, most likely. They grew aggressive when she confronted them. They didn't hurt her, but she was badly frightened."

"Did she file a report?"

"She wanted to, but I was afraid a visit from the police would only escalate the situation. She agreed, though she didn't want Donnie coming around anymore. I didn't blame her. I told him he had betrayed my trust, and now he had to keep his distance."

"How did he take it?"

"Not well. He said some unkind things about my wife, but I let it go. I was afraid he might try to cause even more trouble, so I postponed travel as much as I could. A few weeks after the incident, the halfway house closed down. The windows and doors were boarded up, and the boys just disappeared overnight. Turns out, some of the other neighbors had been complaining."

"What happened to Brandon?"

"I never knew. Truth be told, I didn't want to know."

"You didn't keep in touch?"

"Not for several years. As he grew older, he would occasionally send a card to let me know how he was getting on. I never responded and I didn't tell my wife. His messages were brief but sometimes troubling. Reading between the lines, he seemed to be taunting me."

"Taunting you how?"

"Vague nuances and innuendos. I thought it best to sever ties completely."

"Did you keep the cards?"

"I burned them as soon as I read them. I didn't want to take the chance that Margaret would find them. She was sick and frail by that time. I wanted to spare her any worry. Hers was a gradual decline but devastating nonetheless."

"I'm sorry for your loss," Sydney murmured.

"No need to be sorry. The end was a blessing for both of us." He took another long breath and released it slowly, as if to expel any residual despair or regret. "A few months after she died, he showed up on my doorstep. He must have been in his early twenties by that time. He seemed different. He wanted to be called Brandon, but his name wasn't the only thing that had changed. He was no longer aggressive or rough around the edges, but a quiet, thoughtful, humble young man. Still charming, of course, and so personable I couldn't find it in me to send him away. I invited him back to the garden. I'm not sure why. Loneliness, I suppose. I did enjoy his company that day. We talked for hours. He seemed genuinely distressed to hear about Margaret. And then he told me the most fantastic story."

Sydney had long since forgotten about the waiting car, the imminent meeting with Lieutenant Bertram and the missing white sandals. She had only a passing thought for Trent and his mission at the storage unit. She ignored her surroundings and the very real possibility that Brandon Shaw could return at any moment. Far better—and safer— to continue the conversation on the other side of the hedge, but she didn't want to give Martin an opportunity to have second thoughts.

"What did he tell you that day?"

"He said he'd located his birth parents through DNA testing. One of those public databases where people can learn about their heritage or search for long-lost relatives. He never knew anything about the circumstances of his birth. He'd been placed in foster care as an infant. He found out his mother was dead, but his father was very much alive, and he agreed to see him. Evidently, he was—is—a very successful businessman. He offered to help Brandon financially, even going so far as to set up a trust fund. I thought he was exaggerating at first. It sounded too good to be true. But his car and clothing looked expensive, and the changes in him were profound."

"Did he tell you who his father is?"

"No, and I never asked. I had a feeling the man's generosity came with a price."

"What do you mean?"

Martin shrugged. "Someone with status and a reputation to maintain might view a long-lost son as an inconvenience. Particularly one with a troubled past."

"You think he bought Brandon's silence?"

"That was my suspicion."

"Is Brandon Shaw even his real name?"

"I only knew him as Donnie. I never heard a last name. The young man you know as Brandon Shaw is very handsome and charismatic. Even as a boy, he had a disarming personality. I'm happy for him if he's truly turned his life around, but you've heard the old saying about a leopard changing its spots."

"You said you believe in second chances."

"In theory, yes, but I also worry that some people can't change their innate nature." He glanced once more over his shoulder as if sensing someone outside. Then he picked up the rake and slung it over his shoulder. "I wouldn't come over here alone if I were you. And I'd be very careful who I let into my apartment."

THE CHANGE TO his whiteboard continued to plague Trent as he left Sydney's neighborhood and headed to the storage unit on the other side of town. His mind drifted back to that moment last night when he'd discovered the subtle addition to his map followed by the dreaded certainty that the killer had been inside his house. He'd come in through a window while Trent had sat only yards away on the patio watching the water. He'd stood in Trent's office studying the series of blue x's that visually represented his seven-

year killing spree. He may even have thrilled to the notion that his work was being researched, analyzed and—in
his mind—admired after so many years. And then, before
going out the same way he'd come in, he'd left a puzzling
yet chilling clue. A tiny black cross had been added to the
map in permanent marker.

The modification was so slight that Trent could have
easily overlooked the icon had he not been familiar with
every nuance of that map. But it was where the symbol
had been placed that mattered. It was what that particular
addition potentially represented that even now turned his
veins to ice.

The line of blue x's along the I-45 corridor represented
the seven original homicides, and the three red x's clustered
around the Seaside area denoted the most recent murders.
The cross had been placed to the left—west on the map—
of the blue *x* that designated the location of where the fifth
victim had been discovered. Tom Shepherd had been the
lead investigator on that case and had later brought in the
FBI to advise, profile and widen the search.

So, why a cross? Not an *x* like the other markers, but a
distinct symbol denoting a possible grave. Was the killer
trying to tell him that he'd already killed again and that
he'd buried the body in the same wooded area where the
fifth victim had been found? Or was the goal to send him
on a wild-goose chase?

The notion crossed Trent's mind that Sydney's initial
suggestion might be spot on. A fan of his podcast had become a little too obsessed and wanted to get his attention
by playing a macabre game of cat and mouse. But that
didn't explain the bloodstained scarf. Would a fan go so
far as to break into his house and plant a fake clue on his
map? Or cruise the bay night after night, stopping in the

same location precisely at midnight? Who would have that kind of dedication?

Instead of heading straight to the storage unit as planned, Trent drove to the edge of town and pulled onto a gravel service road. The wooded area on either side of the narrow lane served as a median between Seaside's industrial area and the interstate. Directly behind him was a row of rundown warehouses, many of them abandoned. In front of him, a metal fence kept motorists from cutting through to the freeway, but he could easily climb over the gate.

He sat peering down the road and into the trees as he consulted his mental map and got his bearings. Dark clouds gathered overhead, and it had started to sprinkle. If he was going to do this, he needed to get a move on before the heavy rain set in.

Chamber-checking his Glock, he got out of the vehicle and stuffed the weapon in his jeans as he glanced over his shoulder to make sure no passersby had spotted him. Scanning the rows of warehouse windows, he could imagine someone standing in one of the vacant spaces watching him. The hair at his nape bristled, but he ignored the sensation as he scaled the gate and paused on the other side to survey his surroundings. The freeway was only half a mile or so straight ahead, but the trees buffered the traffic noise. He might have been miles from civilization, the silence was so complete.

Without sunlight streaming down through the tree branches, the woods seemed thick and oppressive. Or maybe the sense of doom came more from the mystery of what he might find rather than his surroundings. He wondered again about the significance of the cross. For all he knew, he could be walking into a trap. The symbol could represent death, all right. His.

Senses on full alert, he walked deeper into the gloom. Twenty-two years ago, the killer had traversed this same unpaved road. An experienced predator by then with at least four murders under his belt, he'd come in from the freeway side of the woods, using a bolt cutter to open the gate. He'd parked his vehicle on the side of the road and dragged the victim's body into the woods. He hadn't bothered digging even a shallow grave but instead had left her to the elements. A few days later, a motorist who had run out of gas on the interstate found her on his way into town. He'd spotted her right shoe lying in the ditch, along with tire tracks and footprints that had led him to search the immediate area where he soon discovered the body. The fifth victim's death had been the first of three consecutive strangulations. In Trent's estimation, her murder marked an important transition for the killer.

The FBI profiler had theorized that the diverse MO in the four previous murders was a deliberate misdirection by a cunning monster who knew how to mask his identity along with his true nature. A killer so clever that he varied his modus operandi, the location of his murders and his victim criteria in order to fool and elude the police. The profiler determined that they were looking for a male unsub, probably in his late twenties to late thirties—mobile, adaptive and patient. The killer knew how to blend in rather than call attention to himself. And he'd known when to call it quits.

Trent had developed a slightly different theory after he'd interviewed members of the victims' families and some of the detectives who'd worked those early cases. The killer had been clever and cunning, no doubt about that. But he'd also been experimenting and evolving, searching for the perfect method of taking a life that would reward him with the greatest thrill and the longest high.

Strangulation gave him the opportunity to prolong death by easing and increasing pressure on the victim's veins and arteries. It required no special tools or cleanup, and the foreplay could last as long as he wanted. He alone could choose the time of death. Gazing into his victim's eyes, he could relish every moment of her struggle, teasing and tormenting before succumbing to an obscene pleasure as the fight left her body and the light in her eyes faded.

The moment the fifth victim died, the Seaside Strangler had been born. He'd killed twice more in the same manner, and then for whatever reason, he'd gone to ground. Maybe he realized his time was limited. The consistency of his new MO gave him the greatest thrill, but it also put him at risk because it created a pattern. And patterns were too easily traced.

The three recent murders were still a puzzle to Trent. He hadn't yet worked out how everything fit together. Possibly the killer's appetite for taking lives had grown more voracious during his dormancy. That could explain the escalation. Three kills in less than a year.

Or maybe a second younger predator had brought the Seaside Strangler out of hiding to defend his territory. Maybe he didn't appreciate someone invading his turf, muddying his history, stealing his perfected method of death.

But why would the killer contact you? Sydney had asked in response to his explanation about the scarf. Only one person could answer that question, but Trent had a theory about that, too. If the recent murders had awakened a latent hunger, his podcast had stroked the killer's ego. He no longer wanted to blend in; he wanted notoriety on his terms. He wanted his story told. He wanted a legacy.

By this time, Trent was far down the service road and had long since abandoned any thought of turning back. The sprinkles had turned into a light shower. The air felt thick and cloying, but the rain was refreshing. He knew from his many conversations with Doug Carter where the fifth body had been found.

Look for a metal rod in the ground on the left side of the road coming in from town. Tom Shepherd placed that marker years ago. From there go straight into the woods maybe ten or fifteen yards. You should find what's left of a memorial. The last time I talked to Tom, he said he still went out there from time to time to throw away the dead flowers and tidy up around the place. I think those visits somehow made him feel closer to the victim. And I think he harbored a small hope that he would someday run into the killer.

Trent located the iron rod without any trouble and took a left into the woods. He could see the faint remnants of a path where people had once trekked through the trees to visit the area. Seemed a little strange to him. The victim hadn't drawn her last breath or been laid to rest in that spot. Instead, her lifeless body had been dumped and left to the vultures. But maybe that was the purpose of the memorial—to remind people that she was more than a victim, more than a number, more than a vicious killer's prey. She'd been a human being. Someone's daughter, sister, lover, friend.

The deeper into the woods he walked, the quieter his surroundings. He heard nothing at all except for the patter of rain on the leaves. Every now and then he stopped to listen, just to make sure he wasn't so inured in the quiet that he missed the snap of a twig or a footfall. He didn't think he'd been followed. He was adept at spotting tails, but he'd also been a little preoccupied. Not good. He was out here alone, basically at the invitation of a killer. He needed to stay focused.

Shaking off his disquiet, he moved farther along the path, eventually stepping out of the woods into a small clearing. He knew immediately he was in the right place. No mistaking the makeshift altar of stones.

The flowers that had been placed on top of them had long since withered, and the stuffed animals scattered on the ground had lost eyes, ears and stuffing to time and inclement weather. But someone had visited the altar recently. Trent spotted footprints in the damp earth.

The breeze picked up, rattling dead leaves across the clearing. Thunder rumbled in the distance, and he wondered how long he had before the clouds cracked open in earnest. He told himself to get back to the car and touch base with Sydney. He needed to tell her about the break-in at his house the previous evening and the addition of the cross to his map. He needed to make sure she was okay, because he had a very bad feeling they'd misjudged something important.

Instead of listening to that internal warning, he walked slowly around the clearing, looking for signs of fresh digging. Then he hunkered in front of the altar, careful to avoid the footprints, and sifted through the offerings for clues. He was so absorbed in the task that a sudden movement caught him by surprise. His head jerked skyward as a flock of grackles took flight. Something other than the approaching storm had startled them from their roosts.

Someone was coming toward him through the woods.

Chapter Eight

The premature twilight had brought out the predators. Somewhere behind Trent, a barn owl screamed a warning. His spine tingled even as he recognized the eerie sound from the summers he'd spent on his grandparents' farm in East Texas. Deep in the country with no neighbors for miles, the high-pitched screech had been terrifying to a six-year-old boy. To this day, the sound reminded him nothing so much as an uncanny combination of a child in distress, a mythical banshee and the velociraptors from a popular movie.

Feeling exposed, he took cover at the edge of the clearing, positioning himself so that he could keep an eye on the altar and the tree line directly across from him.

The owl screamed again, sending that same icy finger down his backbone. He drew his weapon and kept it at his side. With his other hand, he silenced his ringtone, but he didn't put the phone away. For some reason, he had an almost urgent need to touch base with Sydney. What if he'd been lured out here so that she would be left alone? An absurd notion. He'd come here on impulse. No way the killer could have predicted his plans. Still…

He thumbed a text:

Everything okay?

Her reply was immediate:

Just now getting to the station. I'll let you know how it
goes.

He wasn't about to tell her that a killer might be stalking
him in the woods, so he typed, Meet back at your place
later?

When she sent an okay emoji, he added, Go straight
home. Lock your door. Don't let anyone in until I get there.

?????

I'll explain when I see you. Be careful.

He pocketed his phone as he scanned the clearing.

All was silent now. The owl seemed to have scared away
the wildlife. No birds took flight. No small creatures scurried through the underbrush to safety. It was as if everything that lived in the woods had gone into hiding. He
listened intently for the telltale snap of a twig or the crunch
of leaves underfoot, but the only sound he could distinguish
was the distant hum of a car engine out on the freeway.

He drew a couple of long breaths to slow his pulse. Minutes went by. He wondered if he had imagined a presence.
Probably shouldn't have sent that text. Sydney had enough
to deal with without his overreaction. For all he knew, he
was alone in the woods. And she was at the police station
surrounded by cops. Safe for now. No need to worry. Time
to take a few photos of the area and head back to the car.

Instead, he held his position. He'd been baited into coming out here for a reason. He let another few minutes go
by before he eased through the woods, heading west. The

location on the map put the marker halfway between the clearing and the freeway. He could still be walking into a trap, but he didn't like giving up. Even as he hardened his resolve, he found himself thinking, *Don't let me find a body.*

The farther west he walked, the louder the cars on the freeway. The swoosh of tires on wet pavement mingled with the rhythmic drumming of raindrops on the leaves. The sounds were normal, almost soothing, and he might have let down his guard except for the intrusion of another noise straight ahead of him in the trees. Rustling leaves. A snapped twig. The very signals he had been listening for earlier.

Trent paused. From the muted sounds, he'd judged the person to still be some distance away from him in the woods, yet he could have sworn he heard a hitched breath followed by a soft laugh.

Into the silence came the shrill screech of the owl. The uncanny scream seemed different this time, closer and more bloodcurdling. More human.

It's just an owl, he told himself, but in the next instant, he found himself scrambling through the vines and scrub brush, heedless of the noise he made and the thorns tearing at his ankles. Heedless of what might be waiting for him in the trees.

He warned himself to proceed with caution. Now was not the time to get careless. But what if the scream had come from someone in trouble? He couldn't ignore the possibility no matter how remote.

The rain slackened, but the trees continued to drip. His hair and shirt were soaked by the time he discovered a second clearing. He knew at once he'd found the spot that had been designated on his map. He stopped in his tracks, assuming a shooting stance as he lifted his weapon.

He did a quick scan of his surroundings before letting his gaze move more slowly around the clearing. In the center, a cross had been hammered into the damp ground. The two thin slats of wood had been crudely assembled, unpainted and unadorned except for a dead daisy chain draped over the horizontal arms. A bouquet of wilting white roses laid at the base.

Recognition dawned for Trent as adrenaline started to pump. White roses had been left in Sydney's hospital room after the accident. No way this could be a coincidence.

A connection to a killer who had been active when she was a little kid seemed implausible unless her speculation the previous night proved true. Had he known about her all along? Had he tormented her dad with vague threats and enigmatic clues the way he seemed intent on toying with Trent? Was this just a game to him, or was he working his way up to the next kill?

Trent started toward the cross only to freeze yet again as the feeling of being watched intensified. Someone was nearby, hiding in the bushes.

Scouring the shadows, he waited. Then, turning in a slow circle, he called out, "I know you're there. Who are you?"

No answer. Nothing stirred.

"What do you want?"

He kept his weapon steadied as he moved around the clearing, peering deep into the woods. "I've seen you on the water. You come every night at midnight. Why?"

Silence.

"Last night, you came ashore and broke into my house. You left a clue on my whiteboard. Why a cross? Why *this* cross? Is someone buried here?"

Another beat went by.

Trent's voice rose in frustration. "Coward! Show yourself! Tell me what you want!"

After a few minutes, the feeling of being watched faded. He listened intently for hints of a retreat. No sound came to him, yet his every instinct told him the danger had passed. He was once again alone in the woods.

Lowering his weapon to his side, he made another pass around the clearing, still probing the trees and underbrush for even the slightest movement.

He called out. "Are you there?"

The echo that came back to him seemed like a taunt. *Are you there, are you there, are you there?*

"Why have you been watching me?"

Watching me, watching me, watching me.

"Why run away? Are you afraid of me? You should be. I don't give up easily. Sooner or later, I'll find you."

If the killer still lingered in the woods, the thrown gauntlet should have brought him out into the open.

You're losing it, Trent chided himself. Maybe he'd let his imagination and the desire to catch a killer get the better of him. Make his trek out here had been nothing more than the wild-goose chase he'd feared. But he wasn't imagining the cross or the white roses. Or the dead daisy chain that somehow seemed both sad and ominous.

He continued to circle, muttering questions to himself if for no other reason than to remain focused. "Why did you bring me here? What did you want me to see? The cross? The white roses?"

His head came back up to scour the tree line. His instinct was to plunge into the woods in pursuit. But where to start? Should he keep moving toward the freeway or backtrack to his vehicle? The killer had eluded the police for decades by being both cunning and cautious. He was never going to be that easy to catch.

Tucking the gun in his jeans, Trent walked back to the center of the circle and knelt to examine the cross, checking along the slats of wood for clues before turning his attention to the bouquet of roses. Raindrops glistened on the snowy petals as he parted the stems.

A card had been tucked down among the blossoms. The rain had dampened the envelope and blurred the ink inside, but he could still make out the message: *See you soon, Sydney.*

SYDNEY SENSED AN odd energy in the squad room that afternoon. She wondered if word had already spread about Richard Mathison's lawsuit. A couple of her colleagues waved a greeting, but most kept their heads buried in paperwork or pretended to be engrossed in phone calls. She had to admit, the cold shoulder stung a bit. It was one thing to purposely keep to herself, quite another to be openly shunned.

Her own fault, she supposed. She'd never gone out of her way to cultivate friendships, so why would anyone pretend to have her back now?

Funny how things could go south so quickly. One anonymous phone call, one mistake in judgment, and her career as a detective for the Seaside Police Department was effectively over. No one would be sorry to see her go. A few might view her inevitable termination as an opportunity the way she had when Trent had been fired. He hadn't gone quietly. A part of her had come to admire his departing rant. Or at least to understand it. His assessment of the department and some of his colleagues had been brutal. Sydney would know because she'd been on the receiving end of his disdain.

As satisfying as it might be to go out in a blaze of glory, losing control wasn't her style. She didn't like exposing her vulnerabilities. If she had to imagine herself leaving the building for the last time, it would be with her head high and her dignity, if nothing else, intact.

Keeping her focus straight ahead, she navigated through the crowded desks in the squad room and started down the hallway to the lieutenant's office. She tapped on the glass panel and waited until he responded before opening the door and poking her head in. He was hunched over his desk, phone pressed to his ear. His deep scowl didn't bode well for the nature of their visit. He invited her in with a quick beckoning gesture, then pointed to the chairs across from his desk. She lowered herself onto the one farthest from the door, effectively putting herself in a corner where she could pretend to fade into the woodwork. Then she placed her crutches on the floor as quietly as she could manage so as not to interrupt his call.

While she waited, she surveyed his office. She'd been there many times for a myriad of reasons, yet the amount of furniture crammed into the room always amazed her. Large desk and credenza, printer stand, chairs, filing cabinets. And on the beige walls, clusters of framed pictures, maps and citations.

She tried to distract herself by focusing on a group photograph that included her dad, but her mind kept going back to Trent's enigmatic texts. He'd seen her just a few minutes prior to sending those messages, so why had he felt the need to issue such a dire warning? *Go straight home. Lock your door. Don't let anyone in until I get there.*

Something must have happened after he left her apartment. Maybe he'd found a significant clue among her dad's belongings, or maybe he'd somehow intuited her foray into Brandon Shaw's garage. Those would be some serious precognitive abilities. More likely, he'd made an educated guess based on what he knew about her personality. It didn't take special powers to deduce that sooner or later, she was bound to investigate the premises next door.

She checked her phone. No additional texts or voicemails. His silence should have reassured her, but it didn't. She wondered what the lieutenant would think of her concern for Trent Gannon. An association with the former detective might be the final straw for him.

The lieutenant finished his call and made a few notes on a yellow legal pad before he glanced up. "Sorry about that. It's been one of those days."

She nodded and tried to relax, but instead she found herself sitting straighter as her fingers curled around the arms of the chair. Maybe it was her imagination, but the sound of voices and ringing telephones filtering in from the squad room seemed more chaotic than usual. *What the heck is going on around here?*

"Syd?"

She tried to shake off her trepidation. "Sorry. What?"

"Thanks for coming in on such short notice." He nodded toward her cast. "Can't be easy to get around with a broken ankle. Those stairs outside your apartment must be a bear."

"They're not so bad. You get the hang of it after a time or two. Besides, I didn't think I had a choice."

He folded his arms as he regarded her across the desk. "Of course you had a choice. It was a request not a summons."

"Isn't a request from your boss the same as a summons?"

"That's your interpretation, I guess. Regardless, I appreciate the effort. I wanted you to hear this from me before word gets out."

Her stomach sank as she gripped the armrests. "I have a

pretty good idea of why I'm here, so no need to beat around the bush. If I'm being terminated or demoted, just say so. I'd rather get it over with."

His expression remained annoyingly passive. "You think I asked you down here to fire you?"

She gave him a puzzled frown. "Didn't you? I heard Richard Mathison's press conference yesterday. His ultimatum was crystal clear. Either I go or he files a lawsuit against the department. I just assumed—"

Before the lieutenant could confirm or deny her suspicions, they were interrupted by a sharp rap on the door. Instead of inviting the person in, he got up and went over to answer. The chatter from the squad room filtered in through the open door. The commotion had a frenzied edge that made her wonder again if something major was about to go down. And if the pending event somehow involved her.

He closed the door and came back around to his desk. His brow remained deeply furrowed as he took a seat and swiveled around to face her once again.

Sydney glanced over her shoulder. "What's going on out there? Is it my imagination, or does everyone around here seem more tense than usual?"

His voice lowered to a gruff rumble. "It's not your imagination. There's a lot of buzz about an arrest."

"Must be a big bust. Since when does an apprehension generate this kind of excitement?"

He cleared his throat and straightened the papers on his desk, but his gaze never left hers. "Since it involves Gabriel Mathison. He was brought in on suspicion of murder."

For a moment, Sydney thought she must have misheard. Then her mouth dropped in astonishment. She was so taken aback she could only manage a monosyllabic response. "When?"

"A little while ago. He's still being booked. As you can imagine, everyone is a little on edge."

Sydney sat back in her chair as a myriad of emotions poured over her. Anger, first and foremost. Disappointment, betrayal, disbelief. Not two days after her suspension, the main suspect in a controversial and exhaustive investigation had been arrested, depriving her of the satisfaction of placing him in cuffs and closing her first murder case. She couldn't help but wonder if this had all been carefully orchestrated to take her down a peg or two. Maybe even to drive her out of the department. She thought about Trent's warning that once the wagons started to circle, no one would have her back.

She glanced at the closed door. No wonder the squad room was in an uproar. Gabriel Mathison in custody was big news, and everyone at the station was probably bracing for the fallout.

The lieutenant's gaze narrowed as if he didn't trust her silence. "Well? Aren't you going to say anything?"

She took a breath and counted to ten. "Why now? Why so soon after you took me off the case? You made it clear that Gabriel Mathison was off limits."

"He was off limits to you. He still is. You were suspended because of your reckless behavior. A full investigation is pending. Gabriel Mathison's arrest doesn't change anything in that regard. But he never stopped being a suspect. We just didn't have enough evidence to arrest him until today."

"What changed?"

"Turns out, his alibi isn't as airtight as he led us to believe."

"Let me guess," she said. "One of his friends finally turned on him."

"In a manner of speaking. Instead of partying in the VIP room until four in the morning as he and his buddies previously claimed, we have a witness who says Gabriel left the club shortly before midnight and was gone for over an hour. When he came back, he was visibly agitated. He started knocking back shots and grew more obnoxious and aggressive as the night wore on. The timeline comports with your witness's recanted claim that she saw Gabriel and Jessica in a loud altercation in the parking lot of her apartment complex around midnight."

"What did you mean, 'in a manner of speaking'?"

He paused as if considering how much he should tell her. It was obvious he wanted to keep her away from the case. It was also apparent that he wanted to maintain control by doling out just enough information to keep her from digging on her own.

"The witness didn't come forward of his own volition. He was picked up on a third-offense DWI. Which means he could be facing prison time with hardcore criminals instead of lockup in the county jail with a bunch of drunks. He's talking because he hopes the DA will take his cooperation into consideration."

"Do you think he's credible?"

"As credible as anyone looking to save his own hide. As of now, he's one piece of the puzzle, but he's not the only piece. We also received a tip from an anonymous caller who placed Gabriel's car—or one like it—near the area where Jessica's body was found. The caller said the vehicle was parked on the shoulder of the road with the trunk open. He stopped to offer assistance and saw what appeared to be blood on the driver's shirt. The driver claimed he'd been changing a flat. The jack slipped and cut his hand. The caller said he was only now reporting what he'd seen weeks ago because he recognized Gabriel Mathison from the press conference yesterday."

"Does Gabriel have a cut on his hand?"

"No, but a superficial injury would have had time to heal by now."

"Were you able to trace the call?"

"The caller used a burner. All we could get was a general location from where the call was placed."

"Hmmm." Sydney thought about that for a moment. "Why would someone go to the trouble of buying a disposable phone to call in a tip?"

"Obviously someone who doesn't want to get involved with the police."

"I guess, but all these things lining up at the same time strikes me as a little too convenient," she insisted. "I spent weeks investigating this case and pretty much hit a brick wall at every turn."

He gave her a look she couldn't decipher. She had to wonder what was going through his head at the moment. Just two days ago, he'd lectured her own the virtue of knowing when to back off only to end up arresting her main suspect. She wanted to take satisfaction in being proven right, but something seemed off about Gabriel Mathison's arrest. The timing bugged her as Trent's theory continued to niggle. *What if you're both wrong?*

"I don't know about convenient." The lieutenant's response drew her back to the conversation. "Murder cases aren't solved overnight. Sometimes weeks, months or even years go by before an investigation clicks into place. All it takes is for one person to come forward. Or in this case, two. We may not have a smoking gun yet, but we were able to obtain a warrant to search Gabriel's car. We found traces of hair and blood on a lug wrench stored beneath the carpet in the spare tire compartment. The lab results haven't come back yet, but if the blood matches the victim's DNA, then that tire iron may well be the murder weapon."

"Or it could prove he actually did cut his hand changing a flat." She was only too aware of how their roles had reversed. Since when had she become Gabriel Mathison's advocate? Since the evidence against him seemed a little too pat, she decided. "If the lug wrench was used to knock Jessica unconscious, why would he stuff it back in his trunk?"

He seemed confused by her attitude and rightfully so. "He probably meant to dispose of it somewhere away from the body but, in his agitated state, forgot to throw it out."

"That's a pretty important thing to forget," Sydney said. "How did he explain it?"

"As you would expect, he claims he's being set up."

"By whom?" When he hesitated, she said, "By me? That's ridiculous! How would I have gained access to his trunk?"

"Don't take it personally. He and his attorneys have been throwing around a lot of wild accusations. But at least he finally owned up to leaving the club around midnight. He also admitted to an altercation with Jessica in the parking lot, but he swears she was alive when he left her apartment complex. He says the tire iron must have been planted in his car at a later date."

Sydney tried to remain focused, but the conversation wasn't going at all as she'd expected. Now that she'd managed to tamp down her initial indignation, she was starting to ponder other possibilities. "The nightclub has valet parking. It's conceivable someone took his key fob from the stand and planted the blood in his trunk."

"Someone as in…?"

"Whoever killed Jessica King."

He cocked his head and tugged at his ear. "Hold on a second. I must be hearing things. For a minute there, I thought you said, 'whoever killed Jessica King.' I know that can't be right, because you're the person who insisted for weeks that Gabriel Mathison was our man."

"I know. Believe me, it's weird being on the other side of things. But I can't get past the timing. Two witnesses coming forward at virtually the same time? And what about the other two unsolved homicides? Both strangulations, both bodies found within miles of the Mathison beach home. If someone wanted to frame Gabriel, that's exactly where they'd dump the bodies."

He shook his head in disbelief. "This about-face is making my head spin. What happened since I saw you in the hospital? Two days ago, you were more convinced than ever that Gabriel Mathison was a cold-blooded killer. Not just a killer, but a predator. Now you sound like his attorney. Did he get to you? Did he threaten you somehow?"

"Yes, as a matter of fact he did, but that has nothing to do with my uncertainty regarding his arrest. And for the record, I still think he's a predator. His history of violent behavior speaks for itself. However, information has recently been brought to my attention that has made me question whether or not he's a murderer."

"What information?"

She leaned forward, her pulse quickening in apprehension. "What if I told you that someone credible has come to me with a compelling alternative theory? A premise that links all three murders to a killer who went dormant twenty years ago."

He didn't look impressed. "I'd say you've got too much time on your hands. You need to find a more productive hobby until that ankle heals."

"I know it sounds implausible. I discounted it, too, at first. But just hear me out for a minute." She sat back in her chair and tried not to let his attitude deflate her. He'd been a cop when the original seven murders occurred. He might remember something valuable if she could keep him sufficiently engaged. "Do you remember a series of murders that occurred in the late 1990s to the early 2000s here in Southeast Texas? The bodies of seven young women were found in as many years along the interstate from Houston to Galveston. My dad was lead detective on one of those cases. He was the first investigator to suspect a single killer in all seven cases, and he eventually called in the FBI for support."

The lieutenant fiddled with a pen as he turned to glance out the window. He seemed distracted and not very interested in pursuing an alternative theory. "I remember the murders, but I never agreed with the single-killer theory. There were too many disparities. A lone perpetrator never made any sense to me, and I told Tom so. But he wouldn't listen to reason. No one's opinion mattered but his own. We even had a brief falling out over it."

She said in surprise, "I never knew that."

He shrugged. "We both got over it. We put all that business behind us when we became partners. Tom was the smartest detective I ever worked with, but he wasn't infallible. For whatever reason, he became obsessed with those murders. He lost all perspective. It was like he had a personal vendetta to carry out."

"What do you mean?"

"The investigation consumed so much of his time and attention that he let it become personal. Every cop has a case like that in the course of a long career. The one that gets away. The one that eats at you for years. Tom con-

vinced himself there was an active serial killer in the area
and that he alone could catch him. The righteous crusader
complex. He never gave up looking until the day he died."

There was an edge of disdain in the lieutenant's description that didn't sit well with Sydney. "If he was so obsessed,
why did he never talk about those cases at home? He never
even mentioned them to me after I became a cop."

"Maybe he didn't want you taking up his lost cause."

She frowned at that. "You do know the FBI validated
his theory. When they correlated the casefiles, they found
a common link."

"You mean the missing shoes." His tone remained dismissive.

"A missing left shoe in every single case," Sydney stressed.
"Do you really think that was a coincidence?"

"What I think is that shoes are the first articles of clothing to go missing when a body is stuffed in a trunk or
dragged through the woods. Nothing coincidental or unusual about it."

"But a left shoe is specific," she insisted.

He sighed. "The press got that whole thing started after
the first woman was grabbed leaving a New Year's Eve
party. One of her fancy shoes was found in the parking garage after she went missing. A blue high heel with a crystal bow on the toe. I remember the details because every
newspaper in the area ran a color photo of that shoe on the
front page with a caption about a missing Cinderella. That
was before social media took over our lives, but the photograph found its way into dozens if not hundreds of chat
rooms and message boards. The national news even picked
it up for a minute, but you know how those things go. A
week later, something else captured the public's attention."

Sydney grew even more insistent. "Don't you think it's

possible the killer enjoyed the notoriety so much that he started collecting shoes as trophies from his victims?"

"Anything's possible, but I think it more likely that the idea of a missing shoe was already planted in Tom's head when he started trying to connect the cases."

"The FBI, as well?"

"Your dad could be extremely persuasive. And tunnel vision happens to the best of us. I think they all found what they wanted to find." He gave her a long scrutinizing look. "I can't help wondering who planted the idea in your head."

"Why does that matter?"

"It matters if you've been talking to Trent Gannon."

She gaped in astonishment. "How could you possibly know that?"

He sat back in his chair, still eyeing her with the same speculative expression. "I've listened to his podcast from time to time. He's all about digging through old casefiles and trying to poke holes in the original investigations to prove his superior detective skills. He comes across as a guy with an axe to grind."

Sydney started to protest, but she didn't want to sound overly defensive or too invested. Instead, she said casually, "I was surprised to learn he even had a podcast. He never struck me as the type. How long have you been listening?"

"On and off for a couple of years, mostly out of curiosity."

"You never said anything."

"Why would I bring up some random podcast?" The lieutenant was still fiddling with the pen, but he no longer seemed distracted. Sydney had a feeling he might be more engrossed in the conversation than he wanted to reveal. "For the past couple of weeks, he's been focusing on the seven cases you just mentioned. He even managed to drag a retired detective onto his show, and I hear he's been talking to other law enforcement personnel who were involved in some of those investigations. Considering your dad's role in the single killer fantasy, I figured it was only a matter of time before he contacted you."

"Have you talked to him?" she asked curiously.

"No. The murders occurred before Tom and I were partners." He glanced up. "Whatever he said must have been convincing if he's made you second-guess Gabriel Mathison's guilt."

"I'm just trying to keep an open mind," she said. "Three unsolved strangulations twenty years ago. Three more strangulations in the past year. I can't help but see a pattern." She wondered what he would say about the bloodstained scarf and the midnight boat sightings. As much as she wanted to observe his reaction, she wouldn't go behind Trent's back.

The lieutenant continued to watch her from across his desk. The vibe in the office had changed since she first entered. The look on his face wasn't disappointment or exasperation or even anger. He seemed guarded, as if he no longer felt comfortable in her company. She wondered if he resented the heat that had rained down on the department from her actions or if they were just naturally growing apart. Her dad had been the common bond, and he'd been gone for nearly five years. Without him, what did she have in common with Dan Bertram except for their profession?

"A word of caution?"

She forced a brief smile and a nod. "Of course. I always appreciate your input."

"Whatever you think of Gabriel Mathison's arrest or anything else we've discussed today, keep it to yourself. Don't go around spouting alternative theories. In other words, don't make waves. Why give the review board an excuse to delay your reinstatement?" He paused with another hard scrutiny. "If you're smart, you'll stay away from Trent Gannon. There's a reason he's no longer a cop."

She kept her response neutral. "I appreciate your concern, but by every indication, he's turned his life around. His podcast is successful, and if he's found a niche solving cold cases, more power to him. He was once an excellent detective. Why should his talents go to waste?"

He didn't look pleased by her defense. "He's damaged goods, Syd. Don't make the mistake of thinking you can fix or even trust him. He's the kind of guy who will drag you down with him if you're not careful."

"I'll take that under advisement." She tried not to sound dismissive as she bent to retrieve her crutches, but working with Trent was her decision. She was anxious to get home and find out what he'd uncovered at the storage unit. Not to mention filling him in on what she'd learned from Martin Swann.

"Sit tight," the lieutenant said as he picked up the receiver. "I'll have someone drive you home."

"Thanks."

The conversation seemed to be ending on a strained note. Sydney couldn't help reflecting with a bit of nostalgia that their once close and oftentimes combative relationship had shifted into something more secretive and restrained.

While he made the call, she took out her own phone and glanced at the screen. Nothing new from Trent. She didn't know whether to be relieved or worried—

She jumped as the lieutenant replaced the receiver with a loud bang. Then she heard him mutter an oath a split second before the door to his office slammed against the wall so hard the glass panel rattled. He jumped to his feet, sending his desk chair flying back into the credenza.

Sydney was so taken aback by the commotion and his startled demeanor that she dropped her crutches, adding to the confusion. She braced herself against the back of the chair as Richard Mathison stormed through the door. The officer who trailed him tried to subdue him, but Richard shook him off and strode across the room to plant his hands on the lieutenant's desk, his rage so consuming he appeared oblivious to Sydney's presence.

"What the *hell* is going on around here?" he demanded.

The lieutenant cleared his throat. "I take it you've heard about the arrest."

"Did you think I wouldn't?"

"I'm a little surprised to see you so soon. Your assistant said you were away on a business trip."

"Well, that explains the timing." Venom dripped from Mathison's voice. "You waited until my back was turned, otherwise, you wouldn't have dared."

"If you'll calm down, I'll try to explain what happened." After the initial shock, the lieutenant managed to regain his composure. He rolled his chair back to the desk and sat down, straightened his phone and then clasped his hands on the surface.

Sydney's attention shifted back and forth between the two men. Richard Mathison was an imposing figure, though not so much physically. Like his son, he was an inch or two shy of six feet, slim and athletic with an imperious demeanor. But the gleam of cruelty in his eyes and the sneer of disdain in his voice had a chilling effect Sydney wasn't immune to. Despite her relentless pursuit of Gabriel Mathison these past few weeks, she found herself trying to shrink into the shadows. Her timidity annoyed her. She had to admire the lieutenant's comportment, but then, he wasn't without his own power.

Richard leaned in. "Maybe now is a good time to remind you of all the favors I've done for this department over the years. And for you."

The lieutenant gave a brief nod to the uniformed officer still hovering behind Mathison. The officer retreated into the hallway but left the door open and stationed himself just outside. Sydney wished she could slink out of the office behind him. On the other hand, she was riveted by Richard Mathison's words. What favors?

"Maybe now is a good time to remind you that no one is above the law," the lieutenant countered.

"Get off your high horse, Danny. We both know you've done your share of cutting corners and looking the other way…and worse. Gabriel has his faults, but he's no murderer. If nothing else, he wouldn't have the stomach for it. Until about a minute ago, you agreed with me."

"That was before new evidence came to light."

Richard straightened. "You mean the drunk trying to save his own skin or the anonymous phone call? No judge in his right mind would issue a search warrant on such flimsy evidence unless someone with influence twisted his arm. That had to be you or the chief, and I don't think she's that stupid."

"You're forgetting about the blood sample we collected from his car."

"Undoubtedly planted by one of your officers."

The lieutenant merely shrugged at the accusation. "If Gabriel is innocent, you have nothing to worry about."

"Innocent people get railroaded into prison every day. What I can't figure out is why you thought you could get away with framing him. You know me well enough to realize that an attack on my family is an attack on me."

"Is that a threat?"

"Wait and find out."

Sydney shivered as Gabriel's warning came back to her. *You have no idea what he's capable of.*

Despite that warning, something about the confrontation struck her as off. She couldn't put her finger on why. Then she chided herself for the suspicion, but she couldn't help eyeing both men with skepticism. She couldn't help remembering Trent's advice about watching her back when it came to Dan Bertram.

"I've given this a lot of thought," Richard was saying. "And I believe I've figured out your motivation. One, it gives you leverage against a lawsuit. And two, you're trying to protect someone. I've been asking myself who would have the most to gain by Gabriel's arrest. Who had access to the victim's DNA?"

The lieutenant's gaze darted to Sydney. Mathison had been so singularly focused on his attack that her presence had gone unnoticed. Whether unwittingly or otherwise, the lieutenant had just given her away.

Or had he?

Richard turned slowly, his knowing gaze meeting hers before taking in her cast and the crutches on the floor. "Well, well, well. If it isn't the erstwhile Detective Shepherd."

She returned his stare without flinching even though his unblinking inspection had thoroughly unnerved her. She tried to stand straighter without appearing to stand straighter. "Hardly erstwhile. I'm still a detective."

"I wouldn't count on being reinstated after this stunt," he said. "Planting evidence in my son's car took guts. I'll give you that. You remind me of your father. Smug and self-righteous but not nearly as bright as you think you are."

The mention of her dad shocked her. She automatically lashed out. "Don't talk about my dad."

His expression altered, hardened. "I'll talk about any-one I damn well please. Do you have any idea what you've unleashed?"

Before Sydney could utter a word in her defense or even steady her balance, he crossed the space between them in two strides. She sidestepped reflexively and her weight came down on her broken ankle. She would have tumbled to the floor if he hadn't grabbed her arms. From the lieutenant's vantage, it would look as if Mathison had caught her be-fore she toppled, but the feral gleam in his eyes told her otherwise.

Blocking her with his body, he slid his hands over her shoulders and briefly cupped his fingers around her neck. He didn't squeeze. To the contrary, his touched was almost intimate.

Sydney shuddered in disgust even as his expression held her enthralled. Something dark flashed in his eyes as he ran his tongue over his lips. His fingers tightened almost im-perceptibly, and then he released her with a knowing smile.

The lieutenant couldn't have seen that smile or Mathi-son's fingers around her neck. He didn't have any idea what had just passed between them in the blink of an eye. Sydney wasn't even certain herself. The one thing she did know— Richard Mathison was in complete control of his faculties. And he was enjoying himself immensely.

"Careful," he murmured. "We wouldn't want you to fall and hurt yourself again."

The moment he stepped back, Sydney's ankle gave way and she crumpled to the floor. He didn't try to help her up but instead turned his back to her. And the lieutenant didn't leap to her aid. For the longest moment, he merely stared down at her from behind his desk. She tried to give him the benefit of the doubt. Maybe he was still in shock from the confrontation.

But for a moment, she could have sworn he looked coldly indifferent to her pain.

Chapter Nine

Trent was sitting on the outside stairs when Sydney got home. He strode down the driveway as the squad car pulled to the curb to let her out. Despite everything that had happened at the station, she felt excited to see him and more than a little grateful that she didn't have to face an evening alone in her apartment.

She murmured her thanks as he helped her with the crutches. Then he closed the car door and put a steadying hand on her elbow until she had her balance. She'd learned at a very young age the importance of self-reliance and had always prided herself on her fierce independence. But she had to admit that every now and then, it was nice to have someone, literally, to lean on.

"You okay?" he asked as the officer drove away. "You look a little flushed."

"Just hot and sticky. The AC was out in the vehicle and the drive home seemed to take forever. We caught every traffic light." She teetered on one foot while she adjusted the crutches. "But I'm here now and I have so much to tell you. You won't believe all that's happened since you left the apartment earlier. It's been a wild afternoon."

"I have a lot to tell you, too, but you first. How did the meeting with Bertram go?" He reached up and absently tucked back a strand of hair that had blown loose from her ponytail. He didn't even seem conscious of the gesture, but Sydney's pulse jumped, and she had to suppress her reaction.

She swallowed. "He didn't fire me. At least, not yet. That's something, I guess."

"Then what was so urgent that he had to see you today?"

"It's kind of a long story. I'll tell you everything, I promise, but I'd like to go upstairs and freshen up before we get into it. I'm hot and grimy, and the squad car smelled like sweat and bad takeout. I need to wash my face and get something cold to drink." *And just sit for a minute and catch my breath.* The confrontation with Richard Mathison had left her shaken, particularly the dig at her dad. No doubt, that had been his intent. He'd instinctively known how to cut her to the quick.

If she concentrated too hard, she could still feel the touch of his hands around her neck, could still see that feral gleam in his eyes as his tongue flicked out to lick his lips in anticipation. She shuddered at the memory.

Her reaction didn't go unnoticed. Trent studied her features. "Are you sure you're okay?"

"Let's just get inside."

He checked their surroundings and gave a tense nod. "Good idea. I'll follow you up the stairs."

Once they reached the top, she unlocked the door and beckoned him in with a nod, but he lingered on the landing. "You go on in without me. Unless you need my help with something."

"I think I can manage a glass of ice water on my own. But…aren't you staying?" She tried to hide her disappointment. "We have a lot to talk about."

"I'll be right back. I just need to get something from the

car." When she waited for an explanation, he said, "I brought some boxes back from the storage unit. I hope you don't mind. I thought we could go through the contents together."

"I don't mind, but I'm surprised you had the patience to wait for me. Ever since you came to see me in the hospital, you've been champing at the bit to get your hands on my dad's files."

"Something came up. Another errand ate up my time, and I wanted to be here when you got back, so I did a quick search. You're right. Your dad was very detail-oriented, and he took copious notes. We can go back to the storage unit tomorrow and take another look, but the files I brought should keep us occupied for the rest of the evening."

Her first instinct was to press him about the other errand, not to mention the enigmatic text messages he'd sent earlier. Instead, she nodded and left him at the door. Plenty of time to get into all that later. Right now, she needed a moment alone to pull herself together. The ride home wasn't the only thing that had left her feeling grimy.

She shivered as she stood at the bathroom mirror and stared at her flushed reflection. Then, propping her crutches against the wall, she undid her collar so that she could examine her neck. No marks, of course. Mathison had applied just enough pressure to make her skin crawl. The image repelled her and made her queasy. Unclean. She bent to splash cold water on her face, and then she got out a washcloth to scrub her neck where she imagined the imprint of his fingers lingered.

What would have happened if he'd caught her alone? Would he have been able to restrict his anger to a taunt, or would he have wrapped his hands around her neck and squeezed the life from her?

And what was going on with Lieutenant Bertram? Why

had he hesitated so long to come to her aid when she fell? She hated to think that Trent could be right about him, but she was starting to wonder if she'd ever known the real Dan Bertram. Had her dad?

She had no idea how long she'd been in front of the mirror lost in thought when she spotted Trent's reflection. He stood in the living room staring down the short hallway at her.

"Sorry," he said when their gazes connected. "I didn't mean to intrude on your privacy. The door was open, and you looked upset."

"I'm fine. Just trying to freshen up a bit." She kept the washcloth at her throat as their gazes met again in the mirror. "You made quick work of the boxes."

"I brought up a couple that look promising. Some interesting photographs to sort through. I'll go down and get the rest later."

She nodded as she leaned against the sink for balance. Hard to believe she'd initially had reservations about letting him go through her dad's things. Now she was eager to join him in the hunt. Her change of heart was a prime example of how quickly her feelings for him had evolved. Maybe too quickly. From disgraced cop to trusted partner in just two short days.

If she'd given him any thought at all in the years since he'd left the department, it had been the passing worry that she might find herself on a similar path. That she might reach the peak of her profession only to flame out in her thirties as he had. The attributes that drove her to compete and succeed were also the flaws that could end her career as a detective.

She wasn't proud of the fact that she'd passed judgment on him without bothering to dig into the specifics of his downfall. His appeal had caught her off guard because she'd primed herself to dislike him. His attractiveness only seemed unassuming at first, but then his magnetism had a way of hitting like a ton of bricks. How had she never noticed back in the day how truly beautiful his gray eyes were? Or the sensuous shape of his lips and the strong line of his jaw? The hint—just a hint—of swagger in the way he carried himself?

His hair was tousled as if he'd been driving with the windows down, and his shirt was untucked and unbuttoned, revealing another worn T-shirt beneath. What she'd once considered a careless and lackadaisical approach to his appearance now seemed understated and unaffected. A man who was comfortable in his own skin.

All this flashed through her head in the blink of an eye as he held her gaze in the mirror. Then he came down the hallway slowly, pausing in the doorway as if worried he might be overstepping his bounds. Her bathroom was a private domain, after all. But she didn't utter a word of protest when he moved up behind her and rested his hands briefly on her shoulders.

Reaching around, he gently parted her collar. "What happened to your neck?" His voice was both hushed and sharp. His gaze probed her reflection. "How did you get those marks?"

"It's not what you think. Not entirely what you think," she amended. "I got a little aggressive washing up."

"You call that washing up? It looks like you tried to scrub off your skin." His hands slid back to her shoulders, and he squeezed ever so lightly. "What happened at the station?"

She felt a shiver go through her at his touch. "I hardly know where to start. It was a very strange afternoon."

And getting stranger by the minute, she decided. Trent Gannon in her bathroom making her go weak in the knees every time their gazes met in the mirror.

"Start anywhere," he said. "Just tell me what happened."

He dropped his hands from her arms and reached for her crutches. A part of her wished that he hadn't. The gentle pressure had been reassuring. Cleansing. She sighed again and accepted the crutches. "Let's go into the other room where we can get comfortable. I'll finish up in here and be out in a minute."

He left her alone and closed the door behind him. She finished washing up. When she came down the hallway a few minutes later, he stood at the window with her dad's binoculars looking down on the property next door.

"What's going on?"

He answered without turning. "Just wondering if your neighbor is home. I can't tell from here if his car is in the garage."

"He left earlier right after you did," she told him.

He swung around at that. "*Right* after?"

"A few minutes later. Why?"

"I'm curious about the timing." He lowered the binoculars as she came up beside him. "What did you mean when you said you'd had a wild afternoon? What happened at the station?"

"The lieutenant had me come in so that he could tell me Gabriel Mathison has been arrested for murder."

Trent looked taken aback by the news. "When did that happen? How did it happen?"

"I was surprised, too," she said. "Stunned might be a better word. Apparently, one of his friends contradicted his alibi. Once his lie was exposed, he came clean about his whereabouts on the night in question. He admitted to having an argument with Jessica King in the parking lot of her apartment complex, but he swears she was alive when he left her."

"That's a pretty big admission."

"Though not a confession," she pointed out. "But get this. Right after the friend came forward, an anonymous caller placed him in the vicinity of where her body was discovered. The police were able to get a search warrant and found blood and hair on a tire iron in the trunk of his car."

"The victim's DNA?"

"We won't know for certain until the lab report comes back."

"That could take a few days." His posture seemed relaxed, but his expression turned pensive. "You said an anonymous caller placed him in the vicinity?"

"Yes, and the caller used a burner phone. The lieutenant thinks it was probably someone who doesn't want to get involved with the police—or the Mathisons—but it just seems a little convenient. I worked on that case for weeks only to have witnesses recant or move out of town. It was like banging my head against a stone wall. Now all this damning evidence turns up out of the blue once I'm off the case."

Trent gave a vague nod as he rubbed a hand across his chin, still deep in thought. "What did Gabriel say about the blood on the tire iron?"

"Naturally, he claims he's being set up. By me, incidentally."

"Of course, he does." His tone was gratifyingly dismissive.

"My history with the Mathisons makes me an easy target," she said. "Who has a better motive to frame him than a suspended cop looking to clear her name? I never thought I would say this, but he may have a point. The evidence could have been planted by someone intent on making him a scapegoat. Maybe the person who murdered Jessica or someone looking to take advantage of an opportunity. Someone with a grudge, maybe. I don't know. All I do know at this point is that the timing worries me. And, yes, I'm well aware of how improbable that sounds coming from me. Two days ago, I literally staked my career on Gabriel Mathison's guilt. Now…" She frowned as she stared down into the backyard. "I want to believe the police have the right man, but something seems fishy about the arrest. I don't trust either of the witnesses or the evidence. I'm not even sure I trust Lieutenant Bertram."

Trent's brows soared. "That's quite a turnaround."

"I'm having to eat a lot of crow lately. It's an acquired taste," she said.

He flashed a grin. "Mathison's arrest was the only reason you were called in?"

"As far as I could tell, but I managed to ask about the cold cases during the course of the meeting. Don't worry—" she was quick to assure him "—I didn't mention anything about the boat or the bloodstained scarf or any other specifics, because I promised you I wouldn't. But I also didn't want to pass up an opportunity. Dan Bertram worked with my dad for years. They were partners for a good amount of that time. I thought he might remember something that could prove helpful."

"Did he?"

She sighed. "Not really. He says he never put much stock in the single-killer theory. It was apparently such a point of contention that he and my dad had a falling out over it. He claimed Dad became so obsessed with those cases that he lost all perspective. Finding the killer was like a personal vendetta for him."

"Your dad was a homicide detective. Of course it was personal. He became the voice of the victims," Trent said. "It doesn't get more personal than that."

She gave him a grateful nod. "The lieutenant insisted that the whole missing shoe thing started when the first victim's fancy high heel was found in a parking garage and the press ran with an abducted Cinderella story."

"Sounds like he went out of his way to try and discredit your dad's entire investigation. Were you aware of any bad blood between them?"

The question surprised her. "Not really. I mean, they had their disagreements. They could both be stubborn and strong-willed. But even after they were no longer partners, the lieutenant would come over for dinner at least once a month. He was there for my dad when my mom walked out, and he was there for me when Dad passed away. He's the one person I thought I could always count on. But today..."

Trent's tone gentled. "Today?"

"Something was different. I can't really put my finger on it, but he seemed distant. Secretive. Maybe he's starting to resent all the trouble I've caused him. Or maybe he was just tense about the arrest. He had to know Richard Mathison would raise hell when he found out. And, boy, did he ever."

"You saw him?"

She grimaced. "I couldn't avoid him. He stormed into the office while I was there. The odd thing is, he was so focused on tearing the lieutenant a new one that he didn't seem to notice me at first. At least that's what I thought. When he finally turned to acknowledge my presence, I had a feeling he'd known all along I was there."

"What did he say when he saw you?"

Her hand crept back to her throat. "He came at me so quickly I was caught off guard."

Trent's gaze narrowed as his voice hardened. "What do you mean, he *came* at you?"

"I thought he was going to attack me. I tried to jump out of the way and lost my balance. He grabbed my shoulders and made it look as if he tried to keep me from falling. But I saw a look in his eyes, and he actually licked his lips when he put his hands around my throat—"

"He did what?"

Trent's outrage caused Sydney to jump.

"Sorry," he muttered.

She laughed nervously. "Not your fault. I'm still a little jittery, I guess. He didn't hurt me, and the whole thing was over in a flash. No one else even saw what he did. Somehow, that made his actions even creepier. That he could be so blatant and sneaky at the same time. But in hindsight, a part of me wonders if I overreacted. Maybe I saw him as a monster because that's how I've begun to think of him."

"Maybe you've begun to think of him as a monster because he is one." Trent's eyes glinted dangerously. "You were right when you said these are not good people. Maybe Gabriel's violent history is learned behavior."

"Like father, like son?"

"Nurture over nature. It's a cycle," Trent said. "What I want to know is, where was Dan Bertram this whole time? Why did he let Mathison get that close to you?"

"He was behind his desk and couldn't see what was actually happening. And I think he may have been as startled as I was at first. Mathison obviously wasn't trying to hurt me. His fingers were around my throat for only a split second, and he didn't apply pressure. It was almost as if he caressed me. Between that and the lip-licking—" she gave an exaggerated shudder "—I think I would have preferred he strangle me. It was like waking up in the hospital to find Gabriel staring down at me. Nightmarish and creepy. Maybe you're right about a cycle. There is something seriously wrong in that family."

"Maybe we need to do a deeper dive into Richard's background," Trent suggested. "What do we even know about him except that he's a rich entrepreneur with enough shady ties and ready cash to get himself installed as a city council member? Not a bad position to have if one needs to keep tabs on current police activities. Or hide sleazy business dealings."

Sydney nodded. "I did some research when I first started investigating Gabriel. Richard and his first wife split years ago when Gabriel was still a kid. Richard sued for full custody and won. I don't think his ex could compete with his high-powered attorneys."

"Is she still in the picture?"

"Not that I'm aware. If she is, she keeps a low profile."

"Where is Richard Mathison now?"

"At this minute, you mean?" Sydney shrugged. "I have no idea. I left the station almost immediately. I didn't see him again."

"And Gabriel?"

"He's in custody until bail is set. The hearing could take up to forty-eight hours."

Trent turned to stare down at her, his expression troubled. "I feel like this is my fault."

She shivered at the intensity of his gaze. "Your fault? How do you figure that?"

"I should never have come to see you in the hospital, let alone at your apartment. I feel like I brought all this to your doorstep. It was never my intent to put you in danger. I hope you know that."

"Of course I know that," she said almost fiercely. "Richard Mathison was gunning for me long before you came into the picture. You didn't bring anything to my doorstep. I knew the risks when I went after Gabriel, but I did it anyway. I don't always do the safe thing or even the smart thing. I do what feels right at the time. If that gets me into trouble, so be it."

He allowed a brief smile. "Maybe we're too much alike to be partners."

"Just a few short days ago, I would have taken exception to that comparison," she admitted.

"And I wouldn't have blamed you." His hand came up once more to smooth back her hair.

"Trent?"

"Yeah."

"I'm going to say something that might make us both a little uncomfortable. Which is surprising. I'm not usually so bold. But I feel like in our case we'd both rather have everything out in the open."

"Speak your mind."

She drew another long breath and released it. "Is it my imagination or is something happening here? Between us, I mean."

His response was instant. "It's not your imagination."

She didn't know whether to be relieved or agitated. "The lieutenant warned me about you."

"What did he say?"

"That you're damaged goods."

His voice lowered to an intimate murmur. "He's not wrong. Maybe you should listen to him."

"You're not damaged. You're wounded. There's a difference."

"Is there?"

"Yes," she insisted.

Something flickered in his eyes. Doubt? Regret? Unease? She suddenly had second thoughts about her own honesty.

"Now I really have made you uncomfortable."

"I'm not uncomfortable. Surprised, is all. Maybe even a little humble. That's a new one for me," he added with irony. "At the risk of sounding like a jerk, I think we should just relax and take our time. See what happens. You've had a shock. Your judgment might be a little off-kilter. Now is probably a good time to remind yourself that you've known me for all of two minutes."

"Two long minutes. Look at all that's happened since you came to my hospital room. That seems like a lifetime ago."

"That's my point. You've been through one traumatic event after another. What you're feeling right now may be a reaction to all that stress."

"Are you trying to convince me or yourself?"

He searched her face. "Both, I think. I'm no expert on relationships, but I do know this. Rushing headlong into any situation with little regard to possible consequences is rarely a good idea."

She nodded. "On that we agree. My impulses have a tendency to get me in trouble. And, full disclosure, I've never been that great at relationships of any kind. Any partner that's ever been assigned to me usually ends up hating or resenting me."

"I doubt that's true."

"It is, and you know it. I had a reputation even before you left the department, and it hasn't softened over the years." She paused. "For whatever reason, you and I work well together. I don't want this other thing to screw that up."

"I don't want to screw it up, either."

"So…" She shrugged.

"So we relax, we take things slow, and for now, we get back to work," he said. "Does that sound right to you?"

Yes, of course, it sounded right and logical and smart. And disappointing. "Where do we start?"

He nodded across the room to where he'd stacked boxes on the floor by her dining table. "We have a lot of information to sort through. Your dad's files are the first priority."

A spark of anticipation ignited despite her deflation. "Okay, but you still haven't told me about your afternoon. What was the task that ate up your time?"

"We'll get to that. Are you hungry? Maybe we should order dinner before we get started."

"Let's wait. I don't think I could eat a bite at the moment."

The return to more mundane conversation helped restore her equilibrium. He was right. Taking things slow was the smart thing to do—not just for her but for him. She wasn't such a prize in the romance department. She had trust issues, probably abandonment issues, and over the years, she'd become far too suspicious of any act of kindness. But—and this was hard to ignore—Trent wasn't like any other man she'd ever dated. His outer appearance to the contrary, he was deep, pensive and insightful. He'd known instinctively that her dad's vendetta against the killer stemmed from his resolute commitment to the victims and that meant more to her than she could say.

Her past perception of him as a disgraced cop had been replaced by the reality of a selfless man who'd given up his dreams—essentially his life—to care for his young sister. A man who had hit rock bottom in grief but managed to lift himself up without becoming bitter or jaded. Sydney had an image in her head that only grew stronger the longer they were together—Trent at his sister's bedside, holding her hand, reading to her, administering whatever comfort he could give her. Then Trent alone in his car on the long drive home when hope had been lost and the only thing left was to wait.

That was the Trent Gannon she'd come to know in just two short days. That was the man she would readily trust with her life if it ever came down to it.

Rather than joining him at the table. She moved across the room to the hallway, turning to glance over her shoulder until she had his attention. He was on the phone. He laid it on the table and followed her to the bedroom without a word.

Chapter Ten

He took her crutches and propped them against the wall. Then he lifted his hands to cup her face and kissed her for the first time. Maybe it was the moment, maybe it was the adrenaline, maybe it was Trent himself, but she couldn't remember ever responding to a kiss so intensely.

His hands slid around her waist as his tongue probed deeper. Balancing on one foot, she wrapped her arms around his neck and leaned into him, shivering when he lifted her. It was still daylight outside, but the bedroom was cozy and dim. They fumbled with buttons, snaps and zippers. Laughing at the struggle of tugging pants over her cast. Then crawling between the cool sheets.

Sydney turned on her side, and he draped his arm over her breasts and nudged her neck with his lips.

"Top drawer of the nightstand on your side," she said.

The drawer slid open and closed. "Full box," he said. "Should I be intimidated?"

"Full *unopened* box, so no. I'm not very sociable."

"Is that what the kids are calling it these days?" His arm came back around her.

"At the risk of spoiling the moment, can I just say something?"

"I doubt I could stop you."

Rolling to her back, she gazed up at him. "Earlier when you were waiting for me, I could tell you were worried. That's why you sent those text messages, isn't it? That's why you wanted to be here when I got home."

His expression sobered. "I was worried. Maybe that's something we need to get into before we go any further."

"That's not why I mentioned it," she was quick to explain. "We don't need to talk about at this very minute. I've more to tell you, too, but we've got all night for that. I only brought it up because I wanted to say…thank you."

"For what?" He sounded surprised.

"For giving a damn about what happens to me. It's been a long time since anyone cared enough to worry."

"That can't be true."

"It's only a slight exaggeration," she insisted. "The indifference to my suspension hit hard earlier at the station, but I've only myself to blame. I've never gone out of my way to make friends at work or anywhere else. People think I'm standoffish and competitive, but mostly I'm just wildly insecure."

"That could probably be said for most of us."

The intimate timber of his voice made her shiver. "Anyway…thank you."

He was silent for a moment. "This day has taken more than its share of unexpected turns."

She couldn't help but laugh. "An understatement if I ever heard one. Lying naked in bed with Trent Gannon…who would have ever thought?"

"Second thoughts?"

"Nope. You?"

"Not a one." He leaned down and kissed her until she was breathless, and then he trailed his lips over each breast, teasing with his tongue before gently nipping with his teeth.

He moved lower still, parting her thighs and lingering there, too, until her soft sighs turned into sharp gasps.

Plunging her fingers in his hair, she pulled him up and into her. He obliged, dipping his head to kiss her again. Moving in such a way that had her trembling from head to toe. He was good. Very, very good. The tension became white hot. She lifted her arms and clutched the headboard as her body shuddered in release.

THEY GOT UP at some point and showered. Trent helped her with the plastic cast cover and all the minor tasks that she'd taken for granted before the accident. Afterward they went back to bed and napped. When Sydney woke up, it was dark outside, and she was alone.

Her phone was in the other room. She had no idea what time it was, but she had the sense that it was still early. She dressed and tottered down the hallway to find Trent at the table going through her dad's files. He glanced up when he heard her come in, smiled in that way he had before he beckoned her to join him.

"What time is it?" she asked as she crutched around the sofa.

He glanced at his phone. "Nine thirty-three."

"When did you get up?"

"A little while ago. I wanted to get in a few hours of work before I have to leave." When she lifted a brow, he said, "I need to be home by midnight."

"The boat. Of course," she said with a nod. "Why didn't you wake me up? I'm supposed to help with those files."

"You were sleeping peacefully. I figured you needed the rest, and I felt pretty energized. Thank you for that," he added with a knowing smile.

"If only I could take credit," she countered. "We both

know the real reason for your excitement. You couldn't wait to dig into these files. That's not an accusation, by the way." She moved up behind him and rested a hand on his shoulder as she peered down at the open folder in front of him. "Find anything interesting?"

His hand came up to briefly rest on hers. Then he released her and was all business. Fine by her. They had a lot of work ahead of them, and she was as excited as he was by the prospect of the hunt.

"The files were a bit of a mess," he said. "Did you go through the boxes before they were stored?"

"No. I didn't have time. There was so much that had to be done before I could put the house on the market. Why?"

"Your dad's notes are thorough, but the condition of the files leads me to wonder if he went through the boxes looking for something in a hurry. I found dozens of loose photographs. For whatever reason, he never went back and refiled them. I've done my best to label them." He indicated three separate stacks on the table. "For our purposes, I've grouped them into crime scene photos, victim photos and miscellaneous. The next step is to locate the corresponding casefile and return them to the proper folder."

"Doesn't seem like something Dad would do," she said. "He was always so organized. Everything in its proper place at home and at work. What do you think he could have been looking for?"

Trent shrugged. "Your guess is as good as mine. Maybe we'll figure it out as we go along."

"What's in the miscellaneous stack?" she asked.

"Photos that don't fall into either of the other two categories but, for whatever reason, piqued my curiosity. I figured they must have had some significance to your dad's investigation if he kept them with his notes."

She sat down at the table and leafed through the crime scene photos. An image jolted her as she flipped back through. Pulling the photograph from the stack, she placed it face up so that Trent could see the one that had caught her attention.

His expression turned grim. "The second victim. She stands out from the others because the savagery of the attack appears to be an anomaly. Much more violent and graphic than any of the other murders. I think I've figured out why. The first victim—"

"The missing Cinderella," Sydney interjected.

"Correct. She was executed with a single gunshot to the back of the head. The detectives who investigated the case could never find motive. No enemies, no nefarious connections. For years, they believed her death was either the result of mistaken identity or she'd been caught in the wrong place at the wrong time. Maybe she saw or overheard something that got her killed. The second murder nearly a year later and thirty miles away was an entirely different situation as you can see from that photograph."

Sydney's gaze dropped back to gruesome image. "We call this kind of brutality overkill. Usually the result of rage or revenge. A crime of passion. The first murder appears to have been a cold, premeditated execution. No wonder the cases were never connected. Different jurisdictions, completely different MO."

"If not for your dad's persistence, no one would have ever suspected a single perpetrator. You should be proud of him," Trent said.

"I've always been proud of my dad." She returned the photograph to the proper stack. "If the second victim was the only one subjected to that level of savagery, maybe the killer knew her. Maybe the attack was personal."

"That's one explanation," Trent said. "But I think in those early years he was still evolving. Experimenting. Searching for the perfect method of taking a life that would give him the greatest thrill. Try putting yourself in his head for a moment."

Sydney shivered. "I'd rather not."

"Then let me do it for you." He lowered his voice as his gaze held hers across the table. "Let's assume you've never killed before—"

"For the record, I haven't."

"Let's *assume* you've had a dark urge for as long as you can remember. A need that has only grown stronger with each passing year. You try to assuage the hunger by fantasizing and possibly stalking, but a day comes when those fantasies no longer cut it. The desire to take a life becomes overpowering, all-consuming. You begin the hunt for a victim. Now that the decision has been made, the craving intensifies. But you're smart. You realize the importance of planning and a meticulous attention to detail. Nothing left to chance. You wait for the perfect opportunity in order to minimize exposure and the risk of getting caught. But as careful as you are, it's your first time and you're nervous. Strung out on adrenaline. You've had months if not years to work up the courage, but when the moment is finally at hand, you just need to get it over with before you lose your nerve. Like ripping off a bandage."

Sydney stared at him in silence.

"Death is quick and clean," he continued. "One shot to the back of the head and it's done. But the initial high begins to fade rapidly. You're left frustrated. Unfulfilled. You watch and you wait until you find a second victim. The scrupulous preparations only heighten the anticipation, so you take your time. When the moment finally arrives, you're more excited than nervous. Almost euphoric. The adrenaline is pumping so hard you find yourself losing control, overcompensating for that first sterile kill. Not quick and clean like before, but in the end, still unfulfilling because the rage you've worked yourself into steals the moment. You may even have blacked out at some point. Afterward, you have nothing but a few hazy images to sustain you until the next kill."

Sydney muttered an oath. "You made that seem too real."

"Just getting my point across."

She let out a slow breath. "You've given this a lot of thought."

"Yes." His gaze met hers. "It's become personal for me, too."

"No wonder. He left that scarf at your house. He's been watching you and your neighbors. He's probably been listening to your podcast. I'd take it personally, too, if he sought me out."

"That may have been my motivation at first, but the longer I study these cases, the more I realize how forgotten these victims are. They still need a voice, and if not me, then who? It's like I said before, no one else is out there looking for the killer. It's just you and me."

"Then we need to find him," she said. "For the dead, for their families and before there are any future victims."

He nodded. "And for your dad."

"For my dad." She glanced at the stack of files. "You said you thought the killer was evolving and experimenting in the early years. Why do you think his last three kills were strangulations?"

"Clean but not quick. He could remain in control of his faculties and prolong his victim's death for hours."

"If he *is* active again, things have changed," she said.

"He's older now. It can't be as easy to subdue his victims. Have you considered the possibility of a partner?"

"He's older but not elderly," Trent said. "Probably somewhere in his early fifties to early sixties. Still vital if he's taken care of himself for the past twenty years. But the partner thing is an intriguing idea. That's only one of the reasons I like working with you. You aren't afraid to consider possibilities that on first mention seem remote."

"The lieutenant would probably tell you that's a flaw not a virtue," she said dryly.

"Then he'd be wrong. And speaking of Dan Bertram, I need to show you what I've found." Trent removed a photograph from the miscellaneous stack and handed it to her. "I doubt this has anything to do with your dad's investigation, but for whatever reason, he stuck the picture in one of the boxes. No names on the back, just an address. Does it mean anything to you?"

She stared down at the outdoor shot of a group of thirty-something men standing in front of a corresponding number of adolescent boys. The photograph fascinated Sydney. She said almost in awe, "The man on the far left is Lieutenant Bertram, as I'm sure you've already determined."

"Any idea who the others are?"

She scanned the faces before glancing at the back of the photograph. The scrawled address shook her. "That's the house next door."

Trent nodded. "I thought so."

"I didn't recognize it at first." She flipped the photo back over and focused on the surroundings. "It was taken in the backyard before the pool was put in. The landscaping looks completely different now, and the house has been painted white. I don't know the other men, but—" she tapped the visage of one of the boys "—I think that's Brandon Shaw."

"What?" He took the photograph from her hand. "How did I not notice him before?"

"He was just a kid and looks change over time. A lot of things change. He was called Donnie back then."

He glanced up in surprise. "How do you know that?"

"I had a long conversation with Martin Swann this afternoon."

"The landlord?"

"He caught me sneaking into the garage next door," she said.

Trent gave her a look that seemed to mingle frustration with a hint of amusement. "And here I thought you were going to play it safe unless I'm around to have your back."

"I fully intended to, but the opportunity presented itself and I couldn't resist."

"I guess you'd better tell me the rest," he said with a resigned sigh.

"I was just going to have a quick look around while I waited for my ride, but then Martin came into the garage behind me. Snuck up on me, actually. I'd just opened the freezer lid—"

"Opened *what?*"

"There's a huge chest-style freezer in the garage. Coffin-size, you might say. It struck me as odd that Mrs. Dorman would need that much storage space. And then the possibility occurred to me that I might find her body stuffed inside."

"I guess that's not entirely irrational."

"Martin came in and startled me before I got a good look at the contents. I told him that I'd walked over to ask about Brandon's online class."

"Did he buy it?"

"I'm not sure. He said he needed to get a garden rake that he'd loaned Mrs. Dorman before she left. We got to talking, and with a little coaxing, he told me about Brandon's history. He didn't live next door with his family like he claimed. The place was once a halfway house for adolescent boys being released from juvenile detention. Martin said the kids were each assigned a mentor. Someone known and respected in the community. An authority figure."

"Like a cop," Trent said.

"Or a coach or a businessman, but, yes, like a cop."

"Did Dan Bertram ever say anything about being a mentor?"

"Not to me, but he's pretty private when it comes to his personal life."

"Your dad must have known," Trent said. "How do you suppose the photograph came to be in his possession? And why keep it with his murder file?"

"That's a very good question." Sydney took the photograph from Trent, letting her gaze linger on Brandon Shaw's youthful visage. Even at so tender an age, he'd had those piercing eyes. She took a second, closer look. "That's not possible," she said in a near whisper.

"What isn't?"

"No wonder he looked so familiar when we first met. I couldn't put my finger on why. Hold on. I need to check something." She opened her laptop and searched through her image folders until she found what she needed. "The eyes are a dead giveaway. Why didn't I see it before?"

"See what before?" Trent demanded.

Her voice rose in excitement. "Do you remember when I told you I'd researched Richard Mathison's background? He and his wife divorced when Gabriel was just a kid. Twelve or fourteen, I think. This is a photograph of father and son leaving the courthouse after Richard was awarded sole custody. That trial was pretty sensational for Seaside. The local paper carried all the sordid details for weeks." She enlarged the computer image and turned the screen toward Trent. "Look at Gabriel's eyes. And Richard's, for that matter."

He studied the screen, then picked up the photograph of Brandon Shaw. His gaze darted back and forth between the images before he glanced up. "They could be brothers."

"What if they *are* brothers?"

He repeated the obvious. "Brandon Shaw and Gabriel Mathison?"

"Martin told me that Brandon showed up at his place years after the halfway house was shut down. He claimed he'd found his biological father through a public DNA database. He was a rich businessman who helped Brandon out financially. But according to Martin, the money didn't come without a price. He thought the father had bought Brandon's silence in order to protect his reputation."

"And you think that rich businessman was Richard Mathison." It was a statement not a question.

"It explains why Brandon looked vaguely familiar when I first met him. You saw it, too."

"If you're right, you have to wonder if Richard knew he had another child or was the return of the prodigal son a surprise?"

"I bet he knew," Sydney said. "There were accusations of serial adultery at the trial. Maybe Richard was already married to Gabriel's mother when Brandon's mother got pregnant. Rather than owning up to his responsibilities, he incentivized her to disappear."

"Incentivized her how?"

She shrugged. "Money, threats...probably both. Who knows how Brandon ended up in the system? Maybe his mother died, or for whatever reason, she thought he'd be better off in foster care. I doubt he found Richard through a DNA database. He probably searched for years. He may have even seen a photograph of Gabriel in the paper and put two and two together."

"So he turns up in Seaside to…what? Put the screws to Richard?"

"Makes more sense than returning out of nostalgia," she said. "Instead of giving him money outright, Richard offered him the job of spying on me. Or maybe Richard sought *him* out. He needed someone he could trust to do his dirty work."

"This is nothing more than wild speculation," Trent said.

"I prefer to think of it as brainstorming. Taking all the tiny and obscure puzzle pieces we've collected so far and trying to make sense of them."

"I need to add a piece to the puzzle," he said. "And just to be clear, I haven't deliberately withheld the information. We've had a lot to go through."

Sydney gave him an accusing look. "Shoot."

She listened in fascination as he told her about witnessing trash bags being thrown overboard from the cruiser the night before, the subsequent break-in at his house and the clue that was left on the whiteboard in his office. Then he recounted his solo foray into the woods that afternoon and the cross he'd found in the clearing that corresponded to the icon on the map. When he described the feeling of being watched, she felt a shiver go through her.

"You never saw anyone?"

"No. For a while, I thought I'd imagined the whole experience, but I didn't dream up that cross or the bouquet of wilted roses that someone had place at the base. *White* roses."

"*White* roses?" she repeated with the same emphasis.

He pulled a plastic evidence bag from one of the boxes and handed it to her. "There's a card inside the envelope.

The ink is a little runny from the rain, but the message is still legible."

"What does it say?"

"You should probably take a look for yourself."

She opened the bag and removed the card from the damp envelope. Her heart was already pounding by the time she deciphered the smeared message: *See you soon, Sydney.*

Chapter Eleven

A little while later, Sydney stood at the window peering down into the dark backyard. Trent was still at the table sorting through the boxes. He seemed tireless in his mission.

"What's going on over there?" he asked without glancing up.

"Looks like he's home. There's a light in the sunroom."

"I wonder why we didn't hear his car drive up."

"Maybe he's been home this whole time." She heard a chair scoot back from the table, and a moment later, Trent joined her at the window.

"You can see right into his house when the lights are on," he said.

"Which means he can probably see right into mine. Maybe we should move away from the window." But they both remained in place, as if glued by a morbid curiosity that rendered them immobile.

"I'm still trying to make sense of something." She shifted her body weight to a more accommodating position on the crutches. "The message you found on the card with the roses is identical to the one left in my hospital room. And it's the same catchphrase Brandon Shaw uttered from the bottom of the stairs when I first met him. That's one of the reasons I've been so suspicious of him. I don't think the phrasing or the timing was a coincidence. To take it a step further, if he's the one who lured you into the woods this afternoon, was he also the intruder who left the cross symbol on the map in your office? Is he the person piloting the boat night after night?"

"All very good questions," Trent said.

She gave him a sidelong glance. "Here's an even better one. How did he manage to get his hands on a scarf that belonged to a woman who was murdered twenty years ago? As you pointed out earlier, he would have been a kid back then."

"A troubled kid with a cop for a mentor."

"Meaning?"

He frowned. "I keep going back to that photograph. I have to believe your dad kept it for a reason. And I'm starting to wonder if he and Dan Bertram were as close as you thought they were."

"The lieutenant did say they had a falling out over my dad's single-killer theory. He also said they put any hard feelings behind them when they became partners."

"Maybe they became partners because your dad felt the need to keep a close eye on him."

She shot him a glance. "You're not suggesting what I think you are."

"I'm thinking out loud," he said. "You mentioned earlier that you're starting to have doubts about him."

"About his honesty and his relationship with Richard Mathison. Not about *that*," she insisted. "Being a bent cop is a far cry from being a serial killer."

"Like I said, just thinking out loud."

"Then think about this. Richard Mathison accused me of being smug and self-righteous just like my dad. I had no idea they even knew each other."

"Maybe that explains the photograph," Trent said. "If

your dad noticed the resemblance between Brandon and Gabriel, he could have started digging into Richard Mathison's past."

"But why?"

Trent shrugged. "Maybe we'll find that out somewhere in his notes. Did Martin say what happened to Brandon after he left the halfway house?"

"They lost touch for years, apparently. Then Brandon showed up on his doorstep one day with the news about his biological father."

"And then a few years after that, he turns up again in the house next door."

Sydney's attention was still fixated on the lighted sunroom. "We need to get a sample of his DNA."

She felt Trent's gaze on her. "That would require a break-in. If caught in the act, you'd be fired for sure, and we both might end up in jail."

"Or we could just go through his trash," she suggested.

"Even if we could get our hands on a viable sample, we'd still need Richard Mathison's DNA for comparison. Or Gabriel's. But neither is likely to volunteer a swab."

"What about the bloodstain on the scarf? I don't suppose you've heard back from the lab yet."

"Probably not until the end of the week. Why?"

"I'm working on a theory of my own," Sydney said. "It's a little out there, so keep an open mind."

"My mind is open," he assured her.

"It involves the recent murders. Two homicides that appeared to be drug-related and then Jessica King. All three bodies were dumped close to the Mathison beach house. I figured it was a matter of convenience or hubris on Gabriel's part, but my perception of that case is also evolving."

"You think someone has been setting him up all along?"

"Setting him up or trying very hard to get Richard Mathison's attention." She scowled down into the backyard. "Do you know the reason cats leave gifts of dead rodents on their owner's doorstep? It's not about hunger. It's about instinct. It's about sharing skills with the family."

"Nature versus nurture," he murmured.

"The first two victims were deliberately chosen because of their ties to the drug trade. The killer knew the police would draw the most obvious conclusion, but he wanted Richard to know the truth. That's why he dumped the bodies near the beach house, as if to say, 'See, Dad? I'm just like you. You gave away the wrong son. The superior son. The only son worthy of your legacy.'"

Trent turned to face her. "Brandon is jealous of Gabriel and decides to take him out of the picture by framing him for murder."

"Exactly."

"That's some theory," Trent said. "Mind open, mind blown."

"It is just a theory," Sydney reminded him. "No one will believe any of this without concrete proof."

He glanced at his phone. "Speaking of proof... I need to get home before the boat makes an appearance. Who knows? Tonight could be the night when he finally shows his hand."

"I don't like the sound of that," she said.

"And I don't like leaving you alone with a broken ankle. I'd ask you to come with me, but considering the events of the past two evenings, I think you'll be safer here behind a locked door."

At any other time, Sydney would have insisted on accompanying him, but she was realistic about her current immobility. She didn't want to put his life in danger by slowing him down. "I'll be fine. You're the one I'm worried about." She put a hand on his arm. "I'm serious, Trent. Please, please be careful. We could be entering a dangerous phase of the investigation. We're starting to put the pieces together, but we don't yet have the big picture. We don't know who the killer is or who we can trust. We do know he's getting bolder. Brandon Shaw may have moved next door to spy on me, but you're the one the killer has contacted."

"I'll be careful," he promised.

She said in a hushed voice, "The light just went out in the sunroom."

Trent reached over and turned off the nearest lamp.

"The kitchen light," she whispered.

"Why are you whispering? He can't hear us." But Trent complied, circling the room until all the lights were off and they were in total darkness. He came back over to the window. "Can you see anything?"

"It's pitch-black in the yard with the pool lights off."

A moment later, they heard the rumble of the garage door.

"What time is it?" she whispered.

He checked his phone. "Nearly eleven."

"Does that give him enough time to drive to the marina, launch the boat and get to your house by midnight?"

"If he knows what he's doing."

"What *is* he doing?" she murmured.

"Hold on." Trent headed toward the door.

"Where are you going?"

"Just taking a quick look. I'll be right back."

She followed him out to the landing and watched as he slipped through the hedge. Silencing her phone, she eased around the corner. The overhead light in the garage next door was off, but she could see the dim glow from Brandon's open trunk.

Her first thought was that he might be loading a body. She had a sudden vision of Mrs. Dorman's frosted eyes staring up from the bowels of that giant freezer.

Trent returned a few minutes later. He hurried up the steps, and they pressed against the wall as the car backed down the driveway and into the street. The lights were still off as Brandon Shaw sped away from the house.

"What happened?" she asked anxiously. "Did you see anything?"

"He loaded something into his trunk. I couldn't tell what it was."

"Mrs. Dorman," she whispered. "He got rid of her things. Now he's going to dump her body in the bay."

SYDNEY WAS ALONE in the apartment. She hadn't turned the lights on after Trent left, and now the darkness seemed to close in on her as she settled in the recliner and propped up her foot. Her phone was nearby. Trent had promised to keep her apprised of his movements. Not that she would be able to assist if he ran into trouble while tailing Brandon, but at least she could call 911 if he failed to touch base.

She got out her laptop, intent on listening to some of Trent's older podcasts, but she couldn't concentrate. Her mind kept wandering back to their previous discussion. So many questions lingered. Why had the killer gone dormant twenty years ago, and what connection did he have to Brandon Shaw?

On and on her thoughts churned until a sound caught her attention. The same muted thumping she'd heard the night before. She couldn't seem to pinpoint the direction or source. A tree limb bumping against the side of the apartment? A loose shutter somewhere down the street? Nothing suspicious. Nothing to worry about. Except…the wind had died down after a brief rainstorm that afternoon. The night was still.

Easing out of the recliner, she moved to the door and peered through the peephole, then glanced out the side window. No one was around. No one she could see.

She went back to the other window and stared down into Mrs. Dorman's backyard. The lights were still off, and Brandon's car hadn't returned. An inner voice warned her against acting impulsively, but it was nearing midnight. If her suspicions were right about Brandon Shaw, then he would be headed for the marina with Trent not far behind. She would have plenty of time to scoot down the steps, check out the noise and maybe the freezer in his garage and get back upstairs before he returned.

She hobbled down the hallway to retrieve the penlight she kept in her nightstand. A more powerful beam would have been helpful, but she was limited by what she could carry on crutches. Besides, a brighter light might attract attention.

Maybe it was her imagination, but the thumping seemed louder in the bedroom and, to her mind, more frantic.

She followed the sound into the closet. Still muted, still nothing to worry about. But…

Setting her crutches aside, she lowered herself to her stomach and put her ear to the floorboards. The thumping stopped.

She waited. Nothing. No sound at all except for the thud of her heartbeat.

Scrambling to her feet, she grabbed the crutches and went back down the hallway to the front door. She took another quick glance through the peephole, then exited her apartment.

Going down the outside staircase was a little more nerve-racking in the dark. She slid the crutches down first. Without them she felt vulnerable and exposed. She was already agitated, and the rush of adrenaline made her jittery. But she made it to the bottom without incident and grabbed the crutches, feeling more confident as she slipped them in place.

Her initial intent had been to check the freezer before Brandon returned. But she couldn't get that strange thumping out of her head. Maybe something directly beneath her apartment had caused the noise. Like Mrs. Dorman, Martin Swann had converted his detached garage into a workshop and storage space for his gardening equipment. Sometimes her lights flickered when he used his power tools.

Maneuvering around the corner of the building, she tried the side door. It was unlocked, which struck her as odd. Martin was usually fastidious about securing his tools. She only meant to glimpse inside. But then she heard the thumping. Still so muted as to be her imagination. *It's nothing. Go check out that freezer before it's too late.*

She paused just inside the door to the garage to listen once again. Nothing came to her except the low hum of an appliance. A refrigerator? A window fan?

See? Just your imagination.

Reaching behind her, she closed the door to block the glow of her flashlight. Then she swept the narrow beam around the room. Like Mrs. Dorman's garage, the walls were filled with gardening equipment. The space was smaller than next door and an unpleasant odor permeated from the shadows. The smell made her nose itch and her stomach churn. *Probably fertilizer. There's nothing here, so move on.*

She made another pass with her penlight. At the back

of the workshop, another door opened into what she assumed was a storage room. Again, she told herself to go
next door and check the freezer. She hadn't left the safety
of her apartment just to wander around in her landlord's
garage. But now that she was here…

A padlock on the storage room door had also been left
open. That really was odd. Why the need for a second lock
when he was usually so diligent about keeping the outside
door secured?

Sydney approached carefully. She didn't know what she
expected to find inside, but the shelves of chemicals and
fertilizers seemed almost anticlimactic. She supposed it
made sense that he'd double his efforts to keep poisonous
pesticides from curious neighborhood children.

She started to back out of the space when the beam of
her penlight sparked off a small metal ring in the ceiling.
On closer inspection, the ring appeared to be attached to
an attic door. But there wasn't an attic above the garage,
just her apartment. The best she could tell, the door was
directly below her closet.

Her adrenaline was really pumping now. She had a very
bad feeling about that door.

Retracing her steps into the workshop, she searched the
walls of equipment until she found the metal garden rake
that Martin had taken from the garage next door. She managed to drag it back into the storage room—no easy feat
on crutches—and then positioned the penlight on one of
the shelves so that she could see the metal ring. Balancing
on one foot, she hooked a tine through the ring and pulled.

The folding stairs slid down silently on well-oiled
hinges. She grabbed the flashlight and angled the beam
up through the opening. Leaving her crutches behind, she
used her good foot and the handrails to pull herself up. By

this time, she was half convinced she would emerge inside her closet. How a trap door in the floor had gone unnoticed all this time was beyond her, but...

She heaved herself through the opening and sat on the edge as she panned the area with the penlight.

Not her closet after all, but a crawl space that had been constructed between her apartment floor and the ceiling of the garage. She shined the light up and over the walls, where narrow shelves displayed a killer's trophies.

She counted seven shoes, including a blue satin high heel with a rhinestone buckle.

The revelation hit her with the force of a physical blow. Martin Swann was the killer her father had hunted for years. All this time, she'd been living above his lair with no clue of his true nature.

She could almost hear her dad's voice in her ear. *There are no coincidences, Syd.* Then, *Get out of there now!*

She had to get to safety and then call the police—

Thump...thump...thump.

The sound came from directly behind her. She turned in dread, moving the beam slowly over the tight space. From the darkest corner, eyes gleamed back at her.

Chapter Twelve

Sydney was so startled she almost dropped the light. She collected herself and focused the beam back into the space where a young woman lay bound and gagged on the floorboards. Sydney thought she must be dead, but then the eyes blinked. Even with the light in the captive's face, she didn't seem to register Sydney's presence. The woman was either drugged or had been there for a very long time. She was so weak, she could barely lift her hand to knock on the wall. *Thump, thump, thump.* Pause to rest. *Thump, thump, thump.* When she moved, the chain attached to a shackle around her ankle rattled.

Sydney swung her legs up and through the opening, then crawled on all fours back into the narrow space. When the woman finally noticed her, she scooted deeper into the corner. The sounds coming from behind the gag were inhuman, like an animal caught in a trap.

"It's okay," Sydney whispered. "I won't hurt you. I'm here to help you. I'm a police detective."

After a moment of frantic keening, the woman seemed to comprehend and quieted.

Sydney lifted her hand to the gag. "I'm going to remove it, but you can't scream."

She nodded, tears rolling down her cheeks.

Sydney couldn't undo the knot. She ran her hand underneath the cloth and managed to work it loose enough that she could slip the gag from the woman's mouth and down her chin.

Her voice was raspy when she spoke. "Can you get me out of here?"

"Yes, but we have to be careful." Sydney checked her phone. No bars. Whatever had been used to soundproof the space also blocked her cell phone signal. "Do you know how long you've been up here?"

"Since last night, I think. We must have been drugged. When I came to, I was chained to the wall. I don't know what happened to my friend—" Her voice caught. "Do you think she's okay?"

"I don't know," Sydney said.

"We just wanted to have a little fun, you know? Unwind in the pool, have a few drinks. But I should have known something was off. A guy like that doesn't need to pick up women in a bar."

"Did he give you his name?"

"Donnie. Just…Donnie." She drew a gasping breath. "We need to find my friend. Maybe she's still in the house. Maybe they haven't come for her yet."

"They?"

"I remember two male voices," she said. "Do you think I dreamed the other guy?"

"I don't think so. But right this minute, we need to focus on getting you out of here."

"Can you call the police?"

"Yes, but I'll have to go downstairs. I can't get a signal up here." Sydney adjusted her position so that she could check the lock on the shackle.

"Can you unfasten it?" the woman whispered.

Sydney followed the chain to a heavy bolt in the wall. "Not without tools. I need to find something to snap the links."

The woman clutched her arm. "Please don't leave me here."

"I'm coming back. I won't leave without you, I promise." She gently pried the woman's fingers from her arm. "Just stay quiet, okay? I'll be back before you know it."

She scooted backward across the rough boards until the lower part of her body was through the opening and she felt for the steps with her foot. A rustling sound caught her attention a split second before a hand closed around the cast and yanked. She screamed in agony and flailed for the railings as she crashed through the opening and landed on her back at the bottom.

A light came on in the storage room. Martin Swann put one foot on either side of her legs and adjusted his glasses as he peered down at her.

"I've waited a long time for this."

Sydney used her elbows to propel herself backward.

"No use trying to escape. You won't get very far on that ankle."

"I know who you are. *What* you are." She nodded toward the opening in the ceiling. "I saw your trophies up there. I saw her."

"I don't think of them as trophies. They're my memories."

"I think of them as proof," she said. "The kind of hard evidence that will put you away for the rest of your life."

"Maybe, if they were to ever see the light of day. But I'm good at keeping secrets. I know how to fade into the background. I'm the kind of guy no one ever notices. The quiet neighbor who keeps to himself. Your dad was the only one whoever got close to finding out about me. So close, in fact, he forced me into retirement. A part of me had to admire him for that. Too bad a heart attack took him out of the game before he knew what I had in store for you. Although I did warn him once."

Don't let her go outside until we catch the bastard.

She inched backward. "Why surface now? You were home free."

"Let's just say the timing was right. The stars lined up. You were always meant to be my last. The daughter of my old nemesis. A fitting swan song."

Sydney's hand bumped against something on the floor. Her fingers closed around the rake handle. The tool was heavy and bulky. Hard to swing from her position. She'd have to be quick—

A whimper came from the crawl space. A tiny sound that drew Martin's attention for one split second. That was enough. She swung the rake against his legs, then into his groin. When he dropped to his knees, she aimed for his head. Blood gushed from the wounds left by the metal tines.

By the time he toppled to the floor, she was already on her feet. She grabbed one of the crutches, tucked it underneath her arm and limped toward the outside door.

She was running, hobbling, stumbling toward the stairs when Brandon emerged from the hedge next door. Fear froze her for an instant, and then she plunged on, ignoring the searing pain in her ankle and the screams from inside the garage. Ignoring the bloodlust in Brandon Shaw's eyes as he dashed toward her. She beat him to the stairs, scrambling up several steps before she heard him behind her. She kept going. If she could just make it to the top and lock herself inside—

Up another step and then another. Almost there—

He had deliberately slowed his pace, enjoying the moment. Relishing the foreplay.

She was almost to the top when he grabbed her broken ankle and twisted. She screamed in agony and rolled to her back, lashing out with her other foot as she hoisted herself onto the landing. He came at her quickly. She grabbed each banister and lifted her body, kicking him square in the midsection with the cast. He faltered, then stumbled back a few steps before he caught his balance.

She was on her feet in a flash. Without crutches, she had to put her full weight on the wounded ankle. She couldn't let that slow her down. Brandon was already taking the steps two at a time. She barely made it inside before he slammed his shoulder into the door. Twisting the dead bolt, she staggered back as he rammed the door a second time.

Whirling, she limped down the hallway to the bedroom. Ignoring the pain. Ignoring the sound of splintering wood. She went straight for the revolver in her nightstand. *Stay calm. Stay calm. Stay calm.* Hard to keep her cool when a killer was crashing through her front door at that very moment.

She barely had time to steady the weapon before he appeared in the doorway. It was dark in her apartment, but she had no trouble finding her target. "Don't move. Don't you dare take another step."

He laughed. "Or what? You'll shoot me on the spot? Not possible. Open the cylinder and check your ammo."

"I said don't move!" she yelled when he took a step toward her.

"Did you really think I'd leave a loaded weapon in your nightstand?"

Was he bluffing? Her hand started to tremble.

"Never mind. I'll save you the trouble." She heard what

sounded like bullet casings hitting the hardwood floor. "See? I told you. You can't stop what's coming with an empty gun."

"But I can," Trent said from the hallway. "Fifteen rounds aimed straight at your back."

"In that case..." Brandon lifted his hands.

Sydney didn't trust his surrender. He had to be up to something.

Trent must have thought so, too. "The police are on the way," he warned. "I wouldn't make any sudden moves."

"They can hold me for twenty-four hours, and then I'll be out and long gone before you even have time to catch your breath."

"Don't count on it," Trent said.

Brandon was still facing Sydney in the dark. "Did you really think I'd start all this without an endgame? I have resources you can't even begin to imagine. You can spend the next twenty years looking, but you won't find me. You won't even know I'm around, but I'll be watching you." He laughed softly. "See you soon, Sydney."

SYDNEY AWOKE TO the unpleasant familiarity of a hospital room. But no Gabriel Mathison watching her sleep this time. No scent of roses permeating the small space. She wasn't alone, however. She could see Trent's silhouette at the window. She called his name and he turned with a smile.

"Hey."

"Hey." She rubbed her eyes. "How long have I been asleep?"

"A few hours. How do you feel?"

"Groggy. What did they give me anyway?"

"Something strong." He sat down on the edge of her bed.

"You were in a lot of pain. They had to remove the old cast and reset the bone."

She sat up suddenly. "The woman I found. Is she okay? They brought her here, too, didn't they?"

"Physically, she's fine. Mentally…that'll take a while."

"And her friend…?"

"The police are out looking, but I'm afraid they won't find her alive."

"That's my fear, too." Sydney lay back against the pillows. "I heard her underneath the floor last night. I thought I'd either dreamed the sound or it was nothing more than a branch brushing against the wall or a loose shutter or…" She trailed off. "I should have investigated. Maybe I would have found both of them alive."

Trent frowned. "Don't do that. Don't fall into the what-if trap. You saved a life tonight. Probably two, if you count Mrs. Dorman."

She said on a gasp, "You found her?"

"She's in Florida with her sister. But they were never going to let that old woman back into her house. As you pointed out, Brandon was already getting rid of her stuff. You saved lives tonight, and you closed nearly a dozen unsolved homicides. Your dad would be proud."

"I wish he could have known justice was coming."

"He knew."

"Martin told me that Dad was getting close. That's the reason he went to ground. I was supposed to be his swan song."

"I've been thinking about that photograph in light of what's happened," Trent said. "Brandon—Donnie—must have found out about Martin. That's how he came to be in possession of the bloodstained scarf. Maybe he squirreled away pieces of evidence as insurance if Martin ever turned on him."

"Or for blackmail."

"That too. I wonder if Brandon said something to Dan Bertram when he was a mentor at the halfway house. Just a throwaway boast that meant nothing to Bertram, but it put both Brandon and Martin Swann on your dad's radar."

"My ending up in that apartment was no coincidence," Sydney said with a shudder. "Martin has been watching me all these years, and I never suspected a thing. Stranger still that he's at this very moment in the same hospital getting the finest medical treatment taxpayer money can buy. Doesn't seem fair. Doesn't really seem like justice."

"You nearly took his eye out with the rake, so there's that. I have a feeling the real justice will be swift when it finally comes," Trent said grimly. "Serial killers don't tend to fare well in Texas prisons."

"And Brandon Shaw? Do you think Richard Mathison will help him disappear? Will I need to watch my back for the rest of my life?"

"Richard may not be willing to help once he finds out Brandon tried to frame his other son. But if it makes you feel any safer, I'll be watching your back, too." He squeezed her hand. "You have more people watching out for you than you know. Bertram came by earlier to check on you. I don't know if he's crooked. My gut says he has a few skeletons. But either way, he seems to genuinely care about you."

"Thanks for that."

Trent stared down at her for a moment.

"What?" she demanded.

"You should know your mother was here earlier, too. Evidently, Bertram called her."

Sydney opened her mouth in astonishment. Then she turned her head to glance at the door. "Where is she?"

"She said she'd be back in the morning. There's been a steady stream of officers coming by to check on you, including the chief. I wouldn't be surprised if you're reinstated without a hearing. You may even get a promotion."

"I didn't do any of this alone," she said. "I would have been blindsided by Martin Swann if you hadn't brought these cases to my attention. You can probably have your old job back, too, if you want it."

He shrugged. "I loved being a cop and I was good at it. But that's in the past. These days, I'm more into looking toward the future."

She gazed up at him. "Can I ask you something?"

"Go for it."

"Is this real? You and me, I mean. Did we ruin things by moving too fast?"

"Time will tell. All I can say for certain is that nothing has felt this right in my life in a very long time."

She nodded. "I feel the same."

He bent and kissed her. "You should get some rest. It's been a long night."

"Will you be here when I wake up?"

"I'm not going anywhere."

She sighed deeply and closed her eyes.

* * * * *

What Lies Bellow
Carol Ericson

MILLS & BOON

Carol Ericson is a bestselling, award-winning author of more than forty books. She has an eerie fascination for true-crime stories, a love of film noir and a weakness for reality TV, all of which fuel her imagination to create her own tales of murder, mayhem and mystery. To find out more about Carol and her current projects, please visit her website at carolericson.com, "where romance flirts with danger."

Visit the Author Profile page
at millsandboon.com.au.

CAST OF CHARACTERS

Heath Bradford—A developer tasked with buying up property on Dead Falls Island for a casino project, Heath comes to the island with a different set of priorities, and meeting up with the "Tree Girl" only strengthens his resolve, even though his desire for the truth puts them both in danger.

Willow Sands—An ecobiologist, the "Tree Girl" loves the land she studies and protects, but an unlikely alliance with Heath Bradford puts them both on a path that could destroy them before it destroys the land they seek to preserve.

Toby Keel—Willow's neighbor winds up dead, and the police can't decide if his death is a homicide or an accident, but it does set off a chain of events that threaten Willow and her property.

Paul Sands—Willow's father left a complicated will that only serves to pit Willow against the man she's falling for.

Jessica Bradford—Heath's mother died under mysterious circumstances, and Heath's search for the truth leads him to a dark side of the island he loves.

Lee Scott—This member of the Samish Nation is its primary advocate for building a casino on the island, and he'll do whatever is necessary to achieve his goal.

Ellie and Garrett Keel—Toby's niece and nephew expected to inherit their uncle's property on his death and reap the rewards of its sale, but when a twist in the will disrupts their plans, they vow revenge.

Chapter One

Apollo sensed the intruder before she did. Willow Sands's dog cocked his ears forward. His nostrils twitched, and he let out a soft whine.

When a twig cracked, Willow sat forward in her camp chair and placed her hand on top of Apollo's broad head. "What is it, boy? Is that a coyote out there?"

Apollo's whine morphed into a growl in the back of his throat, and his fur stood on end. Coyotes didn't usually make Apollo nervous. Her Rottweiler might be old, but the coyotes in the area showed him respect, never encroaching on his territory.

Willow shoved her feet into her Birkenstocks and pushed up from her camp chair. Apollo's tail stirred up little eddies of dirt as he thumped it on the ground. "So, you're happy I'm investigating instead of you?"

Shuffling toward the tree line that ringed her property, Willow whistled through her teeth, the sound piercing the silent night. "Scram! And don't leave any rabbit carcasses around my cabin. Doesn't impress me."

Apollo had followed her lead and stood next to her, his body stiff, his fur tickling her leg.

She flicked his ear. "Don't go chasing after anything out there. I don't want to have to rescue you."

Typically, when Apollo sensed an animal in the woods, he'd bark to warn it off, as his hunting skills weren't what they used to be. When he sensed a human, he acted like this. On high alert but no barking, as if waiting for the person to make the first move.

Willow didn't like waiting for others to make the first move. She did better on offense than defense. Peering into the darkness, she shouted, "I don't want my dog chasing you, but I wouldn't mind some rabbit stew. Don't make me go for my rifle."

She was totally bluffing—not about the rifle; she had one and knew how to use it, but she'd never kill a rabbit or any other type of animal. Humans were the trespassers in the forest, not the rabbits or deer or coyotes or any of the other fauna that roamed the island.

Willow huffed out a breath after realizing she'd been holding it. Her release seemed to set the forest in motion, as a flock of birds winged it skyward and a chorus of crickets and frogs competed for dominance with their song. Beneath the cacophony, Willow detected branches rustling and some earthbound creature retreating along the carpet of dense, rotting organic material.

Apollo shook himself and circled back to his spot next to her chair. He collapsed, exhausted from doing his duty, his head shoved beneath the seat. If her dog no longer detected an interloper near their cabin in the woods, she could relax, too.

She scanned the forest one more time and then joined Apollo, plopping down in her chair. "We showed him, didn't we, boy?"

Apollo snorted, halfway to a snore, and Willow tried to roll the knots out of her shoulders.

When her heart stopped galloping, she wedged her feet against the rocks ringing her campfire and flipped open the notebook in her lap. She scribbled a few more notes in the margins of the table she'd worked on today while surveying the summer flora and fauna of Dead Falls Island, where she returned every June after her classes at the university ended. She'd grown up on the island in this very cabin, taking care of her father after her mom had left them.

She couldn't blame her mom for taking off. Mom had grown weary of Dad's drinking and mental instability—both of which worsened in the wake of Mom's departure. But Willow did blame her mother for leaving *her* behind.

Of course, Willow had always been closer to her father than her mother. If Mom had offered her a seat on the ferry that had carried her away from the island, Willow probably would've declined it anyway. Someone had to watch out for Dad.

That task had fallen to her until just after her eighteenth birthday, when she'd been debating whether or not she'd be able to attend the University of Washington, leaving Dad behind to fend for himself. Perhaps sensing her dilemma, Dad had made her decision easy by drinking himself to death that winter.

As she'd reached the legal age of adulthood, social services couldn't do anything about her decision to remain in this cabin to finish high school and then attend UW for what turned out to be a full ride.

Now she'd never give up this cabin, her land or the island—not to build something bigger and shinier and certainly not to those greedy developers who wanted to bring tourism to this side of the island, along with the Samish people's plans for a casino.

As she smacked her notebook shut, she startled Apollo, who jerked his head up. "Sorry to disturb your hundredth nap for the day."

When her dog lumbered to his feet and let out a loud bark, she realized she wasn't the one who'd awakened him. She dropped her notebook on her chair and jumped to her feet. Why had her cabin all of a sudden become the hot gathering place for all the critters in the forest?

Apollo put his nose to the ground, and she followed him to the tree line. He stopped, tilted his head back and barked again. This was more like his animal-alert stance.

"Keep barking, boy. If you get lucky, you won't have to give chase." As she scanned the tree line, a pair of gleaming orbs appeared among the bushes.

An animal edged into the clearing, and Apollo jumped into action, racing toward the creature. Willow tried to call him back, but when she saw Luna, Toby Keel's mutt, she stopped yelling at Apollo.

Willow crouched and whistled softly. "Come here, girl. Does Toby know you're out and about?"

The white dog of indeterminate lineage loped toward Willow. Luna's ears folded, and her tongue hung out of her mouth. She'd been a shy dog ever since Toby, Willow's nearest neighbor, rescued her from the bay. They both theorized that some holiday boaters must've tossed her overboard, so Toby made up for that abandonment by spoiling Luna every day. She rarely left his side.

Snapping her fingers, Willow said in a low voice, "C'mon, Luna. Did you get lost chasing something in the woods?"

As Luna made her way toward Willow, Apollo sniffed

the other dog. At least he'd stopped barking. Had Luna been skulking around the cabin before, too afraid to make herself known?

When Luna reached Willow, she nuzzled her outstretched hand and whimpered. Willow stroked her back. "What is it, girl?" Willow's hand skimmed across Luna's wet, sticky fur. She peered at her palm, stained with a dark substance. "What did you get into?" Hooking her fingers around Luna's collar, Willow pulled the dog toward the glowing light of the fire. She inspected the dog's fur and sucked in a breath. "Are you injured?"

Blood streaks marred Luna's fluffy coat. Willow ran her hands down Luna's legs, and she felt the pads of her front paws. Luna stood patiently while Willow used the flashlight from her phone to inspect the rest of her body. She couldn't find any injuries on the dog, but when Luna panted, the drool that hung from her jaws had a red tinge.

"Did you unleash on a rabbit?" Willow swallowed hard. Luna did not possess the hunting gene. She might give chase but wouldn't know what to do with a wild animal if she actually caught it. "Did you come across something dead in the woods?"

Not that Luna could answer her, but the better questions would be why had she left Toby's cabin and where was Toby? Willow wiped her hand on one of the rocks ringing her campfire, and then cupped that same hand around her mouth and shouted, "Toby? Toby, you out there? I have Luna."

Luna whined again as Apollo cocked his head, listening for an answer to Willow's call. No sound came from the forest, so Willow flipped over her phone and checked for a signal. Getting cell phone service on this

side of the island was a dicey proposition, and Toby had
his phone turned off most of the time, anyway.

Standing up, Willow held her phone in the air, but that
last-ditch effort didn't fly out here. Wasn't that why she
and Toby liked this location?

She shoved the phone in the back pocket of her jeans.
"Looks like we're going to have to take a little evening
stroll."

Willow headed into her cabin to grab a proper flashlight and yank a flannel shirt from a hook by the front
door. She needed the long sleeves more as a buffer against
the branches and spiky leaves in the forest than protection against the elements. June had ushered in a warm
spell on the island, even at night. She tied the laces of her
hiking boots and locked up.

Once outside, she flicked on the flashlight and stuffed
her arms into the flannel, which she left unbuttoned over
her T-shirt. She patted her thigh. "C'mon, guys. Let's
take Luna home."

And find out why Toby hasn't come after his dog.

Toby Keel, a member of the Samish Indian Nation,
had bought his property from her father for a song. Dad's
family had been big landowners on Dead Falls Island.
Slowly, the Sands family holdings had been parceled out
and sold up. By the time her father inherited the family
assets, the acreage on this side of the island comprised
the last of the Sands land.

Paul Sands had no inclination to sell or develop his
parcel of dirt. If Toby hadn't been Samish, her father
never would've parted with the land. He always figured the Samish had more rights to the land than he did.

Shattered from his deployment during the Gulf War,

Willow's father wanted only to be left alone, and he'd found his perfect paradise at the edge of the forest on Dead Falls Island. He and Toby were two of a kind.

Willow's hiking boots crunched through the mulch on the forest floor as she trod the well-worn path between the two properties. Much like her father, Toby wanted to be left alone, so she obliged during the summer months when she took up residence at the cabin. But Toby's dog had arrived at her place smudged with blood. That necessitated an impromptu visit.

As they drew closer to the clearing for Toby's home, Luna picked up her pace and Apollo followed.

"Wait up, you two." In her haste to follow the dogs, Willow tripped over a rotting log, saving herself by wedging her hand against the nearest tree. The rough bark scraped her palm, and she rubbed the sting against the thigh of her jeans.

She slowed her pace as the dogs disappeared ahead of her. She didn't need a broken ankle out here. Aiming the flashlight at the ground, she picked her way over the tangled roots that marked the end of the path to Toby's cabin. He'd allowed the forest to encroach on his land even more than her father had, so the edge of Toby's cabin sat close to the tree line.

Willow's steps faltered as the dogs started barking furiously. Luna sent up a spine-tingling howl that hearkened back to her wolf ancestry, and Willow pressed a hand to her chest, where more than just physical exertion had her heart thumping against her rib cage. Something had clearly disturbed Luna, and Willow dragged her feet the final fifteen yards to Toby's clearing, dread pounding a beat against her eardrums.

When she parted the branches and peered at Toby's cabin, the flickering flames of his campfire cast a burnished glow on the dogs' fur as they circled the ground. She crept into the clearing. "Toby?"

Luna threw her head back and howled again. Willow felt like doing the same, but she proceeded to the other side of the fire where the dogs paced.

As she drew closer, Apollo turned and trotted toward her, allowing her to see Toby's body crumpled on the ground.

Gasping, she circled the fire and crouched beside him. She gripped his shoulder, shaking him. "Toby? Toby?"

Luna nudged Toby's head and came away with blood on her snout. That was when Willow noticed the cut on the side of Toby's head, and the sharp rock that lay inches from his scalp.

She pressed her fingers against his throat but couldn't feel a pulse. Had he tripped and fallen in a drunken stupor? Had a heart attack? A stroke?

As she fumbled for her phone, a low growl rumbled from Apollo's throat. Willow glanced up to see a dark figure coming from the other side of Toby's cabin, and she screamed loudly enough to rival Luna's howl.

Chapter Two

The woman's scream pierced his brain, and Heath Bradford tripped to a stop, his flashlight falling to the ground. The rolling light illuminated flashes of a woman on the ground, her mouth agape, and two big dogs circling her, barking and howling.

Heath dived for his flashlight and raised it, stalking toward the chaotic scene. He'd never hit a dog before, but he'd never encountered one attacking a human. He stomped his booted foot. "Get! Get out of here."

At the sound of his voice, the woman and the two dogs stopped their caterwauling and pinned him with three sets of eyes, two of those pairs gleaming in the dark. As the dogs no longer seemed to be menacing the woman, Heath lowered his flashlight and aimed it at the group.

That was when he noticed another figure sprawled on the ground behind the woman. He flicked the light over the prone form, and his pulse jumped. That had to be Toby Keel, and this did not look good. "What's going on? Does he need medical attention?"

The woman drew her knees up close to her body and wrapped one arm around her bent legs. "Who the hell are you, and what are you doing here?"

He hadn't expected that response, and his senses ramped up. Had he stumbled on a domestic? Had she just taken out Toby? He waved his free hand. "Hang on. Before we get to that, I think we should take care of Toby. Looks like he's out cold."

Her eyes narrowed as she jumped to her feet, one hand on the Rottweiler's head. "He's dead."

His hand tightening on the flashlight, Heath lunged forward. "Are you sure?"

Both dogs growled but stood their ground as he brushed past the woman and dropped to his knees beside Toby. He felt for a pulse, and then put his ear to the man's mouth, which was slightly ajar. His gaze flicked to the rock next to Toby's head and the blood soaking into the dirt.

"What happened to him?" Heath cranked his head around to take in the woman, standing stiffly behind him. Maybe he shouldn't turn his back on her.

"Good question." She folded her arms. "You tell me."

"Me?" He thumped his chest. "I just got here and found you and the dogs howling over a dead body. I'm completely in the dark."

"Same." She yanked on the Rottweiler's collar as the beast took a step toward Heath and the body. "His dog, Luna, came to my cabin about fifteen minutes ago with blood on her fur. Cell service being what it is out here, I decided to hike to Toby's to find out what was going on."

Understanding dawned on Heath, and he studied the woman standing before him, her spine erect, shoulders pulled back. Her dark hair swung from a high ponytail, random wisps framing the delicate features of her face. Shorter hair, riper body and attitude to spare, but he'd never mistake the Tree Girl for anyone else, even several years after he'd last seen her.

He wiped his hand across the chest of his flannel shirt and extended it to her. "You're Willow Sands, aren't you? Heath Bradford."

She went up on her toes like a startled doe prepared for flight. Then she tilted forward, thrusting her own hand toward his. "Right. I know you. Bradford and Sons Development."

If she spit the words at him, they couldn't have sounded more venomous coming from her lips. He expected that. When he took her hand in his, her slender fingers delivered a death grip. He *didn't* expect that.

When she released him, he flapped his hand. "Ouch. Quite a handshake you have there. Makes me think maybe you are strong enough to kill a man by smashing a rock against his head."

Her eyes widened, and she stepped back. "You think *I* had something to do with Toby's death? I told you. He was dead when I got here. Probably dead by the time Luna made it to my place."

He nodded. He didn't really think the Tree Girl was capable of murder. She probably avoided stepping on ants. "We need to get to someplace that has cell service and call the cops. Regardless of how Toby died, he is dead."

Stuffing her hands inside the arms of her shirt, Willow asked, "Do you really think someone bashed him on the head? I sort of figured he hit his head on that rock in a fall. Toby had heart issues…and drinking issues. I know that."

Heath lifted his shoulders. "Probably, but that's for

the cops to figure out. My vehicle is parked on the road behind Toby's cabin. You know better than I, but we should probably be able to get service from the road. I'll take you and the dogs."

"Luna's bloody, Apollo's dirty." Her lips twisted. "You sure you want them in your nice ride?"

"My truck is no stranger to filthy animals. My two Labs like frolicking in the river—mud and fur everywhere." He jerked his thumb over his shoulder. "I'm sure you know the way. Will Luna leave Toby's side?"

"She did before." Willow tugged her dog's collar and whistled. "C'mon, Luna. You can't help Toby now."

Luna snuffled around the body and planted herself next to Toby. Heath said, "I don't think she's leaving him this time."

"Doesn't look like it. I'll lead the way back to the road."

Willow stepped past him, and Apollo's tail thwacked Heath's leg as the dog curled his lip. Didn't seem Willow's dog liked him any more than Willow did.

Their two flashlights picked out the trail beneath their feet as they wended their way to the road that wound behind Toby's property. Heath clenched his teeth as he followed Willow. Just his luck that Toby would die right before their meeting. What were the odds of that happening? Heart issues. Who knew? Maybe the thought of discussing business with someone from Bradford and Son had stressed the guy out.

Heath crimped the edges of the note in his pocket. Or maybe it was that other business.

He glanced at Willow's swinging ponytail and huffed out a breath. Bradford and Son would have to shelve the notion of developing this side of Dead Falls Island. If his father thought Toby Keel would be a tough sell, wait until Heath told him about Willow Sands. Of course, that might depend on who just inherited Toby's property. They could still develop with one parcel, but definitely not without the two adjoining pieces of land.

As they emerged from the forest, Willow called back, "I see your truck. We can try our phones now."

Heath plucked his phone from the front pocket of his shirt and checked the bars on his display. "Not yet. Do you have the number for the Dead Falls Sheriff's Department, or should we call 911?"

"I've got their number." She stamped her boots on the asphalt and held up her phone. "And I've got service. I'll make the call."

While Willow called the DFSD, Heath scratched a spot behind Apollo's ear, trying to get on his good side. The dog looked too old to do much damage with an attack, but Heath had other reasons for currying favor with Apollo. If the beast liked him, maybe his owner would soften toward him. Maybe she wouldn't capitulate enough to sell her land to Bradford and Son, but she might agree to dinner.

A guy could hope.

She ended the call and spun around. "They're coming out. The sheriff himself is on the way. New guy, who's supposed to be proactive."

As she started to plunge back into the trees, Heath held up a hand. "Why don't we wait in my truck? We can lead the sheriff to Toby's body when he gets here. I've got some water, some wipes for your hands."

Willow turned her palms up and gaped at the blood streaks staining them. "I—I didn't realize…"

"I don't know if you've recovered from the shock of finding Toby and then seeing me materialize in the darkness. I know I scared you by showing up." He touched her arm. "Why don't you have a seat in my truck before the sheriff arrives?"

Her shoulders sagged, and she sniffled. "I can't believe he's dead. I mean, he was kind of cantankerous, not too friendly, but every summer I knew he was on the other side of the forest from me."

"Come on." Heath jingled his key ring. "We've both had a shock."

And a disappointment. He pivoted toward his truck parked up the road from the trailhead and heard her footsteps shuffling behind him. When he reached his vehicle, he put down the tailgate. "Will Apollo jump in?"

"It's too high, and he's too old."

He opened the passenger door, leaving it wide as he circled around to the driver's side. As Willow hopped into the seat, her dog collapsed on the ground beside the truck. Heath twisted around and reached into a cooler for two bottles of water. He handed both to Willow. "One for you and one for Apollo, if he'll drink from the bottle."

"Thanks." She took one. "He can drink from mine. Don't you want one?"

"I'm not thirsty. Looks like you two need it more than I do."

She grabbed the second bottle and pressed it against her cheek. "Everything happened so fast. I think Toby's death is hitting me now."

"Yeah, honestly, you seemed more concerned with my presence there than you did with Toby."

She whipped her head around. "I'd already checked

Toby. I knew he was dead. What I didn't know was what you were doing near his cabin while his body lay on the ground. You still haven't answered that question."

"Toby and I had a meeting scheduled for nine o'clock tonight."

Taking a gulp of water from the bottle, Willow raised her eyebrows. "Odd time to take a meeting."

"His choice." Heath spread his hands. "I offered him a lunchtime meeting, dinner, cocktails at the Harbor Restaurant and Bar. He chose his cabin at nine o'clock."

"And because Bradford and Sons wants his land, you jumped." She snorted. "He was just toying with you. Toby was never going to sell that piece of real estate."

"I proposed the meeting, and he agreed." Heath shrugged. "I guess I won't know if he was toying with me or not."

Toby had another reason for meeting with Heath, but Tree Girl didn't need to know about that.

With the bottle halfway to her mouth, she jerked her hand, and the liquid spilled down her front. "Now that he's dead, his heirs can do whatever they want with the property."

"Whoever they are." He pointed at Apollo. "I think he wants some water."

"Sorry, boy." She cracked open the other bottle and tipped it for him to drink. He took the bottle opening between his teeth and took probably one sip for every two that dripped from his jowls.

Patting Apollo's head, she said, "Am I next on your list? I know what Bradford and Sons wants."

"Son."

"What?"

"Son. It's actually Bradford and *Son*, singular." He raised his hand. "I'm it. One son."

She studied his face, as if trying to catch him in a lie. "That's right. You were a few years ahead of me in school—before you went to some posh boarding school—and I don't remember that you had any siblings. Only child...like me."

"I think for similar reasons." He clenched the steering wheel. He didn't know why, but he felt cut off from the world here in his truck with the Tree Girl, as if they were the only two in the forest.

She snorted. "Was your dad an unstable alcoholic, too?"

"My father..." He was saved from explaining anything about his father by the rotating red-and-blue lights that approached them from behind. "Sheriff's here. What's his name?"

"Sheriff Chandler." She stepped out of the truck, nudging Apollo with her foot. "Don't bite the sheriff."

Heath followed her and introduced himself to Sheriff Chandler after Willow greeted the man. A patrol car pulled behind the sheriff's SUV.

After a handshake, Chandler nodded. "Heath Bradford—I know the name. You're a client of Astrid Mitchell's, aren't you? Interested in the Misty Hollow property."

Heath gave the sheriff a tight smile as he felt Willow's stare burning a hole in his cheek. The island hadn't changed since the time he'd spent here—small-town gossip got around quickly. "That's right. Astrid showed me the property the other day, and it has a lot of potential."

"Potential for what?" Willow wedged a hand on her

hip. "You do know that's the site of a family massacre, don't you?"

"I've been informed." He pointed to the trailhead. "Toby's cabin is this way, Sheriff. We had a meeting scheduled for nine o'clock tonight. I arrived a little late and found Willow screaming and the dogs barking."

"I'll lead the way." Willow looked over her shoulder and said, "And I didn't start screaming until I saw you lurking behind his cabin."

Chandler asked, "Why'd you scream, Willow? Did Heath startle you, or did you suspect some foul play regarding Toby's death?"

"Foul play? I don't think so." She tossed her ponytail over her shoulder. "Toby does have a head injury, but he's lying beside a rock. Looks like he could've fallen and hit his head on it. He's had heart issues for the past few years, and a drinking problem for longer than that."

As Heath was bringing up the rear with the two patrol officers behind him, Chandler turned to look back at him. "Is that what you saw, too? Head injury, rock, blood?"

"Yeah, same. The only weird thing I noticed was his lack of footwear."

"He was barefoot?" Chandler tripped over a root and righted himself by grabbing a branch. "Did you notice that, Willow?"

"I did, but I didn't think it was unusual. It's the beginning of summer. It's not hot, but it's definitely not cold. Toby's accustomed to this weather. If he was barefoot in his cabin and then came outside to do something, he might not put shoes on. I've seen him walking around outside with no shoes before."

"Okay. We'll take a look. I called for an ambulance. Next of kin?"

Willow answered, "Toby was divorced a long time ago, no kids, but he does have a niece and nephew. They're probably his closest relatives. Toby is Samish, but the niece and nephew don't live here on the island. They left the rez after high school. His brother, their father, is dead, as far as I know."

"Okay. Maybe he has something in his cabin that will allow us to contact them, or we can get the info from his phone. Do you know the names of the niece and nephew?"

"Ellie and…" Willow snapped her fingers. "Can't remember the nephew's name."

"Garrett." Heath kicked a rock out of his way with the toe of his hiking boot. "Garrett Keel."

Chandler said, "Thanks. That's helpful."

Heath ignored the intense look from Willow's green eyes as she turned to stare at him over the sheriff's shoulder. If Sheriff Chandler didn't care how he knew that nugget of information, he didn't owe anything to Willow Sands.

Heath kept his eyes down and his mouth shut the last several yards of the trail. When they broke through to the clearing, Toby's dog, Luna, barked at them from her position next to Toby's body.

"Was the dog here before?" Chandler approached the mutt, his hand held out.

"I told the dispatcher that's how I found Toby," Willow said. "Luna came to my place. She followed me back, and Heath and I left her here. She wasn't budging."

"Do you think she'll come to you now?" Chandler

had reached Luna, and she sniffed his hand. "I'd like to have a look at the body, take some pictures."

"Luna." Willow made kissing sounds with her lips.

Heath swallowed. He'd follow that sound anywhere, and Luna agreed with him. The dog peeled herself away from her owner's body and trotted toward Willow.

She grabbed the dog's collar. "You stay with me, girl."

Chandler took charge of the scene, ordering Heath and Willow to stand back with the dogs and telling his deputies to enter Toby's cabin. "Make note of any disturbances in there and see if you can locate a cell phone. Doesn't seem to be one with the body."

Heath straddled a picnic table bench and slid his fingers beneath Luna's collar. "I'll hang on to her. You already have your hands full with Apollo."

Willow released Luna's collar as soon as her fingers met his and rubbed them on the thigh of her jeans as if he had cooties. "Are you really interested in buying the Misty Hollow property?"

"It's a prime piece of real estate. I'd tear down the house and outer buildings, just like anyone would, I assume."

"Prime piece of real estate for what purpose? I thought Bradford was done developing that side of the island and had set its sights on this side."

"Misty Hollow isn't part of our plan. I'd be buying it for personal reasons." When he came back to Dead Falls Island this time, he discovered he'd missed it. Now, after seeing Willow Sands again, he missed it even more.

He'd had a thing for Willow in high school, but she hadn't socialized with his group of friends. She hadn't socialized at all. She'd lived with her father and spent most of her time in the woods, collecting specimens, cataloging, photographing. The other kids shunned her for what they deemed her *weirdness*, but she'd always intrigued him.

Sheriff Chandler stood up and called out for his two deputies, still inside Toby's cabin. "Stop what you're doing and secure this area. I think we've got a murder scene here."

Chapter Three

A chill snaked up Willow's spine, and she jerked away from Heath, who was sitting way too close to her. "M-murder?"

"I have to call in some resources, and I need you two to leave the scene. Drop by the station tomorrow, so I or someone else can take your formal statements."

Heath pushed to his feet, his fingers still curled around Luna's collar. "What makes you think there was foul play, Sheriff?"

"Rather not discuss that right now. Can one of you take Toby's dog?"

Willow licked her dry lips. "I think she'll come home with me."

"Thanks." Chandler dismissed them, turning to his wide-eyed deputies and giving them instructions.

"I'll give you a ride back to your place." Heath leveled a finger at the trail where one of the deputies was heading with his phone.

Her mind still whirling from Sheriff Chandler's news, Willow rose unsteadily to her feet. "I can walk back through the woods to my cabin."

He raised his eyebrows, and one disappeared beneath a lock of dark hair that curled over his forehead. "Toby may have been murdered—probably moments before you discovered him. I don't think it's a great idea for you to be plunging into the forest in the dark with two spooked dogs as your only protection."

Willow's gaze traveled to the tree line on the other side of Toby's property that led to her cabin. The path she took couldn't even really be called a trail. She hated to admit it, but Heath had a point. Toby's killer could still be wandering around.

Was Heath anxious to get her away from the scene of the crime? Did he want to grill her about what she saw? Why had he been coming from behind Toby's cabin instead of the end of the trail?

She scooped in a deep breath. Heath Bradford might be a scummy, money-grubbing developer, but she had a hard time envisioning him as a killer—and it wasn't just because he was so damned attractive.

She'd witnessed Heath's sensitive side more than once when they were young and he still lived on the island. She'd even seen him off on his own crying once—although she'd never told anyone, especially not him. She'd thought his grief had to do with his mother disappearing, just like hers did. Maybe that was what he meant by their similarities.

Ever since that day, she'd watched him, taken notice. Not that the very handsome, very popular Heath Bradford would ever give the Tree Girl two minutes of his time back then.

"Well?" He tugged on Luna's collar. "You might also have a hard time getting Luna away from here."

"You're right. I'll take the ride, but only if you fess up and tell me how you knew the name of Toby's nephew." She waved her hand in the air. "We're leaving, Sheriff Chandler. I'll be in touch tomorrow."

Heath called to the sheriff, "Me, too."

Chandler gave them a thumbs-up and returned to ex-amining the area around Toby's body. Willow gave a lit-tle shiver. "I can't believe Toby was murdered. It's not like he has anything worth stealing."

"Maybe Chandler's wrong. He's gotta err on the side of caution and secure the scene just in case." Heath hung back at the trailhead and pointed his flashlight at the ground. "Lead the way."

They said little on their way back to the road and Heath's truck. He had a struggle on his hands with Luna, leading her down the trail. She seemed reluctant to leave Toby, and Willow's heart hurt for the dog.

When they got to the truck, Heath lowered the tailgate and Luna jumped inside. "Will Apollo let me pick him up and will he stay in the truck bed once I get him there?"

"I'm sure he will, but he's a solid dog. Don't let his age fool you."

Heath crouched down and gathered Apollo around the middle. With the dog's legs dangling, Heath hoisted him into the truck bed. When both dogs were settled, he stroked them both, murmuring in a low voice, before closing the tailgate.

He opened the door for her and went around to the other side. Punching on the engine, he said, "Tell me where to go."

As her mouth quirked into a smile, he jerked his head toward her. "I saw that. I meant literally give me direc-tions."

She slid a sideways glance at him. "You know, you're not going to be very popular here, trying to develop this side of the island."

"You'd be surprised. We have a lot of support. The Samish are looking to cash in with a casino on the island."

She pulled her mouth down in a sad face. "Nobody I know is in favor of that. Besides, the Samish Reservation is on the other side of the island."

"They hold a plot on this side, too. The properties could dovetail—casino on Samish land and hotels and restaurants on Bradford land." He shrugged. "That kind of development would benefit their casino."

"Oh, I get it now." She tapped the window with her fingernails. "Toby's property and mine sit between the Bradford holding and the Samish land. Am I right?"

"Yours, Toby's, a couple of others."

She squinted at him in the darkness of the cab. "Is that how you know Garrett Keel? Have you already spoken to him?"

"I haven't spoken to Garrett. I just know he's on the title of the property with his uncle. We make it our business to know who we have to deal with. With Toby the one living here, we figured it was best to talk to him first."

"Might as well start with the hardest nut to crack, right?"

Heath's teeth flashed white in the low light, and she poked him in the thigh. "What's so funny?"

"We never figured Toby would be the most stubborn." He flicked a finger at her. "That would be you."

She snorted. "I'll save you the trouble, Bradford and *Son*. I have no intention of selling my property to you or anyone else—especially not to someone ready to destroy the ecosystem of the forest and put up a bunch of horrid hotels and cheap restaurants."

"We've developed other areas with the environment in mind, actually enhancing the habitat for the plants and animals and protecting them from wildfires and other natural disasters. Some of our resort areas have actually seen an increase in the population of some species." He stopped to take a breath and glanced at her face. "Not buying it, huh?"

"Is that the pitch you were planning for me?" Tilting her head, she wrapped her ponytail around her hand. "What pitch did you have in store for Toby? Were you going to tell him all his Samish brethren were on board for the casino? That he'd be impeding progress for the Samish Nation?"

"Close." He adjusted his mirror to check on the dogs when she told him to take the next turn. "You don't even live here, right? Aren't you a professor at the University of Washington?"

Her heart did a little skip that he'd kept tabs on her, but the euphoria fell flat when she reminded herself that he would know all about her just like he knew all about Toby Keel. "I am, but I'm writing my second book on this area and return often for research. I've been coming back to Dead Falls Island every summer since my dad passed away."

"I was sorry to hear about your father."

His softened tone made her nose tingle, and she drew the back of her hand across the tip. "Ah, you mean you weren't one of the ones to nod sagely and opine that Paul Sands, the resident eccentric of Dead Falls Island, had cirrhosis of the liver coming to him."

"Not at all." The truck bounced as Heath took it down the final unpaved stretch to her cabin. "And your dad wasn't eccentric. He was a fascinating man with a vast scope of knowledge behind an eccentric manner."

He threw the truck into Park, and Willow sat still in the idling vehicle, staring at Heath's chiseled profile. "You knew my father?"

"I wouldn't say I knew him. I'm not sure anyone really knew your father, but I talked to him many times while I lived on the island. He was generous with his time." He cut the engine. "I'll help you with the dogs."

Willow opened and closed her mouth. She wanted to ask Heath under what circumstances he had talked to her father, but he didn't seem inclined to share. Her father certainly never told her he'd had conversations with her secret high school crush.

When Heath cranked open his door, the noise startled her into action, and she grabbed the handle of the passenger door and shoved it open. By the time she circled to the back of the truck, Heath already had the tailgate down and Luna had jumped out of the truck and was sniffing the ground.

Leaning into the truck bed, Heath coaxed Apollo, "C'mon, old boy. You don't have to jump."

Willow blurted out, "Where are your dogs now? Home with the wife and kids?"

Heath clicked his tongue softly, luring Apollo to the edge of the truck bed and then scooping him up and lowering him to the ground. "They're at my house in Seattle with my buddy's college-age daughter, who's dog- and house-sitting for me. I'm sure she's spoiling them."

No wife and kids. She closed her eyes and eked out a small breath. That wasn't too obvious at all. "Thanks for the ride and the help with Apollo. I'll be going to the station tomorrow to give my statement."

"Whoa. Wait a minute." Heath stood in front of her cabin, turning in a circle, his arms outstretched. "You're out here on your own?"

"I have Apollo." She rubbed her knuckles on the top of her dog's head. "And now Luna."

"Luna couldn't help Toby, and no offense to Apollo, but it looks like his personal protection days might be behind him." To lessen the blow, Heath cuffed Apollo's ears, his fingers running over Willow's.

She snatched her hand away from Apollo's head and Heath's electric touch. Must be all those unresolved adolescent issues. She cleared her throat. "I also have a few weapons, and they're loaded and ready to go."

"The Tree Girl is locked and loaded?" Heath widened his eyes in mock surprise.

"Tree Girl? Wow. I haven't heard *that* name in quite a while."

Heath covered his mouth with one hand. "Sorry. I didn't mean that as an insult. I've always thought of you that way."

Always? He always thought of her?

She waved a hand in the air. "I don't care. Didn't care back then, either."

Heath ran a hand through his hair. "I—I'm sorry. I mean it as a compliment, not an insult."

Laughing, she said, "Forget it. Just haven't heard anyone call me that in years."

"Understandable. Just know I didn't use it to insult you, and I'm relieved that you have firearms. Keep them handy tonight. It'll make me feel better about leaving you out here on your own."

"I'll be fine. Apollo may not look like much these days, but he's still a good watchdog." She nodded toward her dog, now collapsed at Heath's feet, his head resting on his hiking boot.

"So, he'll at least alert you if someone's in your area." Heath wiggled his foot. "When he wakes up."

"Yeah..." She stopped and caught her lower lip between her teeth. Had there been someone near her cabin earlier, before Luna showed up? About the time Toby died?

Cocking his head, Heath said, "What's wrong? Can we count on Apollo to keep watch?"

"Yeah." She shook her head. "Yeah, he can handle it. You'd better head back to your hotel and let the rest of the suits at Bradford and Son know that your meeting with Toby didn't work out the way you wanted it to... or maybe it did."

"Hey, that's a low blow. We wanted the guy's property for a fair price, not his death."

"But his death makes it more likely you'll get that property."

"Not necessarily. I don't know a thing about Ellie or Garrett Keel."

"Except their names."

"Yeah, well, names alone don't tell if they're going to be any more willing to sell the property than their uncle." Heath brushed his hands together. "You know what? I gotta go. You be careful out here."

He turned on his heel before she had a chance to respond. She guessed she deserved that. She'd practically just accused him of murdering Toby to get his land.

When Heath cranked on his engine, she shaded her eyes against the headlights flooding her yard and waved. She couldn't see if he responded or even saw her.

She sighed and scratched Luna behind the ear. "C'mon, you two. It's probably better to have an adversarial relationship with Heath Bradford if he's trying to develop this side of the island. No fraternizing with the enemy."

Apollo whined as he sat at her feet while she unlocked the door to her cabin. "And that means you, Apollo. I saw how you were looking at him."

After she settled Apollo and Luna in side-by-side beds in the living room, she yanked open the door to the closet by the front door and grabbed her father's pump-action Remington. He'd taught her how to use it, and she cleaned and loaded it at the beginning of each summer visit.

She'd never slept with it beside her bed—until now. Placing the rifle on the floor next to her, she slid between the sheets. If Toby was murdered and his killer got any bright ideas about her, she'd be ready for him. She *wasn't* ready for Heath Bradford.

THE FOLLOWING MORNING, not one dog but two woke her up. Willow scrambled out of bed and opened the front door for them. She didn't know Luna's routine, and until she had time to learn it, Toby's dog would have to follow Apollo's schedule.

As the dogs sniffed around outside, Willow put away the shotgun. It had made her feel safer after last night's events. When she went to the DFSD today, she'd nose around a little to find out if Sheriff Chandler had decided Toby's death was a homicide.

Hard to believe anyone would want to kill Toby, but then, she didn't know much about the man's past before he bought that property from her father and took up residence there. The guy preferred to be alone, so something or someone must've driven him to that solitude.

She shook out enough dog food to fill two bowls and set them outside on the porch. As she gazed out at the tree line ringing her house, an eerie feeling settled on her skin. Who or what had been out there last night before Luna showed up? Could it have been Luna sniffing around before she made her presence known?

Willow dipped back into the house to grab her long-sleeved flannel from last night and stuff her feet into her hiking boots. The dogs didn't even look up from their breakfast as she ducked through the opening that led to the path to Toby's cabin.

The tree canopy shadowed the ground, but enough light seeped between the branches that she didn't need a flashlight to see. She took the same path she'd hiked last night after Luna showed up, taking her time and looking for snapped twigs and trampled undergrowth. She discovered a little of both.

Had something or someone come this way last night, or were these the signs of her own trek through the forest? She glanced up after stepping over a complex root system blocking her path, and something red flapping from a tree branch caught her attention.

She made a beeline for the Pacific madrone and reached out for the piece of cloth hooked on a small branch jutting from the reddish trunk. She rubbed the flannel material between her fingers. It had come from a shirt, most likely. She held the bit of cloth to her nose and sniffed, and then smoothed it against her palm. This clean, fresh-smelling piece of fabric hadn't been out here long.

The hair on the back of her neck quivered. The material had probably been here since last night—when someone had been watching her cabin.

Chapter Four

Heath grabbed his red flannel shirt from the hanger in the closet and tossed it over the back of a chair. The meteorologists on TV had been predicting a warm start of the summer months on Dead Falls Island, but when it came to the islands of Discovery Bay, warm was relative.

His father, vacationing with his new wife, hadn't been happy when Heath told him about the complications with Toby. His old man would be even less happy to discover Heath's other business with Toby.

Even though Dad had also ordered him to track down the niece and nephew and start working on them, Heath decided he'd wait a few days before approaching the relatives. If Sheriff Chandler did rule Toby's death a homicide, Toby's family would be in shock and grieving. Not the best time to bring up a land deal. But minutiae like murder never stopped his father.

He checked his phone for messages, thought about texting Willow to find out if she'd made it through the night okay and then just as quickly discarded that idea. Not only did his company and business disgust her, she also had him pegged as a killer.

Had he really called her Tree Girl to her face? He

didn't need to give her more reasons to dislike him, but he was batting a thousand.

His stomach grumbled when he left his hotel room, but he wanted to get to the sheriff's station to give his statement before he did anything else. He didn't exactly have an alibi for the time of Toby's...death, but the GPS on his truck should show the time he arrived at Toby's place. He wanted to get in the clear with Chandler in case the sheriff had the same line of thought as Willow.

He tucked the phone into his pocket and grabbed the flannel on his way out of the hotel room. He drove through the town of Dead Falls and along the winding coastal road to the sheriff's station.

When he got out of his truck, he gazed at the harbor and bay below the cliff. The station had one of the best views in town. The land would be worth a lot of money today—almost as much as Toby's.

As he pushed through the door of the station, he almost ran straight into Willow, dressed in jeans and boots again—not that the casual look didn't suit her. He had a hard time dragging his gaze from her fit body to meet her eyes.

"Sorry." He held out a hand as if to steady her, but the cold look in her green eyes ended that courtesy. "Everything okay last night? Luna good?"

She tugged on the flannel he grasped in one hand. "I don't think you'll need this today."

He flattened the crumpled shirt against his chest with his arm. "I remember island weather as unpredictable. Are you all right?"

"I'm good, yeah." She rubbed her palms on the thighs of her jeans. "Luna seems to want to go back to the scene of the…Toby's death, but I've been distracting her. You here for your statement?"

"I am. Happy to hear Luna's doing okay. Let me know if you need any help with her." He took a step away from her and the weird vibe emanating from her stiff frame.

Reaching out, she grabbed his sleeve. "Do you mind if I wait for you while you give your statement? Th-there's something I want to ask you. It shouldn't take you too long. I'll buy you breakfast or a coffee when you're done."

He schooled the surprise out of his face. She wanted to buy him a meal? She looked like she wanted to stab him with a small, sharp object. "Sure, you can wait. I could use something to eat. How long were you in there?"

"About fifteen minutes."

"Did the sheriff give away anything about Toby's death?"

"Nope." She tilted her head and a cascade of auburn-tinted brown hair fell over her shoulder. "He's going to check out your alibi."

"He probably will. He can look at the GPS on my truck, so he can try to pin down the time of death or at least some kind of timeline." He leveled a finger at her. "Did he check yours, too?"

"Moi?" She slapped a hand against her chest. "I didn't have any reason to kill Toby."

"Yeah, well, neither did I." He cocked his head toward the front counter. "I think they're ready for me."

"See you when you get out."

As Heath walked through the swinging doors to the offices in the back, he glanced over his shoulder. Willow sank onto a chair in the lobby, the calculating look still playing across her face. He didn't know why he should have breakfast with a woman who suspected him of murder. Maybe he just wanted to prove her wrong. Maybe he just wanted to prove something to Willow so she'd stop eyeing him like a bug. Wait, no. She liked bugs a helluva lot more than she liked him.

His conversation with Chandler didn't last even fifteen minutes. He repeated what he'd told the sheriff last night and offered to share his GPS data with him. Chandler didn't give any hint which direction the investigation was headed and was impervious to Heath's hints.

As Heath stood to leave, the note from Toby burned a hole in his pocket. Should he share it with Chandler?

The sheriff asked, "Anything else?"

"No. That's all I have. I'll be on the island for a few more weeks. Let me know if you have any more questions for me."

They shook hands, and Heath exited the office and strode toward the station's lobby. He caught his breath at the sight of Willow still seated on one of the hard chairs in the front.

She looked up from her phone. "That was fast."

"Guess Sheriff Chandler wasn't as interested in my alibi as you thought he should be."

She bustled out of the station, and he followed her.

As they stood outside beneath the emerging sun, he dangled his flannel from his fingers. "Doesn't look like I'll need this after all."

"Before I go anywhere with you—" she snatched the shirt from his hand "—I need to have a look at this flannel."

He didn't even try to hide the surprise from his face

this time. His mouth dropped open as she examined his shirt. "What are you doing?"

"I'll tell you over breakfast. You're driving." She tossed the shirt at him, and he caught it in one hand.

As he settled behind the wheel, he asked, "Where to? It's been a while for me. Some things look different."

"Yeah, and we want to stop that from happening to the other side of the island." She tapped on the glass. "Let's go to the Harbor Restaurant. It's close, just up the hill, and they have a good breakfast."

If the DFSD had a good view, the Harbor Restaurant and Bar had a better one. Floor-to-ceiling windows looked over Discovery Bay and Dead Falls Island's harbor.

He'd left his flannel shirt in the car. He didn't know what Willow expected to find in it, but he didn't want to trigger her.

After the hostess seated them by a window and the busboy dropped off a couple of waters, Heath planted his elbows on the table. "Do you want to tell me what's going on?"

Willow reached into her purse and pulled out a scrap of red material. She waved it over the table. "Look familiar?"

Pinching the cloth between his fingers, he tugged it from her grasp. "Looks like a piece of red flannel, but it's not from my shirt. This one has like a yellow stripe running through it. Mine has a black one."

"I figured that out. Plus, your shirt isn't missing a piece."

He took a sip of water, feeling exonerated. "You wanna tell me where you found that?"

"I found it on a branch, ringing my property." He'd

dropped the flannel on the table, and she smoothed it with her fingers. "Looks clean, doesn't it? I don't think it had been there long."

"Significance?" He flipped open the menu the waitress had dropped off and ran his finger down the breakfast items.

"Last night, before Luna ran to my place and before we discovered Toby, Apollo was whining about something in the woods outside my house. I forgot about it until I got back. So, this morning, I went to the general area where he was alerting, and I found this." She dragged the piece of cloth across the table toward her with one finger.

"You think someone was watching you?" He closed the menu and folded his hands on top of it.

"Maybe. Apollo usually barks when there's another animal. He saves his whines for humans, and he was definitely whining."

Heath picked up the piece of flannel and folded it in two. "Did you tell Sheriff Chandler about this?"

"No." She snatched the material from his fingers and shoved it into her pocket. "I wanted to check with you first."

"When you saw me with my red flannel shirt today, you figured I was the one skulking around your property?"

Two red spots formed on her cheeks. "It was a coincidence, don't you think?"

Cranking his head from side to side, he said, "Almost every person in here is wearing or carrying a flannel shirt, and red is a popular color."

"But I don't know anyone in here who was also at Toby's cabin last night." She shifted her attention from him to the waitress approaching their table. "Good morning. I'll have the avocado toast and a cup of hot tea—herbal, if you have it."

The waitress reeled off several herbal teas, took Willow's order and turned to him. "What would you like?"

"Banana pancakes, bacon on the side and some coffee." He turned his coffee mug upright on the table as the waitress walked away. Seemed like he wasn't the only one keeping secrets from the sheriff. "Why didn't you tell the sheriff?"

"I told you. I wanted to ask you about it first." Avoiding his gaze, she took her time tapping her straw on the table and peeling the paper away from it before plunging it into her glass of ice water.

He narrowed his eyes. "You really thought it was me out there and wanted to trap me before I could ditch the flannel."

"Trap you?" Her lips puckered around the straw as she took a sip of water. "I'm not Nancy Drew. I just wanted to see first if you had a chunk of material missing from your shirt. I could already see before you went in to talk to the sheriff…West…that your shirt looked intact."

"But you invited me to breakfast just to make sure." He thanked the waitress as she filled his coffee cup and set down Willow's hot water.

"I invited you to breakfast to…" She lifted one shoulder. "Not sure why. Maybe just to discuss what we saw last night. See if we're on the same page. Did West give you any indications which way the investigation was going?"

"Nope." He tipped some cream into his coffee. "Tight-lipped. So, you said Luna's okay?"

"A little nervous. She looks to the forest and whines

but hasn't tried to go back home yet." Willow stirred her ice with the straw, clinking it against the glass. "What did you see last night? I never asked you. You seemed to be there before me because you came from the back of Toby's cabin."

The food's arrival saved him from the quick retort on his lips. She seemed determined to suspect him of something. He took his time slathering butter on his pancakes and pouring a little pool of syrup on his plate.

Willow pointed her knife at his plate. "You missed a spot."

He smeared a thin glaze of butter over the very edges of the top pancake and sliced through a corner of the stack. Then he swept the pancakes through the syrup and held the impending bite over his plate, watching golden beads drip onto his bacon. "What did I see when I got there? I saw you screaming and crouching over someone on the ground while two dogs bayed into the night like a couple of mutts from the Baskervilles."

Ignoring her own food, Willow placed an elbow on the table beside her plate and wedged her chin on her palm. "I meant prior to that. You were there before I was. I saw you coming from behind his cabin."

"Ah…" He dabbed his sticky mouth with a napkin. "You're assuming I ended in front of Toby's cabin when I came off the trail. You'd be wrong. That last part of the trail is confusing, maybe on purpose. I forked off in the wrong direction. I found my way to the back of Toby's cabin by following his lights through the trees. I realized my mistake and walked around to the front… and saw you."

She picked up her knife again and cut her avocado

toast in half. "I guess that makes sense. I know that part of the trail can be baffling, and yeah, Toby probably made it that way."

"Look, we're dancing around each other, giving each other the side-eye…"

"Me?" Her voice squeaked. "You're giving me the side-eye? I don't have any reason to harm Toby."

"I wouldn't say that. What if Toby told you he was ready to sell his property to Bradford and Son? You two had a heated argument." He drew a finger across his throat. "Sale canceled."

"You're ridiculous." She bared her teeth and took a bite of her toast.

He didn't believe for one minute that Willow Sands could harm a flea on Apollo's back, but if she suspected him of killing Toby, he wanted her to know what it felt like.

"What I was trying to say is that maybe we're getting worked up for nothing. Chandler's the new sheriff in town. He probably just wants to get this right. Toby's death could be an accident or natural causes. He did have health issues."

"I guess we'll find out." She dusted crumbs from her fingers onto her plate and tilted her chin at the door. "They sure got here quickly."

Heath swiveled his head to the side, his gaze landing on a couple by the hostess stand, the chic woman pointing to a table by the window and the man, overdressed for the island, burying his face in his phone.

"Who are they?" he asked.

While Willow flapped a hand in front of her mouth, indicating she was still chewing, Heath watched the couple as the woman, her eyes wide, jabbed the man in the arm with her elbow. Her companion followed her pointing finger and bobbled his phone as he zeroed in on Heath and Willow. With two spots of color high on her cheeks, the woman grabbed the man's arm and marched toward their table, bumping a chair and causing a waiter to zigzag out of her way.

Heath tapped the handle of his knife on the table in front of Willow. "Incoming."

Willow glanced up from her dangling tea bag and whispered, "What the heck?"

The woman landed next to their table, her chest heaving, her dark eyes flashing. "There you are, you conniving witch."

Chapter Five

Willow's hand jerked, and her tea sloshed over the rim of her cup, flicking hot droplets of liquid on her knuckles. "What? Excuse me?"

"Hey. Back off." Heath sat forward in his seat, holding up a hand in Ellie Keel's direction.

Willow didn't need his protection from Ellie or her brother, but his gesture caused a warm glow in her belly.

Garrett shuffled his feet beside his sister, as his gaze took a quick inventory of Willow from hair to chest. "Hello there, Willow, all grown up."

Dabbing her hand with a napkin, Willow swallowed. Ignoring Garrett's leer, she said, "I don't know what you're talking about, Ellie. I'm sorry for your uncle's death, but he was already dead when I found him. There's nothing I could've done to help him."

"This is Ellie and Garrett Keel?" Heath's eyes narrowed as he took in the fuming woman beside their table and her slick brother next to her.

"Wait a minute." Ellie jabbed a finger, topped with scarlet nail polish the same shade as her sneering lips, in Heath's face. "You're Heath Bradford of Bradford and Son. What is going on here?"

Willow raised her eyebrows at Heath as they exchanged a glance. "Why don't *you* tell *us*? You're the one who came charging up here, interrupting our breakfast."

"Business meeting?" Ellie tapped a nail on the table as the waitress squeezed past her to raise the coffeepot at Heath.

"More coffee?"

Heath shook his head. "No, thanks."

"Hon?" Ellie grabbed the waitress's upper arm with her talons and nodded toward a window table two down from theirs. "Can you make sure we get two coffees and waters at that table?"

The waitress glanced at the hand clawing her arm and rolled her eyes. "Sure, *hon.*"

Tipping a little more hot water from the mini teapot on the table into her cup, Willow said, "This is not a business meeting, Ellie. I don't know why you're upset with me. I'm sure your uncle's death was a shock…"

Ellie's nostrils flared. "Don't be coy, Willow. You must've known about Uncle Toby's will. Hell, you probably helped him write it."

"Your uncle's will?" Willow tilted her head. Ellie's statements were getting more and more bizarre. "Again, I don't have a clue what you're talking about. Toby died yesterday, and you're already checking his will?"

"We've been suspicious for a while, so of course we wanted to confirm things with his attorney this morning on our way out to the island." She smacked the table with the flat of her hand. "Suspicions confirmed."

"Still don't know what you're talking about, Ellie." Willow shook her head and took a calming sip of tea.

"Why so much drama, Ellie? Spit it out." Garrett stuffed

his phone in his pocket. "Uncle Toby left his land to you, Willow. All of it."

Willow choked on her tea and clicked the cup back in its saucer. "You're not serious."

"Deadly, as it turns out." Ellie wagged her finger between Willow and Heath. "You two already working out some deal? The laugh's on Uncle Toby, huh? I'm sure you coerced him into leaving the property to you once you assured him you'd protect it against all the mean developers."

Willow's mouth hung open until she stole a glance at Heath, who looked equally surprised. And suspicious? Did he believe Ellie that she knew about Toby's will? She snapped her mouth shut.

"I didn't know anything about your uncle's will, Ellie. He and I never discussed his business, although he probably figured I wouldn't be as eager to sell off the property as you and your brother." Willow deliberately picked up her phone and stared at it. "Imagine that. Toby hasn't even been dead for twenty-four hours, and you already know what's in his will."

Ellie sniffed. "Some of us weren't privy to it in advance."

"Okay, that's enough." Heath sliced his hand through the air, as if to dissipate the tension and anger. "You'd better go claim your table before someone else takes it."

"We're not done here, Tree Girl. We plan to fight this." Ellie spun around, crooking her finger at Garrett.

Garrett winked at Willow before joining his sister.

"Wow. What a surprise. I don't blame Ellie for being angry, but it's not like she or Garrett ever visited Toby or spent much time with him." Willow stuffed a bite of avocado toast in her mouth, the crunching from her chewing reverberating like falling boulders in the silence.

As she swallowed, she watched Heath break off a piece of bacon and crumble it in his fingers.

She dropped her toast onto her plate. "What? What are you thinking?"

"Like you said, it's a surprise." He blotted his greasy fingers with a napkin. "It just...changes a lot."

"Before you ask—" she held up a hand "—I'm not interested in selling the property to Bradford and Son. I mean, if Ellie's challenge to the will fails. If it's successful, I guess you'll have to take it up with them."

His whiskey-colored eyes picked up the light from the window and practically glowed as he studied her face. "Did you really not know about Toby Keel's will?"

"I didn't look shocked to you? I'm not that great of an actress." She circled a finger in the air, encompassing Heath's suspicious face and questioning gaze, a sticky patch of syrup on his lip. "You don't believe me. You think I sweet-talked Toby into leaving that property to me, and then what? I killed him to make sure I get my hands on it, all to protect it from greedy developers like you and the casino expansion?"

He snorted. "Of course not. I don't believe for one minute you'd harm Toby...or anyone else. Although the way you're drilling me with those stormy green eyes of yours right now, I might be inclined to hire protection."

She dropped her gaze to the mangled toast on her plate. He might've misinterpreted the look in her eyes. She did have an inclination to devour him, but not out of anger. Sighing, she shoved her plate away and curled a finger around the handle of her teacup. "I don't know what Toby was thinking. I hope Ellie and Garrett are mistaken, even though they'd probably sell you that land in a heartbeat."

"They're both older than I expected. Harder to handle, I imagine."

"They are the children of Toby's older brother. There's probably less than fifteen years' age difference between them. Toby wasn't that old, just in poor health."

Heath steepled his fingers. "If they do launch a lawsuit, you wouldn't fight it?"

"Oh, sure I would, but that fight might be better than being the landholder and reviled on all sides." She swirled her tea before taking a sip of the lukewarm brew. "I suppose I'd better find out who Toby's attorney was and make a call."

"You might want to tell Sheriff Chandler about this development before the damning duo does their damage—unless they've already told him." Heath signaled to the waitress with a raised finger.

"You're probably right. If I'm the new owner of that property, I'd rather be the one to give West the news." She reached for the check the waitress slid onto the table. "Do you really think the sheriff is going to see that as a motive for me to kill Toby?"

He snatched the bill from her hand. "We don't even know yet if anyone killed Toby, but I'm sure the sheriff will perform his due diligence. Seems like an okay guy, unlike some of the other sheriffs we've had on the island."

"You say that as if you're a local." Willow pulled a ten and a five from her purse and shoved them at Heath. She couldn't have him thinking he could buy her off. "You weren't here that long, as I remember it."

"I lived here for a few years as a teenager. That was when my parents were trying to work things out. My mother grew up on Dead Falls Island, and when she... got sick, she wanted to return to her childhood home. My father, in typical Brad Bradford fashion, bought her a huge house in a new development, thinking that would satisfy her."

"I take it the house didn't work."

Heath blinked and swept up her money while replacing it with plastic. "Didn't work."

As Willow gathered her purse in her lap, she felt her phone buzzing in the side pocket. Wrinkling her nose, she studied the unfamiliar Seattle number. "I'd better answer this, given the circumstances." She spoke quietly into the phone. "Hello?"

"Is this Willow Sands?"

"It is."

"Glad I reached you. This is Jason Hart, Toby Keel's attorney."

Willow clutched the phone as she watched Heath sign the check and pocket his credit card. "I was actually going to call you once I found your number."

"Oh? Did Toby already inform you of his plans?"

"No. I had no idea what was in his will. We never discussed it, but I was attacked by Ellie and Garrett Keel this morning, accusing me of all kinds of things."

He cleared his throat. "That's why I wanted to contact you so quickly. I gave them the bad news this morning after they called and gave me the worse news about Toby. Didn't think they'd track you down so fast."

"They were speedy."

"I have some papers for you to sign, Ms. Sands, but

I'll come to you. I have plans to head out to the island anyway. Can we meet when I get there?"

"Of course. Call me when you arrive, and we'll set up something. Just so you know, I didn't discuss Toby's land with him at all."

"Oh, I know that. He had some arrangement with your father. He bought the land from him, right?"

"Yeah." Willow wrinkled her nose and shrugged at Heath, watching her closely. "I was unaware of any kind of arrangement with my dad."

"I'll tell you about it when I get to the island."

"Okay, Mr. Hart. Thanks for the call."

"Call me Jason, and I'll see you in a few days."

Willow ended the call and tapped the edge of the phone against her chin. "That was weird."

"Toby's attorney?"

"Jason Hart. He told me Toby and my dad had some kind of arrangement."

"Regarding the land?"

"You know, my dad sold it to him originally."

"I don't remember that, but it makes sense that he left it to you, then. Maybe that was the agreement."

She scooted back from her chair, suddenly anxious to get away from all the turmoil. "My father never told me about it."

Heath put a hand on her back as they passed the table where Ellie and Garrett were sitting, both on their phones and oblivious to everything around them. His firm hand steered her toward the entrance as if protecting her against a couple of wild bears.

Once in his car, he turned to her. "Are you going to

tell the sheriff about the will when I take you back to the station?"

"The sooner, the better." She snapped her seat belt. "Where does that leave you?"

"Soundly on this island. I still have some business to conduct." He winked at her. "And don't discount my powers of persuasion so easily."

Shifting in her seat, she stared out the window. When a simple wink from Heath Bradford's eye sent flutters to all the right parts of her body, she had no doubts at all about his powers.

He pulled up to the station, his engine idling. "Do you want me to go in with you? I can at least be a witness to the Keels' animosity toward you."

"That's okay. I'm sure Ellie's animosity will come out when she sues me for that land." She slid from the truck, and resting a hand on the door, she said, "Thanks for the ride and the verification that you weren't lurking in the woods outside my cabin."

"Glad I could clear myself, but if I wasn't the one in the woods, who was?"

She shrugged and slammed his door. As she meandered toward the entrance to the sheriff's station, she fingered the soft piece of cloth in her pocket. She couldn't run around and invite every man…or woman…with a red flannel shirt to breakfast to interrogate them.

Her visit to the station didn't last long, as Sheriff Chandler was out. Nobody else could or would give her any information about the investigation into Toby's death.

She'd lost a morning's work, so she headed straight back to her cabin. She'd left the dogs on a couple of long leads—long enough to reach their water and beds outside, but short enough to keep them out of the woods. She didn't want Luna snuffling around Toby's cabin.

As she drove up to her place, she hunched over the steering wheel to look for the dogs. Apollo knew enough to not run toward her truck, but Luna was probably still feeling displaced and anxious.

She eased back when she spotted them both asleep near the firepit. As she parked and swung open her door, she braced for Apollo's assault. He always hobbled over to greet her.

Her heart jumped when she shut the truck door and still neither of the two dogs stirred from their nap.

"Apollo! Luna!"

Dropping her bag, she rushed toward the dogs lying on their sides, the ropes still attached to their collars. Had tying them up left them as prey for some forest predator?

She crouched beside them and sucked in a sharp breath as she wiped bubbles of foam from Apollo's mouth. She placed her hand on his barrel chest and gave a sob when she felt the gentle rise and fall of his breathing.

She crawled to Luna, who whimpered in her sleep when Willow touched her face. Prodding the dog did nothing to rouse her. She ran her hands along Luna's fur, much like she did last night, but didn't feel any wound or even see any blood this time.

Willow sat back on her heels and surveyed the ground around the two sleeping dogs. No signs of a fight or scuffle or animal attack. Her gaze tripped over a lump of something organic a few feet from Apollo, and she lunged toward it.

She grabbed the bloody piece of meat in her hand

and squeezed it through her fingers. A blue pill oozed out of the mass.

On her hands and knees, she searched the rest of the yard for any vestiges of the drugged lures. She scooped up a few intact balls of meat with the same blue pills embedded in the middle.

She rose to her feet, shock making her movement and thoughts lethargic. Someone had come onto her property and drugged the dogs. Why? Her gaze floated from the tree line to her truck to the firepit to the dogs and then finally to her porch, littered with splintered wood.

The mess on her porch gave her a shot of adrenaline, and she darted toward her cabin. Kicking aside the wood, she pushed open her damaged front door.

As she stood on the threshold, she gaped at the upheaval before her. Someone had ransacked her place.

Chapter Six

"The Samish call this 'where the mist meets the earth'?" Heath's gaze dropped to the white tendrils circling the ground, the swirl of it almost hypnotizing.

His Realtor, Astrid Mitchell, cleared her throat. "This particular area is called Misty Hollow. I think you'll find that Samish description applies to many locales on the island. What do you think?"

Heath thought he'd like to start digging right now. "I like the location. The aspect is great. I know a two-story house won't give me a view of the falls, but it wouldn't be half bad."

"So, you're thinking residential instead of commercial property, right? You can go commercial here, but that means pulling a few strings with the zoning commission." Astrid cupped a hand over her sunglasses and stood on her tiptoes. "We have a visitor."

"Not competition for the property, I hope." Heath turned toward the oncoming SUV plowing through the mist.

"Nope, Sheriff Chandler just bought another property on the island." She waved as the sheriff pulled up.

He stepped out of his vehicle. "Sorry to interrupt, babe,

but I was in the area and I knew you were showing out here. Hey, Heath."

Heath let out a breath. These two must be in a relationship, and that was how the sheriff had known about his interest in the Misty Hollow site. "Sheriff. Good to see you again. Anything new on Keel's death?"

"Nothing yet, and call me West. Sorry to barge in. I'm taking my girl to lunch, but you two carry on. I can wait."

Her face now beaming, Astrid turned to Heath. "Is there anything else I can show you, Heath? Once you get past the property's ghoulish history, it's a great location."

Heath turned in a slow circle, taking in the land and the ramshackle ranch house. Did this property hold even more ghoulish history than the family massacre that had taken place twenty years ago? Were other secrets buried here? Would those secrets be buried with Toby Keel?

"I'm good, Astrid. If you don't mind leaving me behind to wander by myself, I'll have another look around. You go have lunch with West." Heath held his breath as the sheriff walked past the bed of his truck, hoping he wouldn't notice or ask about the shovel and pick stowed there.

"Look around all you like and call me if you have any more questions." She hooked her arm around West's. "Where to for lunch, Sheriff? I'll follow you."

West's cell phone rang loudly, and he twisted his lips. "You might be able to stay here with Heath after all. Chandler here," he said, answering his phone.

Heath turned away as West paused on the phone. He hoped the sheriff would take Astrid away for lunch and leave him to explore the property on his own.

"Willow Sands's cabin? Again, out there? What the hell is going on? I'll be right there."

Heath spun around and said, "Is Willow okay? I just saw her for breakfast this morning."

"She's fine. Cabin was ransacked." West kissed Astrid on the forehead. "Meet you at the Grill in about an hour?"

Astrid huffed out a breath. "Of course. I hope Willow is all right."

"I'm following you over there." Heath held up his hands. "I won't interfere, but I want to check on Willow. What about the dogs?"

"My deputy didn't say anything about the dogs. You can come, but stay out of her cabin until we're done with our investigation."

"Got it." Heath thrust out his hand to Astrid. "Thanks for meeting me out here again. Any objection if I mosey out this way later and have another look?"

"None at all. I want to make this sale, Heath." She winked at him and waved at West.

Not that he needed to this time, but Heath followed West out to Willow's cabin, his thumbs drumming a beat on the steering wheel. This assault on Willow's home obviously had something to do with Toby's death. Was it some kind of warning, or was someone looking for something?

Was his father capable of threats like this? He knew his father was capable of many deeds that made Heath's continued employment and association with Bradford and Son almost untenable. Did he have the guts to follow his principles and make a move? Could he drive the old man out of his own company?

If Dead Falls Island gave up its secrets to Heath, he

might have all the ammunition he needed to oust his father from Bradford and Son.

By the time he reached Willow's property, minutes behind the sheriff, Heath had convinced himself that Bradford and Son had something to do with this recent threat against Willow. He hadn't quite persuaded himself that the company was also responsible for Toby's death, but the idea had occurred to him that someone might have discovered that Heath had been in touch with Toby for reasons other than the land deal.

One look at Willow's ashen face as she sat on the ground with Apollo's head in her lap banished every other thought in his head except the desire to protect her and make everything right. If the intruders had also killed Apollo and Luna, Willow would be devastated.

He scrambled out of his truck and rushed to Willow's side. "Are you okay?"

She nodded. "I'm fine. I got here after the fact. Didn't interrupt anyone doing the deed, but I wish I had been here."

"I'm glad you weren't." He stroked Apollo with one hand and Luna with the other as a substitute for what he really wanted to do—take Willow in his arms and hold her close. "The dogs aren't dead. What happened to them?"

She pointed to a plastic bag containing raw meat. "Someone wrapped up some pills in meat and tossed it to the dogs. I'm saving that for the vet. She's coming to look at the dogs but said as long as they're breathing steadily and not vomiting or foaming at the mouth, they'll probably be fine. They've just been in a pretty deep sleep since I discovered them."

"So someone incapacitated the dogs to get to your

cabin and what?" He pried open Luna's eye, and she
stirred and whined. "West said your place was tossed."

She flicked her fingers at West talking to one of his
deputies on the porch as he examined the splintered door.
"Is he consulting with you now?"

He felt her barb pierce his chest. Their easy cama-
raderie over breakfast had ended with a busted door. "I
was with Astrid Mitchell at the Misty Hollow property
when the sheriff drove up. I guess the two of them are in
a relationship and had a lunch date. He got the call when
he was standing there, and I insisted on following him."

Her green eyes narrowed to a cat's stare. "Why?"

Shoving a hand through his hair, he said, "Chill, Willow. I wanted to make sure you were okay after what
we witnessed last night. That doesn't make me a stalker
or someone complicit in the break-in. Is that what you
think?"

"Did you tell your daddy that I was the lucky recipi-
ent of Toby's land?"

"No." As Willow sank back next to Apollo and rubbed
his head, Heath said, "But I did call the office. Of course
I did. That's just business."

She shot back up, her spine erect. "Shady business.
You tell your cronies at Bradford that I inherited Toby's
property, and minutes later someone drugs my dogs and
trashes my house."

"Exactly." He rolled his eyes in relief. She'd just van-
quished any suspicions he had of the company being involved here. "*Minutes* later. Think about it. Do you really
believe Bradford and Son has a goon squad on call to
perpetrate violence against land holdouts?"

Leveling a finger at him, she said, "*You* think about it.

If that goon squad was already in the area to take care of Toby, they wouldn't have had to go too far, would they?"

"The company doesn't have an enforcement division waiting in the wings." Even as the words left Heath's mouth, dozens of dirty tricks he'd suspected Bradford of perpetuating marched across his brain.

He tipped his head toward a white van rolling up, with the words Mobile Vet inscribed across the side in blue. "I think your vet's here to check out the dogs."

"Willow!" West gestured with his hand in the air. "We need you to check for missing items."

"You go." Heath nudged Willow's shoulder with his elbow. "I'll handle the dogs."

On her way to answer the sheriff's questions, Willow stopped to talk to the vet, who had the lowdown by the time she reached Heath and the two sleeping dogs.

"Hi, I'm Dr. Jaimie. Willow told me what happened."

"I'm Heath. If you need any help with the dogs, let me know. Do you think you'll be taking them into the van?"

"From what Willow told me and the looks of these two, I don't think so." Dr. Jaimie reached over and opened the plastic bag with the meat. Running her thumb across one of the blue pills, she squinted at it. "This is a tranquilizer, not poison. Even if the dogs ate several of these, it won't kill them. Whoever did this wanted to knock out a couple of guard dogs, and that's what they got."

"Just a long nap."

"Pretty much."

The vet grasped the stethoscope around her neck and proceeded to check the vitals of each animal. Luna stirred several times and whimpered in her sleep. Even Apollo snorted a few times as the doc prodded him.

Heath glanced over Dr. Jaimie's head as Willow exited her cabin, her face set in a scowl. *Must be bad in there.*

She and West approached the vet together, and Jaimie turned her head to greet the sheriff. "How's Sherlock doing, West?"

"He's doing great. Follows Olly around everywhere." West explained to Heath. "Olly is Astrid's son, and Sherlock is a stray they adopted."

Dr. Jaimie ran her hand through the fur of a still-groggy Apollo. "I hope nobody is running around the island drugging pets."

"I think that's reserved for my pets." Willow crouched beside the vet. "Are they okay? Will they need any treatment?"

"Their vitals are strong. Luna is already showing signs of coming around, probably because she's younger than Apollo, but he's doing okay. They just need to sleep it off." With two fingers, the vet picked up the plastic bag with the meat and dangled it in the air. "Is it okay if I take this, West? I can tell by the markings on the pill that it's a tranquilizer, but I'd like to test it."

"Unless there's another one, I'm going to have to take it for evidence."

"There was another one." Willow jerked her thumb over her shoulder. "I gave it to Deputy Fletcher when he first showed up."

"Then keep it, Jaimie." West squeezed Willow's shoulder. "I think you should invest in a security system, Willow."

Willow pulled her bottom lip between her teeth. "I can't even get Wi-Fi out here."

Heath said, "There are still security cameras that record directly to a hard drive. You don't need Wi-Fi. I can handle that for you."

"I think I can figure that out myself." Willow jumped to her feet, dusting the knees of her jeans.

As she and the vet talked, Heath edged closer to West. "Was anything taken from her cabin?"

"Not that she could tell. Computer, guns, a few expensive jewelry items—all safe." Hooking a thumb in his belt loop and tilting his head back, West surveyed the remote property. "You should encourage her to get a camera up sooner rather than later."

"As if I have any pull with her." Heath spread his arms. "She has the idea that Bradford and Son is responsible for this."

"There is some high-stakes land grabbing out here, isn't there?" West raised an eyebrow in his direction. "Are you sure your company *isn't* involved?"

Heath let that go. At least the sheriff wasn't accusing Bradford and Son of murder...yet.

Dr. Jaimie and Sheriff Chandler wrapped up at the same time, and pulled away from Willow's property one right after the other, leaving Heath alone with Willow, crouching over the dogs.

"Let me at least get the mutts comfortable." Before she could protest his help, Heath scooped up Apollo and carried him to a bed near the cabin's porch. He followed suit with Luna, placing her down gently on the sheepskin. "They'll probably be thirsty when they wake up."

"At least they're going to wake up." She pushed open her damaged door, and Heath peeked inside the cabin, his eyes widening.

"They did a number on your place. Do you need help cleaning up?"

Wedging a hand on her hip, she looked him up and down. "First the security camera, now the cabin cleanup. Do you feel guilty or something?"

"I just wanna help." He crossed his arms over his chest. "And I'm going to start with that door. You need to get it fixed before night falls. Is Gem Hardware still in town, or are you going to have to get a door from the mainland?"

"Gem is still there." Her tense shoulders finally dropped. "Why are you so invested in helping me?"

"I don't see anyone else stepping up."

"You're assuming I can't handle cleaning up and getting the repairs done myself."

"Why should you do it alone?" He squeezed past her and inspected the doorjamb. "Someone kicked this in or used some kind of battering ram to break it apart."

"That's what West figured." She waved a hand behind her at the disheveled cabin. "I don't think they were looking for anything, or at least, I can't imagine what they hoped to find. I believe this is just an intimidation tactic—sell the land or else."

"There are several interested parties here, not just Bradford and Son." He held up a hand and ticked off his fingers. "Ellie and Garrett are mad enough to take some kind of action. Then there's the Samish. It's in their best interest for Bradford to develop this land for the casino."

"The Samish are going to build that casino with or without the adjacent land."

"True, but they'll realize bigger profits from the casino if Bradford can add some hotels, restaurants and infrastructure to support it." He stepped into the room and plucked up a throw pillow. "I'll start with the easy stuff."

He darted around the room, stuffing cushions back onto sofas and chairs, righting tables and stacking papers. He picked up a few books pulled from a shelf and slotted them back in place. Several framed pictures on the shelf had been knocked down, and he studied one photo as he turned it over.

Tapping the unbroken glass on the frame, he asked, "Is this your mother?"

"Yeah, before she took off for greener pastures." Hugging a pillow to her chest, Willow stood on her tiptoes and peeked over his arm.

"D-did she disappear, or do you know where she is? Have you had contact with her since she left?"

Willow dropped down to her heels, barely reaching his shoulder. "Of course I know where she is…or mostly. She's in Central America right now. Costa Rica, I believe. I'll have to check her blog to find out for sure."

"Your mother has a blog?"

"A vlog, actually. A travel vlog for single women of a certain age." She tossed the pillow onto a love seat. "It's quite popular, actually. She even earns enough to support herself."

"Good for her, I guess. Not so much for you."

Pushing her hair back, Willow made a sad face. "It hurt when I was little. Now? Not so much. Your mom left when you were older, right? When you were living on Dead Falls."

"That's right, but the difference is I never heard from her again. She disappeared."

Willow's mouth dropped open. "What do you mean, disappeared?"

"Exactly that. She left one day, leaving a note for us, and we never heard from her again. At least, I didn't."

"Did your father?"

"I don't know. He won't talk about it, but a few years ago after no contact, he had her declared dead." Heath choked on the words and coughed to hide it.

"That's...that's terrible." She rested her hand on his back with a featherlight touch. "What did the note say?"

"It said she was going to end her life."

"Heath, no." She covered her mouth. "Do you think she was serious?"

"My mom suffered from depression. She'd been in therapy, had medication, but nothing seemed to work. My dad thought being back on Dead Falls would help. It didn't."

"But suicide." Willow's eyes shimmered with tears. "Her body was never found? Did she leave the island?"

"The sheriff at the time conducted a cursory investigation. A ticket purchased shows she took a ferry back to the mainland, but she'd left her phone at home. Her purse and credit cards were gone, but she never used them."

"I'm so sorry. I had no idea at the time. I guess I'd heard that your mom left, but I didn't know the details."

He rubbed a hand across his mouth. He hadn't meant to get into this with her. "Nobody did. My dad kept things pretty quiet."

"I thought losing a mom the way I did was bad, but at least I can visit her vlog to check on her." She patted his back awkwardly. "If you want to pick up that door at Gem Hardware, I'll give you my debit card, and you can knock yourself out. Hell, if they have a home security camera there—the low-tech kind—you can pick up one of those while you're at it."

A smile stretched his lips. "Do you think I told you that sad story so you'd let me help you?"

"I don't know, but it worked." She snatched the frame from his hand and adjusted it on the shelf.

HEATH SPENT THE afternoon making Willow feel better—or at least more secure. While she finished putting her place back together, he drove into town and purchased a replacement door, which he loaded into the back of his truck, and a security camera that fed to a hard drive.

When he got back to her place, the dogs were stirring. She helped him hang the new door and install the camera above it. She insisted on treating him to pizza from Luigi's for dinner to reward his efforts. It almost felt like a date, and his pity party had softened her stance toward him—not that he intended that result.

He hadn't meant to spill his guts at all about his mother. All anyone knew around these parts, if they remembered at all, was that his mother disappeared in the fall and never returned. His father sold the house on Dead Falls Island a few years later, but Heath never forgot it.

Apparently, Toby Keel had never forgotten it, either.

Heath collected their plates and brought them to the kitchen. "Thanks again for the pizza."

"Thanks for everything else." She joined him at the sink and held up his half-full wineglass, the red liquid catching the light and reflecting it in her eyes. "You sure you don't want to finish this off?"

"I have some work to do tonight in my hotel room, and I need a clear head for the numbers."

"I have my new door, new locks, new camera, refreshed dogs, and I don't need a clear head for anything." She tipped his glass back and gulped the rest of the wine.

He laughed. "Don't get too tipsy to handle that rifle."

"I'd probably need a few more glasses to actually shoot someone coming through the door."

"Just remember what they did to Apollo and Luna." He flicked the empty glass with his fingernail.

"You're right." She growled. "Bring it on."

"That's better." He loaded the last of the dishes in the dishwasher. "You have my number now. If you need anything, don't hesitate to call me."

She stood with her back to the counter, her hands loosely clasped in front of her, her lush lips stained with red wine. "Are you doing all this to get my property?"

The hell with the property. He had completely different motives now. He dragged his gaze away from her pout. "Told you I could be persuasive."

She showed him to the door, and he paused on the porch. "Be careful, and I mean that. Call me for anything."

Saluting, she said, "You got it, Bradford."

He cuffed Apollo's ear and loped toward his truck. As he backed up, he waved out the window. He left it open for his drive and inhaled the fresh air. He needed to clear his mind for the business at hand.

The drive to the other side of the island took longer in the dark, but he didn't want to get pulled over for speeding. Not that carrying a pick and shovel were illegal or even suspicious on Dead Falls Island, but he didn't want to draw attention to himself or his mission.

He flicked on his wipers as he crossed the bridge, the falls to his right sprinkling his windshield. Then he made the hard turn left to Misty Hollow and the cursed property.

He pulled his truck into position, facing the two big-leaf maples, and left his headlights beaming into the dark. He thumbed on the dome light and pulled the scrap of paper from his pocket, its edges soft and worn. He held it under the light and read the words aloud for the hundredth time. "'You'll find your mother where the mist meets the earth, between the giant maples.'"

The mist met the earth here, and two huge maple trees towered in front of him. Even though Toby Keel hadn't lived long enough to verify his riddle, Heath felt confident he'd found his mother's resting place.

He jumped from the truck and peeled back the tarp he'd bought at Gem Hardware today to reveal his tools. He hoisted the shovel and pick from the truck bed and strode toward the space between the two trees.

Then he plowed the shovel into the ground and started digging.

Chapter Seven

The following morning, Willow sprang out of bed to check the video footage from the night before. She scanned through the recording, noting the night critters that darted in and out of view and the mist that rolled across the ground. Nothing human crept up to her cabin.

Sighing, she slumped in her chair. Anyone could spot the camera above her porch, so it might work more as a deterrent than a spy.

Luna called her to the front door with a scratch, and she pushed up to her feet to rescue the dog.

Willow stood on the front porch, her toes curled over the edge of the top step, as she watched the dogs go about their business. They didn't seem any worse for wear after their ordeal yesterday. Who ran around drugging dogs?

She glanced over her shoulder into her cabin. The intruders must've been trying to spook her with their break-in. As far as she could tell, they'd taken nothing of value. Their tactic didn't make much sense to her, though. A few thugs ransacking her summer house were not going to suddenly convince her to sell her land… or Toby's.

Had they been looking for something else? When Dad

died and she'd come back here that first summer after her freshman year in college, she'd cleaned out a lot of his items—but not everything. Maybe his papers contained something of value that she'd missed.

Dad's family, the Sandses, did have a lot of wealth and property at some point. Mom had told her that Dad had sold it all off except this plot and the one he eventually sold to Toby. But Mom didn't always know all of Paul Sands's business.

Dad's will had kept things simple. He'd left all his worldly possessions to Willow, and he'd already put her on the title for this property, so there was no paperwork to go through at the time of his death, except to remove his name from the title. He didn't have stacks of cash or stocks or Swiss bank accounts—as far as she knew.

But maybe someone knew something she didn't.

Rubbing the back of her neck, she strolled into the house. She'd have to dig out Dad's old stuff to see if she could find something. The trespassers had gone through some papers, as they'd strewn the evidence across her floor, but they probably hadn't gone through the old suitcase where she'd stashed most of her father's paperwork.

She filled the dogs' bowls with food and refreshed the water in the tub outside. Then she made herself a smoothie for breakfast and carried it to the small bedroom. The cabin had only two bedrooms—the large one, which she'd taken over from her father after his death, and the smaller one, which had been her room growing up.

She placed her breakfast drink on the white nightstand with flowers painted on the drawer and sat crosslegged on the floor beside the double bed covered with a yellow comforter. The invaders had tossed this room, too, but mostly for show. They'd rifled the bookshelf, knocking over a few vampire books from her teen years, and had pulled a couple of items, mostly sports gear, from the closet.

Flipping up the comforter, she felt beneath the bed until her fingers found the handle of the battered suitcase that had belonged to her father. She curled her fingers around it and dragged the bag from under the bed.

She'd never put a lock on the suitcase but figured it had been a step up from the cardboard box where she'd found most of her father's business. He'd left the only important paper, his will, in a kitchen drawer, and had made sure she knew where to find it. She'd grabbed handfuls of this other irrelevant paperwork and shoveled it from the box into this brown suitcase.

Flipping the suitcase open now, she studied the paperwork scattered in the bottom. Did it seem like there were fewer papers in here? She wouldn't have a clue. She'd tossed these items in here, helter-skelter, figuring if someone asked for something important later, she could go through it at that time. Nobody ever had. She grabbed a piece on top, scanning a letter about brush clearance from the Forest Service. How would she know if someone had gone through this mess?

Dropping the Forest Service letter on the floor, she noticed her dirty fingerprints on the page. She hadn't dragged this suitcase from its hiding place for years, and it was dusty. If someone else had been here before her, there should be more fingerprints.

To avoid leaving more prints, she grabbed the shredded silky lining inside the lid of the bag and tugged it down, removing her fingers at the last second when it closed. A few eddies of dust floated upward with the closure, caught in the rays of sun from the window, but not a lot.

She squinted at the top of the suitcase, making out her fingerprints on the edge of the lid, left when she'd opened the bag. But her marks in the dust weren't the only ones there. Larger swaths of dust had been removed, as if other prints were left in the general area of hers, but then wiped out with a sleeve or a cloth. Or perhaps the thief had worn gloves and had cleared the dust off with his hands.

Her nose tingled with the release of the dust in the air, and she rubbed it with the back of her hand. "Well, I'll be damned."

The intruders had found this case and opened it. Whether or not they'd taken anything would have to remain a mystery, as Willow had no idea what she'd shoved in there.

Should she tell West? She played out that absurd conversation in her head and rejected it. The strangers, in the course of going through her cabin, had also looked into this suitcase, but she didn't know what had been in it or if anything was now missing. She pushed the case back under the bed and wiped her hands on her pajama bottoms.

The dogs started barking out front, and the growl of an engine carried into the cabin. Willow grabbed her smoothie and scurried to the front door, which she'd left wide open.

When she spied Heath getting out of his truck, her heart still beat furiously, but in a different kind of pattern. It seemed as if they'd just parted company hours ago, and here he was again. He either really wanted to see her, or he wanted to keep applying some subtle pressure on her.

She plucked at her flannel pajama bottoms but took some pleasure in the fact that his hair stood on end and he needed a shave. She could put down her own appearance to a couple of glasses of wine the night before, but he'd pretty much abstained. What was his excuse for his tired appearance?

Cupping a hand over her eyes, she said, "What brings you out here so early? I'm still not selling."

"Early?" He rubbed the top of Apollo's head. "It's almost eleven o'clock."

The dogs had barked at the arrival of his truck, but he'd already earned their trust and devotion. Once they saw Heath get out of the truck, they'd stopped barking.

"Is it?" She took a sip of her drink and caught a drop of the thick smoothie at the corner of her mouth with her tongue. "I swear, I haven't gotten any work done out here."

"What's been going on hasn't exactly been conducive to cataloging flora and fauna." He made a circling motion in the air. "Everything go okay with the camera setup?"

"I looked at the footage this morning, and except for a skunk drinking from the dogs' water dish, nothing much happened."

"That's good to hear. Just wanted to make sure the security system was in working order. It'll at least function as a deterrent." Heath clapped a hand over his mouth and yawned.

"You must've had a lot of work last night."

Dropping his hand, Heath jerked his head up. "Why do you say that?"

"Um, because you told me you had work to do, and this morning you can barely keep your eyes open." She tipped her head toward her open door. "Would you like some coffee? I haven't made it yet. Clearly, I haven't done much of anything this morning, but it'll just take a few minutes."

"I'll take you up on that. The coffee from the hotel lobby was so vile, I couldn't stomach it." On his way to the porch, he crouched down to give Luna a hug.

Must be missing his own pooches.

Once inside, Heath sank into a chair at the kitchen table. "No leftover pizza for breakfast?"

"Leftover veggie pizza is kind of gross. You should've taken the pepperoni that was left over. I'll never eat it."

"I'll take it now." He brushed past her in the small kitchen and opened her fridge. He snatched up the plastic bag that contained the leftovers from their meal last night.

She punched the button to start the coffee brewing. "Do you want to heat that up in the microwave?"

"Negative. Better cold." To prove his point, he bit off the tip of a piece of pepperoni pizza straight from the fridge.

While Heath ate his breakfast, Willow watched the coffee drip into the pot. She poured two cups and carried them to the table. "Cream or sugar?"

"Black." He curled two fingers around the handle of the mug and lifted it. "Breakfast of champions."

Tapping next to a blister on his finger, she said, "That looks nasty."

"Yeah, well, I'm not above manual labor, as I proved yesterday. Must've gotten that while I was hanging the door." He blew on the steam wafting from his cup and took a sip. "So much better than what the hotel has to offer. Anything more from the Keels after yesterday's ambush?"

"No, but Toby's attorney, Jason Hart, called me and wants to meet this afternoon. I'm hoping he can explain what's going on." She clicked her fingernail against her mug, watching the cream swirl in the mocha-colored liquid.

"What's wrong? Feeling guilty about inheriting that property? I can assuage you of that guilt." Heath quirked his eyebrows up and down.

"N-no. I'm just coming to the realization that I didn't know much about my father's affairs."

"Why would you? You were just a teenager when he passed. You didn't get any help from the adults in your life at the time, did you?"

"My mother was in Bali at the time." She twisted her lips into a semblance of a smile.

"You're lucky, though. Other than this house and the strings attached to the property he sold Toby, sounds like your father's assets were simple and straightforward." He plopped another slice of pizza onto his plate.

"I thought so, but…"

Apollo cut off her confession with a high-pitched whine, and she scrambled from her chair. Standing at the front door, she called to Apollo, pacing in front of the tree line. "What's wrong, boy? Where's Luna?"

Heath came up behind her, cradling his coffee mug. "What's he crying for?"

"Not sure, but I don't see Luna anywhere."

"The way Apollo's stalking the edge of the forest there, I'd bet a few bucks Luna headed into the woods, probably back to Toby's."

"That's what I've been afraid of. That's why I kept her on a lead yesterday, which probably made it easier for the intruders to drug them."

"The DFSD must be done processing that scene by now. Hell, it may even just be the scene of an accident. I don't think there's any harm in Luna going there."

"Probably not, but I don't want her going through the forest. She's completely domesticated." She whistled for Apollo, and he loped to her side, head hanging. "Don't worry, Apollo. We'll bring her back."

"I'll drive you over in my truck." Heath popped the last bit of crust into his mouth and brushed his hands together. "Get dressed. I'll take care of the dishes. You see? Luna's not the only one who's domesticated."

"I thought you were a bachelor."

"Bachelors have to be even more domesticated, or we'll end up living in squalor." He nudged the small of her back. "If you want to take a shower before you get dressed, I think Luna will be fine."

"That sounds like a broad hint. I must smell like dog, wine and sweat."

"Whatever it is, I like it." He took her coffee cup from her as they entered the house and made a beeline for the kitchen.

"You are really working it, Bradford. I might just make you believe there's hope to keep the groveling coming."

He parked himself in front of the sink. "I obviously have to work on my sincerity."

She couldn't wipe the smile from her face as she traipsed into her room to gather some clothes and cranked on the shower for a quick wash. The man had charm to spare, and its effect was dizzying.

She still had no plans to sell either property to Bradford and Son, but how far would Son go to change her mind?

As HEATH RINSED the dishes, he ran a thumb over the blister on the side of his finger. His digging last night had yielded nothing...except this blister. He'd looked over the land but didn't see any other pair of maple trees together. Had Toby been messing with his mind?

Toby had been the one to contact Heath with his cryptic, unsigned notes. Heath had only figured out that Toby Keel was his anonymous pen pal by luck. When his father had told him to start securing the properties on the west side of Dead Falls Island to dovetail with the Samish casino plans, Heath had recognized Toby's handwriting from several documents.

Toby had admitted to being the author, and the two had planned to meet so that Toby could come clean about what he knew regarding the disappearance of Heath's mother. Toby's death had put an end to that. Had someone made sure that Toby would die with his secrets?

Luna's escape gave Heath an excuse to check out Toby's house. Willow owned the property now. Why shouldn't she be there, and why shouldn't he be there with her to collect Luna?

He poured himself another cup of coffee and scrolled through his phone as he waited for Willow. Now he just needed an excuse to get into Toby's house. He wanted to search through the man's things to see if he'd intended to send Heath any more clues about his mother.

Why hadn't Toby just come out and told Heath what happened and where his mother was buried? He must've had something to do with his mother's death. Maybe he knew he was dying, and his conscience forced him to come clean before his death. Only he hadn't had time.

"You seem engrossed. Playing a game on your phone?"

He lifted his head as Willow walked into the kitchen, her hair swinging in a ponytail and jeans encasing her slender legs. Tilting his phone back and forth, he said, "Reception is spotty. Can't get new mail or messages."

"That's a problem out here. Hike or drive?" She pointed to two pairs of shoes stationed at the front door—white tennis shoes and scuffed hiking boots.

"Let's walk over. You can show me where you found that piece of flannel. Did you ever tell West about that?" He dumped his coffee down the drain and chased it with a blast of water.

"I gave West a call and told him everything—about Toby's will, the anger of the Keels, and I handed over that scrap of material after the break-in yesterday." She sat down on the edge of a chair and stuffed her stockinged feet into her boots. "I can't run around grabbing everyone with a red flannel."

"Just me, but you can grab *me* all you want." As Willow's cheeks turned pink, he shook his head. "I mean, if you ever need help or...anything."

"I'm not selling, Son."

Crouching in front of Apollo, he cupped the dog's head and touched his nose to his. "A guy can't get a break around here, dude."

"And don't try to get Apollo on your side, either. He can't be bought with cheap affection." She raised a finger. "Don't even go there."

Heath left Willow's cabin with a lighter step than when he'd arrived. He'd plastered over his fatigue and disappointment with a quick smile and a jovial attitude, just like he always did, but several minutes in Willow's company turned the cover-up into reality. She had a way of making him feel at ease. The whole island did, and he'd turned her into some kind of woodsy representative of Dead Falls.

As they tromped through the woods, Heath tried to keep his gaze on the trail in front of him instead of on Willow's pert backside in those tight jeans. He'd still want her even if she didn't own one blade of grass on this island.

She stopped suddenly, and he almost plowed into her. "Whoa."

She glanced at the hand on her hip he'd used to avoid knocking her to the ground. Then she flicked a skinny branch with her fingers. "I found the flannel material here."

Taking a step back, he surveyed the area. "No reason for anyone to be hiking this trail unless he or she was going from Toby's place to yours, right?"

She rubbed her chin. "I mean, yeah, but it's part of the National Forest. Anyone has a right to be here."

"You didn't find anything else suspicious?"

"Nope. Could've been some hiker, but I thought it was a coincidence."

"I agree, especially as someone trashed your place yesterday. They must've known you were out, known about the dogs, known they were tied up." He snapped a twig between his fingers. "Like they were watching you."

"I know." She hunched her shoulders. "Let's get to Luna."

Ten minutes later, they emerged from the tree line onto Toby's property. Yellow crime scene tape sagged between a post and the picnic bench, and Luna lay beside the firepit where they'd found Toby's body just two nights ago.

Willow dabbed the corner of her eye with the tip of her finger. "That's so sad. She's waiting for Toby to come back."

Heath crept toward the dog and hunched beside her. "It's all right, girl. You don't need to protect him anymore."

Leaning above him, Willow circled her finger in the air over a spot on the ground. "West took the rock. I imagine the medical examiner is going to determine if Toby fell on it or if someone used it to bash his head."

"West is being tight-lipped about it." Heath rose to his feet, his gaze darting toward Toby's cabin. "Do you need to get anything out of Toby's cabin for Luna?"

"I have everything I need for her—" Willow shoved her hands in her pockets and kicked at one of the stones circling the firepit "—but I might need her vaccination records."

Heath lifted his shoulders. "It's not really breaking in if he left everything to you."

She pulled her hand free from her pocket and dangled a silver key in front of him. "We don't need to break in. I have a key to the cabin, just as Toby had a key to mine."

"Even better."

Willow ordered the dogs to stay as she bobbled the key in the palm of her hand. When they reached the entrance, she slid the key home and pushed open the door.

The layout of Toby's cabin mirrored Willow's, but the resemblance ended there. While Willow had turned her space into a cozy, charming, neat forest retreat, Toby had stuffed his place full of junk. Towers of books lined one wall without the benefit of a shelf. On one crowded table, Samish relics fought for space with bits of flora from the forest.

Heath wiped his forehead with the back of his hand. If he thought he was going to find any evidence of his mother's mysterious disappearance here, he'd been grossly mistaken. He whistled through his teeth. "What a mess."

"Kind of a controlled chaos." Willow picked up a red file folder from a desk and thumbed through it. "It would take weeks to find anything in here."

Throwing her a sharp look, he said, "You mean Luna's records?"

"Yeah, yeah. Luna's records. I'll just ask Dr. Jaimie. She probably has all that." She swept several folders from the desk, including the red one, and tucked them under her arm. "Maybe Toby's attorney needs some of these papers."

Heath turned his back on her and scanned the rest of the cluttered room. It felt like he wasn't the only one compelled to search through Toby Keel's life for clues. No wonder he hadn't had to twist her arm to get in here. But he couldn't do much of a search with her hanging over his shoulder.

As they stepped out of the cabin, a chill permeated

the air, and the sun struggled to reach the ground, now swirling with mist. He glanced up as moisture caressed his face. "That was fast."

"Toby's property dips just enough to be susceptible to the moisture from the ocean that gets trapped inland. He had a name for this property when my father sold it to him. I don't remember the Samish name, which is more poetic, but he called it *where the mist meets the earth.*"

Chapter Eight

Heath froze beside her, and she stumbled to a stop, nearly tripping over Apollo. "Did you forget something?"

He turned in a circle and pointed to a thatch of trees near a creek that ran through the back of the property. "Are those maple trees?"

"Yes." She grabbed Apollo's collar to prevent him from backtracking to Heath. "The two big ones are big-leaf maples. Are you having second thoughts about tearing everything down and putting up a parking lot?"

"I see them around a lot. Thought they were maples but couldn't remember. There are a couple on the Misty Hollow property, too."

"They're all over." She tilted her head toward the trail back to her place. "You ready to go, or have you decided to do a nature inventory here? If that's the case, I can put you to work."

"Yeah, let's get going. I'll take Luna with me, so she doesn't make a beeline back here. But how are you going to stop her from going back home?"

"Food, warmth, affection. I guess I have to expect she'll return here occasionally and just hope she doesn't get attacked by anything feral."

"Hey, you two."

Willow spun around at the sound of a voice, slip-ping the file folders inside her flannel. She swallowed as Lee Scott ambled toward them, the silver from his bolo tie glinting through the haze. As the business rep for the Samish, Lee always dressed sharply. No quick getaway, but a swift offense always trumped a back-pedaling defense.

"Hi, Lee. What brings you out here?"

"I could ask you the same." Lee nodded at Heath. "Hello, Heath. Checking out the property again now that Toby has passed?"

"I guess introductions aren't necessary." She wagged her finger between the two men. "You guys know each other?"

Heath reached forward to grab Lee's hand. "Of course we do. Similar interests."

Willow thunked her forehead with the heel of her hand, even though she knew all about their shared in-terests. "That's right. Lee's the one leading the charge to get a casino on the island."

"We'll get it done one way or the other, Willow, with or without your land." He pressed his thin lips into a smile.

"Is that why you're here? To drool over your prospects with Toby gone?" She tugged her shirt closed, folding her arms over the files.

Lee put his hands together. "I'm here to pay my re-spects. Even though Toby and I were on opposite sides of the issue, he was still a brother. And you?"

Heath jingled Luna's collar. "Came to retrieve Toby's dog. Willow is keeping her for now, but she insists on going home."

"Poor thing." Lee advanced toward Luna, who bristled and snarled at him.

"I guess she's still protective of the area." Heath smoothed his hand over the top of Luna's head.

Willow glanced between Luna and Lee, narrowing her eyes. "We'll leave you to…pay your respects in peace, Lee."

"Take care, Willow. Good to see you, Heath. We might have to schedule another meeting soon."

Willow plunged into the forest with Heath hot on her heels. When they got some distance from Toby's cabin, she hissed over her shoulder. "Did you see how Luna behaved toward Lee?"

"Like a dog defending her people and property."

"Or like a dog reacting to her owner's killer."

Heath tugged on the tail of her shirt. "Now you've pegged Lee Scott as Toby's murderer? Next, you'll be pawing through his wardrobe looking for a red flannel. He's probably not even going to get the land now."

"*He* doesn't know that, does he?" She snorted. "Do you think he would've been all nicey-nice with me back there if he knew Toby left the property to me?"

"Lee Scott is an astute businessman, not a killer."

"He's got a lot riding on that casino. He wants to maximize its profits." She flipped her ponytail over her shoulder and plowed forward.

"If we ever do have that meeting, I'll see what I can find out. But I think you'll be suspicious of anyone with connections to the land. The sooner West Chandler and the medical examiner release a manner of death, the sooner we can all move on."

She shot back, "Unless that manner of death is homicide."

When they got to her cabin, Heath helped her corral the dogs inside.

As he eyed the stack of file folders she put on the kitchen table, she moved between his line of sight and the table. She didn't want to explain to him why she wanted to look through the folders or why she'd hidden them from Lee. Bradford and Son didn't need to know everything about these properties.

"I need to get ready for my meeting with Jason Hart," she said. "Thanks for coming with me to rescue Luna."

"Anytime. I hope you get the property. I really do."

"I might be a long way from that if Ellie and Garrett challenge the will, and I'll have to stand up to the likes of Lee Scott."

"I'm sure the Keels plan to contest, which will end up keeping Lee at bay. Keep me posted." He let himself out and waved.

As soon as the door closed behind him, Willow pounced on the folders. Plopping down in a chair, she flipped open the first one.

She ran her finger down a bunch of meaningless expenses and then thumbed through the rest of the papers in the folder. More of the same. Before she could get to the next folder in the stack, she glanced at her phone and cursed softly.

She had only a few minutes to get ready for her meeting with Jason Hart. She didn't plan to dress up too much, but she could at least pluck the leaves and twigs from her hair.

Ten minutes later, dressed in a pair of blue slacks and

a white blouse, she secured the dogs in the house and jumped in her truck.

Hart had an office in Seattle but kept a small home on the coast near the harbor for frequent visits. He'd chosen the Harbor Restaurant and Bar for their afternoon meeting between the lunch and the dinner crowd, and Willow wheeled into the parking lot. She grabbed her purse from the passenger seat and slung it over her shoulder. She hadn't brought the file folders with her. She had no intention of sharing them with Hart until she had a look at them herself.

As she barreled through the door, she spotted Hart at the bar. He'd told her he'd be nursing a drink, wearing a black hat. She raised her hand in his direction, and he slid off the stool, holding up his highball glass.

"Can I get you something?" he asked her.

"Let's grab a table. I'll order something then." She took his proffered hand, his fingers damp from the glass he'd just switched to the other hand. "Good to meet you."

"Nice to meet you, too, Willow." He swirled the drink, and ice clinked against the glass. "I know it's a little early, but I'm on vacation and just took my boat over this morning."

"I don't need any explanations—as long as you're sober enough to tell me what the hell is going on with this property." She pointed to a table by the window in the half-empty restaurant. "Okay if we grab that?"

The hostess hurried over with a couple of menus. "No problem."

Once they were seated, the hostess returned with a cocktail napkin for Jason's drink. He set his glass on the napkin and reached into a satchel on the seat next to him. "I have the papers for the transfer of property with me. Please remember, I wasn't your father's attorney, just Toby's. At the time your father sold the property to Toby, his attorney sent paperwork to Toby's attorney, and that's what I have now. Toby's attorney retired, and I took over."

"My father's attorney? Wasn't her name Jordan or something like that? I dealt with her when I was a teenager, so it's been a while."

"Tabitha Jordan. Sadly, she passed away."

"Did anyone replace her? Did she work for a firm?"

Jason took a sip of his drink and raised his eyebrows at her over the rim. "The dead don't need attorneys, Willow. Once I settle Toby's estate, he won't need me, either."

Willow ordered an iced tea and a salad from the waitress, while Jason ordered another Scotch.

She chewed on her bottom lip, selecting her words before blurting out anything. "Is there any reason why someone would want to see papers on the house? I mean, if someone found another will that came after the one you have, could that cancel my ownership of the property?"

"Nothing can cancel that ownership, even if Toby made twenty wills. The paperwork your father and his attorney drew up upon the sale of the property to Toby is ironclad—at least for now. No other will can supplant it."

"Why do you say 'at least for now'?"

Jason thanked the waitress as she set his second drink in front of him. He poked at the ice in his glass with a stir stick. "Ellie and Garrett Keel are going to challenge your father's will. They've already put me on notice."

"I figured they would." She took a sip of her tea. "I'm

just wondering why my father set things up this way. If he wanted Toby to have that land, he should've sold it to him with no strings attached. At the time, he couldn't have known about the plans of the Samish and predatory developers."

Jason spread his hands. "Maybe he took a good guess."

"He sold off other plots with no such stipulations. Why this piece of land?"

"I don't have the answer to that, but if you'll excuse me, my understanding is that your father had to sell off that land to live. He wasn't working, and he owed some money to your mother for the divorce."

"You don't have to tiptoe around." She chewed on the tip of her straw. "I know better than anyone that my father had issues."

"I can't help you with the whys. I'm here to satisfy the terms of Toby's will and get this property in your name, regardless of what the Keels do down the line." Jason creased his damp cocktail napkin with his thumb. "Do you have a will?"

"Me? What? No." She pushed her place setting to the side when the waitress showed up with her salad. "I'm not married. No kids. There's really just my mom."

"You should get on that. You're a woman with two very valuable properties now. If you die intestate—" he put a hand over his heart "—God forbid, but if you do die without a will, your mother will be your beneficiary, but she'll pay some heavy taxes for the privilege."

A little chill zigzagged down her spine, and she stabbed a piece of lettuce with her fork. "I could bypass my mother and leave the property to the university or something, couldn't I?"

"Of course you can." He toyed with his drink for a few seconds before taking a sip. "And make sure everyone knows it."

The zigzag turned into a river, and Willow clenched her teeth. "Why do you say that?"

"I don't know. Just seems like everyone has some kind of interest in those properties. If you leave them under the protection of some entity, maybe that interest will die down. In the meantime, the Samish can do whatever they like with their land."

"True, but Lee Scott has made it clear that profits will be maximized with the development of the lands adjoining the casino property."

"I guess that's Lee Scott's problem, then, isn't it? Don't make it yours." Jason rattled his glass one more time before draining it of the last bit of Scotch. "Do you mind if I abandon you here to finish your salad on your own? I'll leave the paperwork, of course, so you can look it over. I'll be on the island for a few days if you have any questions, and you can return everything to me in person before I go."

"No problem. Quick question." She slid the packet of papers to her side of the table. "Will you be representing the Keels when they sue me?"

"One thing at a time." He pulled several bills from his wallet and dropped them on the table. "Lunch is on me."

When Jason left, Willow flipped through the papers while eating her salad. Her father had indeed stipulated that the property return to his daughter if both he and Toby preceded her in death. Well, that happened.

So, really, Paul Sands's agreement with Toby Keel looked more like a long-term lease than a sale, and the price reflected that. Her father had charged Toby one dollar a year for the cabin and the land.

Sighing, she pushed the papers away from her. Dad never did have a head for business, but he'd gotten what he wanted in the end. That land would remain undisturbed and immune to the development that had occurred on this side of the island. And, to be on the safe side, Willow would contact an attorney when she got back to Seattle at the end of the summer and draw up a will or living trust.

She finished her salad and ordered a refill on her iced tea, as she shoveled the files Jason left into her oversize purse. She sipped her drink and scrolled through her phone, stopping at Mom's Instagram account.

Mom's latest posts detailed several hikes in Sedona. Hopefully, she was still on this side of the world. As Willow brought up her contacts, someone rapped on her table.

Willow glanced up, her stomach sinking at the sight of Ellie Keel hovering over the booth.

Ellie's nostrils flared. "I ran into Jason Hart in the parking lot. You didn't waste any time, did you?"

"Give it a rest, Ellie." Willow massaged her temple with two fingers. "Jason called me yesterday to let me know he'd be on the island this week. He wanted to handle your uncle's business as soon as possible. Think of it this way—the sooner I take possession of the property, the sooner you can get down to the business of suing me."

Undeterred, Ellie wedged a hip against the banquette. "I also saw Lee Scott."

Willow murmured, "You've been busy."

"He said you and Heath Bradford were nosing around Toby's house."

"Did he?" Willow leaned back in her seat and folded her arms. "Seems like he was the one nosing around. We were there to retrieve Luna."

"Who?"

"Luna, Toby's dog. I can see how well acquainted you were with your uncle's life. We went to collect her and ran into Lee *paying his respects*." She huffed out a breath. "I don't think Lee ever respected Toby when he was alive."

"Lee was probably there making plans. We'd already made it clear to him that we were trying to convince Uncle Toby to sell."

"Were you pressuring Toby all this time?" Willow dug her fingernails into her biceps.

"We were discussing, not pressuring. He was family." Ellie leveled a finger at her. "Just be prepared. We're coming for you."

"Maybe you already started. Did you and Garrett break into my place yesterday?"

"Break into your place?" Ellie's face grew still and she stopped tapping her foot. "Someone broke into your cabin?"

"Drugged the two dogs and ransacked my house."

"What did they take?"

"The dogs are fine—thanks for asking." She held up her phone. "You need to leave. I was about to make a phone call."

Ellie leaned forward, and Willow could already smell the booze on her breath emanating from her parted, bright red lips. "Was anything stolen?"

"Bye." Willow wiggled her fingers in the air.

Ellie flounced off toward the bar, and the man who'd been waiting for her. After several seconds of gesturing toward Willow, Ellie perched on the bar stool and took a few gulps of her Bloody Mary.

What was it with the early drinkers on this island? Everyone was too stressed out.

Willow went back to her phone and called her mother. To her surprise, Mom picked up on the second ring. "Hello, darling."

"Hey, Mom. Saw you were in Sedona, so I thought I'd give you a try. It's not often we're in the same time zone."

"Actually, that was two days ago. I'm at the Grand Canyon today, trying to book a mule trip down to the canyon, the overnight one. It's summertime, so you must be on the island—cold, dreary place."

"It's June. The weather is great."

"Ha! The weather is never great on Dead Falls Island, Willow, unless by *great* you mean *misty, gray, cool.*"

"Yeah, I get it, Mom. You hate it here and always did." Willow shook her head and swallowed some tea. "There's been some…upset here on the island this summer. Toby Keel died."

"Oh, God, Toby Keel. That's a name from the past I'd rather forget."

Her mother never had anything good to say about anyone on Dead Falls. "You knew Toby?"

"Toby made it his business to know all the women on the island—him and his creepy nephew."

Willow choked on her tea. "Toby was a womanizer?"

"Yes, runs in the family, and that's all I'm gonna say about it. How'd he die? Shot by an irate husband?"

"Mom!" Willow dabbed the liquid on her chin. "He fell and hit his head on a rock, or someone bashed his head with that rock."

Mom gasped. "I told you. It was probably some man who got fed up with Toby feeding his wife mystical Samish crap."

"Just stop. The medical examiner hasn't pinpointed manner of death yet. We're still waiting, but Sheriff Chandler is on it."

"Mark my words." Her mother crunched on something. "I heard that new sheriff is a hot commodity. Do you know him?"

"I know him, but he's already in a relationship with Astrid Mitchell."

"Hmm, you'd think that girl would've learned her lesson with cops, but I hear Chandler is the real deal."

Willow rolled her eyes. "How do you know all the Dead Falls gossip, anyway?"

"I have my sources, but they obviously dropped the ball since this is the first time I heard about Toby. What about his property? Is Garrett finally getting his hands on it?"

Her mother didn't know everything that went on here. "Yeah, about that. Dad worked out some plan that gives the property to me when Toby dies."

"Your father. He would do something like that. I wondered why he'd turn that parcel over to Toby in the first place. It's a lot more valuable than the one you're sitting on."

"No, it's not." Willow waved off the waitress bearing more iced tea. "My property is a little bigger, and the cabin is much nicer—thanks to me."

"Yeah, but Toby's property has all that other stuff. I guess it doesn't matter, as it's yours now. Makes sense why Paul would ensure it went back to you. You're just like him. You'll never do anything with that land, even though you could earn a mint from it."

Willow cocked her head. Mom was losing her. "You mean sell it for the Samish casino development."

"Casino? That's small potatoes compared to the rest of it."

"The rest of what, Mom? I have no idea what you're talking about."

She clicked her tongue. "Maybe Paul didn't trust you after all, if he didn't tell you."

"Tell me what?" Willow found herself gripping the edge of the table.

"That land—Toby's and now yours—it's full of nickel, and your father owned the mineral rights. Probably worth millions."

Willow reached for her empty glass and knocked it over. A piece of ice skittered across the table. "A-are you sure?"

"Positive. It came up in the divorce proceedings, but I couldn't touch it—not that I wanted to. Look, I'm not fond of the island, but even I didn't want to see an ugly nickel mine gouge out that side of Dead Falls."

Pinching her bottom lip with her fingers, Willow thought about the search of her cabin. Were the intruders looking for the mineral rights to Toby's property?

"Why don't I know about the mineral rights if I own the property? Toby's lawyer never mentioned anything about it." As Willow asked the question, she pulled the legal paperwork from her bag and scrambled through it.

"I don't know that much about it, but I do know that mineral rights can be held separately from the property. Maybe your father sold them off to someone else." A man's voice intruded on the conversation. "Darling, I have to go. Congrats on getting that property back, and let's meet up soon."

Her mother rang off before Willow could answer. If other people knew about the nickel vein on the land, that could explain a lot. She needed to learn more about mineral rights in general and who owned them on Toby's property—because she was pretty sure she didn't.

The waitress approached again with a pitcher of tea. "Did you want more? My shift's over in about ten minutes."

"I'm sorry to keep you. I'm done."

The waitress tipped her chin toward the window. "Looks like fire season is getting an early start."

"There's a fire?" Willow twisted her head to peer out the window. Her stomach knotted when she spied a thin trail of black smoke reaching into the sky.

"Don't worry. It's not close to us. I heard it's on the other side of the island, the less populated side."

"I know exactly where it is." Willow sprang from her seat, keeping an eye on the smoke unfurling into the mist to create a gray haze that hovered over the trees. "I live there."

Chapter Nine

Heath plunged his shovel into the ground and hit rock. The reverberation reached his shoulder. He'd need the pickax for this land. Why would someone bury his mother's body out here? Was he even looking for his mother's body? Toby Keel had talked in riddles. Maybe he didn't literally mean that Heath would find his mother here, but he'd find something.

He took a deep breath and brought the shovel down a few feet from his first attempt. It sank into the dirt easier this time, so he pulled up a shovelful of dirt and tossed it to the side. He dug down a few more feet, and then started another hole in the same area.

After about thirty minutes of work, his nostrils twitched, and he stepped back from the little mound of dirt. Had Lee Scott started a fire when he was here? Heath walked to the firepit filled with cold ash and prodded a stump of scorched wood with the toe of his boot.

When he turned in a circle, he caught sight of a plume of smoke rising above the trees—from the direction of Willow's cabin.

His adrenaline pumping, he ran to the back of Toby's cabin and stashed his tools there, propping them against the side of the house. Then he charged toward the trail leading to Willow's property. He'd been on this trail before, but this time he plowed through it, leaping over gnarled roots and ignoring the branches that grabbed at his clothing and slapped his face.

Panting, he stumbled into the clearing that ringed her place. Lifting his head, he spotted a hooded figure running for the road. He started to give chase, the smell of the fire and some kind of chemical accelerant permeating his senses.

The dogs howling from the cabin stopped him short.

He let the assailant escape and spun around toward the flaming house. The smoke had intensified since he'd first noticed it, and his eyes stung as he battled his way to the front door. Fire engulfed the back of the cabin, and a window on the side of the house shattered, but the front door remained clear.

Heath snatched a log from beside the firepit and clutched it in both hands as he scrambled up the porch. He swung the log like a Louisville Slugger at the front window and smashed it in. The dogs could survive a few shards of glass. They wouldn't be able to survive this inferno.

He shoved his arm through the hole in the glass, and with his body halfway into the house, he reached around and unlocked the door. He pushed it in, and Luna rushed past him. Smoke billowed from the back of the house, and Heath called for Apollo.

The dog answered with a whine, and Heath followed the sound, almost tripping over him huddled in a corner of the room. Heath grabbed his collar. "It's okay, boy. Come out with me this way."

As he led Apollo to the front door, Heath heard sirens wailing and Luna's echoing cry. He got Apollo outside and corralled both dogs away from the house and the road where a fire truck careened to a stop. Helicopter blades thwacked above him as the chopper dumped red fire retardant into the trees at the edge of Willow's property. The sticky substance floated his way, and he threw an arm across his eyes.

As the firefighters rushed in, something exploded in the house, and another burst of flames shot from the roof. The chopper swooped in and doused the fire from above.

Heath tried to keep himself and the dogs away from the activity at the house. They had taken refuge beneath the picnic table, and he parked on top of it, pulling his shirt over his nose and mouth. They couldn't leave the area. He'd parked his truck on the other side, near the trail leading to Toby's house, and he couldn't take the dogs past the fire engines on the road. Right now, fear paralyzed them, but that same fear could send the dogs into a panic and out into the wilderness.

Heath lifted his head as footsteps approached him, and he raised his hand at Sheriff Chandler.

West stopped next to the table. "Are you okay? Do you need medical attention?"

"I'm fine." Heath held his arms in front of him. "Just a little sliced up from breaking the window. Nothing serious."

West asked, "Are you the one who called 911?"

"Never had a chance and don't think I can get service, anyway. I saw the smoke and ran over when I realized it was Willow's place. I saw someone running away from the fire, but I heard the dogs yelping and couldn't leave them."

West's brows shot up and disappeared beneath his hat. "You're kidding. You saw the arsonist?"

Spreading his arms, Heath asked, "You don't think this happened naturally, do you? Not after the break-in yesterday. Someone is trying to smoke Willow out—literally."

"Did you get a good look at this person?"

"Nope. He was running away. Had a black hoodie on, black pants. That's all I saw." Heath coughed. "If we can salvage the footage from Willow's security camera, you might get a look at him, but I doubt he was smiling for the camera."

"You sure the arsonist was male?"

"Are you thinking Ellie Keel is behind this?" Heath shrugged. "Could've been a woman."

A commotion erupted from the road, and Willow barreled into the clearing. "My dogs! My dogs!"

Hearing Willow's voice, Apollo lumbered from his spot beneath the table and trotted toward her.

Sobbing, she fell to her knees and wrapped her arms around her pet's neck. Willow wiped her nose on Apollo's fur and looked up. "Luna?"

"She's right here. Safe." Heath reached down and rubbed the top of Luna's head with his knuckles.

West cleared his throat. "Heath saw the arsonist running from the scene, Willow."

Her eyes widened. "Did you see who it was?"

"He was covered up. Disguised." Heath pushed to his feet. "Do you have any more questions for me, West? I think we need to get Willow away from here until the… rubble cools, and the dogs don't need to be here."

"Away from here?" Willow turned her head to take in the smoldering heap that used to be her summer home. "Where are we supposed to go?"

West snapped his fingers. "Why don't you stay with Astrid? She and her son have Sherlock. I'm sure she won't mind another couple of dogs, and I know Olly won't. Astrid's brother is still in DC, so she and Olly have the place to themselves."

"I'm not going to descend on Astrid."

Heath said, "Stay at my hotel. I know there are vacancies."

"The Bay View Hotel is not going to allow a couple of mangy mutts to roam their halls."

"If you don't want to stay at Astrid's, at least leave the dogs with her, and you go to the hotel." West adjusted his hat and glanced at the ruined cabin. "Might be a good idea for you to stay in town until things get…settled."

"I guess." Willow chewed her bottom lip. "You don't think Astrid would object?"

"Absolutely not." West pulled out his phone. "I'll call her now. You sure you don't need medical attention, Heath?"

"I'm good."

Willow turned her gaze on him for the first time since she rushed onto the scene. She studied him from his still-tearing eyes to his soot-stained shirt and his battered arms. "Why are you here, and how'd you save the dogs?"

"Saw the smoke, noted the direction and ran over. Heard the dogs yelping in the cabin, so I let the arsonist go to get the dogs." He pulled up the hem of his T-shirt to wipe his face. "You're welcome."

"I mean, yeah, thanks for rescuing the dogs. What

kind of person drugs dogs and then sets fire to a house with them in it?"

Heath eased out a long breath. "Someone desperate to chase you off this property. If you don't have a place to live here, maybe they think they can force you out."

"That's not gonna work with me." She dug her heels into the dirt and wedged her hands on her hips, looking like she'd never leave.

"Maybe they don't know who they're dealing with." He tugged on Luna's collar. "Let's get out of here. Breathing in all this stuff can't be healthy."

West strolled over from where he was talking to the fire captain. "Definitely arson. The perpetrator used accelerant. Captain Foster said you can come back tomorrow to sift through the remains. Much of the living room survived intact, although I'm sure the water got to some things. The firefighters pulled out and bagged your laptop."

Willow waved her hand. "All that stuff is on the cloud. At least the dogs are safe."

"Which reminds me. Astrid said she has no problem taking the dogs, and you're more than welcome to stay with them."

"As long as the dogs are secured, I'll stay at the Bay View."

"Let Astrid know if you change your mind." West held up a finger. "Let me get your laptop."

Willow urged Apollo toward the road. "I might just have to wait until all these vehicles leave before getting the dogs in my truck. Where's your truck? I didn't see any other vehicles on my drive."

"I left it up the road. I didn't know where the fire was headed or how fast."

Batting at a bit of floating ash, Willow asked, "Do you want me to take you to your truck on my way to dropping off the dogs?"

"No. You go ahead. I'll make sure there's a room waiting for you at the hotel. I think the fire captain wants to talk to me again anyway."

West walked toward them, a large plastic bag swinging from his hand. "The firefighters grabbed a few other things, too, some files on your table that looked important."

"Thank you." Willow took the bag from West and, with the sheriff and Heath's help, coaxed the dogs past the fire engines to her truck and into the bed, giving Apollo a boost.

Heath waved her off with a sense of relief. Then, with just a couple of firefighters left on the scene, he plunged back into the forest and retraced his steps to Toby's place. He'd have to come back later to continue digging. He stashed his tools in the back of his truck and drove to his hotel.

The ready smile on the hotel clerk's face vanished when Heath strode into the lobby. He must look worse than he felt.

"A-are you okay, Mr. Bradford?"

"You know that fire on the other side of the island? I was there."

The guy clicked his tongue. "I heard about it. Just glad it didn't start a forest fire."

"No, but it badly damaged my friend's cabin, and she's going to need a place to stay. Do you know Willow Sands?"

"I know of her. We'd be happy to offer her something here."

"Put her room on my credit card."

The clerk clicked his computer's keyboard and, without looking up from the screen, said, "We have a room on your floor, just a few doors down."

"Even better. You can give me the key card. I'm meeting her here in the lobby."

The clerk finished the transaction and slid two cards across the counter. "Let me know if we can do anything else for you or Ms. Sands."

Heath jerked his thumb toward the alcove stocked with drinks and snacks to the right of the front desk. "Put a couple of waters on my room, too."

After he gathered two bottles of water from the fridge in the little market, Heath dropped down on a sofa in the lobby, exhaustion rolling through his body. Confusion and frustration beat against his temples.

His father had sent him here to pressure Toby Keel and Willow Sands into selling their properties to Bradford and Son, so the company could work with the Samish to develop the land for a casino on the island. At the time, Heath's father had no idea that Heath would discover that Toby had been the one sending him anonymous messages about his mother. As soon as Heath figured that out, his mission on the island changed.

The mission also changed as soon as he met up again with Willow Sands.

His eyes flew open as someone touched him on the shoulder. "Sorry it took so long." Willow's voice was quiet. "Had to get the dogs settled, but I think they'll be okay there. They're getting all kinds of attention from Astrid's son."

"That's good." Heath sat up and rubbed his eyes. "Can't believe I just dozed off in a hotel lobby."

She sat beside him and squeezed his thigh. "You were a hero saving Apollo and Luna. I think you deserve some rest—and some first aid."

"Just a few cuts and scratches." He squinted at his arms. "And some singed hair. Don't know how that happened. I wasn't running through the flames."

"Well, I smell like an ashtray, and I wasn't there as long as you were. There was hot debris floating around. A few of those fire flakes probably landed on you." She called to the front desk. "Hello! Do you have a first aid kit? Just a few bandages, antiseptic and burn cream."

"We do. Take it up to your room and return it whenever. I'll go get it." The clerk disappeared in the back and then walked over to them with a white plastic first aid kit.

Heath said under his breath, "I think he wants me out of his lobby."

"Of course he does. You look a mess." She prodded his shoulder. "Your place or mine?"

"Mine. I can change my clothes, too." He handed her the key cards to her room, and they took the elevator up to the fourth floor, where her room sat a few doors down from his.

He flashed his card at the door and pushed it open. "You can check out your room. I'll be fine. Put your things away."

"No way." She squeezed past him and placed the first aid kit on the credenza, dropping the plastic bag West had given her. She flipped the kit open and rifled through the contents. "You should wash your injuries with soap and water first."

"Good idea." He walked into the bathroom and whistled. "No wonder I scared that hotel clerk. I look like hell."

"There's some burn ointment in here, some antibiotic cream, bandages, ibuprofen."

Heath pulled his T-shirt over his head and hitched it over the shower rod. He ran warm water in the sink and soaped up a washcloth with the bar. He ran it across the scratches and cuts on his hands and arms, wincing at the stings.

Blotting himself dry with a towel, he slung it over his shoulder, then splashed some water on his face. Finally, he ran his wet hands through his hair. The next best thing to taking a shower.

When he walked out of the bathroom, Willow was standing in front of an array of first aid items. She glanced up, and he felt the heat from her gaze that swept across his bare chest almost as intensely as he'd felt the fire in her cabin today.

Tapping the credenza, she said, "Burn ointment?"

"On the backs of my hands and a few spots on my neck."

"Sit." She nodded at the bed.

He perched on the edge of the mattress and held out his hands while she plucked up a white tube. She squeezed some gel on the tips of her fingers and dabbed at some red marks and blisters on his hands. Then she shuffled closer and tapped at a few spots on his throat.

She spun around suddenly and dropped the ointment on the credenza. "Do you need antibiotic cream for those cuts?"

He inspected the red welts on his arms and one slice where the glass from the window cut him. "Just on this one spot, I think. I can get that if you put a little cream on my hand."

"I got it." She turned back around, pinching another tube between her fingers. She leaned over him and patted some of the cream on the cut. "This one's different from the others. This one is a cut. The other smaller ones are scratches. You got those from reaching through the shattered glass?"

He got those from racing through the woods, and she probably suspected that. "No clue where those came from. They might even be old scratches."

Finished tending to his wounds, Willow packed up the first aid kit and ducked down to the mini fridge. She held up a beer. "I think you deserve this."

"Sure." Heath yawned. "Join me?"

"If you don't mind paying minibar prices for a bottle of beer."

"This could be considered a business meeting. I'll expense it." He gestured for the bottle, and she handed it to him.

While he stayed on the bed, she sat on the desk chair with her beer. "What do you think is going on? Why would someone set fire to my cabin?"

"Probably to put pressure on you." The few sips of alcohol trickled down to his nerve endings and dulled them. He'd been so tired the past few days, creeping out, digging holes. And he didn't even know what he was looking for. His lids felt heavy, but he took another slug of beer.

"Does this person or group think because I don't have a place to live on the island that I'll just give up?"

"How'd your meeting go with the attorney? Did he shed any light on the situation?"

"Not really. The property is legally mine according to the will, but it doesn't mean the Keels can't challenge." Willow picked at the label on her bottle, opened her mouth and then shut it. Whatever she was going to say, she'd decided against it.

He couldn't blame her for that. Plenty of secrets swirling around this island, and he didn't know if he could handle one more.

He finished off the beer in two more gulps and collapsed, flat on the bed, holding the bottle loosely in his hand. "I think that fire did me in. I was already tired, but that adrenaline spike drained me."

Willow took the bottle from his hand, and he heard her voice through a drowsy haze. "I'm going to let you get some sleep. You started the day tired, and it doesn't appear that it got any better for you. Thanks for booking the room."

As she closed the door with a whisper, he was already trailing off to sleep.

WILLOW THUMBED ON a light as she walked into her hotel room. She placed the plastic bag on the desk. It contained her laptop, Toby's files and a few toiletry items and food that Astrid had pressed upon her. She fished out her computer and a sandwich. She was actually more grateful that the firefighter saved those files than the laptop—especially after what she'd learned from her mother.

She plugged in the computer, and it flickered to life. She entered the Wi-Fi password from the hotel and launched a search engine. A quick probe confirmed that just because a person owned the surface of a property didn't mean that person also owned the mineral rights on that property.

Her exploration had also delivered the bad news that the

owner of the mineral rights could exploit those rights, regardless of the wishes of the property owner. Big trouble.

Who else knew about the nickel vein and that she probably didn't own it?

She slumped in the chair and unwrapped the sandwich Astrid had packed for her. Peeking inside the pita bread, Willow smiled. Knowing her preferences, Astrid had slathered the pita with hummus and added some diced tomato, onion and cucumber. What a mom.

She devoured the sandwich, then bit into an apple, her leg bouncing up and down. After her cabin had been ransacked and set on fire, she couldn't just sit here. Her gaze wandered to the bottle of water Heath had procured for her, and she grabbed it.

What had he been doing near her cabin? She'd taken note of the road when she left for Astrid's and didn't see his truck parked there. He must've been at Toby's for some reason.

She noted the setting sun out the window, gulped back some water and shoved the hotel key in her back pocket. With both Lee and Heath nosing around that property, she figured it was time she did her own reconnaissance out there. She'd already signed the paperwork Jason had given her. Hell, she owned that land.

Before she slipped out the door, she grabbed Toby's files and shoved them into the hotel safe. She couldn't trust anyone right now.

She made the forty-five-minute drive back across the island and parked on the road that led to Toby's trail. Tilting her head back, she sniffed as she hiked in, the acrid odor of the fire still permeating the air.

By the time she reached the clearing where Toby's

cabin huddled, the sun had sent out its last rays, caught in the mist that hugged the ground. Willow's flashlight played over the front of the cabin. Had Heath broken into Toby's house after she and he had left earlier? Had he seen something during their search?

She stomped up the steps and tried the door. The knob resisted her attempts to turn it, and she didn't have her key. Hunching forward, she cupped her hand over the window and peered inside. Nothing looked disturbed or any different from this afternoon's visit. She turned around, and leaning against the door, she scanned the front of the property. The yellow caution tape had sunk to the ground, weighed down by the moisture in the air.

She descended the porch and circled behind the property. That was where Heath had come from on the night of Toby's death. Had he come back today to finish the business he started?

She flicked the light toward the two maples towering near the edge of the forest. Heath had seemed unusually interested in those trees today. In fact, his whole demeanor had changed after they left the cabin.

She was about to shine her light on the other side of the cabin when some lumpy objects on the ground near the trees caught her attention. Holding her flashlight in front of her, she crept toward the maples.

When her light picked up mounds of dirt next to several holes in the ground, she almost dropped her flashlight. Had Heath been digging out here? She didn't remember seeing this disruption a few nights ago. But had she walked back here? Maybe Toby had dug those holes.

She could think of only two reasons to dig holes in the ground: either you were burying something or retrieving something. She scuffed toward the pits and knocked some dirt back into one with the toe of her hiking boot as she peered down with her light. Dirt and more dirt.

Had the digger found what he was looking for? Or had a fire interrupted his search?

She knew where Toby kept his tools, and she crossed the back of the property to a dilapidated shed, its door hanging on one rusty hinge. She pulled open the door, which squealed in protest, and lit up the cobwebby interior with her light.

"Two can play this game." She grabbed a shovel, which had seen better days, leaning against the wall of the shed and dragged it outside. She tromped back to the site of the little treasure hunt, the shovel heavy on her shoulder.

She placed her flashlight on a log, pointing in the direction of the excavation area, and plunged the shovel in the dirt. As soon as the shovel met solid resistance, she knew why the initial excavator had stopped. You couldn't dig any farther once you hit the rock beneath the dirt.

She shuffled to the right and tensed her muscles to have another go. As she lifted the shovel, a loud popping noise startled her at the same time she felt something hot whiz by her ear.

Someone was shooting at her.

Chapter Ten

The sound of gunfire had Heath diving for cover on the trail, but Willow's scream juiced him up. He jumped to his feet and ran toward the sounds, pulling his own gun from his jacket pocket. When he reached the clearing of Toby's cursed property, he dropped to the ground again and army-crawled toward the cabin. He called out, "Willow! Are you okay, Willow?"

He got a muffled sob as an answer, and then… "I'm okay. Was that a gun?"

. "That was a gun. Where are you?"

"I'm behind the house, over by the maple trees you noticed today."

Heath swore under his breath. "I'm by the cabin's porch. Can you crawl over here? Flat on the ground."

"Wh-what if the shooter comes out of the woods and finishes what he started?"

"I have a gun." He yelled loud enough for every creature in the forest to hear him. "Stay down. If someone comes out of those trees, I'll take care of him."

He heard scraping and scuffling noises, so he shimmied toward the back corner of the cabin. The rising moon shed enough light on the scene that he could see Willow make her way toward him.

When she reached his position, he wrapped an arm around her. "Sure you're okay?"

"No, I'm not okay, but I'm not hurt. Let's get the hell out of here."

He pushed her toward the trail that led to the road and duckwalked in a crouch behind her, his weapon ready for an assault. After a few feet of scrabbling along the forest floor, he poked her thigh. "Get up slowly and then run like hell. I've got your back."

Willow galloped through the woods like a sprightly fawn, leaping over roots and fallen logs, bobbing and weaving away from the branches that reached out for her. Heath followed her at a slower and much clumsier pace, but he kept his gun ready in case someone decided to come after them.

When Willow reached the road, she continued running to her truck, which he'd spotted earlier. When he'd seen it, he almost turned around, knowing full well she'd find the holes he'd dug previously. He was happy now he'd followed that sixth sense in his head, telling him to go after her.

When he caught up to her, bent over, hands on her knees, panting, he leaned against her truck. "What happened out there?"

She coughed. "I'm not talking here. Meet me in my hotel room. You have a lot of explaining to do."

He holstered his gun and tapped the phone in his pocket. "Should we call 911? Someone fired a weapon at you, and I doubt it was a stray hunter."

"Wild turkey hunting ended in the spring, and other game hunting doesn't start until fall. Summer is a no-go season, but I guess human prey is year-round." She grabbed his hand hovering over his pocket. "Don't call the police—at least, not until we talk."

"Fine by me." He blew out a long breath. The last thing he wanted to do was call the police and try to explain his excavation site on Toby Keel's property.

He followed her truck back to the hotel, with one eye on his rearview mirror checking for a tail. He didn't believe anyone would be following them—whoever shot at Willow knew exactly who she was and probably where she was staying. But did they know why she was digging? Had they been waiting for Heath to show up?

By the time he pulled into the hotel parking lot, next to Willow standing beside her truck, he'd decided to come clean to her. Why not? He didn't owe Toby Keel anything.

They walked side by side into the hotel, silently. When they got to the elevator, Heath turned to Willow. "Why'd you go out there tonight?"

The doors opened. Willow entered the car and jabbed the button for the fourth floor. "I didn't believe your story this afternoon. I figured you'd been at Toby's place again. I just didn't know why. I still don't know why."

When they got to her room, she sat on the edge of a chair, folding her arms.

He took the corner of the bed. "You know I was digging on Toby's land."

"What are you looking for?"

"My mother."

Willow's mouth dropped open, and she stopped kicking her leg. "Your mother is buried on Toby's property?"

"I don't know." The hand he plowed through his hair came away dusted with soot. He rubbed his palms together. "Toby knew something about my mother's disappearance. He started sending me cryptic notes several months ago. When I pinned him down, shortly before I showed up on Dead Falls Island, he told me that he and my mother had been friendly. That they'd had a special relationship."

"An intimate one?" Willow chewed on the side of her thumb. "They were having an affair?"

"I'm not sure about that. He said my mother would confide in him about her bad marriage, her unhappiness, her depression. He tried to help her, but she was determined to kill herself."

"Wasn't much help. Do you believe him? Did he tell you your mother committed suicide?"

He nodded as a sharp pain shot through the back of his head. "He said she'd spent a lot of time at his place to get away, and when he got home one day, he found her dead."

Willow gasped and covered her mouth. "Why didn't he call the police?"

"Because she told him she just wanted to disappear." Hunching forward, he braced his elbows on his knees and clasped his hands.

"And then what? He buried her behind his house. He kept mum when everyone was looking for her." Willow wound a strand of hair around her finger, her gaze never leaving his face.

"He never claimed he buried her."

"Then why are you digging? Where is she?"

"That's what I was trying to find out the night he died. I didn't go to his cabin to talk about the land deal. I told him I wanted answers." He stood up and shoved his hand in his pocket, withdrawing the frayed piece of paper. He thrust it toward Willow. "This was his last note to me."

She smoothed out the paper and read the words aloud. "'Where the mist meets the earth, between the giant maples.'"

"He told me I'd find my mother there. I don't know if he meant her actual body, something belonging to her, or if he just meant it metaphorically. I went to his cabin to find out."

"Oh my God, Heath." She crumpled the paper in her fist and moved from the chair to a position next to him on the bed. "That's terrible. He's evil for putting you through this, for playing games with you."

His heart thumped painfully in his chest. "Do you think he was playing games? Maybe this was all some sick joke to punish me for being Brad Bradford's son."

"Toby was a strange man. I don't think anyone ever really knew him. My father probably got the closest to him. Even my mother shared with me today that Toby was a womanizer. Got the impression he may have hit on her, too." She tossed the balled-up note onto the table. "Maybe your mom rejected his advances. Maybe this is his revenge on her, on you. Who knows?"

"I have to find out for myself." Heath pinched the bridge of his nose.

"And to do that, you're going to excavate Toby's property—I mean, my property."

"I didn't think it would be such a big deal to dig a few holes...but someone doesn't want me digging."

Clasping her hands between her knees, she twisted her head to look at him. "You mean that bullet wasn't meant for me?"

"I mean, someone has an eye on Toby's property, saw you digging and took a potshot at you. Maybe they didn't even mean to hit you. They just wanted to drive you away."

"Like the fire drove me away." She pulled her bottom lip between her teeth. "Do you think the two incidents are related? I'm the common denominator. It might not have anything to do with the holes. With Toby gone, why would anyone care about your mother? Sorry—except you, of course."

"I don't know." He pressed the heels of his hands into his eye sockets. He'd dozed off when Willow left his room but hadn't slept very long, his dreams compelling him to wake up and finish what he'd started.

Willow encircled his wrist with her fingers. "You know you still have soot in your hair and your hands. Now you're getting it all over your face, and you still look exhausted."

"This hasn't been the best day of my life." But her understanding and gentle touch had just made it a whole lot better.

"Have you even eaten since your heroic rescue of the dogs? Unless you grabbed something between your nap and your heroic rescue of me at the excavation site, I don't think so." She nudged him. "Go take a shower, and I'll order you some room service."

He pushed up to his feet. "428."

"What does that mean?" She jumped up and grabbed the phone by the side of the bed.

"That's my room number for the room service. Burger and fries are fine and another beer, unless you want to give me one from your minibar."

She placed two hands flat on his back and pushed

him. "You can clean up and eat here. That shooting incident still has me rattled. I'd rather not be alone right now, and you do have a weapon."

"Are you sure?" He glanced at her bathroom door. He didn't want to leave her alone, either, but his motivation was purely selfish.

"I'm sure. I haven't even had time to use the shower yet, so knock yourself out." She waved the phone at him. "I'll order the food."

As she spoke into the phone, Heath toed off his shoes and shut himself in the bathroom. He stripped off his clothes and stepped under the warm spray of the shower, the coils in his shoulders loosening for the first time today.

He should've told Willow sooner. It felt good to have someone on his side.

WILLOW ORDERED THE food and collapsed into the chair. Whatever motive she'd imagined Heath had for digging those holes, looking for his dead mother was not on her bingo card. What was Toby playing at? Had he told Heath some tall tale about Jessica Bradford to distract him from the land deal?

News like that would take Heath right out of the game of pressuring Toby to sell his land—and it had. His meeting with Toby that night was supposed to be about his mother, not the casino deal.

Was that another reason Toby didn't want to sell the land? He didn't want the developers to make any discoveries on his property, like a dead body.

With Toby dead, who else would want to stop that discovery? Heath could be completely wrong about the shooter. That bullet could've been meant for her, regardless of what she was doing. The fact that she was back on the land could've been motivation enough for someone to take a shot at her.

The shower stopped, and Willow held her breath. For a second, she'd thought Heath would refuse her offer of showering and eating in her room. He had a perfectly good shower two doors down. She knew playing to his protective instincts would get him to stay.

Was she really afraid to stay here by herself? She didn't believe the shooter or the arsonist, whether that was the same person or not, would track her down to the hotel and finish his business, but it eased her mind to have Heath here.

The hair dryer whirred from behind the closed door, and Willow shut her eyes for a second, indulging in the fantasy of Heath Bradford naked in her bathroom. That vision could keep her warm on a cold, rainy Seattle night.

The door cracked open, and Heath stuck his head into the room. "Is the food here yet?"

She spied a lot of bare skin in the sliver of that opening and swallowed. "Not yet. Take your time."

Five minutes later, when he stepped out of the bathroom on a cloud of citrus-scented steam, he'd left just his feet bare. The T-shirt and clean pair of jeans he'd changed into after the fire covered the rest of him.

He cocked his head back and forth as if releasing a kink in his neck. "That feels better. I'm halfway to human."

"Eating a cow is going to complete the process?"

"I think that should about do it."

"Start with one of these." She held out a cold beer to him, the cap popped.

Studying the label on the bottle, he said, "I don't know. The last time I drank one of these, it knocked me out, and you sneaked back to Toby's to find out what I was up to."

"You were dead on your feet then. You've been revived by a gunshot." She clinked the neck of her bottle against his and took a gulp of beer.

The knock on the door startled them, and they both rose to answer. Heath held out a hand. "I'll get it."

Pressing a hand against the door, he peered through the peephole first and then stepped back to open it.

A hotel employee rolled a cart, a white tablecloth flapping around it, into the room and parked it by the window. After he transferred the contents of the cart to the table, Heath thanked him and handed him a wad of cash.

When Heath saw the waiter out of the room, he returned and whipped the silver domes off the two plates. He snatched a french fry from a heap of them stacked next to a mile-high burger and nudged the other plate, overflowing with a garden salad, in her direction. "Is this yours?"

"It actually came with the burger and fries. It's all yours." She wrinkled her nose.

"Did you eat before swinging your shovel at the ground?" He rubbed his hands together and pulled a chair up to the table, setting his beer next to the plate of food on the tray.

"Astrid packed some food for me when I dropped off the dogs."

"Nuts and berries?" He cut into the burger, and pink juices flooded the plate.

"Hilarious." She jabbed a finger at the mess on his plate. "I ordered you a medium rare. Too pink?"

"It's perfect." He tapped the edge of the salad plate with his fork. "Help yourself. I doubt I'm going to eat that."

Picking up a fork, she took the seat to his left. "Do you need this fork?"

"I'm a real man. I eat with my hands." He pounded his chest.

"Okay, Tarzan."

She let him eat in peace as she picked at the salad. This was the most relaxed she'd seen him all day. Why would Toby tell him he could find his mother here on the island? It seemed almost like torture.

Heath practically inhaled one half of the burger and started on the second half. He washed a bite down with his beer and said, "Do you want some fries?"

"I'm fine." She dabbed her mouth with a napkin. "Are you going to keep digging? What if you don't find anything?"

"I'll keep digging. My father was satisfied to have my mother declared dead a few years ago, but I can't let go as easily as he did."

"What exactly does he think happened to your mother?"

"He believes she committed suicide and made sure nobody found her body." He pushed away his plate with the rest of his burger.

She'd meant to allow him to eat without dwelling on his mother or Toby's sadistic clues. She picked up one of the fries and nibbled on the end. "Why would she do that?"

"I don't know." He raised and dropped his shoulders quickly. "My father said she always threatened to go out that way. And I'm not saying my father was lying. My mother was an unstable woman, but you know…"

"I do know. She's still your mom." She plucked up another fry and held it out to him. "I'm sorry. I didn't mean to ruin your appetite. Finish your food."

His gaze shifted from the french fry in her hand to her eyes as he leaned forward and opened his mouth. She put the fry to his lips, and he took in the whole thing, his salty lips meeting the tips of her fingers.

She didn't snatch her hand away. Instead, she traced his mouth with the pad of her finger.

His whiskey eyes darkened. "Would you kiss me now, even though I just ate a hamburger?"

She raised her eyes to the ceiling. "I think my vegetarian taste buds could handle that."

Tossing his napkin onto the tray, he stood up and circled behind her chair. He leaned over her, tilted her head back and kissed her upside down. He deepened the kiss, stroking her neck with his hand as her heart thundered in her chest.

She'd imagined a few kisses from Heath Bradford—then and now—but even her fantasies never felt like this. A tingling sensation started in her toes and buzzed through her entire body, although his mouth never left hers and his hand didn't trail down any farther than her throat.

Straightening up, he moved his hands to her shoulders, tucked them beneath her sweater and massaged her skin. The touch of his hands against her flesh set the blood in her veins afire, and the heat coursed through her body.

Closing her eyes, she released a sound from the back of her throat—something between a sigh and a groan.

He returned to the front of her chair and knelt before her. "You don't know how long I've wanted to touch you."

She touched the dark stubble on his jaw. "Two days?"

Running his hands along the outsides of her thighs, he said, "A lot longer than that. I was just a stupid kid who didn't know how to approach the most fascinating girl I'd ever encountered."

Her lips twisted into a smile. "I'm sure your popular friends would've had a lot to say if you'd started dating the Tree Girl."

"Maybe. I wasn't as bold or independent as you. Following the clues to my mother's disappearance instead of doing my father's bidding is the closest I've come to rebelling against him."

"Is that what this is?" She cupped his jaw. "Seducing me to get back at Daddy?"

"This is—" he kissed her forehead "—me—" he kissed her cheek "—seducing you—" he kissed her throat, where her pulse throbbed "—because I want you more than anything right now."

She draped her arms over his shoulders. "Then be bold and independent and take me."

With a grin on his face and a light in his eyes, Heath scooped her off the chair and hoisted her in his arms. She wrapped her legs around his waist as he carried her to the bed. He swung around so that he was sitting on the edge of the mattress with her curled around his body.

He sealed his mouth over hers in a kiss that seared her soul, his pent-up longing drowning her previous reservations about him, about her feelings for him, her long-smoldering desire for the teenage boy leaping to an urgent need for the adult man.

Heath brushed a loose strand of hair away from Willow's face, his touch gentle and full of affection. His thumb traced a delicate path along her cheek, and she closed her eyes, savoring the sensation.

Willow placed her hands against Heath's chest, feeling the steady rhythm of his heart beneath her fingertips, his body heat ferocious beneath the material of his shirt. She pulled the shirt over his head and tossed it over her shoulder.

She dipped her head and placed a trail of kisses along his collarbone, skimming her teeth along his flesh.

He fell against the bed, and she straddled him as he unbuttoned her shirt and peeled it from her shoulders. She unhooked her bra for him, and his hands cupped her breasts. He ran the pads of his thumbs over her peaked nipples, and she squirmed against him.

He sucked in a breath. "You're driving me crazy."

Curling his hands around her waist, he lifted her from his lap and positioned her on the bed next to him. His clumsy fingers grappled with the button on her jeans, and she swatted away his hands.

"We'll be here all night if I leave this to you."

"What's wrong with that?" With a much defter touch, he unbuttoned his own jeans and pulled them off, along with his black briefs.

She left her jeans gaping as she drank in the sight of his naked body stretched out on the bed. "I'm pretty sure you didn't look like this in high school."

"I didn't." He tugged on a lock of her hair hanging over her shoulder. "Now who's taking too long?"

She whipped off her jeans and snuggled next to him. Heath's hands moved to the small of her back, drawing her closer until there was no space left between them. Their bodies molded together, fitting perfectly like pieces of a long-lost puzzle. Their lips met again with a newfound urgency, a shared yearning fueled by the danger and uncertainty of the past few days and the desire to connect with someone safe.

As their kisses deepened, the room seemed to disappear for Willow, leaving only the two of them, lost in each other's embrace. Dead Falls Island, the land, Toby, the secrets, all of it faded into insignificance, and all that mattered was the two of them in this moment.

Heath's hands roamed across her body, and he brought her to climax with his touch. Before the haze of content completely settled, she reached for him and guided him inside, where he opened her and filled her at the same time, bringing her a sense of completeness.

As he plunged into her over and over, she curled her fingers into his backside, digging her nails into his flexing muscle. He released, and she wrapped her legs around him, riding him until the end. They lay side by side, their limbs entwined, murmuring silly things to each other until they drifted off.

What seemed like seconds later, Willow jerked awake. She squinted at the clock to discover they'd been asleep for about an hour.

Heath's arm draped heavily over her hip, and Willow scooted away, trying not to wake him. His nighttime excursions had left him exhausted. She didn't want to keep the poor guy awake, even though her greedy gaze skimmed across his body splayed on the bed.

She tiptoed to the bathroom to freshen up. Then she yanked one of the fluffy white hotel robes from a hook on the door and wrapped herself in it before returning to the main room.

She cleaned up Heath's meal from the table and set the tray on the floor outside the door in the hallway. She grabbed a water from the mini fridge and sat down at the table, sliding Toby's file folders in front of her.

The game Toby and Heath were playing explained why Heath had been interested in entering Toby's cabin with her, but she got to his files first. If Toby did have anything about Jessica Bradford in his papers, she'd share it with Heath. She couldn't imagine what he'd been going through. At least when her mother took off, Willow had known exactly why and where she'd been headed.

The desk lamp illuminated the top of the folder she'd thumbed through before. It contained receipts and not much more. By the time she reached the third file, things got more interesting. It held legal documents about the property, verifying the terms of Toby's possession.

With a renewed sense of determination and Heath breathing heavily behind her, she dived into the next folder. Her pulse picked up when she recognized documents containing geologist reports and maps. Toby knew about the nickel on the property. Had her father left the rights to Toby but not the property? If so, Toby's attorney, Jason Hart, didn't know anything about it.

When she got to the bottom of the sheaf of papers, Willow's heart skipped a beat. She picked up a document and held it beneath the lamp. It was a mineral deed.

She scanned the legalese until she reached a name at the bottom. An icy finger seemed to stab her chest when she read the name, and her gaze slowly turned to the man sleeping in her bed—the man who owned the mineral rights to her property.

Chapter Eleven

A bright light flashed down on him, and Heath squeezed his eyes, seeing black dots behind his lids. An insistent voice prodded his eardrums in time to a determined prodding of his shoulder.

"Wake up. You knew. You knew all this time."

Willow's words pierced his sleep haze, and he peeled one eye open to find her hovering over him like an avenging angel, her lips pursed and a glint in her eye. He'd remembered a much different look on her face when he made love to her.

He closed his eye again and rubbed it. When he opened both, the same sight still met his gaze. He pulled the tangled sheet over the bottom half of his body. "What? What's going on?"

"This." Clutching a piece of paper in her fist, she waved it in his face. "The mineral deed to my property. *My* property."

"Okay." His eyes darted around the room looking for the punch line. "The mineral deed?"

"You knew. All this time you knew, and that's why you were digging around." She crumpled up the paper and threw it at him. "You didn't have to dig. It's on the map. It's all on the map."

Heath sat up, scrunching up a pillow behind his back. "I don't know what you're talking about, Willow. You're going to have to start at the beginning."

"Me? Why don't you start at the beginning—the beginning where you bamboozled my father out of those rights."

"I didn't bamboozle your father out of anything. Can we just…? Can I just…?" He plucked at the sheet covering his nakedness. "Let me put some clothes on."

"Please do." She crossed her arms and pivoted toward the window as he staggered from the bed.

He swept up his jeans and briefs on his way to the bathroom. He splashed some water on his face, sluiced back his hair and rinsed out his mouth for good measure.

When he eased open the door, he felt as if he was entering the lion's den. What had set her off? What mineral rights was she talking about?

"Is it safe?" He poked his head into the room.

Willow spun around, dragging her hair into a ponytail and clutching it like she was going to pull it out. "I dug through Toby's paperwork some more and found something very interesting."

"Obviously. Something about mineral rights on Toby's land."

"I already knew about that." She waved her hand up and down in his direction. "You can put your shirt on, too."

"Okay." This must be bad. He stepped over the bed-covers in disarray on the floor, his head down in search of his T-shirt.

"Here it is." She ducked down and picked up his shirt

where she'd thrown it before in a moment of passion. She chucked it at him, and he caught it in one hand.

A different kind of passion had her enflamed now.

He pulled the shirt over his head. "You already knew about mineral rights on the land? You didn't tell me that."

"I didn't—" She scooped up the crumpled piece of paper from the floor and bobbled it in her hand. "I didn't want to tell anyone just yet. Didn't want the property to become even more valuable to outsiders, but now I know."

"What is it you think you know?"

"You own the mineral rights, and you were aware of that all along." The finger she leveled at him felt like a poke in his eyeball.

"Honestly, Willow. I have no idea what you're talking about. I didn't know Toby's property had any minerals on it and neither did Bradford and Son." The last words stuck in his throat. Had his father known? "What kind of minerals are we talking about?"

She spit out one word. "Nickel."

"Can I see the paper?" He held out his hand, and she slammed the balled-up wad into his palm.

He picked open the mass and smoothed it on the table. "A mineral deed. I've seen a few of these with some other land deals—not this one, though."

"Keep reading, all the way to the bottom."

He ran his finger over the legal verbiage until he reached his own name at the bottom of the page. "I'll be damned."

"That's all you have to say about it?" She narrowed her eyes, and her nostrils flared. "Why were you digging? All you had to do was visit some county clerk's office to get the maps and a copy of this deed. Toby has the map, too. I'm sure it details the location of the ore deposits."

"I'm sure I could have, and I'm sure the map is useful—except I didn't know that I had the mineral rights. Look—" he drilled a finger into the middle of the paper "—if I'd known about this, I would've already played that card to get the property over to Bradford and Son. Can you imagine the leverage I'd have?"

"Do have." Her chin jutted forward. "The leverage you *do* have, Heath."

"I don't care about that now. I want you to believe me, Willow. I knew nothing about any nickel on that property. I was digging because Toby was sending me mysterious notes about my mother's disappearance. If you don't believe me, you can go out and have a look at the Misty Hollow property. I was digging there first before you told me Toby referred to his property as *where the mist meets the earth*. I thought that clue meant Misty Hollow."

She sank onto the edge of the tousled bed like a deflated balloon. Maybe he'd gotten through to her. Covering her face, she fell back. "Make it make sense. Why would my father deed his property over to Toby with the stipulation that upon his death the surface property go to me, while knowing all the while that he'd already deeded the mineral rights to the same property over to you?"

"Wait." He picked up the paper and brought it close to his face. "Your father or Toby left the mineral rights to me?"

"It must've been my father. I don't think he gave Toby that kind of control over the property. Toby didn't have the power to leave the property to whomever he wanted, and I'm sure the mineral rights were already tied up."

"Why would he do that?" Heath hunched over the open folder and paged through the rest of the papers. Willow had been correct. Several of these pages contained maps. Who else knew about this?

"You tell me." She rolled onto her side, propping her head up, chin in hand. "You were the one having secret conversations with him when you were a teen."

"Secret conversations? H-he was just helping me out at the time I lost my mother." Heath's nose stung, and he cleared his throat. He was done showing vulnerability to Willow. "Your father was an adult voice of reason and compassion, someone who wasn't my father. We certainly never discussed property. I probably even told him I had no intention of going into business with my father and Bradford Associates."

"Yeah, how'd that go? Bradford Associates is now Bradford and Son. Bet my father never imagined that."

He cut a hand through the air. "Let's just stop with the accusations for a second. We don't even know if these documents Toby had are legal. You saw his cabin. Complete mess. This stuff could be old and out-of-date."

"There's a way we can find out. I've been doing a little research on mineral rights since I discovered the land contained these nickel deposits."

"When Toby's lawyer told you about the mineral rights, why couldn't he tell you who owned them then? Why the big secret?"

She swung her legs off the bed and planted her feet on the floor. "Jason Hart's not the one who told me."

"Then someone else does know about this. Who told you?"

"My mother."

His head snapped to attention. "Why didn't she tell you I owned the rights?"

She lifted her shoulders to her ears. "She didn't know you did. She just assumed I was in the know and would inherit the rights along with the property, but she didn't seem surprised that I didn't have a clue about the nickel."

"Your father, Toby, my father—why all the secrets?" He scuffed his knuckles against his chin.

Did his father know about the mineral rights? He found it hard to believe Brad Bradford wouldn't research every aspect of every property that came across his desk for a deal. And knowing about the rights, he must know who owned them. That kind of information was public record, but you had to know about it to look for it. His father had his ways.

Willow hopped up from the bed and took a turn around the room, tightening the belt on the robe that enveloped her small frame. "Do you think Toby was leading you on a wild-goose chase in a search for your mother when all along he knew about the nickel? Maybe he wanted you to dig to find the nickel deposits."

Heath's gut churned. "That's assuming I'd know what a nickel deposit looked like if I plunged my shovel into it. I wouldn't have any idea. I was a business major, not a geology major. I don't know how Toby could expect me to dig a hole on his property and say *eureka*! And why would he even go that route? If he wanted me to know I owned the mineral rights on his property, he should've told me."

"How does this affect the casino deal?" Willow reached past him to grab a bottle of water next to the files on the desk. How long had she been awake, poring over these documents?

"I would think this would put an end to the casino deal. I mean, if whoever owns the mineral rights, and I'm not saying it's me, decides to exploit the nickel, that would end any plans for hotels and restaurants to support the casino." Heath smacked the table with his palm. "I think that's the first order of business. We need to find out who really owns those mineral rights."

"And if it is you?" Willow's gaze never left his face as she tipped the bottle into her mouth.

"Before anything else, I wanna know why. Why would your father put those rights in my name?" He drummed his thumbs against the edge of the desk. "Something happened on this island at the time my mother disappeared, maybe even before, and it's now rearing its ugly head, causing mayhem and violence. We need to sort it out before someone else gets hurt."

"Maybe it's the sorting out that'll get someone hurt."

"It could be, but we have to take that risk." He rose from the table, pushing the folders away from him. He grabbed his shoes and headed for the door.

Willow called after him, "Y-you're going back to your own room?"

He kept plodding toward the exit, his gaze straight ahead, willing himself not to turn around. "We both need to get some sleep. We'll attack this tomorrow."

"Heath, what about…what about what happened between us?"

He pressed down on the handle of the door and yanked it open. "I think that was a mistake."

THE FOLLOWING MORNING, Willow stood in front of the mirror brushing her teeth. She'd screwed up big-time last night. She'd seen that deed with Heath's name and lost it. If only she'd taken a breather before shining a spotlight in his face to wake him up like the grand inquisitor.

What he'd said made sense. If he was already aware that he held the mineral rights to the property, he wouldn't be digging little holes in the ground. He would use the map and do a proper survey.

Of course, he could've known about the nickel deposits *and* be searching for his mother. She spit in the sink and rinsed her mouth. Even after making love with him last night, she still had her doubts. What he'd said on his way out the door was right. Having sex with Heath had been a big mistake.

From here on out, they'd better keep their relationship in the business zone. At least he still felt comfortable including her in his search for answers. His answers could turn out to be her answers. Someone had searched her place, burned it down and taken a shot at her. That couldn't be because Heath owned the mineral rights to her property, but she felt the two were somehow connected.

Her cell phone rang in the main room, and she jumped. When Heath left last night, he promised they'd attack this together but hadn't mentioned who would call whom. Her heart dropped when she spun the phone around to face her and saw her insurance company calling her back.

While she finished relaying the details of the fire to her insurance agent, someone tapped on her door. She wrapped up the call and peeked through the hole. She eased out a long breath when she saw Heath on the other side.

She flung open the door. "It's safe."

He gave her a tight smile and held up a white bag and a cardboard tray containing two cups. "Bagels and coffee—chai tea for you, if you drink it."

"I do, thanks." She ushered him into the room, relieved she'd taken the time to straighten the bedcovers after their roll in the hay last night. They didn't need that awkwardness between them right now.

He set the bag on the table and took one of the cups. "I did a little research last night when I got back to my room."

So while she'd been tossing and turning, alternately reliving and anguishing over their moments together, he'd been...researching. "I'll bet you did," she murmured under her breath.

Raising his eyebrows, he said, "Sorry?"

She coughed. "That's good. What did you discover?"

"I found out that we can research mineral rights on the Mineral and Land Records System website. You can also get the same information faster if you go to the county records office."

"Faster? Our county records office is on San Juan, isn't it?" She popped the lid from her tea and inhaled its spicy aroma before taking a sip.

"Literally a fifteen-minute flight from Dead Falls Island."

"I know you haven't lived here for a while, but San Juan Airlines doesn't make that trip every hour, or even every day."

"I've already arranged the flight." He snapped his fingers. "Private pilot is taking us over in about an hour. Will you be ready?"

She glanced down at her jeans, still smudged with soot from yesterday. "I was hoping to buy a few clothes this morning in case mine are burned to a crisp or water-logged."

"We can stop somewhere on the way to the airport." He opened the white bag and shook out a little container of cream cheese and some packets of butter. "That's why I brought breakfast with me, so we could get going."

"Are they expecting us at the county office?" She flattened a paper napkin on the table and hooked her finger around a poppy seed bagel from the bag.

"I arranged that, too." He claimed the remaining bagel and dug a plastic knife into the cream cheese. "I just need to bring my ID and a legal description of the property, which you should have from Jason Hart, right?"

"I'll bring my whole set of documents from Jason if that's what it takes." She smeared some cream cheese on one half of her bagel and scraped off some poppy seeds with her fingernail. "I'm sorry about last night—not the first part. I'm sorry about the second part...later. When I saw your name on that mineral deed, I don't know. I kinda saw red."

"You jumped to the worst conclusion...about someone you just slept with." He took a big bite of his bagel, and the cream cheese squished out the sides. He had to lick it off with his tongue—damn him.

She closed her eyes to block out the sight of his tongue and the sensations it stirred up in her belly...and below. "I think that's why I went there."

"You normally interrogate men in your bed?" His tongue darted from his mouth, catching a crumb in the corner of it.

He was just torturing her now, and she deserved it.

"No. I guess my first thought was that you'd taken advantage of me, that you'd kept this secret from me."

He dropped his bagel. "You think I took advantage of you last night?"

"Not at all." She'd meant to apologize, and she'd made the situation worse. Her awkwardness with boys... men...had never left her. "I have an issue with feeling that love and affection are always given in exchange for something else. It's my go-to in relationships, which explains my single status."

The lines bracketing his mouth softened. "I get it. Are you going to eat that bagel or dismantle it?"

"Eat it."

They finished their breakfasts, and Willow grabbed her purse, shoving the documents inside. They took Heath's truck to the airport and stopped on the way at a vintage clothing store.

As they walked up to the entrance of Second Hand Sadie, Heath eyed the beaded cocktail dress in the window. "Are you sure about this?"

"I've shopped here before, and I know they have some jeans and tops I can scoop up." She waved to Sadie at the counter. "Hi, Sadie. I need an outfit that I can wear out of the store."

Sadie came around the counter and gave Willow a hug scented with patchouli. "I heard about your cabin. First Toby and now you. What's going on out there?"

"Have you heard anything more about Toby's death?"

Willow glanced at Heath. Had West been holding out on them?

"Just through the grapevine. You know everyone around here likes drama. Apparently, someone from that greedy development corps, Bradford and Sons, is out here, nosing around for land, and he murdered Toby to get his hands on it."

Willow covered her smile as Heath raised a hand. "That would be me."

"Sadie, this is Heath Bradford, and he's not all that greedy."

Sadie turned pink up to the roots of her pink hair. "Foot in mouth. I'm sorry, but you know how locals are."

"I know, and it's okay. We *are* nosing around for land— but we don't murder people."

Willow laughed. "Okay, let's forget about this greedy bastard for a few minutes and find me some clothes to wear."

Fifteen minutes later, dressed in a pair of bell-bottom jeans and a blouse with geometric shapes on it, Willow emerged from the dressing room. "I'll take this and throw in the denim trucker jacket in case this glorious sun goes away."

"It's Dead Falls Island—guaranteed to go away at some point today." Sadie patted a stack of clothes on the counter. "These, too?"

"Might as well. I'm not sure when I'm going to go back to my place and what my wardrobe's going to look like."

"And to prove I'm not a greedy bastard, I'll pay for Willow's stuff." Heath reached for his wallet and pulled out several bills.

"You don't have to do that. Sadie doesn't think you're greedy. Do you, Sadie?"

"No, but if a hot guy wants to buy you some clothes, girl, you let him." Sadie snatched the money from Heath's fingers and gave him change.

As they walked back to his truck, a plastic bag from the store swinging from his fingertips, Heath said, "Wow, this is a tough crowd. How do they feel about the Samish developing their land?"

"Most aren't happy about it, some are, and some believe the Samish can do whatever they want with their land, including building a casino. There are some Samish who disagree, too. Toby was obviously one of them. So no matter what Lee says, he doesn't speak for the entire Samish nation on this island."

They settled in the truck, and Heath punched on the ignition. "I wish the medical examiner would announce a manner of death for Toby. If the DFSD announces Toby's death was an accident, it will quell some of the suspicion."

"Including ours, but someone still searched my place and set fire to it. Those incidents have to be related to Toby's death, accident or not."

"His death could've definitely precipitated those actions. Maybe someone already knew Toby's land was going to you, and when he died, you became the focus of the intimidation."

"Lucky me."

They drove past the harbor to the small airport on the island. Several private planes, and some for hire, sat on the tarmac, ready to puddle jump to other islands and even to Seattle.

As Heath parked his truck, he pointed to a Cessna with red stripes. "That's ours."

"Fifteen minutes, huh?" Willow eyed the small plane and the man under the wing.

"Up and down. No time for complimentary drink service."

Five minutes later, they approached the plane. The person who'd been tinkering with it turned and wiped his hands on his overalls. "Heath Bradford?"

"Yeah. Thanks for taking us on short notice." Heath shook hands with the pilot. "Willow, this is Captain Mark Santos. He's flying us to San Juan today."

"Captain." Willow gingerly took his still-oily hand.

"Sorry about that." Mark glanced at his palms. "There are some wipes in the plane, and you can call me Mark. I'm just finishing my preflight. You can go on board."

They climbed onto the plane and took two of the four available seats. Must've cost Heath a bunch of cash to charter this plane to San Juan, but if the nickel in the rocks beneath that property really was worth millions, and he owned the rights, he could afford it.

As they settled into their seats and secured their seat belts, Heath handed her a headset. "Can get noisy in these things."

Nodding, Willow took the headset with a smile that masked her anxiety, but the plane took off smoothly, with just a few bumps and dips. Willow eased back in her seat as the emerald jewel of Dead Falls Island receded and other islets dotting Discovery Bay emerged through the mist.

The landing proved to be a tad rougher, and she didn't

uncurl her fingers from the armrest until the pilot rolled to a stop.

Heath squeezed her hand. "Not so bad, huh?"

She licked her lips and unhitched the seat belt. "How far to the county seat?"

"Far enough to take an app car."

They clambered out of the plane, thanking Mark, and Heath pulled out his phone to find them a ride. Fifteen minutes later, they were on the way to the county courthouse.

Heath approached the counter with authority, or at least as someone who had an appointment. When a clerk at another window called him, Heath tugged on Willow's sleeve. "Come with me."

The woman behind the glass smiled, her eyes crinkling at the edges. "After your call, Mr. Bradford, I was able to look up the records."

He said, "Great. Is the information clear-cut, or so bogged down in legalese, I'm gonna need my business degree to decipher it?"

"I don't think you'll have any problem figuring out that you're the legal owner of the mineral rights on that property, currently owned by Toby Keel."

"Not anymore." Willow clenched her teeth. It was all true. Her father had deeded the mineral rights on her property to Heath, a kid he'd talked to a few times.

"Sorry?" The woman tilted her head like a bird and shoved her glasses up the bridge of her nose.

"Toby Keel passed away. I'm the owner of the surface property." The corner of Willow's eye twitched.

"Well, that's perfect, then." The chirpy clerk grinned from ear to ear. "A husband-and-wife team."

Heath had the nerve to chuckle, and Willow felt like elbowing him in the ribs. Easy for him to find humor in the situation. He'd just discovered he owned mineral rights worth a fortune.

"I made you a copy of the documents." The clerk patted a manila envelope before sliding it beneath the window. "Did you lose the other set?"

"Other set?" Heath paused, the envelope clutched to his chest. "What do you mean? This is the first set I've ordered."

"Hmm, well." The clerk adjusted her glasses and peered at the computer monitor next to her. "That's not what I show here."

"Your records show that Heath Bradford ordered this report before?"

"Not exactly. Not *Heath* Bradford but Bradford and Son. Yes, it's right here. Bradford and Son already got a copy of the deed."

Chapter Twelve

Heath felt like Muhammad Ali just landed a punch to his gut, and it took all his control not to stagger back. He opened his mouth, but he couldn't form a sentence or utter a word.

Willow cleared her throat. "The corporation Bradford and Son requested these documents? When?"

The clerk's gaze shifted back to her computer screen. "About six months ago. It was done online, though. Is there a problem? Mineral rights are part of the public record. Anyone with the correct data can look up deeds for any property."

"Yeah, I know that. No problem." Heath held up the manila envelope in a surprisingly steady hand and said, "Thanks for your help."

Willow took his arm as they left the building but kept mum. He appreciated her silence. She could've laid into him with an *I told you so*.

When they reached the sidewalk, Heath took a couple of breaths of salty air. "What the hell just happened in there?"

"You're the proud owner of a vein of nickel, worth millions, running beneath my property, and there's not a damned thing I can do to stop you from mining it." She steered him down the sidewalk. "We might as well have some lunch while we're here."

"Don't play dumb. That part didn't surprise me. After looking at Toby's files, I figured they were legit. But how and why was Bradford and Son looking at this stuff six months ago, and why didn't my father tell me?"

He'd stopped in the middle of the sidewalk, and she pulled him forward.

"Lunch and maybe an adult beverage before I get back on that little death trap again." She pulled out her phone. "My turn. There are a bunch of restaurants near Friday Harbor."

Like a sleepwalker, he got into the rideshare and sat in the back seat, his arms folded around the envelope. "Six months. Little Miss Sunshine back there said the docs were ordered six months ago, right?"

"That's what I heard. What's the significance of that?"

"Six months ago is when Toby started sending me those cryptic notes, only I didn't know it was him back then."

"How *did* you figure that out? Did he confess?"

Squeezing the back of his neck, Heath said, "I know it sounds crazy, but I recognized his writing."

"You're right. It sounds crazy." Willow rapped on the window. "Yeah, this is good. We'll find something from here."

The driver dropped them off at the top of a long street that led to the harbor, lined with tourist shops, bars and restaurants. After perusing a few menu boards outside, they agreed on a place that smelled like fresh fish, with a sunny patio facing the water and the boats.

Once seated with menus and water in front of them, Willow picked up the conversation where they'd left off. "How'd you know it was Toby?"

"My father handed me the files on the two properties—yours and Toby's—and asked me to start preparing offers. Toby's file contained a lot of handwritten notes, most of them telling Bradford to go to hell. When I looked at that writing, which is distinctive, and pulled out the anonymous notes I'd been receiving, they were a match."

"That's crazy, Heath." Willow glanced up at the waitress. "I'll have a mimosa, please, heavy on the champagne, and a caprese salad."

Heath ordered a bottle of beer and a plate of fish-and-chips. Then he slumped in his seat and downed half the water. "Now I'm wondering if my father knew about those notes."

"You never told him?"

"Nope." He ran a hand through his hair. "Did he want me to go digging around for my mother with false hope? What kind of sick SOB puts his son through that?"

"Why wouldn't your father tell you about the mineral rights? Seems to me that would be a done deal for getting his hands on that property."

"Maybe because he thinks I wouldn't go along with exploiting those rights. Maybe because developing the property is more lucrative than decimating it to get to some nickel." He nodded to the waitress as she set their drinks on the table. "I'm going to find out. My father is conveniently on vacation right now, but I can reach him."

Willow held up her champagne flute. "I don't even know what to toast right now."

"How about our joint ownership of Toby's property?"

He clinked his bottle with her glass. "Nobody does anything to that property without our say-so."

"Without *your* say-so." Willow took a sip of her mimosa and crinkled her nose against the bubbles hopping from the glass. "From what I understand about mineral rights, you can choose to exploit those rights, regardless of the property owner's wishes."

"That's true, but I don't want to do anything against the property owner's wishes." He ran a thumb across her knuckles, reveling in the touch of her skin. His pride had forced him to storm out of her hotel room last night, but other parts of his psyche…and his body…wanted to stay with her all night long.

"What about your father's wishes? The wishes of Bradford without the Son?" She circled her finger in the air.

"Without the Son, Bradford's wishes don't count, especially after the underhanded way he went about the entire deal. Why wouldn't he tell me I owned those mineral rights?"

He didn't want to admit to Willow that his father kept him out of the loop on many aspects of their business. His father had brought him in as his partner, but he never treated him like one.

"Do you want my take?" Willow paused to thank the waitress as she delivered the colorful salad and delicious-smelling fish-and-chips.

"Of course…" Heath whipped his napkin into his lap. "…partner."

"Your father probably wants to buy time to wear you down, to work on you. If you believe he wants to develop the land more than he wants to exploit the nickel beneath it, maybe he planned to make some sort of deal with you—get you to threaten the surface landowner, whoever that turned out to be, with mineral exploitation or sell the land for development. Think about it."

She drew a knife through a blob of mozzarella and the tomato beneath it and continued, "If Toby still refused to sell, you could wave those mineral rights in his face and tell him if he doesn't sell, you'll start mining that nickel. He wouldn't want the land crisscrossed with excavation equipment, would he?"

"That's quite a scenario. Why not just tell me that?" Heath stared at his plate, wondering why he'd ordered so much food when his appetite had deserted him.

"C'mon, Heath. Your father has reason to believe Dead Falls Island is special to you. He must understand your hesitance with the idea of developing that property to dovetail with the casino."

"I guess he does." He jabbed at the pile of french fries on his plate with his fork. "You're not going to want half of these again like last night, are you?"

"I did *not* eat half of those fries last night, and no. I don't want anything greasy in my stomach for the flight home." She swirled her drink, causing more bubbles to fizz to the top. "Are you going to call him? Your dad."

"I'll try. He's on vacation in Italy with his new wife, who's a few years older than me, by the way."

"Hey, you can't hold that against the guy. Do you think he'll talk to you?"

"Depends on what kind of voicemail I leave him. If I come on strong, he'll put me on Ignore until he returns. But all of this, my ownership of the mineral rights and my father's knowledge of them, still doesn't explain why someone is targeting you."

"I think someone else knows about the nickel vein on Toby's land, but they don't know who owns it. Maybe that's what they were searching for the first time they broke into my place. The intruders searched an old suitcase that held my father's papers. I don't know if they found anything there or took anything, but maybe the fire was a way to make sure I didn't find anything, either."

"Or the fire was another warning. At least both of those incidents weren't a direct physical threat against you. You were out both times, but the poor dogs suffered."

She tossed back the rest of her mimosa. "I guess I should feel grateful that someone's not trying to kill me...like Toby." Willow raised a finger to the waitress and ordered another mimosa.

"We don't know that yet. I'm not sure what's taking the medical examiner so long to come to a determination. It would help if we knew whether your stalker is capable of murder." He spread his hands. "I mean, I'd go to greater measures to protect you."

She raised one eyebrow at him as he felt his face warm. She asked, "Now he's my stalker?"

"Or she." Heath sprinkled some vinegar on a piece of fish. "Ellie Keel is not happy with you."

"Wait until she finds out *you* own the mineral rights to her uncle's former property. She'll go ballistic."

"Can't wait for that. She and her brother will probably show up to this meeting with the Samish committee for the casino." He crunched into his fish.

"When is that? I got the notice but wasn't planning on attending. Maybe I should."

"You're a major player. The meeting is tonight at the Samish reservation. I'm supposed to present my progress with the adjacent land lots—yours and...yours now. We're opening the floor to dissent."

"I'm going to be even more well-liked than I already am around here." She smiled as the waitress delivered her second champagne flute.

"Are you sure that's the way to deal with your fear of flying?" He tapped the stem of her glass with his finger.

"I don't have a fear of flying regular commercial jets. Those puddle jumpers make me nervous. Flew one over the Cascades once, and I swear the engine sputtered." She shivered and took a generous sip of her drink. "Believe me. This will help for the ride back."

"I think you have more to fear from that meeting."

"I think *you* have more to fear from that meeting than I do." She picked up a piece of basil from her plate with her fingertips and dropped it into her mouth. "Are you going to come out against your own proposal at the meeting?"

"Nope. I'm just going to facilitate. I'm also not going to tell them about the nickel on Toby's property or the fact that I own the rights." Heath finished one piece of fish and eyed the other with distaste. He had knots in his stomach, too, but not from fear of flying.

"Oho, so you're throwing me to the wolves on my own, huh?" She dug her elbows into the table on either side of her plate. "You're going to point the finger at me as the baddie who won't sell."

"Nobody's going to be pointing any fingers. Everyone will have a chance to make their case. If you don't want to go, that's fine. Most people don't expect you to be there anyway. It was always Toby's property that was in play. Nobody ever expected you to sell."

"Unless I'm dead." Willow crossed her arms over her midsection. "Jason Hart suggested I make a will—and he wasn't kidding."

"If you died intestate, your mother would probably inherit. She's your closest relative." Heath tossed his napkin on his plate and finished his beer. "How does she feel about the property?"

Willow's green eyes sparkled as they widened. "You've been thinking about my death? Have it all figured out?"

"I confess. I did work it out in my head, but only for logistical reasons—kind of like Jason did." He grabbed her hand and kissed the inside of her wrist. "It might be what we're dealing with. That's why I want to keep you in my sights."

She didn't pull away, instead curling her fingers around his hand. "To answer your question, my mother hates Dead Falls Island. I'm pretty sure she'd sell that land in a second to fund her vagabond lifestyle. No doubt."

Squeezing her fingers, he said, "Don't tell anyone that."

"Question for you." She ran her fingertips along the length of his hand, giving him the shivers. "Are you going to continue digging? Do you still think Toby was telling the truth about your mom, or was it his way of messing with your mind?"

"I'll keep digging. I don't know what the man was up to, but I can't give up on my mother." He pulled out his wallet and snapped a credit card onto the table. "If it's okay with you."

"Paying or digging?"

He snorted. "I'm paying for lunch. I meant the digging."

"As long as you let me help you."

"Even with people shooting at us?"

"Maybe one of us can be the lookout while the other digs." She wiggled her fingers at the waitress.

"Another mimosa?"

"I wish." Willow winked at Heath. "Just the check."

Before the waitress turned away, Heath handed her his card. "Hopefully, Captain Mark hasn't spent his time on the island downing mimosas."

"He didn't look like the mimosa type." She wiped her hands on a napkin. "Is it time already?"

"We got what we came for—and then some." He paid the bill, and he and Willow decided to walk along the harbor on their way back to the airport.

They ran into their pilot coming out of a pizza place, a square box in his hand. He held up the box. "Leftovers. I can't offer meal service on my Cessna, but you can have it."

Heath answered, "We just had lunch, thanks."

"Did you get your business done?" Mark fell in beside them.

"We did." Heath gave a sharp nod. A slight pounding beat against his temples every time he thought about his father and his deception.

"How often do you make this flight?" Willow tripped over a bump in the sidewalk and grabbed on to Heath's arm.

"This island? A few times a week. More to the mainland. Private is more expensive than the airlines, but you can schedule at any time."

When they reached the small airport that consisted of a tower, a low-lying building, a couple of vending machines and the airstrip, Mark waved to some benches outside. "Hang out here for a few minutes. I need to go inside to file my flight plan."

Five minutes later, Mark emerged from the building pressing a bottle of water against his forehead. "Does it feel hot to you?"

"I'm a little warm." Heath tugged on his light windbreaker.

Mark performed some preflight checks before ushering them onto the plane again. They snapped in and grabbed their headsets. Mark spoke into the mic, and the plane's engines whirred to life. It made a slight turn, picked up speed, and soon after the island dropped away beneath them.

Willow closed her eyes, and Heath rested his forehead against the vibrating window to stare into the bay. Both he and Willow would have to make it clear to all interested parties, including his father, that if the Samish casino went ahead, it would do so without the adjoining land for additional facilities. If the Samish could still make that work, more power to them.

The airplane, which had been climbing, seemed to level off, and Heath glanced back at San Juan, still a visible chunk of land in the bay. Maybe the pilot was going to fly at a lower altitude on the way back, because this didn't seem like cruising.

The wing outside his window dipped to the right, and the plane veered slightly. Were they going back?

Heath tapped his headset. "Mark? Is there a problem?"

Captain Mark didn't respond, and Heath yanked off the headset. Maybe it wasn't meant to communicate to the pilot. He cupped a hand around his mouth and shouted, "Mark? Mark, are we going back?"

The pilot hadn't heard him, so Heath leaned into the aisle to get a clear view of the cockpit. As he did so, the nose of the plane dipped. "Mark!"

Mark didn't turn around or acknowledge him, and the plane had started losing altitude. The sound of the wind outside changed as the craft listed to the right.

Heath scrambled out of his seat, glancing over at Willow, still dozing in a champagne haze. In two long strides, he reached the cockpit and grabbed Mark's shoulder.

The pilot groaned and slumped to the side. Captain Mark was out cold.

Chapter Thirteen

Willow jerked awake. Had they landed already? She glanced across the aisle at Heath and jolted upright when her gaze met an empty seat. The plane dipped, and she dug her fingernails into the arm of her seat. Where the hell was Heath?

Cocking her head to the side, she checked the aisle, and her heart stopped when she saw Captain Mark on the floor, his legs in the cockpit and his torso extending into the aisle. With shaking hands, she clawed at the seat belt around her lap.

As she stood up, the airplane shuddered, and she yelped, making a grab for the headrest on the seat in front of her. Her knees trembled when she took a few unsteady steps toward the cockpit and the prone body of Mark.

"Willow?" Heath waved his hand in the air from the pilot's seat in the front. "Sit down and strap in. It's going to be okay."

"Okay? The pilot's dead."

"Mark's not dead. He can't fly, but I can. I have my pilot's license, and although it's been a few years, I can handle this craft. I'll get us down safely. Sit back down and breathe. I've already radioed ahead."

Willow shuffled back to her seat, dipping her head

to look out the window. Sky met blue water, with not a speck of dry land in sight. Swallowing hard, she dropped back down and snapped the belt, pulling it securely. She braced her forehead against the seat in front of her and murmured a prayer. She had to trust Heath—again.

She balled her hands into fists and buried them in her lap. Squeezing her eyes closed, she kept Heath's advice at the forefront, breathing in through her nose and exhaling through her mouth. The rhythm calmed her, as did the leveling out of the airplane.

Heath seemed to have gotten the situation under control, and the plane had stopped dipping and swaying. What would've happened if Heath didn't know how to fly? And what was wrong with Mark? He'd come out of the pizza place but didn't seem as if he'd been drinking.

After what felt like an eternity, the plane started to descend—in a good way. Willow finally lifted her head, hearing voices from the cockpit. That had to be a good sign.

Heath thrust his thumb in the air. "Coming in for a landing, Willow. I got this."

The plane dropped through the low clouds, turning Willow's world a misty gray. She licked her lips, ignoring the buzzing in her ears. The force of the descent pushed her back against the seat, and she held her breath as the plane wobbled.

She sneaked a peek out the window. Between the wisps of clouds skittering by, she spied the small runway on Dead Falls Island. A lone ambulance waited on the tarmac, its red light a beacon of safety. Was it there in case they crashed, or was it for Captain Mark?

A few minutes later the plane whooshed, and her

stomach dropped. When the wheels touched the ground, she let out a long breath on the tail end of a sob.

When the plane came to a complete halt, she jumped from her seat and made a beeline for the cockpit, where Heath was still flipping switches. She wanted to throw herself in his arms in gratitude and relief, but she dropped to the floor to check Mark's pulse instead. It beat slowly but steadily beneath her fingertips.

She put her face close to his and sniffed the breath huffing from his parted lips. The only alcohol she smelled was the champagne on her own breath.

Heath peeled himself out of the pilot's seat and knelt across from her on the other side of Mark. "Is he all right?"

"Sleeping like a baby. I don't understand."

He reached for her and cupped her jaw. "Are *you* all right?"

"I am now, thanks to you. What other hidden talents do you have?"

He quirked his eyebrows. "Stick around and find out, kid."

The shouting from outside the plane broke the tension between them, and Heath rose to his feet and stepped over Mark's prone form. He opened the door to a clutch of people, all hovering around the plane.

He jerked his thumb over his shoulder. "The pilot, Mark Santos, is on the floor. When I saw what was happening, I eased him out of his seat and laid him flat so I could take his place. I have no idea what happened. He seems to be sleeping. He didn't cry out, foam at the mouth, clutch his chest. He just fell asleep at the controls."

Willow joined Heath at the door, gulping in the fresh

sea breeze. "And he's not drunk. Didn't appear drunk when we boarded, and I just sniffed his breath."

The EMT closest to the plane gestured for them to step outside. "We'll take it from here."

After the ambulance had whisked Mark away, and after a good forty-five minutes of answering questions, Willow finally got her wish. As she and Heath faced each other on the tarmac, he opened his arms to her, and she fell against his chest.

His heart beat strong and steady beneath her cheek. "It gives me the chills to think about what would've happened to us if you weren't a pilot."

"But I am, so don't dwell on it. We're safe. You're safe."

She nestled closer into his embrace. "Did the EMTs say anything about Mark? What caused his collapse?"

"Not to me. Just asked a bunch of questions, which I tried to answer the best I could." He took her by the shoulders and looked down into her face. "Do you think it's a coincidence that we wound up on a plane with a disabled pilot?"

The dread that had been twisting her gut tightened its grip. "I—I don't know. Are you saying my stalker has graduated to murder?"

"Maybe, and he's *my* stalker now, too. I was in the plane with you. Who would've benefited if that Cessna had plunged into the sea?"

A quick breeze gusted up from the bay, and Willow's teeth chattered.

"Are you in shock?" Heath draped an arm around her shoulders. "Let's get in my truck."

She hung on to Heath numbly as he led her to his vehicle. Of course Mark's condition hadn't been an accident. Someone knew what they'd just discovered about the mineral rights. Someone knew they were the two impediments that stood in the way of this great land development—benefiting Bradford and Son, certain factions of the Samish and even the Keels.

Heath helped her into his truck and then slid into the driver's side. He punched on the engine and tabbed a few buttons on the console. Heat rose from the leather seat, warming her thighs and backside.

"This feels nice." She allowed the heat to seep into her rigid muscles, but she couldn't allow herself to get too comfortable. "You asked who would benefit from my death? My mother. As you mentioned before, my mother is my natural heir. She would get that land if I died."

"You really think your mom would put out a hit on you?"

"Would your dad put a hit on you?"

Heath clenched the steering wheel, his knuckles pale. "My father is a lot of things, and we haven't always had the best relationship, but kill his only son for a land deal? No way."

"Same." She curled one leg beneath her. "My mom won't win any mother-of-the-year awards, but she's made a nice life for herself, and we're on good terms now. Not only is she not the killing type, she couldn't care less about this island."

"But you said she'd sell the land if she had the chance, take the money and run."

"Of course she would if it dropped into her lap. But she's not going to take any extreme measures to get it. I'm sure she doesn't even know the drama surrounding this land deal." She stopped and nibbled on the tip of her finger. Or did she?

Heath glanced in her direction. "What? Did you think of something else?"

"Just something my mom said earlier about having contacts on the island. She knew we had a new sheriff, so maybe she does keep tabs on what's going on here." Willow flicked back her hair. "No. She's not going to have me killed to get property on Dead Falls. That's absurd."

"Okay, so we've ruled out our respective parents as murderers. That just leaves a whole bunch of other people."

She said, "Before the meeting, I'm going to my cabin to sort through the mess to see what I can salvage. What are you going to do?"

"I'm going to dig—and I mean that literally."

Wagging her finger in the air, she said, "You're supposed to wait for me."

"Let's do this. We'll regroup at the hotel, swing by your cabin to check it out and then head to Toby's cabin to resume digging."

"Okay. Can we squeeze in a visit to the dogs at Astrid's?" She put her hands together. "I don't want them to think I abandoned them."

"Meeting's at seven. I think we can do it." He gunned his engine. "Let's face the people trying to kill us."

WHEN THEY GOT back to the hotel, Heath retreated to his own room and fell across the bed. He couldn't decide what shocked him more—learning that his father already knew he owned the mineral rights to Toby Keel's property or discovering Captain Mark passed out in the pilot's chair on the Cessna.

Unseeing, he stared at the ceiling. He'd done his best to play it cool around Willow, but he'd been terrified flying that plane. He didn't know if Mark was dead behind him, or if something had been released in the Cessna and he and Willow would be the next ones to collapse. The act of flying had come back to him quickly, even though it had been a few years since he'd piloted a plane on his own.

The weather and course had been his friends today. If they'd had a longer flight or poor visibility, he didn't know if he could've flown and landed that craft safely.

And what the hell had happened to Mark? Nobody could tell him his mission on San Juan and Mark's incident were unrelated. He had to talk to Mark.

Rolling onto his stomach, he grabbed his phone and looked up the number for the hospital. He placed the call and explained to the nurse that he'd been with Mark Santos on the plane and wanted to speak with him.

The nurse wouldn't allow him to talk to Mark, who was resting, but she assured him the pilot would be fine and make a full recovery. She also wouldn't clue him in on what had caused Mark's collapse.

The police on the scene at the airport didn't seem overly invested in finding out what had happened to Mark. They saw it as an aviation issue and under their investigation. That agency would most likely be interested in what and how much Mark was drinking before the flight, or if he had any medical conditions that would preclude him from flying.

Heath was more interested in where Mark went when

he was on the island and who he met. Someone knew he and Willow were headed over there, but Heath couldn't figure out how.

He gave up on the nurse and left a message on Mark's voicemail. If the hospital released him tomorrow or even the next day, Heath wanted to talk to him.

After he changed into a pair of grungy jeans and his hiking boots, Heath went down the hall to check on Willow. He barely tapped a second time when she swung open the door.

His gaze flicked over her outfit, a carbon copy of his own, only she looked a lot better in it than he did. "Ready?"

"Uh-huh. I checked with the fire department, and they told me I could go back inside the cabin. I mostly want to check for photos and my clothes. I can always go back to my place in Seattle to pick up more clothes for the rest of the summer, but I want to salvage what I can."

"And the suitcase that holds your father's papers, right?"

"Honestly—" she let the door slam behind her as she hitched a small backpack purse over one shoulder "—I didn't find anything of importance in there when I looked."

"You should still take it, if the fire didn't damage it."

"Do you think someone searched those papers for the mineral rights?"

He shrugged as he stabbed the call button for the elevator. "At least we know it wasn't my father. He already knew."

Once outside, they climbed into the truck, and Heath's

finger hovered over the control for the heated seats. "You want your seat heated?"

"No. I recovered, sort of." She clicked her seat belt. "Do you see why I don't like flying in those little death traps?"

"It's not every day your pilot passes out." He reached over and squeezed her knee, which was bouncing up and down. "I called the hospital to check on Mark. The nurse wouldn't give me much, but he's out of danger."

"Did you get the impression the deputy at the scene was eager to turn the investigation over to the FAA?"

"Yep. Not his fault, though. Did you want to be the one to explain to him how we went over to San Juan to look up mineral rights, and we suspected that someone was trying to kill us because of that by incapacitating our pilot?"

"No." She twirled an auburn lock of hair around her finger. "But maybe West would be interested in our theory. He, at least, has an idea of what we've been facing."

"I also believe he thinks Toby was murdered. Whether the ME will find for homicide or not, West has a strong suspicion. He would've treated the scene in a different manner if he was sure Toby's death was an accident."

"I agree, so why didn't you report the gunfire last night?"

"You know why. I don't want anyone to know I'm digging holes around Dead Falls Island, not even Sheriff Chandler."

With a later sunset, they didn't need electricity to see inside Willow's cabin. The fire had burned away one wall and portions of the roof, so the sunlight streamed through the openings, giving them a clear picture of the wreckage.

As they stood in the doorway, surveying the damage, Heath entwined his fingers with Willow's. "This is bad. I'm sorry."

A smile wobbled on her lips, and she dashed a tear from her cheek. "It's not my permanent residence, and I'd already gotten rid of most of the furniture from my childhood. At least the dogs are safe, and I have you to thank for that."

He withdrew a pair of gloves from his back pocket. "You wear these while you're mucking around. I'll get the bins from the back of the truck, and you can tell me what to load up."

It took them about an hour to wade through the mess to locate framed pictures, a few salvageable books, dog food and the majority of Willow's clothes, still hanging in the closet in her room.

Outside, she brought a pile of clothes to her nose and buried her face in it. "They don't even smell that bad. I think a good wash will get the smoky smell out of them."

"I'm going back for that suitcase under the bed. You never know." He left her sorting through her clothing and tromped to the bedroom in the back where she'd pointed out the suitcase before.

Crouching down, he grabbed the handle and pulled it from beneath the bed. He glanced over his shoulder once and flipped open the top. Paul Sands had left behind a bigger filing nightmare than Toby Keel. Who could find anything in this mess? But maybe that was the point.

"Are you done?" Willow called from the front door, or at least the space where the front door used to function as a door.

"Coming." He heaved up the suitcase and lugged it

outside. "Why didn't anyone think of putting wheels on suitcases back then?"

"One of the mysteries of life." She shrugged. "Who files paperwork in a suitcase?"

When they finished loading the bins in his truck, Heath stood beside it, one hand on his hip. "Do we take the trail through the woods to Toby's, or should we drive around the bend and park near the other trailhead? I don't like the idea of leaving the truck with all your stuff in the back parked on the side of the road."

"Let's hike in. That way, we can see beforehand if anyone is skulking in the woods with a shotgun."

Their mode of transportation decided, Heath locked up his truck, and he and Willow ducked onto the trail that led to the other property. He carried the shovel and pickax with him. Willow assured him she'd found a shovel on Toby's property and had left it there when the shot rang out.

She said, "I can use that to dig."

He shifted the pickax from one shoulder to the other. "You don't have to dig. Just keep a lookout. Too bad we don't have the dogs with us."

"Exactly. We should've picked up the dogs first."

They emerged into the clearing for Toby's cabin, and Heath's gaze darted around the property. The yellow crime scene tape was even more bedraggled than the previous time he was here, and they still didn't even know if a crime had been committed or not.

He circled around the back of the cabin, and Willow followed him. He dropped his tools near the holes in the ground that he'd dug earlier and that Willow had enlarged. Pointing at the cabin, he said, "Why don't you go inside and look around some more? I'd feel better if you were inside instead of out here in the open."

"What am I looking for?"

He pulled on his gloves. "More documents, maybe some hiding places. Toby was a man with secrets."

"Okay, I'll pretend to be busy while you dig out here. Don't forget. I want to stop off at Astrid's to see the dogs before that meeting."

"I'll be quick." He clapped his hands together, dislodging some particles of dirt from the gloves. "I have a strange feeling about this place."

Heath breathed easier when he heard the cabin door close. Then he got to work. He hadn't been exaggerating to Willow about sensing something about this location. He'd felt it the first night he'd come to this cabin, winding up behind it instead of at the front door. An eerie sensation had made the hair on the back of his neck stand up and quiver. Willow's scream had punctuated that feeling, and finding Toby's body had convinced him that his original unease had been some kind of premonition about the man's death on the other side of the cabin.

Now that he knew this was the location that matched Toby's note, the feeling was back stronger than ever. That conviction gave strength to his efforts, and he plunged the shovel into the earth over and over.

After about an hour of work, during which Willow called out to him a few times and brought him a bottle of water, Heath leaned on the handle of the shovel. He wiped the sweat from his brow with the sleeve of his shirt. He'd made progress, but it would help if he actually knew what he was looking for.

He slid the shovel down the side of one of the ditches

and heard a rustling noise. He aimed his flashlight into
the hole and saw the edge of something blue. Scraping
the point of the shovel across the area revealed a larger
swath of what looked like a blue-and-yellow rug. With
his heart galloping in his chest, he raked the tip of his
shovel across the object, removing more dirt and exposing more of the thick, rolled-up rug.

He dropped to the ground, lying flat on his belly, his
head dipping into the ditch. The beam of his flashlight
swept back and forth across the rug as he stretched his
arm to reach it. Using his fingers, he sifted through some
clods and rocks in the dirt until he met a long, smooth
object.

He scrabbled in the dirt to free the item. Closing his
fingers around it, he pulled himself from the hole.

Sitting back on his heels, he unfurled his hand. He
gaped at the bone in his palm and released an anguished
roar.

Chapter Fourteen

A strangled cry from outside assaulted her ears, and Willow clutched the notebook of recipes she'd found under a floorboard beneath Toby's bed to her chest. She scrambled to her feet and tore out of the cabin, stumbling down the porch steps.

"Heath?" She dropped the notebook as she careened around the corner of the cabin. Relief made her knees weak when she saw Heath crouched next to a ditch, the one he'd been working on the last time she came outside. *He hasn't been shot.*

Scooping in a breath, she charged toward him. "Heath!"

He slowly lifted his head and cranked it toward her like an automaton. His eyes blinked, and he held out his open hand toward her. "I found this. There's more."

She sank to the ground beside him and held out her hand. "What is it?"

Cupping his hand over hers, he dumped his find into her palm. "It's a bone. A human bone."

Willow examined the piece of bone, running a thumb along its concave surface. "I-it looks like a metatarsal bone—from a foot, but I can't tell if it's human. We don't know if it's from a human being."

"Do you know many animals out here that have metatarsal bones?"

"Deer, goats, pigs." She ran a tongue around her dry mouth.

"This long?" He jabbed a finger into the ditch. "And who wraps a dead deer in a rug?"

Willow clambered to the edge of the ditch on her hands and knees and peered into the darkness. It didn't remain dark for long as Heath lit up the area with his flashlight.

Her gut churned when she spotted the rolled-up rug at the bottom of the hole. Shaking her head, she choked. "You can't really believe this is..."

"My mother?" Heath clutched his hair with his dirty hand, and the grime streaked down his sweaty face. "Why else would Toby Keel direct me to this spot? He flat out told me that I could find my mother where the mist meets the earth between two giant maples. And here she is."

"Why? Why?" Willow clutched the base of her throat. "What does this even mean?"

"I'm heading back to the road to call the sheriff. Don't touch anything else." Rising to his feet, he stretched out a hand to her. "In fact, leave it. You're coming with me. I don't want you out here by yourself."

She waved vaguely at the buried rug. "Whoever killed this person—and I'm not convinced it's your mother—is long gone. I think I'm safe."

"Willow, you're not safe." He grabbed her hand and practically yanked her to her feet.

He kept a hold on her until they reached the trail that led to the road on the other side of Toby's property. Then they went single file while he literally watched her back.

She kept her phone out, waiting for a decent signal, and several yards before they hit the road, she got it. "I'm calling the sheriff's department right now."

She talked while she followed Heath onto the road. It took her a few minutes to explain to the sergeant at the desk that they had discovered bones and not a dead body. Once she made that clear, the sergeant's urgency level went down.

Willow rolled her eyes at Heath as he herded her into a turnout. "It's not an animal. The bones are wrapped in a blue carpet. Just tell Sheriff Chandler that the body... bones were found on Toby Keel's property, about twenty feet from where he died."

When she ended the call, she said, "I think I finally got through to him. Mentioning the sheriff helped."

Heath paced back and forth a few steps. "I don't know what this means. Did Toby murder my mother? If he'd just found her body after a suicide, why not report it? Why bury it?"

"Slow down." She rubbed a circle on his back. "We don't even know if that's your mother. Hell, we don't really know if the bones belong to a human. I just bluffed it with the sergeant so he'd get someone out here."

"Are they coming this way?" He jerked his thumb down the empty road.

"Yes. It's always easier to get to Toby's property from this direction."

"You don't have to wait." He glanced at his phone. "I know you want to see the dogs before the meeting tonight."

"Meeting is still on?" She raised her eyebrows. Heath

seemed too shaken right now to conduct a contentious meeting of warring parties.

"Now more than ever. I'm going to announce this development at the meeting and watch what happens."

His jaw tightened, and Willow revised her previous judgment of his emotions. Heath Bradford was determined… and maybe a little mad. Betrayed by his father. Betrayed by Toby. Maybe even betrayed by his mother.

"I'll stay with you. The dogs can wait. Astrid and Olly are spoiling them, from all accounts, and Sherlock likes having more canines in the house." She tucked her hand through the crook of his arm. She didn't want to leave him alone.

He trailed a finger across her cheek and tucked a strand of hair behind her ear. "Thanks."

Several minutes later, Sheriff Chandler himself pulled up in his SUV. He exited his vehicle, shaking his head. "What the hell is going on out here?"

"That's what we'd like to know." Heath strode forward and clenched the sheriff's hand. "Now would be a good time to know if Toby's death was a homicide."

"I can tell you—it's not going in that direction. The ME is stalled on undetermined. Toby had a heart attack. Whether he had it and fell, hitting his head, or when someone knocked him on the head is unclear." He stabbed a finger toward the woods. "How did you happen to come upon a set of buried bones?"

"I dug them up." Heath widened his stance and crossed his arms, as if expecting a physical challenge from West.

West scratched his chin. "Why were you digging on the property?"

"I own the mineral rights beneath the land."

West kept his face impassive, his only reaction the flaring of his nostrils. "So you decided to dig for the gold yourself?"

"Nickel." Heath drummed his fingers against his biceps. "Just curious."

"And instead of nickel, you found human bones wrapped in a rug."

"That's right."

Tipping his head in Heath's direction, West asked Willow, "You're okay with this guy digging trenches in your property to hunt for nickel?"

"We were both curious, West. Now we're even more curious. How are you going to handle this?"

"I'll have a look first, but we'll most likely cordon off the location until we can get some CSI folks from Seattle. We don't have the capability in our small lab to test bones, date them, determine a cause of death." He blew out a long breath. "I have a squad car on the way. Take me to your newest discovery. This is like déjà vu."

In a scene that was eerily familiar, the three of them tromped down the trail to Toby's cabin. When they got to the clearing and circled to the back of the cabin, West whistled through his teeth.

"Looks like you two have been busy." The sheriff crouched beside the ditch and aimed his flashlight at the rug below. "You took a bone out?"

In a macabre gesture, Heath pulled on his gloves and dug the foot bone from his front pocket. He held it up for West's scrutiny.

West swore under his breath and shook out a plastic bag from his pocket. "Drop it in here."

Heath complied and drew back as West pulled on his

own gloves and stretched out on the ground, his head poked below the earth. He shimmied forward until his midsection aligned with the edge of the trench, and then bent forward, the top half of his body disappearing.

Muffled curses reached them on the surface. When he scrambled out, the front of his uniform plastered with mud, he said, "There's a human skull in there."

Shouting from the woods had them all turning their heads, and West clambered to his feet. "Those are my deputies. They're probably lost. I'll be right back."

Looking at Heath's pale face, Willow swallowed. "It *is* human."

Heath glanced at the sheriff's retreating back and dropped to his knees next to the ditch. Mimicking West's position, he vanished into the ground as if being swallowed.

"Heath, what are you doing?"

He didn't answer her, and soon his legs dropped into the hole, too.

"West is not going to like this. You'd better get out before he…"

"Where's Heath?" West came charging back to the scene, a male and a female deputy trailing after him.

Heath's head popped up, dirt smudging his cheeks and sprinkled in his hair. "Sorry. I was having a look, and I fell in." He held up his gloved hands. "I'm wearing gloves, but I didn't touch anything anyway."

"Get out so we can secure this area. I already put a call in to Seattle, and they're going to bring equipment out here tonight so they can excavate the skeletal remains. They don't even want me or my people to touch anything."

"It's all yours." Heath hoisted himself from the grave and clapped his hands together, showering dirt to the ground. "We have a meeting to get to."

"How many more secrets can this island harbor?" West clasped the back of his neck and squeezed it. "That skull looks smallish. I'm hoping this is not another forgotten victim of Dr. Summers's killing spree of young boys several years ago."

"I-it's not a child." Willow twisted her fingers in front of her. If it were a child's skeletal remains, it couldn't be Jessica Bradford, Heath's mother, in there, but how awful it would be if this were another casualty of the sick obsession of Dr. Summers, a serial killer who'd targeted young boys on the island over the course of several years.

"I don't think so, but I'm not sure. That's why we have the experts coming out to excavate and transport the bones to a lab." West sidled in front of the hole and puffed out his chest, as if he feared Heath would make another attempt to dive in. "You two should get to your meeting. I suppose this is going to get out, isn't it? It's Dead Falls Island."

Tugging off his dirt-stained gloves, Heath said, "I think it's important to let all the parties interested in this development know that a body has been discovered on one of the parcels. That could hold up development for quite a while, couldn't it, Sheriff?"

"I thought you *wanted* to develop these properties." West narrowed his eyes, and his gaze shifted from Heath to Willow. "Never mind. I'll keep you posted."

Heath snorted. "Like you're keeping us posted on Toby?"

Done with the two of them, West waved his hand in

the air and addressed the female deputy. "Amanda, can you start marking off this area?"

Willow grabbed Heath's arm. "Let's get out of here."

She made a detour to Toby's porch to scoop up the journal she'd found beneath the floorboards under his bed, rolled it up and shoved it in her pocket. She'd forgotten all about it when Heath yelled. Now it didn't seem that important compared to Heath's discovery.

Lost in their own thoughts on the trail, they didn't talk much on the way back to her burned-out shell of a cabin and the remains of that cabin stuffed in bins and waiting in the back of Heath's truck.

He smacked a hand on the tailgate. "Where are you going to put this stuff?"

"There are storage containers in town. I'll rent one until I figure out where I'm going to stay for the rest of the summer. It can't be that hotel. I'd never get any research done—not that I'm accomplishing much now."

"You're not going to be able to do it before the meeting."

"Are we going to be able to do anything before the meeting?" She brushed a hand down the front of his dirty shirt, and her fingers hit a round object stuck in the breast pocket.

He jerked back quickly and placed his hand over his heart as if to protect the object.

"What is that?"

He closed his eyes, and a muscle ticked at the corner of his mouth.

A breath hitched in her throat. She just wanted to take his face in her hands and kiss away that spot of throbbing tension. "Show me, Heath. I can't help you if you don't share with me. And I want to help you sort this out."

With his eyes still closed, he fished into his pocket with two fingers and withdrew a gold locket on a chain.

Willow watched the necklace glint in the setting sun, her breath coming in shallow gusts. "Where did you get that? What does it mean?"

"I found it amid that pile of bones wrapped in the rug and buried in the ground. It was my mother's."

Chapter Fifteen

Willow pressed her own hand against his empty pocket, over his heart. "You're sure?"

His eyes flew open, and he wedged a thumbnail in a crease in the locket, prying the two pieces apart. He cradled the open locket in his palm and held it out to her. "My picture and lock of my baby hair. She always wore it. Told me even though she couldn't always be present for me, she kept me close to her heart always."

Tears pricked the backs of Willow's eyes, blurring her view of the smiling baby and a lock of soft blond hair on the other side of the locket. She sniffed. "Heath, I'm so sorry. Why didn't you tell Sheriff Chandler?"

"I will." He snapped the locket shut. "I didn't want to get into it with him—how I knew to dig out there. What did I know about her death. I know nothing, but I'm going to find out one way or another."

Hooking two fingers in the front pocket of his jeans, she yanked him toward her. "I'll help. You know I will. I think it's all connected somehow—the properties, your mother, my father, Toby, the stalking and the attempts on our lives. We're looking at the obvious suspects— the people who want to develop the land—but maybe it's not all about the casino project."

He wedged a finger beneath her chin and tilted her head back. He brushed his lips with hers in a gentle kiss. "Thank you for being here. You're a lot like your dad in some respects. He was there for me, too, when Mom disappeared. Now you're here the moment I found her."

A chill zigzagged down Willow's spine at Heath's words. Jessica Bradford's death bracketed by two Sands family members didn't feel like a coincidence. It meant something, but she couldn't put her finger on it...not yet.

"And you'll be there for me at the meeting, too, right?" She tugged on the hem of her sweatshirt. "Not only do we not have time to visit the dogs, but we also don't have time to shower and change."

"I have some wipes in the car. Your clothes don't look bad. I was the one crawling in the dirt." He opened his shirt and shook it out, returning the locket to his breast pocket.

"It's only the outside." She stood on her tiptoes and grabbed the shoulders of his shirt, peeling it back. "I don't think anyone would care if you showed up to the meeting in a white T-shirt. I know I wouldn't mind."

He gave her a crooked smile as he caught the shirt and bunched his hand around the pocket. "Don't want to lose this."

"Absolutely not. Sorry." She held out her hand. "Let me put that in my purse, unless you want to leave it in your truck. You can't keep stuffing it into your pockets."

Heath retrieved the necklace and poured it into her hand, where it pooled in her palm. A sprinkling of goose bumps prickled across her arms as she closed her hand around a locket that had been buried with a dead woman for over ten years.

When they climbed into the truck, Heath pulled a container of wet wipes from the console and offered it to her. "It might be a little harsh on your face, but you only have a smudge of dirt on your chin, probably from my dirty hands."

She plucked a few wipes from the cylinder and scrubbed her hands. As she looked around for a bag for her trash, Heath said, "Turn this way."

She cranked her head to the side, and he dabbed her chin with the corner of a wipe. "There. I think I got it."

"Making me presentable for the drawing and quartering?"

"Any drawing and quartering is going to have to go through me first." He swiped the back of his neck with a towelette and reached into the back seat for a plastic bag. He dangled it from his fingers as he shook it up and down. "You can put your trash in here."

They finished cleaning up, and Heath started the truck. As he turned onto the road, Willow gathered her hair into a ponytail and clasped it over her shoulder. "Do you think Toby murdered your mother?"

"I have no idea. Why would he? But if he didn't, how would he know where she was…buried?" Heath flexed his fingers on the steering wheel.

"You said he told you they were close at the end, that she confided in him." She twisted her hair. "What if… what if he came on to her and she rebuffed him?"

Heath jerked his head toward her. "You mentioned that before. Do you really think that happened?"

"My mom implied Toby was a womanizer. Why would she lie?"

"That guy?" Gripping the steering wheel, Heath sat forward in the driver's seat. "Hard to believe."

"Why? Because he was something of a recluse? Perfect setting, actually. A lot of guys pretend to be a shoulder to cry on just to get close to a woman, gain her confidence, create an intimate emotional bond. Then bam."

"Bam. You mean he uses that to try to take the relationship to a different level, a physical level."

"Maybe your mom thought she had a friend, a confidant, and Toby wanted something more. Maybe he thought your mother was ripe for the picking and then easy to dispose of—" she clutched her throat "—sorry, because she had some mental health issues. Your father knew she had been suicidal in the past."

"You could be right, but why direct me to her grave? Especially me. If he had a guilty conscience after all these years, why not just turn himself in to the police?"

"He was ill, maybe sicker than anyone knew. It could've been the way he wanted to go out." Willow clasped her hands between her knees. "Do you think your mother's death has anything to do with the mineral rights on the property? Why did my father deed those to you? None of it makes sense."

"And why is it all important enough to want to kill two people?" He pointed his finger at her and then himself.

They continued asking each other almost rhetorical questions until Heath passed the stone sign indicating they'd crossed into the Samish reservation.

He made a few turns and tapped on the window. "The meeting is at the community center, and it looks like there's a standing-room-only turnout."

Willow took in all the cars parked at the side of the building and the line of people waiting to get inside. Her belly flip-flopped at the thought of being persona non grata at this event. She murmured, "Maybe I should've gone to Astrid's to visit the dogs. I would've been more welcome there."

"Don't worry." He threw the truck in Park and squeezed her knee. "I'm going to take all the heat off of you."

Placing her hand over his, she said, "Are you sure you're up to this, Heath? You just discovered that your mom is dead. We can leave right now, or you can leave, and I'll face them myself."

He killed the engine and released a long breath. "I always figured she was dead, so that part didn't hit me hard. I also suspected that Toby was sending me on a search for her body. Yeah, I admit actually finding her was a shock, but now I'm determined to figure out what happened to her and who's responsible. I may be way off, but this meeting is a starting point. All of this started when Bradford and Son agreed to partner with the Samish to develop the casino resort. They have to be connected."

"I agree, but you can hold this meeting another day."

"Really?" He slipped his hand from beneath hers and reached for the door. "Someone tried to kill us today, Willow. How much time do you think we have until they're successful?"

"Okay, let's do this." She pushed out of the truck and put her arms through the straps of her backpack purse.

As Heath took her arm to walk through the doors of the community center, Willow pinned back her shoulders and lifted her chin. The crowd parted for them, and she tuned out their chatter. As they ascended the

dais that sported a long table, several chairs and a laptop connected to a projector, Willow caught the eye of
Mindy Whitecotton, a Samish native, who worked at
the university in Seattle.

Mindy gave her a wink, and the knots in Willow's
gut loosened just a little.

Heath pulled out the chair in the middle, in front of
the laptop, for Lee, and Willow slid into the chair on the
end before Heath could get any crazy ideas and seat her
next to Lee. An associate of Lee's sat next to him on the
other side, and Willow flattened her lips when she saw
Ellie Keel take the chair next to him.

As Heath lowered himself into the seat beside her,
Willow nudged him with her elbow and hissed, "What's
Ellie doing up here?"

"Maybe Lee invited her." Heath put his finger to his
lips as Lee tapped the microphone.

"There should be room for everyone. There are a few
empty seats in the front." He cupped his hand in the air.
"Everyone is welcome. Everyone, come in."

Willow gazed at the stragglers squeezing past knees
to grab lone seats. Lee must feel confident that he had
majority support for the casino project. Garrett Keel
raised his hand from his seat in the front row to wave at
her, and she nodded back. Then she folded her hands in
front of her as Lee started the presentation.

When the lights dimmed and the video started, Willow shifted her chair to see the plans for the new casino and the support facilities for it that would never be
built on her property—no matter how many of her cab-
ins burned down.

The video presentation ended, and a buzz of excitement rippled through the room. Maybe Heath should've led with the odds of this thing getting built before Lee drummed up the enthusiasm for it.

Lee smiled and rubbed his hands together. "Beautiful, isn't it? But we can't do it alone. That's why we're partnering with Bradford and Son. So let me introduce you to Heath Bradford, who spent some time here on the island with his family and never forgot its beauty and potential. Let's welcome Heath tonight."

A smattering of applause accompanied Heath as he stood up and took the mic from Lee. When it faded, he said, "Lee's right. The Samish need to partner with a developer, us, to realize the full extent of Lee's…vision. As he mentioned, the Samish have the land for a small casino on the leeward side of the island but will need more land to increase the profitability of the casino with adjacent hotels and restaurants."

Someone yelled from the back. "Do we have Toby's land now?"

"About that." Heath cleared his throat. "As I'm sure all of you know by now, Toby Keel passed away, and he owned one of the properties we were looking into acquiring."

Several people started chanting, "Ellie, Ellie, Ellie."

Ellie Keel jumped up from her seat and waved her arms as if she were at a political rally. She reached over the table and snatched the mic from Heath. "You all know my uncle died, but what you don't know is that he left the property to Willow Sands, the owner of the other property in question."

The room erupted, and Heath sidled behind Willow's

chair and placed a hand on her shoulder. Her hands still folded, Willow gazed out at the agitated crowd.

When they quieted down to a low hum, Ellie continued, "But just to let you know, my brother, Garrett, and I plan to sue to get the property in our names."

Mindy Whitecotton stood up and confronted Ellie. "You and Lee are just assuming all of us Samish want to exploit our land for profit. When did you hold the last vote, Lee? Where are those results? Where's the transparency regarding the support of this abuse of our land?"

More cries went up, and Willow couldn't tell where most people stood. She did mouth a silent thank-you to Mindy.

Heath rapped on the table to restore some order and asked Ellie for the mic, which she grudgingly handed over. "Look, this is an emotionally charged issue. The bottom line is the developers are not going to convince Willow Sands to sell out for this project. Ever. If the Keels are successful in their lawsuit, maybe we have room to move forward. However..." Heath stopped and inhaled, expanding his chest. "...there are new circumstances on Toby's former property that'll put a stop to any designs on that land."

Lee's head shot up. "What are you talking about, Heath?"

A muscle twitched at the corner of Heath's eye, and Willow longed to stand up, take the mic away from him and lead him out of here.

"Skeletal remains were found buried behind Toby's cabin."

The room descended into chaos again, and Willow had had enough. As several people surged toward the dais, smacking the table and shouting questions, she dragged her sweatshirt from the back of her chair. The notebook containing recipes, which she'd unearthed from Toby's cabin, fell onto the floor.

Willow picked it up and smoothed it out on the table, then hoisted her bag next to it. She stuffed the notebook inside the purse; she and Heath could have a look at it later, once she got him back to the hotel and they had a proper meal. She doubted Toby would bother hiding something that was just a homemade book of recipes.

The attendees began to dissipate, but Heath was still in an intense conversation with Lee.

Ellie planted herself in front of Willow. "Just what are you up to now? Are you going to make some sort of claim that the skeleton belongs to some long-lost Samish and that land is sacred burial ground? You do not get to appropriate our culture."

Willow ignored Ellie's finger stabbing at her because she couldn't drag her gaze away from the red flannel shirt draped over Ellie's arm. Was it missing a piece?

"Willow's not even the one making the claim, Ellie, and Heath didn't say anything about a burial place. It's probably another one of gruesome Dr. Summers's victims." Garrett draped an arm over Ellie's shoulder. "Let's go, sis, and maybe let go."

Willow watched them as they turned away and made for the exit, Ellie struggling to stuff her arms into the flannel shirt.

Heath finished his conversation with Lee, who was staying behind with a few helpers to gather their materials and straighten up the community center.

As they walked back to Heath's truck, Willow said,

"I saw Ellie wearing a red flannel tonight, and she sure came in with both barrels blazing."

Heath raised an eyebrow as he opened the passenger door. "I can't see Ellie skulking around the woods outside your cabin in her stiletto heels."

"People can change shoes."

When he settled next to her behind the wheel, he turned to her. "But you're right about her going off. Maybe she mentioned the lawsuit to see how many people are on her side."

"There were a lot in favor of the expanded casino, but there were plenty who seemed okay with the smaller effort or no effort at all, thanks to Mindy Whitecotton." She placed her purse on the floor between her feet. "Do you mind stopping by the storage facility in town? I talked to Levi, who owns the place, when you were digging. He booked a unit for me and said the attendant would be there until midnight. Said I could stop by anytime before then."

"That's fine. As long as you don't mind grabbing a bite to eat in town after we stash your stuff. I haven't eaten since we had that lunch before the plane drama."

"Do you know how Captain Mark is doing?"

"I haven't called again since the earlier call, but I'll try again tomorrow morning. I'd sure like to know what happened in that pizza place before our flight."

"I'm sure he wants to know what happened, too. His pilot's license is on the line if the FAA determines he knowingly drank or did drugs before flying."

As Heath navigated his truck back to town, Willow patted the bag at her feet. "During all the excitement, I forgot to tell you that I found a hiding place in Toby's cabin. I removed the only item that he stashed there."

"What did you find?"

She unzipped her purse and withdrew the notebook with pictures of fruits and vegetables on the cover. She waved it. "It looks like a recipe book. I thumbed through a few pages, and it's filled with handwritten recipes."

"Why would Toby be hiding a cookbook?" He pulled up to the last stop sign before heading into town and glanced at the notebook in her hand.

"No clue. Maybe he had other things stored there over the years, and this was just a leftover. It's odd that he hid it, though." She dropped the notebook on the floor next to her purse and pointed out the window. "Take that turn up there."

She continued giving him directions to the storage containers until he pulled up to the boxy building that sat just outside a locked gate. The glow from the office highlighted a man sitting at a desk.

"He must be the night clerk. I'll jump out and get my key."

Heath pulled in front of the office, and Willow hopped from the truck, dragging her purse with her.

After some exchange of information, Willow grasped the key to her unit and returned to the truck. The gate slid open, and Heath rolled through.

Less than thirty minutes later, her boxes and bins neatly lining the interior of the storage unit, they pulled away from the facility amid a discussion about what to eat.

Heath's preference for bar food won out, so they meandered to the Salty Crab, which boasted a rambunctious crowd long past the dinner phase of their evening.

With most of the clientele watching a game at the bar or playing pool in the back, Heath and Willow snagged a table by the window.

They ordered beers and a variety of appetizers. When the beers arrived, Heath took a long pull from his. "I can't believe the day we had. I feel like we're on a runaway train heading for some catastrophe."

"You and me both." She ran a thumb up the side of her sweating bottle. "The only good thing about this summer is...you."

"I feel the same way. I had such a thing for you back in the day. I even blurted it out to your father."

"Really?" Her face warmed beneath his intent stare, and she wrinkled her nose. "He never mentioned it to me."

He snapped his fingers. "Hey, maybe that's why he left the mineral rights to me and the property to you— so we'd be joined forever."

"It's as good a guess as any." She ran the tip of her finger around the rim of her bottle. "He should've told me. Maybe we could've at least gotten to know each other better."

"We're doing that now, aren't we?"

"Yeah, but it feels..." She lifted her shoulders. "...I don't know...forced, like we almost don't have a choice in the matter."

"Like it's part of that runaway train?" He moved his bottle out of the way to make room for the waitress to put down several plates of deep-fried junk food.

"A little." She pinched a hot onion ring between the tips of her fingers and waved it in the air. "Not to say I'm not fully in charge of my faculties and making decisions on my own."

"I would be surprised if you ever made a decision that wasn't wholly yours." He squirted a puddle of ketchup on the edge of one of the plates.

They concentrated on their food for several minutes, but Willow couldn't stay away from the subject at hand for long. She swiped a napkin across her mouth. "Were you ever able to reach your father and ask him why he didn't tell you about the mineral rights?"

"Nope." Heath crunched into a fried zucchini stick, which they'd ordered at her insistence.

"You're going to tell him about your mom, right?"

"Not immediately. I'll wait until the final identification has been made."

She tipped the rest of her beer into her mouth and grabbed her sweatshirt. "I'm going to use the ladies' room. Be right back."

He circled a finger at her sweatshirt as she shoved her arms in the sleeves and grabbed her purse. "You need a sweatshirt for the restroom?"

"It's out back. This is a high-class joint. Can't you tell?"

As she swept past him, he captured her hand and kissed it. The stupid smile on her face lasted until she pushed through the back door of the bar. The music faded as she crossed the alley to the public restrooms, shared by several businesses on this street.

She reached for the door handle, and a shadow appeared around the corner of the building. As she turned toward the source, she felt a sharp pain scream through her head.

She took a quick, gasping breath before the darkness enveloped her.

Chapter Sixteen

Heath swept the last onion ring through the smear of ketchup on his plate and popped it in his mouth. When the waitress appeared at the table to collect some plates, he stopped her. "Hey, where are the restrooms?"

"They're out the back door by the bar." She rolled her eyes. "We have to share public restrooms with the other businesses, but don't worry. They're all closed now, so those bathrooms are all ours."

"Thanks." Heath glanced at his phone, and a muscle twitched in his jaw. What was taking Willow so long?

He hailed the busy waitress again to tell her they hadn't left yet and to leave the check. Then he made a beeline to the back door. As he opened it, a woman crashed against his chest.

"Whoa, sorry…" he began.

She grabbed a handful of his shirt. "There's a woman by the bathrooms. She's on the ground, unconscious."

Adrenaline surged through Heath's body so fast, his head swam. "Go to the bar and get some help, and call 911."

As the woman stumbled toward the bar, Heath charged outside. The lights from the building illuminated Willow's still form on the ground. He rushed to her side and dropped to his knees.

"Willow! Willow!" As he brushed her hair from her face, his fingers met a sticky wetness.

She moaned, and relief swept through his body.

"Help is on the way. Don't try to move right now. You have a head injury. Does anything else hurt?" He ran his hands over her body and didn't feel any more blood.

The bartender ran outside and hovered over Heath with some towels. "Laila wasn't sure what happened, but she did see some blood. Use these."

Heath tugged a towel from the bartender's hand and pressed it against the spot on Willow's head where he'd seen the blood. "Did you call 911?"

"On the way. Does she need water?" The bartender held up a bottle.

Willow croaked out a few unintelligible words, and Heath put his ear to her mouth.

"Ambulance is on the way," he promised her. "You're gonna be fine."

She curled her fingers around his arm and rasped, "Help me sit up. I'm okay."

"Let's wait for the EMTs. Do you want some water?"

She answered, "Yeah, prop me up, and I'll drink some water."

Heath crawled behind her and hoisted her body halfway into his lap while holding the towel against her head.

Seeing Heath's struggle, the bartender crouched down and held the water bottle to Willow's lips. "Here you go. What happened out here?"

Willow swallowed most of the water, while some of it dribbled down her chin, mixing with the blood that had trickled down her face from her head wound. "I think someone hit me, like with an object on the side of my head. He came up behind me."

The bartender whistled. "That's messed up. Even more reason why we need our own bathroom inside the bar. Did he…assault you?"

"No!" Willow pushed away the water bottle and patted her shoulder and the ground next to her. "Where's my bag?"

Heath scanned the ground. "Your purse?"

"Yeah, the backpack purse I was wearing when I walked out here. At least I had my phone in my pocket." She grimaced and squeezed her eyes closed.

"Don't worry about that now." Heath lifted his head. "I hear the sirens. Just relax."

"Relax?" Willow struggled against him but tired out after a few seconds. "I was just bashed on the head and mugged—for my purse. Why do they want my purse, Heath?"

The bartender scratched his head. "Uh, probably wanted your cards and cash, but you can cancel those cards. It's your head you need to worry about."

Her question confused the bartender, but Heath knew exactly what she meant. This mugging was all part of what they were discovering about his mother, the nickel vein, the properties, the development plan.

When the ambulance arrived, it dispersed the small crowd of people who had gathered in the alley to watch the drama. The EMTs fussed over Willow and walked her to the back of the ambulance while Heath talked to the deputy who'd come out on the call.

"Deputy Fletcher." He shook Heath's hand. "I'll talk

to Willow once she gets sorted out over there, but you said she didn't get a look at her attacker?"

"Saw his shadow, and while she turned, he hit her. Stole her purse."

"You wouldn't happen to know what her purse looks like, would you?" Deputy Fletcher scratched a few notes on his pad.

"It was one of those purses that doubles as a backpack, so kind of big, but I couldn't tell you the color." Heath shrugged. "The purse may have just been a cover. Willow's cabin was ransacked, and then someone set it on fire. This has to be connected to those events."

"Doesn't sound like someone's trying to kill her. He could've finished the job here. You think it's some kind of scare tactic to get her to sell that property for the casino?"

"Sounds like you already know a lot, but not everything." Heath twisted the towel stained with Willow's blood in his hands. "There was an incident on a small plane we hired to San Juan. The pilot collapsed."

Fletcher bounced his pencil on the notepad. "I heard about that. That was you? You have your pilot's license? I'm taking flying lessons right now."

"That's great, but the point is Willow could've died if that plane had crashed, so I'm sure this is more than a run-of-the-mill mugging."

"It might be, but we have no witnesses, no description from Willow, no cameras, no weapon." Fletcher tipped his head toward Willow, sitting on the back of the ambulance, a white bandage on her head. "I'll ask Willow a few questions."

As Fletcher questioned Willow, Heath stopped one

of the EMTs. "Is she going to be okay? What happened to her?"

The EMT tapped his head. "Someone hit her on the side of the noggin with a blunt object. Piece of wood, maybe. Found some slivers in her hair. She'll be fine. Doesn't want to go to the emergency room and doesn't need to. Shouldn't be driving or be on her own tonight, just in case she shows signs of a concussion."

"I'll take care of her. Pain meds?"

"Ibuprofen in another four hours, if she needs it."

The deputy and the EMTs wrapped up about the same time, and Heath and Willow watched them leave from the back door of the bar. He took her hand. "I shouldn't have let you come out here on your own."

"Nonsense. It's a well-lit alley to the bathrooms. Whoever hit me knew we were here and was waiting for an opportunity. He saw it and grabbed it." She tilted her head and fingered her bandage.

"What is it? Do you remember something?"

"Perfume. I smelled perfume before I got whacked. What if it is Ellie? Did you see her tonight? She was livid."

"The perfume could've come from anywhere. Lots of women crossing back and forth in that alley." Noticing the set of her jaw, Heath said, "But we can have West talk to her. Maybe if she suspects we're onto her, she'll back off."

"Why did they take my purse?"

"Like I told Deputy Fletcher, the purse could've just been a ruse to make it look like a mugging in their continuing plan to terrorize you."

"It's all so senseless. After what you sprang on everyone tonight, you'd think they'd just leave this alone for a while." She ran a tongue along her bottom lip. "I'm dying of thirst. Can we go back inside and get something to drink?"

"When I left, I told the waitress we weren't skipping out on the check and to leave it on the table. It's probably still there."

They shuffled back into the Salty Crab, and several people peppered them with questions and offered their condolences. Their table still sported Willow's half-full beer bottle and a pair of bedraggled chicken wings, but no check.

Heath went to the bar to get Willow a Coke. He gave the bartender a fist bump. "Thanks for your help out there, man. You can send the waitress over with our check and add a couple of Cokes to it."

The bartender waved a tattooed arm. "On the house, my man. Hope Willow's okay."

A few minutes later, Heath carried the drinks back to the table where Willow was scrolling through her phone. He put her drink down on a coaster. "Too bad your phone wasn't in your purse. At least we'd have a way to track it."

"Not if they turned the phone off immediately. Then I would've been out a purse *and* my phone." She smacked the table. "My key. The key to my new storage unit. Maybe they followed us there and wanted to search my unit. See what I rescued from the fire."

"I didn't think of that, but the storage facility has cameras. They can't just waltz in there, even with a key."

"Ever hear of disguises? And I had a security camera at my place. Didn't stop someone from burning it down." She sucked down her drink with the straw. "Let's go back to the storage facility."

"Now?" Heath settled back in his chair and crossed his arms. "What do you expect to find there at this hour?"

"Um, someone using my key to get into my storage unit. I still even had the card in my purse with my unit number." Willow was already halfway out of her seat.

Heath gulped down the rest of his drink and followed her. So much for taking care of Willow.

He drove back to the storage facility, with the same attendant in the tiny office. "I'll go in with you this time."

The man in the office buzzed the door open when he spotted Willow out the window. As they entered, he said, "More to load up? Hey, what happened to your head?"

"Hi, Zev." Willow patted her bandage. "Someone mugged me and stole my purse. The key to my unit was in there, along with the unit number, and I'm afraid who-ever stole it is planning to come here and rip me off."

"That's not cool. Nobody has been here this evening since you left, but that key opens the gate to the entire facility. They could come after hours."

Heath rubbed Willow's back. "We can't spend all night out here, keeping watch. You need to get some rest."

Zev spread his hands. "We have cameras, if that helps."

"Someone could come in here with a disguise—a hoodie, a face mask—we wouldn't know who it was." Willow sagged against the desk, her face pale.

"Okay, that's it. You're going back to the hotel now." As Heath curled an arm around Willow's waist, he asked

Zev, "Is there something you can do to prevent the mugger from getting in?"

"I'll tell you what." Zev clicked on his keyboard. "I'm going to assign you a different unit right now. You didn't have much stuff, did you? I'll bring a forklift to your unit and move the contents tonight. If this mugger does come back here, he's gonna find an empty unit. Will that work?"

"But we won't be able to catch them in the act."

Heath placed a finger against Willow's trembling lips. "It'll work for now. Thanks, Zev. We'll pick up her new key tomorrow morning."

They left the unit, and Willow collapsed in his truck. "I'm exhausted."

"Of course you are. I'm running on empty here, and I didn't even get bashed on the head." As he backed out of the parking space in front of the storage facility, Willow's phone buzzed.

"Don't answer that."

She glanced at the display. "It's the DFSD. Hello?" She listened for a few seconds and said, "We'll be right there."

Heath groaned. "What wild-goose chase are we going on now?"

"Someone found my purse down by the harbor and turned it in to the sheriff's department. Maybe they snagged my storage unit key and didn't want to be caught with the purse."

"This is it. The last stop of the day." Heath peeled out of the parking lot and barely stayed within the speed limit on his way to the DFSD.

Deputy Fletcher met them in the lobby. "Good news, huh? I was just getting ready to go off duty when a couple who was spending the night on their boat came in. Found it right by the dock. And your credit cards are still in there, although I do recommend you replace them just in case. Oh, and if you had any cash, that's gone."

Willow thrust out her hand. "Give it over."

Fletcher's eyebrows jumped to his hairline. "Sure, it's behind the desk. Sarge?"

An officer on the phone reached beneath the counter and handed Willow's purse to Fletcher. Willow practically snatched the purse from his hand and carried it to the seats against the wall.

She unzipped the bag and turned it upside down, shaking out the contents onto one of the chairs. Her wallet dropped out, along with a small makeup bag, a sunglasses case, a few pens, some spare change and other odds and ends. Willow pounced on a silver key and held it up. "It's the storage unit key."

"I guess they weren't planning to search your unit after all." Heath crouched down to retrieve a couple of items that had rolled under the chair. "Don't forget these."

Willow stared at the objects in his palm and pinched a silver tube of lipstick between her fingers. "This isn't mine."

"It fell onto the floor from your purse."

She carried the lipstick in front of her as if it was dynamite and parked herself in front of Fletcher. "You said you checked my wallet for my cards. Did you see this lipstick when you did?"

"Oh, that. The couple who turned in your purse said the lipstick was a few feet away from the purse itself. They figured it had fallen out, along with a few coins that had rolled in that same direction. They just dropped it back into the purse."

"It's not mine."

Fletcher shrugged and turned away to finish his conversation with the sergeant, but Heath watched Willow's wide eyes.

"What's wrong, Willow?"

"The lipstick isn't mine, but maybe it belongs to the person who stole my bag." She pulled off the lid and cranked up the scarlet-red lipstick. "And I know who wears this shade."

Chapter Seventeen

Willow waved the lipstick in Heath's face. "It's hers. It belongs to Ellie Keel. She always wears this hideous shade—day or night."

Heath led her out of the station with a backward wave to the deputies. "Maybe it is Ellie's, but why? Why did she take your purse only to dump it? You found your storage unit key, so it's not that. You think she needed a couple of bucks that badly?"

"I don't know, Heath." Willow clutched the bag to her chest. "Maybe she copied the key. Maybe she took my hotel key." With shaky fingers, she unzipped the side pocket of the purse and felt for her hotel key card. She pulled it out. Tears sprang to her eyes, and she slid down the wall of the station into a crouching position.

"Are you all right?" Heath knelt before her on the ground.

"Physically, I'm fine. I'm just so frustrated. What does she want?"

"Physically, you're not fine. I'm taking you back to the hotel now, and I don't care if someone sets fire to your storage unit. We're not making any detours."

She gave in and gave herself over to Heath's tender

care. He helped her to her feet, dried the tears on her cheeks and half carried her to his truck.

When they got back to the hotel, Heath took her to her own room, but he followed her inside. "A warm bath, some hot tea, ibuprofen and rest. Dr. Heath's orders."

She managed a smile. "I like the sound of that."

"Sit." He maneuvered her to the bed and placed gentle pressure on her shoulders. "I'm going to run that bath and have a cup of tea waiting for you when you come out, unless you want something stronger. I'm not sure the EMTs would recommend alcohol for a concussion, though."

"I don't have a concussion, but tea sounds perfect."

She closed her eyes to the sounds of the water running in the tub. When Heath came out of the bathroom, he crouched in front of her and removed her shoes.

"Go relax. I'll make the tea and leave a message for West to look into Ellie Keel. We don't have much proof, but we have the lipstick. He can at least start talking to her."

Willow shuffled to the bathroom, peeled off her clothes and sank into the tub. What was Ellie looking for? Did the woman really believe that if Willow and Heath were out of the way, she could get Willow's mother to sell the property? What good would the casino development do her, even if Mom did sell? Ellie wouldn't get the money from that sale. She must have some other interests in the casino deal. Maybe she'd worked out something with Lee.

These thoughts were not helping her relax. She cupped warm water in her hands and tipped it onto her chest. She took deep breaths through her mouth and exhaled them from her nose. Her muscles still ached with tension, and the questions still buzzed through her brain.

There was only one person who could settle her mind and soothe her body. "Heath!"

He poked his head into the room as if he'd been waiting outside. "Yeah? You okay?"

"You were the one digging today. Don't you need a bath?"

"I thought you'd never ask."

The door flew open, and he had his clothes off by the time he reached the tub. "Is there room?"

"I'll make room."

And suddenly, every bad thought dissipated with the steam.

THE FOLLOWING MORNING, Heath edged out of bed, away from Willow's sleeping form. She still needed her rest. After every crazy thing that had happened to them yesterday, they both should've fallen into an exhausted sleep when they got back to the hotel. Instead, they'd made frantic, passionate love, as if to erase all the bad from their lives.

What had he said earlier? Their relationship, their attraction, seemed to be like a runaway train. And that train had gone off the rails last night.

He had to try to reach his father today. He couldn't keep the discovery of his mother's body to himself or wait for the confirmation. That locket told him everything he needed to know—well, not everything. He still didn't know what had happened to her or who put her in the ground.

His father deserved to hear this from him. Dad had suffered, too. He'd finally moved on with his life, with another woman, and they needed a chance for happiness with a clean slate. Nothing over their heads.

He left Willow a note, anchored by a bottle of ibuprofen and a promise to order her breakfast. She'd planned a nice, peaceful day hanging out at Astrid's and visiting the dogs. He'd take care of getting the key to her new storage unit and talking to West about Ellie's involvement in the campaign of terror against Willow.

Before he left the room, he kissed Willow on the forehead.

Back in his own room, he showered and changed clothes. Then he made the call he'd been dreading since yesterday. He used an app for a face-to-face call with his father.

The old man picked up on the first ring. "Son, it's good to finally hear from you…and see you. You look like hell. Told you that Dead Falls Island was always trouble. How's the deal going?"

"The deal is dead, Dad. Whether Lee Scott and his associates decide to go through with a smaller casino is up to them, but they're going to have to give up on the supporting infrastructure and tourist venues. Those two pieces of land are not for sale and never will be."

"I figured it was a long shot with the Tree Girl, but are Keel's niece and nephew not interested in making a bunch of money?"

"That's the thing, Dad. Paul Sands had some kind of deal in place that left the property to his daughter, Willow, after Keel passed. And that's what happened. She'll never sell."

His father blew a kiss to someone, presumably his wife, before turning back to his phone. "There is a little secret about that property that might just change her mind, Heath."

"It's not a secret, Dad. I found out about the mineral rights—*my* mineral rights. And I'm not going to threaten Willow with the exploitation of those rights to get her to sell for the lesser of two evils."

To his surprise, his father cracked a smile. "Still have a crush on that girl, huh?"

Heath's mouth gaped open for a few seconds. Who *didn't* know he'd had a crush on Willow back then, except Willow? "It's not just that. The island doesn't need any more development."

"Then that's it." His father ran a hand through his salt-and-pepper hair. "One thing I know after running this company for almost thirty years is you can't make people sell their property if they don't want to. Not worth it in the end."

"Th-there's something else, Dad."

"What? You're going to marry this girl?" He crooked his finger, and Heath's stepmother, Lilith, came into view, her head next to his father's.

"Hi, Heath. Are you getting married?"

The two of them giggled like a couple of teenagers.

He shook his head. "Not yet. What are you two doing right now?"

"Getting ready to have dinner and then a gondola ride. I know they're kitschy, but this is Lilith's first time in Italy. Have to do it right. If you're not getting married, what else were you going to tell me?"

Heath rubbed his thumb over the locket in his hand. "It can wait. Just wanted to let you know the deal's off and tell you I knew about the nickel vein. One thing, though."

"Fire away, but make it fast. The pasta here is singing to me."

"Do you know why Paul Sands signed those rights over to me?"

"No clue, son. I know he always felt sorry for you for some reason. Almost like he harbored some guilt when it came to you." He kissed his wife's fingers. "Gotta go. We'll meet when I get back."

Heath said goodbye to his father and Lilith and continued stroking the locket, as if it could give him answers. What did Paul Sands do to make him feel guilty?

His father took the news better than he'd expected him to take it. Marriage had softened his father's outlook. Lilith was young enough to be Dad's daughter, but she seemed to really care about him. She made him happy, and that had to count for something.

Heath texted Willow in case she was awake, but she didn't respond. He let her know he was on his way to pick up her storage unit key and talk to West about the lipstick found near her stolen bag.

As he grabbed a light jacket, his phone buzzed. Mark Santos's number flashed on the display. "Captain Mark, are you okay?"

"I'm madder than hell. I did *not* take any drugs before that flight. I didn't even have a beer."

"Is that what the tests are showing?"

"Tests are showing I had barbiturates in my system. No way. Didn't happen." He hacked a few times. "Just wanted to say I'm sorry about what went down, and I'm so thankful you were able to take over the controls. But I wasn't responsible for that mess."

"I believe you, Mark. Do you think someone drugged you?"

"Maybe. I have no idea who would want to or why, but I can't think of any other explanation for my condition."

"Are you out of the hospital? Can I come and talk to you today? I don't know the who, but I'm pretty sure about the why."

WILLOW BURROWED BENEATH the covers, reaching for the warmth of Heath's body. He'd been the cure she'd needed last night. How had she become so dependent on that man in such a short amount of time?

But her fingers met smooth, empty sheets, so she sat up suddenly, cradling her sore head. Squinting through sleep-encrusted lids, she spotted a square of white paper on the desk.

She inched out of bed to claim it, skimming over Heath's note. So, he'd take care of all the business today, and she'd relax at Astrid's with the dogs. She shook out an ibuprofen into her palm. She'd like to be there to see the look on Ellie's face when West questioned her.

She tossed the gel cap back with a gulp of water and thumbed through her text messages. Determined to make her day stress free, Heath had ordered her a breakfast of oatmeal with bananas, berries, nuts and almond milk. All she had to do was call room service to send it up.

Smiling, she ordered the breakfast and stepped into the bathroom for a quick shower. Different muscles ached this morning from the ones that throbbed with pain yesterday.

By the time she finished dressing and carefully removing the bandage from her head, room service knocked on the door. As she ate, she sent Heath a text thanking him for breakfast, or what had turned out to be lunch, and the other errands he was running on her behalf.

She stacked up the room service tray and fished her makeup bag from her purse. She often used the backpack purse when she had a lot of items to carry. Thankfully, she hadn't stuffed it last night on the way to the meeting.

She took a quick breath and pressed a hand to her chest. The recipe notebook. Hadn't she stashed that in her purse last night at the meeting? No. She'd left it in Heath's truck. Had wanted to show him then, but had gotten sidetracked giving him directions to the storage facility. She'd have to text him to remind him to bring it in with him when he finished his business…or her business.

Toby had to have a good reason for hiding that notebook beneath the floorboards, and it wasn't that he was planning to publish a cookbook and wanted to keep the recipes secret.

The hotel safe beckoned, and she checked the space in her bag. She had room for a gun, and after last night's adventure, she'd feel better with it—even at Astrid's with the dogs. She transferred the gun from the safe to her purse and hung it over a chair.

The sticky antiseptic from yesterday had created some clumps in her hair, so she pulled it into a ponytail. She grabbed her bag, patted the weapon inside and drove her truck to Astrid's. As she stepped out of her vehicle, Luna and Apollo charged toward her, Astrid's dog, Sherlock, trailing after them.

"It's dogpalooza!" Willow crouched down and wrapped her arms around the squirming mutts. "C'mon, Sherlock. You, too."

"They are so happy to see you."

Willow waved at Astrid, posed like a model on the porch that wrapped around the huge cabin. The place belonged to Astrid's brother, Tate, but she and her son had been staying with him for a while, and would continue to live here until Tate returned from an assignment in DC. Willow had a sneaking suspicion that Astrid and Olly would move in with West Chandler when Tate returned.

"You look nice," Willow told her. "Too nice for the rugged outdoors of Dead Falls."

Astrid made a face. "I know, sweetie. I'm sorry. I have a showing in town, and I have to leave. Don't worry. Olly is at his friend's house, and you can help yourself to anything in the fridge for lunch."

"No worries, Astrid. I'll hang out with the dogs. If I leave before you get back, do you want me to put them inside or leave them out?"

"Inside, please. When nobody's home, Sherlock still tends to wander."

"Got it, but if not today, let's catch up soon. I like the new sheriff." She flashed Astrid a thumbs-up. "I approve."

"I'm going to have a get-together when Tate comes home. I'll even invite Heath Bradford." Astrid gave her a broad wink. "Can you hold on to Sherlock while I run to my car? I don't want him jumping on my slacks."

Willow curled her fingers around Sherlock's collar. "I have him."

Astrid minced out to the Jeep in her high heels and beeped her horn when she drove away.

Willow settled in a chair at the edge of the firepit with a couple of balls and a knotted rope. Luna and Sherlock tussled and tumbled and chased the ball, while Apollo lazed contentedly at her feet.

She'd almost forgotten about the outside world when the dogs stopped their play and turned toward the woods, barking up a storm.

"Hey, get back here. You are not taking off on my watch, Sherlock." She grabbed a leash and corralled the big shepherd mix, leading him back to the house. "I'll give you some snacks inside, I'll have lunch, and then we'll resume our romp out here."

She didn't have to coerce the other two dogs. They scrambled after her and Sherlock, and she herded them inside the house.

About to step inside after the dogs, she heard a twig snap behind her and whirled around.

Garrett Keel raised a hand. "Hi, Willow. Got a minute?"

She licked her lips and considered releasing the dogs again, but her gaze flicked to her purse by the chair and the lump from her gun inside. She closed the door and stayed on the porch.

"Hey, Garrett. If you're coming here to put pressure on me or threaten me, give it up."

He slicked back his black hair. "I'm not my sister."

"What does that mean, Garrett?"

He aimed a toe, shod in an expensive cowboy boot, at a rock circling the firepit and then thought better of it. "Ellie has gone off the deep end. She's made some kind of devil's bargain with Lee Scott if she can deliver Uncle Toby's property. I—I'm worried about what she might do next."

Descending the porch as if approaching a wild animal, Willow said, "Is she responsible for the fire at my cabin? The airplane? My so-called mugging last night?"

Garrett pressed a clenched fist against his mouth. "Are you okay, Willow?"

"Is she trying to kill me?"

"She just wants to…convince you to see reason."

"That's not going to happen, Garrett." She edged a little closer to her purse. "And why are you here?"

"I want to get evidence against my sister once and for all. Put her where she belongs—in prison."

"Evidence against Ellie?" Willow spread her hands. "I don't have that. Just her lipstick and maybe a red flannel shirt—weak."

"I—I think you might have it, but you don't know it. Ellie's been searching for it."

"Searching for what? I didn't find anything in my father's papers—or Toby's, for that matter."

"Did you, by any chance, find a homemade recipe book? Handwritten recipes pasted inside a notebook with some food drawings on the cover?"

Willow's mouth dropped open. "I—I don't have it."

The pleasant mask dropped from Garrett's face as he took a menacing step toward her. "Don't lie to me, Willow."

Chapter Eighteen

Heath strode down the dock toward Mark Santos's boat and spotted Mark on the deck of a neat little Catalina 22 Sport. "Nice boat."

"Isn't she?" Mark patted the side. "Don't worry. I'm not going to set sail with you and pass out—unless you also know how to sail a boat."

"I do, but I'm not interested in taking over the controls again." Heath stepped onto the boat, joining Mark. "Tell me everything you remember."

"Took care of all my postflight duties and walked over to Seadog Pizza. They had a couple of games on the TVs there, so I ordered a pizza and a Coke. There were a few of my boating friends there, and we talked some smack for a while."

"Any strangers talk to you?"

"Of course. It's that kind of place—long tables, communal dining and drinking."

"Women?"

Mark cracked a grin. "Always."

"Any get close enough to your drink to slip you something?"

"Sure did. I even went to the john a few times and left my drink unattended. Don't they tell young ladies these days to take their drinks with them when they're in a bar? Should've followed that advice."

"Do you remember what any of these women looked like?"

"One particular blonde caught my eye. I even offered to take her up in my plane." Mark winked.

"No raven-haired sirens?"

"Could've been."

Heath fished his phone from his pocket and brought up a couple of photos he'd snatched of Ellie Keel from the internet. He turned his phone around to Mark. "Did you see her there?"

Mark shoved his sunglasses to the top of his head and squinted. "Naw, I don't think so."

Disappointed, Heath swiped to the next one. "How about this angle?"

Taking the phone from him, Mark brought it closer to his face and used his fingertips to zoom in. "Yeah."

"She was there?" Heath's pulse jumped. They needed all the evidence they could get against Ellie.

"Not the lady, man. The dude. That dude standing behind her was at the Seadog, all dressed up. Looked out of place."

Heath snatched the phone back from Mark and stared at Garrett Keel's face, enlarged. The two of them could be working together.

He smacked Mark on the back. "Thanks, man. I think we can get you cleared with the FAA. You were targeted and drugged."

A surprised Mark yelled his thanks as Heath clambered out of the boat. He had to tell Willow about this new development. He had no proof that Garrett Keel drugged Mark Santos, but they had a couple of starting points for West to dig his teeth into.

Back in his truck, he brought up Willow's texts to let her know about this latest development. He reread her text about the recipe book, and his gaze swept through the cab of his truck. The corner of the notebook peeked out from beneath the passenger seat, and he yanked on it.

As he pulled it free, several pages fell out of the middle of the book, and he gathered them in his hands. He glanced down at the loose pages and dropped them as if they'd scorched his hands.

He'd recognize his mother's handwriting anywhere.

"I'M NOT LYING, GARRETT. I don't have that notebook." Willow drew in her bottom lip, her gaze darting toward her purse.

He cleared his throat and looked at the sky. "I saw you with it at the meeting last night. You put it in your purse. I—I knew you were in trouble as soon as I saw it because I figured Ellie saw it, too. That's why she hit you and stole your purse. So if you just give it to me, you'll be safe from her."

From Ellie or from him?

"What's in that notebook, Garrett? It looked like recipes to me."

"So, you do have it. And you haven't read it. That's good. That'll keep you safe, Willow. Just give it to me, and I'll turn it over to Sheriff Chandler. It'll contain all the evidence he needs—against Ellie."

"What did Ellie do years ago that concerns the property and the casino project today? Why is Jessica Bradford's body buried behind Toby's cabin?"

Garrett's eyes bulged from their sockets. "How do you know that body is Jessica Bradford?"

"We know. Her son knows."

His face a bright red to match his sister's lipstick, Garrett screamed, "Where's the notebook, Willow?"

"It's right here, Garrett." Some branches at the tree line parted, and Heath stepped into the clearing. He raised the notebook in his hand. "I've got it right here… and I've read it."

Garrett staggered back a few steps, and then pulled a gun from his waistband. "Hand it over, Heath. Hand it over, or I'll shoot Willow, right here."

"I don't think you will, Garrett. You're not really a killer, are you? Despite what's in this booklet."

With Garrett's attention on Heath, Willow scooted closer to her purse, her foot inching toward the strap on the ground.

"It's a lie, Heath. I didn't kill your mother. Toby did."

Willow froze. "You killed Heath's mother?"

Heath spread his arms, still clutching the notebook. "You were right, Willow, except it wasn't Toby who came on to my mom. It was Garrett. She rebuffed him. Laughed at him, even, for his youth. Enraged, he tried to assault her, but she fought back. He shoved her, and her head cracked against a rock. An accident, right, Garrett? An accident during the commission of another crime."

"She was using Uncle Toby. She had an unhappy marriage, and she cried on Uncle Toby's shoulder. I told her she could cry on my shoulder anytime. I meant that. I loved your mother."

Heath snarled, "Stop! Your uncle helped you. You both buried her in the back, and Toby told everyone how suicidal she was, how she wanted to disappear and spare her family the grief. He may have even planted that note we found. But Toby wrote it all down, appended to my mother's own diary of events. He kept it in case you ever tried to turn things on him. In case you ever tried to get his property from Willow's dad."

"Willow's dad." Garrett spit out the words. "He knew what happened."

Willow covered her mouth. "My father knew what happened to Jessica?"

Garrett sneered. "That's why he left the mineral rights to her son. Guilt."

"He suspected, Willow." Heath shook the notebook. "He didn't know for sure. He just suspected."

Willow's gut churned. "So, you wanted your uncle's land to *stop* the development so nobody would ever find Jessica Bradford?"

Garrett threw back his head and laughed. "That's my sister's thing. I don't give a damn about this land, never did. But when my uncle threatened to expose me, I'd had enough."

Willow swallowed. "You did kill Toby."

Garrett's voice grew whiny. "It was an accident. The old fool was going to die anyway. His doctor had given him months. He wanted to come clean, clear his conscience—at my expense. I knew he'd invited Bradford over to tell him the truth. We argued. He fell."

"Just like my mother, huh?" Heath said. "People have a habit of falling around you and dying."

Willow taunted, "You should've waited until you found out where Toby kept the diary before killing him."

"I know." Garrett wiped his forehead with the back

of his hand. "When I discovered you inherited the property, Willow, I had to step up my game and search everything. I even drugged the dogs to get access, but I never would've killed them. I'm not a killer. Just in case it was in your place, I set fire to it. I would've torched Toby's place eventually. Guess I was too late."

Folding his arms, Heath clamped the diary against his body. "And the airplane? Mark Santos just ID'd you as being in the pizza place that day. I said before that you weren't a killer, but maybe you just like to do it at a distance or all by accident."

Garrett shrugged, and the gun wavered. "I knew you were going to San Juan Island to look up the mineral rights on the property. I saw an opportunity to take out both of you at the same time. Nobody else would be interested in a diary stuffed inside a cookbook. The mystery would've died with you two."

As Garrett turned his attention to Heath, Willow gestured toward her purse with fingers formed into a gun. Heath gave a quick shake of his head.

Heath coughed and spoke loudly. "What about Ellie? Is she involved in all this?"

"I planted her lipstick by Willow's purse when I dumped it just to shift the suspicion and buy myself time." Garrett snorted. "Not that she didn't enjoy the attacks on Willow. She might've suspected me of those attacks, but she never asked me directly. Like I said, she's all about this land deal. She's having an affair with Lee Scott and will do just about anything…"

While Garrett rambled, his attention on Heath and the notebook in his hand, Willow had snagged the strap of her purse with her foot. It now lay at her feet.

As she started to dip, Heath yelled out and tossed the notebook in the air. "Here you go, Garrett!"

Garrett lunged toward the notebook, still clutching the gun and waving it in her direction.

While Willow scrabbled for the weapon in her purse, Heath charged Garrett, knocking him to the ground. Garrett's gun went off, and Willow screamed.

She pulled her own gun from her purse and hopped up. She aimed it toward the two men rolling on the ground, grappling for agency over the weapon in Garrett's hand.

She ran toward them, her gun shaking. She'd never killed a living thing in her life and didn't know if she could do it now. She yelled, "Stop! I have a gun."

Garrett jerked his head in her direction, and Heath's knee cracked down on his wrist. The gun popped from his grasp, and Willow grabbed it.

As Garrett cowered on the ground, Heath jumped up and loomed above him, fists clenched. "I should kill you for what you did to my mother."

Willow stumbled back from him. A gun in each hand, she put them behind her back. "He's not worth it, Heath."

Garrett started laughing and choking, rolling onto his side. "This island. I hate this island."

Epilogue

Astrid yelled, "Olly, I'm gonna tell you one last time—you and your friends take the dogs in the back and get them away from the food."

A gaggle of boys ran to the back of Astrid's cabin, the three dogs passing them on the way.

Astrid came around with a bottle of wine and refilled everyone's glasses. "So, Garrett started this whole thing by killing his uncle over that diary, but by killing him he also cut off his only chance of finding the diary. Genius."

Heath crooked his fingers in air quotes. "'Accidentally' killed him, just like my mother."

"I'm so sorry about your mother, Heath." Astrid sat beside West and took his hand.

West said, "Forensics is still waiting for her dental records. I'm sorry, too, Heath. I don't know what kind of game Toby Keel was playing."

"I don't think Toby was a very good guy." Willow sniffed. "And I'm not sure about my father, either."

Stroking her arm, Heath said, "Garrett said your father had his suspicions but didn't know for sure."

"He left you the mineral rights to that property based on a suspicion?" Willow took a gulp of wine. "I don't think so."

"You know what I think?" Astrid raised a finger in the air. "I think your father knew about the mutual, unexpressed attraction between the two of you and left Heath those rights to bind you together forever."

"My father, the hopeless romantic." Willow snorted. "I doubt it."

"It's my fiancée who's the hopeless romantic." West twirled a lock of Astrid's blond hair around his finger. "Willow, is Ellie Keel still planning to sue you for the property?"

Willow answered, "I think she's going to drop the idea, just like Lee Scott dropped her. Lee didn't want any connection to the Keels after Garrett's arrest."

"Lee's also putting a hold on developing the Samish plot for the casino." Heath scooped a hand through his hair. "Too much attention, too much bad publicity."

Tilting her head, Willow asked, "How does your father feel about that?"

"Talk about old romantics—my father has new priorities since getting married."

"You hear that?" West leveled a finger at Astrid and then touched her nose. "After we get married, my priorities might change."

"Uh-oh, I thought I already was your number one priority." Astrid dragged his finger to her lips and kissed the tip. Hearing a yelp from the back of the house, Astrid jumped to her feet. "I don't know if that was boy or dog, but we're going to check on both and start cleaning up."

She waved her hand as Willow started to rise. "You two, relax. You deserve it."

Willow sat back down and scooted her chair closer to Heath's until their knees touched. "How'd your father take the news of the discovery of your mother's burial site?"

"He's still waiting on the verification of the dental records, but I told him about the locket. Told him the whole story of Garrett Keel's obsession with her." Heath hunched forward and took her hands. "He was sad. Felt like a failure as a husband all over again, but there's a sense of relief there, too."

"And you? Have you processed all this yet?"

"Selfishly, I feel vindicated in my belief that my mom never would've up and left us with no explanation."

"That's not selfish." She leaned forward and kissed him. "And how about this island? You used to love it. Do you hate it now? Feel like it's cursed?"

He traced a finger along her jaw. "I loved the island because it reminded me of the Tree Girl. It still does. And now I own a piece of it, below the dirt where the mist meets the earth. I'll love any place the Tree Girl calls home…as long as she'll let me."

"I guess we do have a deal, then, Son, because the Tree Girl loves you where the mist meets the earth and anywhere else."

* * * * *

A NOTE TO ALL READERS

From October releases Mills & Boon will be making some changes to the series formats and pricing.

What will be different about the series books?

In response to recent reader feedback, we are increasing the size of our paperbacks to bigger books with better quality paper, making for a better reading experience.

What will be the new price of Mills & Boon?

Over the past four years we have seen significant increases in the cost of producing our books. As a result, in order to continue to provide customers with a quality reading experience, the price of our books will increase to RRP $10.99 for Modern singles and RRP $19.99 for 2-in-1s from Medical, Intrigue, Romantic Suspense, Historical and Western.

For futher information regarding format changes and pricing, please visit our website millsandboon.com.au.

MILLS & BOON
millsandboon.com.au

INTRIGUE

Seek thrills. Solve crimes. Justice served.

Available Next Month

The Sheriff's Baby Delores Fossen
Under Lock And Key K.D. Richards

Smoky Mountains Mystery Lena Diaz
The Silent Setup Katie Mettner

Black Widow Janice Kay Johnson
Safe House Security Jacquelin Thomas

Larger Print

Keep reading for an excerpt of a new title
from the Romantic Suspense series,
PROTECTOR IN DISGUISE by Veronica Forand

Chapter 1

Fiona Stirling's first blind date in the five years since becoming a widow would be the death of her. Death by boredom. The elegant restaurant overlooked Boston Harbor with its seagulls and sailboats and a steady stream of aircraft landing across the water. While the intoxicating aromas from the kitchen encouraged diners to try some of the best seafood in the city, her companion, George, preferred roasted chicken and a beer, and had berated the waiter for not allowing him to order from the lunch menu. Fiona asked for the roasted sea bream and a glass of Sauvignon Blanc from South Africa. Based on the first few minutes, she might need an entire bottle. For an appetizer, they agreed on an order of artichoke dip. She was starving when it arrived. The scent of melted cheese with a touch of white wine filled her with a dozen memories of meals with friends and family. Before she had a chance to taste it, George bit into the French bread, toasted to a perfect warm tan, and spit the bite into his napkin. He waved down the waiter and sent the whole dish back to the kitchen before Fiona could say a word.

"Are you okay?" she asked, her patience evaporating each minute she sat across this man who would never measure up to her dead husband.

He gestured with his hand while he found his voice. "I expect a certain level of quality while dining. This isn't it. The bread is stale."

Fiona bit back the remark burning on her tongue. The Oceanside Grill was her favorite restaurant. She ate there at least once a month with friends or her son or her literary agent, Janet, when she was in town. The bread was never stale. "Was the bread stale or toasted?" she asked.

His expression froze, then he straightened his back and resumed his focus on all the other patrons of the restaurant. "Toast can be stale."

Fiona had a very low tolerance for rudeness. If George acted like a recalcitrant toddler with a piece of bread, how would he deal with more serious issues in life?

Her phone vibrated. She glanced at the text from her son, Matt.

I'm home. Found the lasagna. Thanks.

Although thirteen years old, Matt conducted himself like a seventy-year-old man. He was the kid most mothers wanted their own children to hang out with. Solid grades, a skilled athlete, mild-mannered, preferring an at-home movie or game night to wild parties. Despite all that, Fiona worried about him every second of every day. After already losing one man in her life, she would do everything in her power to keep her son safe.

The waiter brought over a bread basket and placed it on her side of the table. He returned with another glass of wine only moments later. She owed him a very large tip for reading her mind.

As the dinner dragged on, two other guests came

over to the table to ask for an autograph. She smiled, signed a napkin and posed for a selfie. George nodded toward the other guests as though he were harassed by fans all the time. Perhaps he was. A college professor in molecular genetics, he had an impressive résumé and bragged about his soon-to-be promotion to department chair. Fiona asked him about his work, but he dismissed her as though she would never understand such complex issues. Her platinum blond hair and 34D chest precluded intelligence for many people who had imbibed the stereotypes thrown at them for decades. Fiona's deceased husband, Jason, had been the exception. He'd been her biggest champion and a perfect husband in looks and everything else that mattered. To be fair, George was attractive, in a lawyerly sort of way, with his blond hair swooping over his blue eyes like a Wall Street Ken doll. Quite the opposite from her *type*. Jason had sported a permanent three-day beard on his chiseled jawline. His dark hair, dark eyes and intensity had sent Fiona into a sexual meltdown every time he looked into her eyes. In the sixteen years she'd been with him, he'd never said a mean word to her or to anyone around him. He'd been her anchor. Even five years after his death while on a military assignment in Colombia, the grief bowled through her, sending her mind into a glum and restless place.

"…sex on a train?" George was talking about something Fiona wasn't sure she wanted to hear.

To avoid being rude, she snapped out of her memories. "What?"

"The sex scenes you write. Where do you get your ideas?" George lifted his second beer and winked at her.

"Oh." She forced a smile. Her thriller novels often

had one or two sex scenes in them. It spoke volumes that those scenes would be George's focus. She now saw how the rest of the evening would go if she didn't separate him from his assumptions. She leaned forward on her elbows, her arms pressing her breasts together and causing George's attention to drop in anticipation of the rest of the night. "I make up the sex scenes from things I read in books or watched in movies," she said in a low purr. "The murder scenes, however, are carefully orchestrated and practiced. I can slit a throat without breaking a nail." She was a bit rusty, but she was sure she could still handle the task with a three-and-a-half-inch Benchmade blade.

He choked on his beer. It was the first time she laughed all evening.

Her phone rang. Matt. He never called. Ever. "Sorry. I need to take this. It's my son." She pressed Answer. "Hey, honey, what's up?"

"Someone is sneaking around the back of the house." Matt whispered the words. "I saw him by the back hedge after the motion light turned on."

Everything inside her went still. "Where are you?"

"In my room." His nerves traveled to her phone like a high-voltage surge. She always told him to always trust his instincts and she would too.

A wave of panic crashed over her. Nothing mattered to her more than Matt.

She checked the cameras she'd installed around the house. In the backyard by the hydrangeas, a shadowy figure tried to hide, but his solid dark pants and shirt didn't blend into the nuances in the background. "If you hear a window or a door break, run to Meaghan's house.

Otherwise, don't come out until I get home. I'm on my way. Call the police and stay on the phone with them." She stood up and grabbed her purse. "I need to get home. My son needs me."

George finished eating a bite of chicken, then stood too. "Rushing off every time your son has a problem won't prepare him for the real world."

"Fuck off, George." She threw down three twenties to pay for her half of the bill. Her best friend, Meaghan, would be hearing from her about her insistence that George was her *perfect match*.

Once in the parking garage, she scanned the parking lot full of Mercedes, BMWs and Teslas for her ten-year-old Jetta. It may have been smaller and not as luxurious as the cars surrounding her, but it was cheaper to run and could move surprisingly fast. The tires squealed as she circled down three stories of concrete and exited onto the street. As usual, the Saturday-night traffic shuffled along State Street. Fiona couldn't wait. She swerved around several cars and managed to slip through a light as it flickered orange, keeping everyone behind her stalled at red.

Matt's voice pushed her to maneuver like a Formula One driver. He tended to remain calm in most situations, like his father. Tonight she heard apprehension.

She used Alexa to call Meaghan so she wouldn't have to slow down.

Meaghan answered on the second ring. "You better be calling to tell me you just had the best sex of your life."

"Not even close. George is an ass."

"He can be, but he's gorgeous. Couldn't you just ignore everything he said and enjoy the ride?" Meaghan said with a chuckle.

"No. My mind has to be as seduced as my body for me to enjoy sex."

"That must lead to some pretty lonely nights."

"George is not why I'm calling." Fiona wasn't in the mood to discuss her sex life when her son was in danger.

"What's wrong?"

Meaghan was a no-nonsense kind of friend, the only kind of friend Fiona could tolerate, so she just burst right out with it. "Someone is trying to break into my house, right now."

"Oh. My. God. Are you okay? Is Matt okay?" Meaghan, a person who never showed a wide range of emotion, sounded stressed.

"Can you get over there?"

"I wish I could. I'm with a client in Rockport, but I'll tell them I have to go."

"Don't bother. I'll be there before you find your car."

Fifteen minutes later—after a lot of near misses and some angry exchanges with annoyed drivers—Fiona arrived home without a speeding ticket. Their simple one-story ranch house had no lights on, not one. Her neighbors had power and the streetlights still cast a bright ring on the road every hundred yards or so. Fiona rushed to the side door, her eyes scanning her surroundings as she unlocked it. The kitchen was dark with only the external lights casting enough of a glow to make out objects on the counters. The large glass casserole of lasagna she'd made for his dinner sat uncovered on the stove, half-eaten.

"Matt?" She stepped inside, her only defense the keys

in her hand and her small leather purse. She'd never been so unprepared for something in her life.

Before she could call out again, a large arm wrapped around her and covered her mouth. She fought to get free, but another arm locked her body tight against a brick wall of a chest. Her assailant had the physique of a bodybuilder. A burglar? Where were the police? Where was Matt?

The man pushed her forward toward the family room. Fiona twisted and tried to slam the back of her head into his face. No such luck.

They passed the edge of the counter. The darkness hid the colors and details of the interior, but this was her space. She reached behind her and took the ballpoint pen she'd left by her grocery list. One stab to the neck and he'd not only loosen his hold on her, he'd be headed to the morgue, but she'd promised herself she wouldn't kill unless absolutely necessary. So she hesitated, and his grip on her tightened. Before the bastard could crush her ribs, she smashed the pen into his thigh. He stepped back, and she slipped through his arms. Clasping both hands together, she rammed a double fist straight up into the man's groin. He fell forward in pain, but recovered faster than she expected. He grabbed a stool from the table and swung it into her. The hit launched her against the oven, and she dropped to the floor.

Headlights outside the house brought some light into room. The man, his large form coming into focus, wavered. Fiona scrambled back from him. Without a better weapon she stood no chance. But he surprised her. Instead of rushing toward her, he sprinted out of the house into the backyard. Fiona pulled herself up, swallowed her nerves and raced down the hall.

"Matt?" she called out, pushing open his bedroom door. Turning the flashlight on her phone on, she scanned the room. No sign of him. He could have escaped through the window and been safe at her neighbor's, but she paused and waited.

A muffled sound came from under the bed. She dropped to her knees and looked underneath. Behind two flat sweater bins, her son's beautiful brown eyes peeked out.

He pushed his way out of his barricade and stood—he was already a few inches taller than Fiona. She wrapped her arms around him and held him tight as her heartbeat slowed. Having someone invade her space in such a violent manner while her only living relative was home alone shattered the sense of security she'd built around them.

"Are you okay?" She examined his face, his arms, until he pulled away, annoyed enough at her actions to decrease some of her tension. She never should have left him alone. There were too many things that could have gone wrong.

"I'm fine," he replied, "but your nose is bleeding."

She turned away from him and wiped her nose with her sleeve. "Let's get out of here before the beast returns."

"He's still in the house?"

"He escaped out the back door, but I have no idea why he was here so I have no idea if he's coming back." She pointed to the door. "We'll wait out front until the police arrive."

He remained silent as he followed her to the front yard. They stood next to the streetlight, but remained partially hidden by an oak tree on the Murphy's front lawn. Just in case.

It took over ten minutes to hear the sirens. Matt waited with his hands in his pockets, slouched against the tree trunk. He'd always been a calm, levelheaded kid. He had to be deeply processing everything that had happened. In the dark, he looked like a thinner version of his father. If only Jason was still with them. She shook her head. This wasn't the time to be drawn into what-ifs. The *what-is* was too pressing. Someone had broken into their house while her son was there alone. Fiona had never for a moment felt unsafe in this neighborhood, but now, the house where she'd lived these past five years had a shadow over it, one that wouldn't lift. The police arrived, and two officers came out of their car, hands on their revolvers. She announced herself before moving around the large tree in case she surprised them. Matt followed behind her.

The police officers looked past her to Matt, and the older one, about forty-five years old, spoke first. "I'm Officer Dunlop. Did you call 9-1-1?"

He nodded and turned to his mother. Fiona squeezed his arm and stepped forward. "Someone broke into the house and attacked me."

"Where is he?" Dunlop glanced over her shoulder toward the house.

"I don't know. He ran away after I stabbed him with a pen. His blood should be on the floor."

He sent his partner, about ten or so years younger, toward the house. Fiona gave the officer as complete a description of what happened as she could. Matt offered little help as he'd hidden immediately and remained hidden while the man rummaged through several rooms.

She was proud of him. Had he tried to stop the man, he would have been seriously injured or worse. The man who had attacked her was not playing around.

A second police car arrived. The additional blue lights swirling through the neighborhood brought out several neighbors.

The lights flickered on inside the house, which meant her tormentor had only flicked a switch. She'd been so concerned about Matt that she hadn't checked the circuit breaker. Several minutes later, the younger officer returned alone. He strode over to Dunlop and Fiona. "The scene is clear. The circuit breaker was switched off."

Several officers present spread out and searched the neighborhood for "A male suspect, approximately twenty-five years of age, over six feet, black T-shirt, Caucasian, dark hair," as Dunlop had reiterated what Fiona told him.

She looked around. A maze of streets created an easy escape for someone who had left a car one or two blocks over. "You should be able to get his DNA off the blood on the floor."

Dunlop's partner shook his head. "There's no sign of any forced entry and nothing in your house looks disturbed."

"I stabbed him in the leg. There had to be blood on the floor or on the pen. I dropped it after he hit me with the stool."

"Can you show me inside?" Dunlop asked.

Fiona hesitated. She didn't want to be ambushed again, and despite the police officer's presence, something felt off. She told Matt to remain outside with the other officers as she reentered the premises with an armed guard.

The entire scene appeared quite mundane under the five cool-toned track lights illuminating every surface in the kitchen. After her eyes adjusted from the dark, she scanned the room. Not a drop of blood anywhere. It was as though her brain had malfunctioned and now everything was back in order. Even the stool had been placed back next to the island. Officer Dunlop remained beside her, watching over her shoulder, glancing in every direction she looked.

The kitchen floor was cleaner than it had been when she'd left for her dinner date. The man who had assaulted her didn't do this. It would have been too much detail work for someone with an injury. The first officer didn't have time to turn the room over in the five minutes he was in the kitchen before coming outside. Someone else?

"Where's the lasagna?" she asked.

"Lasagna?" Officer Dunlop shook his head as though he were being baited.

"There was a half pan of lasagna on the stove. Right there." She pointed to where she'd seen it when she walked into the room. It wasn't in the sink or the re-frigerator. Her stomach twisted as she opened the trash can. Not there either. Even more than having a stranger in her house trying to harm her and her son, the loss of the lasagna scared the hell out of her.

Subscribe and fall in love with a Mills & Boon series today!

You'll be among the first to read stories delivered to your door monthly and enjoy great savings.